The storm howled and the freezing seas came rushing over our half-deck. I looked aghast at my hands, and found I could see right through the flesh to the shape of the bones beneath! I briefly saw the dancing flaming leaping skeletons of my crew in that instant before the ocean fell on me and sucked me into its commotion.

Suddenly the world was no longer there! I seemed to be suspended in a universe of flame and strange distortions. I seemed to be looking down, down, down into an unfathomable abyss. And even as I was aware of looking down, I fell, spinning, so dizzily wrenched that all thought left me completely. I fell into the abyss, and it twisted me, and tore me apart.

Berkley Books by Stuart Gordon

FIRE IN THE ABYSS
SMILE ON THE VOID

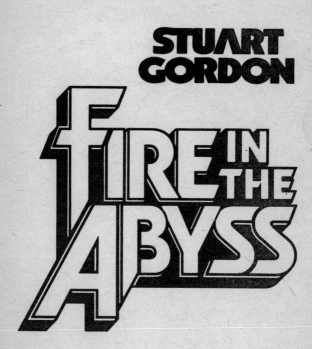

STUART GORDON

FIRE IN THE ABYSS

BERKLEY BOOKS, NEW YORK

FIRE IN THE ABYSS

A Berkley Book/published by arrangement with
the author

PRINTING HISTORY
Berkley edition/August 1983

—

ISBN: 0-425-06081-0

For Luke & everyone at Hinman Lane

with love & thanks

HVMFRIDVS GILBERTVS MILES AVRATVS EQ

Quid Non

GILBERTVS ciues alium deduxit in orbem
Quó CHRISTI imbuerit barbara co'da fide AB

SIR HUMPHREY GILBERT.
From Holland's "Herwologia Anglica."

CONTENTS

⊷❧❲ INTRODUCTION ❳❧⊷

Equinox

The spare, greybearded man awoke soon after sunrise. The windows of the small flinty moorland house were rattling in the spring gale, fertile storm was running in from the west, banks of dark windwracked cloud came spilling by with watery sunlight breaking through from time to time. The rattling had been drumming him from his dreams, gradually, but it was a pale bright sunray, casting through the uncurtained upper window and falling on the man's face, that actually awoke him.

Abruptly, shocked, he sat up straight from his sleep. With a lost look, his lips moving, he stared at the again-misted eye of the sun. Red, it swam warningly through the silhouette firs at the bottom of the yard, above the pearly two-dimensional layers of wooded sodden pasture and bare sodden hills. "Strange light!" he muttered, tugging at his moustache, at his neat sparse goatee, his voice dubious and slightly wild, "and stranger night!"

Even as he watched the appearances changed. The sun and its direly delicate radiance were swallowed by a great onrushing dark whale of cloud, and heavy penumbra returned. He nodded. His lean and high-coloured face grew firm as he drew himself together. Briskly naked he got up from the cool bed and went to the window, impetuously pulling it wide open, breathing deep as the fresh wet blast gusted in, stretching, gasping, his body cracking all over, vociferously shocked now wide awake. He shut the window quickly, shivering and rubbing his slender, calloused hands as he went and pulled on a warm flannel dressing-gown. Then, after hunting and finding separated slippers, he went quickly down the twisty stairs to the stone-flagged kitchen, talking to himself. "Yes!" he told himself sharply as he stoked up the Raeburn, opened the flue, filled the kettle, and put it on, "Yes! Today's the day! The humour's right. It's a hawkish day. If I don't begin now I never will. And when did I dream of her last? Oh yes, it's a sign, begin it, why not? I'm harebrained already, so why fear the Moon?"

Tall, with his proud, preoccupied, lined face, he took his tea to the bathroom behind the stove. He ran hot water then lay in it, his mind faraway, and he was silent save once when adding more water, he stopped himself as he turned the tap.

"The lost can seek truth. But what truth do dogs chew?"

He dressed in boots, dungarees, a thick white cableknit sweater. He ate a breakfast of porridge and toast. Then, excited, putting on coat and knit cap, he went out into the wild invigorated day.

The house stood on its own in a shallow dip. An unpaved road, overgrown, ran out west past two ramshackle sheds through a gate to the alder marsh lower down, and past this unhealthy place, round a hill, to Gwernacca Farm and the way to the outside world. He walked halfway to Gwernacca before cutting over a fence and up winter's faded fields to the top of a rocky bare mount. There he stood some time by an old standing stone, attentive to the moods of the swift vital weather, to the alternations of sun, rain, mist, rainbow, light, and shade, to the birds winging like bullets above, and to the white dots of shaggy blackface sheep at their perpetual munch-munch-munch on the steep slopes. A few early lambs braved the weather to frisk, but as yet there was little new growth. Not yet. In England, yes, but not yet in these parts. He turned to the old stone, wonderingly ran his long weathered brown hands over the rough quartzite surface. "Heretic," he murmured, "Once I'd have been burned for what I hold now. Heretic, more pagan than Christian. If Tari was pagan, then so am I. What would Dee have said? I cannot put it off any longer. Pagan, heretic, Christian, ancient, or modern or whatever, I gave Michael my word. Yes!"

With reluctant eagerness he turned back to the house even as a fresh storm came billowing in, obscuring the day with heavy rain. And it was with uncertainty that, once back and out of his wet clothes, he set the ream of paper on the wide oak kitchen table, and the sharpened pencils alongside. For some time he did not sit down, but busied himself with trivial tasks.

Finally there were no more trivial tasks. Keyed up, he sat and picked a pencil, and pulled a sheet of paper to him.

Chewing his lower lip, he thought for a while, then wrote:

"THE JOURNEY OF HUMPHREY GILBERT, KNIGHT"

PART THE FIRST

◆━❰ 1 ❱━◆

Humf's Declaration

When I was first in this age, shocked and shaved and imprisoned at Horsfield, it was Herbie Pond who had the gall to call me "Humf."

Over five years have passed since nine of us escaped that fearful place, and it may be that now I alone am left alive of all the Eighty-Seven of us plucked from the sea by the U.S. Navy in the aftermath of Project Vulcan.

Yes, I am Humf, and sometimes John Loomiss, but I started life as Humfrey Gylberte, or Humphrey Gilbert—spell it as you wish: we had no fixed convention in such matters. That was long ago, and here and now I begin my account of Project Vulcan and the DTIs, a matter which certain agencies have tried to keep secret ever since it happened. Their methods have included denial and worse; nonetheless our existence has been rumoured internationally. There have been books, movies, questions in the U.N.; there have been innumerable claims and counterclaims that we *do* exist, we *don't* exist, we *can't* exist; or that we are hoaxes, part of a Communist conspiracy to undermine the U.S.A. with chrononuttery; or that we were sent by the *Illuminati* to dupe and discredit the U.S. Government in some convoluted scheme for world takeover. So, how tall can tales get?

It is more than hoax or dream, though.

Professor Michael Greene has persuaded me here to this small house he rents, alone in the north part of Wales. He says I must write this account to reveal the truth of Vulcan and win justice for the DTIs. I tell him he is an optimist. "Then," he says, "do it to lay your ghosts!" Yes. But I have been full of objection. How to tell what I do not clearly remember? Why expose what has already been exposed and successfully denied? Why cause myself needless pain, why court more danger? I am tired. I want peace and quiet.

Yet what's to lose? What's a little more danger now? For words may knit webs that dreams and understanding will cling to, and without our dreams we're lost. As for Michael, he wants to pin down that butterfly, Truth, and since the Regis Clinic results and our day at Compton—in fact, since he began to believe me (unwillingly: he said as much)—he has pressed me to start this. So, a week ago he won my reluctant agreement and drove me here from York, leaving me with supplies, promising to return after a month. I know he fears I'll be gone when he returns, that I'll have slipped away on my wanderings again. I have seen it in his eyes. Perhaps at heart he hopes I *will* decamp. God knows we have strained each other; I make him doubt his own sanity as well as mine; I threaten his position and reputation; his good wife Ursula fears what I'm doing to their lives. Perhaps I *should* slip away. But there is a bond of honour. I gave him my word I would do this, and that is that.

It is problematic. For a week I have hemmed and hawed. Yet last night, for the first time in years, Tari visited my dreams. She showed me a book with my name on it, but the pages of the book were empty. *"What's so sad as an empty page?"* she asked—then I awoke with a weird sun in my eyes, to the blast of fresh spring gale; and I walked up the hill with the pagan stone at its summit, and I looked over the ancient ageless land— and as I looked I felt a new force birthed in me! The Fire of the Ram! Today is the first of that sign under which I was born, the first day of spring—what better day to begin?

But how to begin? With *Truth?* A fine word! Let us begin with Truth, by all means! The truth is that my memories are tangled, my mind confused and multiplied into many warring points of view, like scattered fragments of a jigsaw puzzle, each fragment blindly claiming to be "myself." Truth is hard to find. Then, what of Fact? It seems to be a fantasy of this age that Truth is measurable by Fact alone, so let me join in the game. Here is *Fact:*

It is seventy-five months since the Eight-Seven of us were snatched from our various ages by Project Vulcan; and, as I

said, over five years since a few of us escaped the secret New
Jersey jail at Christmas of 1984. Since then I have been fugitive,
and most of the time on my own. And it is hard to believe
what I remember. Sir Humfrey, the Queen's man, seized from
1583 to 1983 by Vulcan-fire? How can the heart accept such
a thing? How can I believe that others can believe it? In their
place I would not. The world is trouble and amazing enough
without events like this. But *Truth! Fact!* Believe it I must,
for here I am, uniquely, four centuries out of my proper time.
How can I understand? Tari said there is meaning in it, and
tried to convince me, often, but we were ambushed in Denver
and I forgot all she said, being shot nearly to death. I never
saw her again. Later I heard she was killed, but I lack proof
of this. Yet what's the meaning in murder? And what of the
others? I know what happened to Herbie and Utak, yes, and
the Dancer may be alive: he had the power. But Jud, Lucie,
Clive, Jim? And all the rest of our friends we left at Horsfield?
I know nothing.

Yet Tari has returned to my dreaming.

Nefertari Mery-Isis was wise. She warned me not to let my
heart grow sour, yet I grew hopeless after our bloody separa-
tion, and in the mirror it is still a stranger who sees a stranger.
For how can Humf be that man who lived and moved four
hundred years ago? What am I now but a mass of undigested
meals? Like a babe I've sponged up all I can, I've intoxicated
myself with modern image and media, I can use gadgets and
turn off the TV. But I am not modern. My emotions refuse the
present as my reason rejects the past. So I stay split.

But Michael presses me, and Tari shows me the blank page.

Fact. It is near two years since I left San Francisco in a
hurry and reached England with a U.S. passport in the name
of John Anthony Loomiss. *Fact.* It is nine months since I
crawled bleeding into the parlour of Michael and Ursula Greene,
seeking refuge from the troops. *Fact.* Since then there has been
food in my belly, and a rebirth of hope, but still my dreams
are dire. Often I burn in the fiery furnace of Vulcan, awakening
electric and confused, pins-and-needles tingling through me.
Must I awaken the past? Yes, I begin to see I must, for it roosts
uneasy in me: I'll never rest again if I cannot admit it and
marry it to the present. Last night I dreamed of Tari, which is
good, but lately the nightmares of Anne have been terrible—
Anne as pretty as the day we married, calling to me from a

green hill on a sweet summer's day. I hasten instantly to her as I never did then, I who ruined her purse and affection with my enthusiasm for Discovery, but always I get there too late, to find summer turned to winter, the green hill concreted over, no warm wife to greet me, but instead a crow-picked skeleton, a grinning skull that hisses, *"Too late!"* Then in my dream the horrid skull takes on the faces of my enemies: haughty Mendoza who intrigued against my New World expeditions; that cunning man who foretold my sea-fate when I was at Eton; the immunity-suited Horsfield doctors who emptied us of History and filled us with Interferon. Yes, Michael. Sometimes at York, amid our tests to prove I am who I was, I have awoken from these dreams with utter hate at this modern world: hate like a poisoned robe, with anger for a staff and nothing under my feet at all.

But I tire of hate and anger. I have seen too much. *Honni soit qui mal y pense.* If I hate the fools who cracked us with Vulcan's whip, I must also hate the face in the mirror. I too thought myself righteous in the Sight of the Lord; I too advised piracy as patriotic duty, advocating England's seizure of other lands and peoples; I too despised others not like myself. Now I find myself done to as I did, living in a society created by God-fearing Christians like myself. What is hate but blinkered vision? *"...A defect of memory is the origin of opinion..."* wrote Macrobius long ago. Exactly. Much has changed, much has not. My age was better and worse than this, the same and different. Now buildings rise higher, more folk move faster, plague is replaced by cancer, and the Devil we feared in loins and bowels and hell of our guilt is mutated into The Bomb that hangs over the world. Science is wonderful at materialising what was latent in us. It was in my time that Doctor Faustus horned his way up, full of hunger to *know* and *control*, whatever the cost. Now he thinks he owns the world because of the bargain he made, but the joke's on him, for still the world's a bewildering maze of terror and joy, like an infinite onion. Yes! For every layer of ignorance we peel away we find another, more profound and mysterious yet! The human heart is no bigger or smaller; every year still has its dark nights, its sunny days, its Maytime and its winter! Yes, still we dance on the bridge we dream out of Abyss, though the WHY of it remains a mystery....

Tari said this present age is a womb in which History comes

together in a mating. She said an egg is laid from which the Phoenix strains to hatch and burst forth, more gloriously than ever before, flaming in *Manas,* Mind, the Eternal Thinker; and in *Manus,* Hand, the Doer; which two, joined together by Heart and Courage, make *Man.*

Who can tell? Not I. Yet I may do my best, and so now try to light my own small phoenix-fire, telling my tale in tribute to dear friends departed, hoping that my wit and memory may improve in the telling, and that some will read it who find it good.

2

On His Ancestry, Habits, & Name

Most of all I remember that terrible night, the first half of which was September the ninth of 1583. My tiny *Squirrel* foundered in the Atlantic storm and we were all cast into the sea with the witchfire eating in our bones, to our drowning, as I was sure. Yet for myself at least the fire proved stronger than the water. It was the fire of Time unhinged, of Project Vulcan, that ate me up and delivered me through, maddened, to night and sea again, to the early hours of December the twenty-seventh, 1983. And I brought with me not so much as a shred of clothing, not even a flea.

But I am not yet ready to speak of it, nor is this the place, for I knew more than forty years of active life before it happened.

It is most probable I was born in April 1539, though there is no sure proof of it, my mother being most curiously vague about such things as dates and numbers, reckoning instead in seasons, events, and circumstances. She told me I came "on a wild spring night about a week after the chimney caught fire," and when I pressed her for greater precision, she would say, "Oh, a year or so before that whipjack Cromwell went to the block, as he deserved," or, "About the time Coverdale's Bible was brought me to read, though it might have been before that." As for my father, he had no notion of such things, he was more interested in the hunt, and anyway, he died when I was quite young. So, my chart and date of birth are speculative, though the cunning man at Eton Fair said I am of Aries, and much later Doctor Dee affirmed that choleric nature is in many ways typical of the Ram. You may ask: why no record in a register? Well, parish registers were often kept by incompetents, or not kept at all, and much was destroyed during the years of turbulence and reform after our break with Rome. Yet, this is when I was born: sixty years after Caxton, forty years after the Brothers Cabot made their first English landfall in the Americas, twenty years after Luther's rebellion and Magellan's circumnavigation, and about twelve after the sack of Rome by the Imperial troops. I was born at the end of the decade in which King Henry declared himself Supreme Head of the English Church, dissolved the monasteries, divorced one wife, beheaded another, and had Thomas More executed too. Now they say it was because he was mad with the pox. Well, perhaps, it is how history proceeds. But never mind that. I was born Protestant at the time when Calvin published his *Institutes*, when Copernicus was about to declare his new theory, when that damned Cromwell pioneered Machiavelli in England. I was born, most important, in a time of ferment and change and Discovery, with Spain stronger every year from the gold of America.

Yet then in England there was no mad fever for search in the Unknown World. Elizabeth was still a bastard babe; we were a small poor land on the edge of the world, and had need of every man and woman and child at home. None of us could come and go as we pleased. Emigration was not allowed, permission was needed to travel or study on the Continent, patriotism lay in staying at home and diligently tending the land, as my older brother Sir John did, all his life. It was not quite yet time for the great broadening of our horizons. There was no money for great expeditions. People were more concerned with the revolution at home, in their hearts and souls.

But I was born in Devon, near Dartmouth, and grew up among men of every class who were sea-rovers like their fathers before them; bold and skillful men who seemed like giants to me. Especially I admired the fishermen who went out to the Newfoundland Banks where the codfish teemed. Every summer, some went out, and every autumn, some returned, their tiny barks wallowing with dried and salted fish for the profitable new markets. And those who returned brought their tales of the strange New World, so that from an early age my mind was naturally turned outward. I was drawn by the fabulous tales as much as by the more sober seafaring discussions always to be heard—but in particular I was drawn by the mystery of the empty ocean horizon. It was not often, when I was young, that I was allowed to Berry Head or Dartmouth Castle to spend hours gazing out over the sea, but many times in summer I would go down where the lawns of my father's Greenway estate met the fringe of the placid Dart, which there was more like a lagoon than a river. There I would stretch out to watch the boats going down to the sea, or close my eyes to dream of the marvellous discoveries I was sure to make one day. I was always a dreamer, lured more by the invisible than by the already-known, and so I was not old when in my own mind it was decided: when I grew up I would be the first Gilbert to explore the New World.

My father Otho had the same name as his father and grandfather before him. He was a man of position in the West Country, with the Castle at Compton, and manors at Greenway, Galmeton, Sandridge, Brixton, Hansford, and elsewhere, all by inheritance of land we'd held for generations. For my family, being Norman by the male line, (and still in our time we had close ties with our Huguenot cousins), was already set in Devon by the time of Edward the Confessor. When the Conqueror came in 1066 we supported him vigorously, to our advantage, so that in Domesday Book, by which he registered the land, the entry under Gislebert is considerable. But soon the name "Fitz Gislebert" was discarded, we came to write our name "Jilbert," "Gelbert," "Gylberte," or "Gilbert."

What is this gibberish?

Family trees! The Past! Who cares?

It's a trap, a mire, my head aches, I tremble, outside the storm still blows. My Past is all so faraway and useless—and yes, I *do* fear to stir it up. And, pathetic, also I fear my languid style cannot appeal to modern taste. I'm caught between the worlds, I don't belong anywhere! Yes, and I have raised these doubts before! "Just be yourself!" you told me so heartily, Michael. I laughed. "How can I possibly know who 'myself' is?" I demanded. "I was legion enough before Vulcan and those Horsfield doctors made it ten times worse! Now I am Humf, and Humfrey, and Sir Humphrey, and King Fool—I know not which, nor which voice should prevail! What style? What voice? What's the point?" And you shrugged.

"Simply tell what happened," you said, "and don't ramble

too much. Remember most folk now are in such a rush they don't even have time for headlines. Just tell your story as it happened."

Just tell my story as it happened!

Greene, sometimes I fail utterly to understand your modern English irony and cynicism, far less your underlying desires. I think you are a good man, but misguided by romantic notions. *You* don't have to tell my story! As for myself, I feel no passion for it at all, only fear of what happens if I dig too deep. Yet of course we've been through that. I have to face it! I must break out! I'm armoured, rusted. Oh God. A drink would help. We've been through that as well. You call it my "weakness." No wine, no spirits, nothing to make me rave. There's only a crate of *lager* in the fridge. Piss-water! In America it's even worse. What they call beer there is but babe's puke! I like marijuana well enough, having been introduced to it in California, but there's none of that here, only *lager* and tobacco and some Valium pills Ursula pressed on me to help me sleep. Sleep! Well!

But I digress. You want Fact. You want History. You want inedible dates and objective account!

So, as I said, for five hundred years the Gilberts had responsibility in the West Country, and for twelve generations our seat was at Compton, which we got by marriage in the reign of Edward II, that unlucky sodomite buggered to death by a redhot poker in 1327.

No Gay Lib then.

Enough! Hold to your course, man!

In a nutshell. Otho begat Otho begat Otho my father, who married my mother Katherine, daughter of Sir Philip Champernoun of Modbury in Kent. My father broke tradition by moving the family from Compton to Greenway by the Dart, a pleasant-enough place where my mother gave birth to Katherine, John, myself, Adrian, and Otis, who died young. In 1547 my father died, in 1549 my mother remarried, to Walter Raleigh of Hayes and Fardell, bearing him Carew, Walter, and Margaret. My mother was a remarkable woman, I say it flatly, and she bred and raised us accordingly, to courage and virtue, and of course my half-brother Sir Walter became the most famous of us, and is so still, his name being used in America to sell tobacco. It is amazing. Walter was born in 1552, some thirteen years my junior. He *never* lived at Greenway, as some biographers attest, and it is true that many notions ascribed to him originated with myself, and true furthermore that he was always faithful to me, and supported my schemes with his influence at Court. Let historians say what they will! As for the rest of us; sister Katherine married George Raleigh, Walter's half-brother; while John conscientiously tended the estates all his life, he would never support me, save when my mother made him do so for the family sake, as happened in 1578, when Walter and Carew and myself commanded three of the seven ships in my first Atlantic expedition—that black failure! Not the first, not the last: I have always been accomplished at failure—of the spectacular sort, you understand, like not quite returning safely to the Earth from the Moon, or to England from the Newfoundland. Oh yes, I am well acquainted with failure, and I know I got myself the reputation of a difficult, touchy man. I never got on with John, that stolid countryman; Adrian was my best friend in the immediate family. He too was a soldier, then sailor-adventurer; though in character he was much different to myself, being known throughout England as a great buffoon. If I am a buffoon, it is involuntary, I assure you. Yes, I am Humf now, I know—but once, had you called me that, I'd have seen you out on your arse with a cut lip!

But times change, now we are all socialists and clapper-dudgeons, beggars born and fiery men, due I think to pressures of population, cruelties of the tyrant Reason and his henchman Industry, and to rise of the Repressed. Now I am Humf. No doubt had I the vote I'd cast it for that most interesting fellow, Mr. Tony Benn.

Yes, why not?

I have been through the mill these last seven years. Politics is rarely better than self-interest. But I've found it hard to find a wider point of view. My mother would have adapted more bravely, as Tari did. Perhaps the experience women have of men makes them naturally more democratic. I don't know. At any rate, my mother did not disdain the poor as (I suppose) I did.

Once in fact in Mary's reign my mother won fame by going openly to pray with Agnes Prest, a poor woman cast into Exeter jail for her Protestant faith and later burned for it. My mother declared her sympathy and spoke out against the Persecution, winning great respect, thus to risk her life. This happened about October 1555, when I went from Oxford to Hatfield to start service as a page in the household of Princess Elizabeth, who was also in much danger during those mad years.

Such hurlyburly and confusion to recall! I'm all ahead and behind of myself! Fire, rebellion, persecution, ranting fanatics, lunatics and libertarians. It makes me shudder! It is with us now!

The storm has dropped. Now I will drop too, and eat.

◄►[3]◄►

Compton Castle, & How
the Viper Did Not Strike

Well, last night with my efficient modern dentures I chewed at tasteless frozen stuff, then walked out beneath the moon, and then went straight to bed. But my memory was enflamed: I could not rest. For hours I tossed and turned, beset by whispering phantoms, till I was so frayed I reckoned myself haunted by that entire hellish crew with which my mother's maids once terrified me—bugaboos, puckles, imps, urchins, hags, sprites, hellwains, firedrakes, bull-beggars, Boneless, Hobgoblin, and Robin Goodfellow himself. Affrighted, down to the kitchen I went, and made tea, and sat by the fire, and tried comforting myself with a tape of the music I knew, played by the lutenist Julian Bream. But that only hurt and confused me worse with a general disorientation: I stopped it and instead turned to what I'd written, read it, and almost fed it to the fire. Somehow I stayed my hand, breathed deep, and back to bed I went. In time I met that uneasy sleep in which you cannot tell if you wake or dream.

But dreaming I must have been: at one point I saw Tari again, or the shade of her, at the foot of the bed, with a pale glowing light from her by which I could see. Her hair was like white wool, which is how it grew back on her after our escape from Horsfield, where they kept us bald; she was slim and dark as I knew her; but she was dressed in a way I never saw before, in robes of midnight blue, with a horned silver crown on her head, and a silver orb between the horns—the very epitome of her goddess, Isis. She carried a scroll, which she unrolled, and from it read me something (but not with her voice) about remembering, which of course I cannot now remember. Wake up, Humf! I tried speech with her, but of a sudden everything changed: I found myself walking down a long dark passage with my mother, who kept pointing ahead, saying, "The New World lies this way, Humphrey," so we continued, but there was no end to the passage. And when I looked around she was gone, and I was a boy again, and the passage had become the low dank secret tunnel at Compton which once I feared and loved to explore.

Then I seemed to be awake, in bed, but cannot have been, for I clearly heard brother Walter's voice, saying he has spoken with Her Majesty, and that she is willing at last to grant me and my heirs forever letters-patent and Rights of Governorship in the New World. But when I sat up in stupid false elation, looking for the source of the voice, it changed straightaway to another that I knew, that chilled me, though I only ever heard it once, when I was eleven:

"Was I not right?" it cackled, "Did I not speak truth?"

It was the voice of that cunning man at Eton Fair who read my palm, who told me my sign and fate! When I heard this I truly awoke, in a sweat, to the echo of my fearful shout!

Now it is day. I have been up for hours. I have walked for miles. Yes, old man. You spoke truth. You dogged me all my life and even now the prediction's come to pass you won't let me alone.

Well, today I am going to exorcise and banish you!

But first things first. I must find a pattern of telling, or this hundred-head will overwhelm me; the tale'll have more heads than legs, all braining each other. There is an order. Old man, you told me my destiny near Mayday of 1550, but what you told me I knew already, though sleepily, through the dark senses.

I met destiny soon after my father died in the early summer of 1547. His will directed Adrian and myself to the guardianship of our Uncle, Philip Penkewell, a sombre man, whose house wasn't far from Compton and the Castle. Even then the Castle was my favourite place inland. "Cold and out-of-date," said my father when I asked why we no longer lived there, and I suppose it was. But I loved it. The walls were strong and four-square, fortified after an earlier style, with portcullis and bar-tizans and four stout towers, ivied, and standing up amid a clearing in the woods. Even then the clearing was becoming overgrown through my father's abandonment and preference for the gentler modern life at Greenway. It was my mother who took me there first, I think, when I was very young: there is no time I cannot remember it. I explored it and dreamed in it as often as I could; its brooding air influenced me as much to the past as the mariners' tales of Golden Ships and the New World tended me to the future, and in later life I considered myself "Gilbert of Compton," though in fact my father willed Compton to John, as well as Greenway, and I got Hansford, where I rarely went. It is the spirit of the thing: John owned Compton but cared more for his turnips, while my heart was always there—and more than my heart.

The day I found I had destiny was the fourth Sunday after Pentecost in the year my father wasted and died. It was some weeks after Adrian and I had been delivered to Uncle Philip. One morning I awoke knowing I must go the Castle, alone, secretly, not telling Uncle in case he refused me. I had not been since before my father died, now the need was strong, like a starving man's need for food. So, after Matins, I slipped into the woods, taking lantern and tinder, for I meant to explore the underground passage, and bread and cheese filched from the kitchen. I went with beating heart, expecting fuss when I got back, but soon I forgot all that as I went deeper into the dells. The day was very hot and heavy, thunderous high summer, the woods so drowsy and rich-smelling that soon my anxious pace became a yawning lazy amble. After a time I came on a ferny bee-droning glade, full of wild roses. I lay down in the cool mossy shade of a fallen oak and fell deep asleep.

Some strange tremor stirred me. I awoke. I felt alarm, but could not tell what caused it until, blinking, I looked down the length of me—and what I saw had me yelling and jumping away so fast I bashed my head on a branch and knocked myself half-silly.

The viper slithered away just as quick, and doubtless just as shocked, for in my own sleep it had come and coiled up against my body-warmth, most contentedly—until my shout, my convulsion! And it had not bit me! I stood up shuddering and shaky, my head ringing.

But yes, he has bit me! came the cold thought as hammering of heart subsided. *He has marked me, for he did not bite me*

to death! By not biting me he is my friend, which is fatal, for
the Serpent is the Enemy of God, and that means now I am
too, because in Genesis III the Lord says that . . .

I was precocious, yet this logical approach died suddenly
as I noticed something new in me. Amid all the fright and
excitement my boyish loins had awakened. It was another shock,
for there had never been such a stirring before. I did not quite
understand, so felt, and found my throbbing club. It was not
so much, but seemed enormous to me, and I was amazed,
fearful, and delighted. Yes, I knew what it was, we were not
hidden about the body and its doings, it was before the Puritans
infected our minds with their sackcloth hygiene. I'd seen men
and women hump, as I'd seen them shit and piss and eat and
drink and fight and work and sleep and play. Yes, and of course
we brothers had played the games, Who can raise their Peter
Pan, the Little Man, and so on. Whoever human did not?

But I didn't know what to do. There I stood in the grass,
doubly shocked and aroused, one snake by other, body on fire
and throbbing with life, every sense acute, Christian doubt too
refined and pale to survive, for the drowsy bees were part of
my body-hum, they seemed to be part of the song my virgin
cock was trying to crow. And I was bees, winging on the scent
of the roses to alight and drink at the summer cups—then very
suddenly, with intensest vision, I was in beds, in a bed in
particular that smelled of roses all summer long, Annie Pen-
ruddock's bed. She was a Keltic lass, maid of my mother's,
who wetnursed me for a time, and after that for years I liked
to creep into her bed on dark nights. "Frightened by the Grumpit
again, are we? Come to play with Annie's poosie, have we?"
She gathered fresh wild rose and strewed the petals between
her sheets, yes, I liked it there, playing with her poosie, until
Mother quite suddenly found fault over something else, a minor
thing, and amid great explosion of tears and bawling sent Annie
packing back to Cornwall. Yes, Mother knew, and hated it,
though she never said why, or mentioned it again at all. But
she could not send Annie packing from my memory, and in
the glade I stood there, then I lay down in Annie's bed, all a-
throb with longing, with new emotions bursting up, wanting
something I couldn't define—in her, with her, beyond her—
I saw a sun set in the fiery ocean—there was a great surge
into intolerable brightness and night together, and Annie's voice,
like a shower of many-coloured roses: *"Hide your soul in a*

*secret place known only to you. It is what my folk do, so that
we don't forget Mother when Father's unwell."*

So I came for the first time, and went to hide my soul. I
did this with strange ceremony, dreamily, gravely, at a certain
place not far from the Castle, and still in a dream I gave thanks
to the serpent for sparing me.

Then the thunder broke, and so did the spell. All the way
back through the woods I pelted, terrified in the downpour,
certain the Lightning of God's Wrath would strike me dead,
which it did not, but yes, I was thrashed and questioned—not
for the last time!—and no, I said nothing of any of it, nothing
of the viper, nor of Eros, nor pagan commitment, far less my
sense of being marked by the Devil. I'd lost lantern and tinder,
I'd found something I could not tell anyone. It was an initiation,
awakening of sense of destiny, and I could never forget it,
however much I buried myself in Latin.

Michael, I was never just a simple Protestant sailor.

Perhaps now you see why I was in such fuss of temper when
we went to Compton two weeks ago.

You tried to understand my agitation, until you lost your
own calm, but you could not fully grasp it any more than I
could explain it. The truth is I feared to meet my ancient buried
soul. I feared it might enter me then leap out of my eyes and
drop me dead, as part of me says I deserve. I think it is Guilt,
that I did not drown with my crew, that the Serpent did not
kill me. But never mind it. Guilt is murky and impenetrable,
which is why it is Guilt: if it were clear, people would gladly
rid themselves of it.

Or would they?

Michael, it is my business where I hid my soul. Look to
your own. I say there is Public Man, and Private Man. Are
Secrets always such evil things? Must we shine light in the
soul's every corner? The soul must have her dark side too, for
light to shine at all. Without Dark there is no Light—so let
the Darkness be! It fertilises! It brings rest, and it cannot be
scalpelled by Scientific Investigation, for it is protean, evasive,
this-and-that; if you try laser-light on it then it'll blight you
with nightmare and sore misunderstanding! So let it be!

Michael, it is nine months since I stumbled through your
door, not knowing you, and you a historian of my times.

Karma, they'd call it in California. *Synchronicity*.

What do you call it, Michael? Do you disagree if I say these events are somehow *directed?* Being a humanist, no doubt you'd not commit yourself—but I can see in your heart. You know that I am your Fate. You know I didn't ask for it, you might even deny it—but your inner humours resent it. From nowhere I appeared to plague you with doubt and upset your comfortable life. In return you have taxed me most heavily in your drive to prove me a Genuine Historical Relic. You have thrown me to graphologists, linguists, hypnotists, anthropologists, and doctors. You took me to Eton, where I played my turn for the College Historian, telling how it was under Udall, and he was amazed. You took me to Cardiff to be "regressed" to my "past lives," and to general astonishment it turned out not only have I been Sir Humphrey, but also a Mayan astronomer, an Egyptian priestess, an American rum-smuggling pilot, etc. Well, I told you about the Circle at Horsfield, but that you cannot believe. Then we went to the Regis Clinic in London, for analysis of every part of my body. They clipped my toes and hair and skin and blood and my brain as well. They had me drink radioactive barium to trace me deep, and then by analysis of clippings declared I'm a marvel of "minimum contamination by modern global-industrial environment." They determined that the levels of lead, DDT, sulphur, radioactivity, etc., in my natural body are so low as, by their measurements, to prove that I can be no more than seven years old! Precisely!

"From a cellular point of view," said that doctor called Johns, hiding his amazement, "You shouldn't be alive at all."

"Then your cellular point of view is wrong!" I said, and fled. Science is admirable, but it cannot answer people. You won't get me back there again, I can assure you! Nor are you going to persuade me back to Devon again!

It's a wonder you got me there at all. Perhaps I felt I owed it. I found your "lost secret tunnel" for you. Yes, you organised it well, calling the National Trust with your cock-and-bull tale of the astrologer Maplet's newly found diary and its coded directions to vital documents hidden, yes, in a lost tunnel at Compton. You played your prestige, and won, and along I went on your dangerous game, as a "research assistant"—though to the Castle caretaker who supervised us that horrid wet day you confided I was a dowser. Maybe you also told him I am a little cracked. I see you had to tell him something, for I was upset by ghosts as soon as we got there. And nothing was the same, inside or out. But I found your tunnel. I knew its line, toward Berry Pomeroy, in relation to a hill in the east. After much anxious casting-about I located a place inside, at one end of a hall full of eighteenth-century portraits, and mounted muskets, shields, swords and so forth. "H-h-here!" I stuttered like a man in a fit, which I was, "T-t-try here!"

Yet I could not help you prise the flagstone up. I stood there mumbling and shivering as the pair of you sweated and strained—and then the flag burst up, and there it was, descending, a black hole with a dead smell that struck me faint with vertigo even as I glimpsed it. Memory flooded me with a nauseous intensity. I could not look. You took photographs while I walked up and down and the caretaker stared at me as if I might be dangerous. *"No . . . no . . . no . . ."* I was mumbling, or something of the sort.

You pretended you sensed nothing wrong with me.

"Well, I think we should get down in here!" you declared with a jarring false heart. "Humf, do you have the lamp handy?"

"There's nothing down there!" I shouted, *"Nothing!"*

"Damn queerest dowser I ever seen!" the caretaker muttered to himself, but I heard him, my senses are of great acuteness when I am nervous; I heard him, it was the straw that broke my back.

"Sir, I am no dowser!" I snapped at him. "I am Sir Humphrey Gilbert, I have been kidnapped through time by the U.S. military and their cursed Project Vulcan! You will have heard it rumoured on TV! I escaped America, sir, and as to my identity, *sir,* I am who I am, and here I lived at Compton four hundred years ago! *That* is how I know about this tunnel!"

"Right, mister, that's right!" He was younger than I am, in a grey uniform, with sleek parted hair. "I like a good laugh meself." He backed off until the gaping tunnel-pit lay between us. "But mister, you can't be right about living here, everyone knows it was Sir Walter lived here, and . . ."

"Damn you, Raleigh!" I roared, red with rage, and I leapt over the pit and grappled with this silly knave who thus abused me with his ignorance. Raleigh! They say he lived at Greenway, they say he lived at Compton, they say colonising was his idea, they say everything I did was his idea!

Well, you had to drag me off the idiot. You were furious. Yes, I'm not proud of it. You placated the man, and paid him, and then for the sake of appearances you had to crawl down the tunnel, to find only an utter caving-in after some yards. I

would not go down or even watch: I waited outside in the
twilight fog until you came out, covered in the shit and mildew
of five or six centuries. The horrid stench turned me dizzy
again, and I had to walk away, insulting you to greater anger.
Like an officer you seized me by the shoulder and marched
me to your car. I know not why I suffered this: when you
climbed in with your stink of buried history I rolled down the
window. You roared the engine. "Humphrey!" you snapped,
"We're not on the high seas, nor in America! Please roll up
that bloody window! You can't go about assaulting people who
offend you! What if he goes to the Press?"

"Well and good if he does!" I snapped back as you drove
off in lurches that almost broke my back as well as my patience,
"I am not your jackanapes! I am done with lies!"

"Humphrey, if you start attacking government officials and
ranting about being a DTI, that's it! We're finished! I might
as well ring the *Daily Mirror* and say I've got a UFO at the
bottom of my garden, and a man from Betelgeuse in my guest-
room!"

"UFO! DTI!" My dignity was icy as you drove like a madman down the narrow winding misty lane. You drove as wild
as Herbie did that night we took our leave of Horsfield. "Is
that all I am to you, sir? A Distressed Temporal Immigrant?
A category of research? Michael, if you want to be rid of me,
and my risk, then stop the car, now, and let me go! I promise
you'll see me no more!"

You slowed down. You did not stop. You tried to soothe
me. "Soon we'll have enough to go before the U.N. Human
Rights people!" you said. "We must be patient!" Michael, what
sort of game do you think this is? I shut my mouth and sat in
silence all the way back to York. You had a great row with
your wife about me, then your Chancellor called. You took
the call in your study and came out furious and tightmouthed,
and it was next day you suggested I should come up here on
my own for a while to *get myself in order* until *things have
cooled down a bit*.

Michael, you are a clean man, a good man, but you know
nothing about the big bad world, and I fear for you.

Now, the cunning man.

⋯⋙［ 4 ］⋘⋯

A Farthing for His Fate
at Eton Fair

In the year 1549 I saw terrible sights. Guns and the sword
broke many poor bodies and the gibbet broke more. The land
was blighted, with only a boyking, and Warwick at Protector
Somerset's neck for the power, and all preaching licences suspended, and mass uprisings against Cranmer's Prayer Book
and reforming ordinances. It was in the west, in Devon, that
the poor folk rose first; in fact it is how Raleigh of Hayes got
the fame that met him with my mother. He was seized and
shut in the parish church by the rebels for bluntly telling an
old woman that her beads were idolatrous and now illegal; he
was held in great danger until the commotion was bloodily
ended, four thousand rebels being slain near Exeter by the Royal
Army.

In our parts the sailors and merchants and privateering families like ours were Reformed; we had no love for Spain and
the Pope, and we thought the rebels dangerous fools, abandoning their lives for a Mass and likely to turn us all over to
Spain should Mary ever become Queen. It was a great confusion while it lasted. Adrian and I should have been at Eton,
which he had attended one year, and I for two, but outbreak
of plague had shut the College, so we were in Devon when Sir
Peter Carew's "conciliatory" measures turned isolated riots into
general revolt. After Raleigh was seized, Uncle kept us to the
house, though himself he was out continually riding patrols
with others during the week the robbing ranting hordes poured
through our area on their way to Exeter. I thought them fools,

but was uneasy, the more so when our stableboy Thom went with the rebels, saying he must do it for his soul. We never saw him again, but a week after the slaughter, as Adrian and I went by guarded train back to Eton, to loyal Windsor, we saw hundreds of the broken poor limping fearfully home: a miserable sight . . . yet not as dreadful as the one that met our eyes months later when we came coaching home for Christmas through the snowy dark land. Every mile along the road we met a gibbet with chained bones still dangling. The sight moved me with a panic fear that infuriated me. "Why are the poor folk so stupid they'll die rather than give up their old ways?" I demanded, and Adrian giggled, for he was young, and the gibbet-bones disturbed him too. "To feed the Old God of Crows?" he suggested, and I could not answer, I clutched my Seneca and my new-printed copy of Cranmer's Breviary more tightly, and I thought about the sea.

As for Eton, it is an achievement I never ran away, as many did, and forever after it was a question on my mind: how to improve education, so that much later, during my idle Lime-hurst years, I wrote a treatise giving all necessary detail for a new sort of Academy. I prescribed new subjects, and the salaries and duties of the professors, requiring them to publish their study-results, and also requiring every printer in the land to supply the Academy with one copy of every work they printed. I went deep into it, for in my time what passed as education for sons of gentry was barbarity and waste, producing bullies and good-for-nothings. But my effort was ignored. After it I wrote a treatise of a different sort, on how to pillage Spain and seize the West Indies. This was received with enthusiasm, and won me my Charter.

I was a Foundation scholar, living in College. Life was easier as an *oppidan*, in outside lodgings, but Mother would not pay for it, saying I must learn some facts of life. This I did. In College we slept in huge chambers, freezing in winter. Each morning at five a praepostor came about, bellowing *"Surgite!"* If you didn't *surgite* fast enough, well, Friday was flogging day. Each morning we rose and dressed and made our beds, all the time reciting prayers in verses alternating between one side of the chamber and the other. If you fumbled a line, or anything else . . . yes, I think you understand the principle.

It did much to form the English character. *"Untruss your points, boy!"* —the continual flogging command, for it was held that knowledge is best beaten in. Thus to our days: Lily's *Grammar;* the *Eclogues* of Baptista Mantuanus; the *Zodiacus Vitae* inflicted on the world by Palingenius; the hornbooks and parsings, declensions and floggings, the food and other things I'll not mention. As for our famous headmaster, well, Nick Udall wasn't a bad sort: he wrote and produced plays in which he had us act, I remember *Ralph Roister Doister* and *Ezechias;* and if he also mounted private productions with the prettier of us in his bed, so, at Eton buggery was part of the *curriculum vitae* along with grammar and the floggings. Yes, I broke virginity with another boy; it was after a class on Ovid. Quid non? There were no doxies to be had unless you risked the town stews, which usually meant Pox Romana, leading to discovery and expulsion. Some thought this the best way out, most made the most of it, for we had hardly more than a month of freedom each year, save in summers when plague flared worse than usual. We got but eighteen days at Christmas, twelve at Easter, and nine at Whitsun. Thus for eleven months a year and for four years I had opportunity to study the making of English gentlemen, always in good Latin. And it is true that in general I was seen as a mild fellow, often deep in his books but not likely to rat.

The cunning man? Yes. Good friend Simon got us into that.

It was like this. On our birthday we got pleasure of an afternoon out of College with the friend of our choice, and could also get cake and such sent by our families. But I wasn't sure of my birthday, though I said it was April the ninth, and in any case Mother would never send me cake, saying it would make me soft. Instead often she sent books, chiefly by the Greeks, for which I was grateful, but my lack of cake and ignorance of my birthday were a joke to my friends, particularly to Simon Speke, a big and ruddy tow-haired lad from Nottingham, my friend from our first term.

The day we met the cunning man was beautiful, turning May, the world blossoming again, and frightful gibbet-winter behind us. It was Simon's birthday, and he asked me to share his afternoon out of College with him. He told me what he had in mind, and I gladly said I'd chance it. So out we went, and at the gate told the praepostor, the senior boy on duty, that we would walk along the Thames, then through the woods towards Windsor Castle. He believed it, for Simon and I were not thought daring. But it was spring, when even mice will dare, and so, after walking some way into the woods to be sure nobody followed, we turned to a forbidden part of town—the Fair.

All year round there was trading in a wide and muddy marketplace that verged on the fields between Eton and Windsor. Here there was villainy, drinking, and prigging of pockets, and often enough fights and murder. But this day we went to the Fair, Simon's birthday, was six days after St. George's Day, and two before Mayday: we were amid a week of sport and play, with many more folk in town than usual all come to enjoy the processions, the dancing, the preparations for the festivities round the Maypole—how could we not go to the Fair? So out of the woods we came, and cautiously along a filthy alley past the stinking workshops of dryers and soap-boilers, our eyes sharp for praepostors, with bells ringing, and suddenly Simon, laughing, said:

"Well, if your mother cannot or will not tell you the hour you were born, perhaps here we'll find a wizard who can!"

He was joking, or thought he was, for there were laws against all such arts, people being so readily moved to revolt by prophecies and magical utterances, as we had seen the year before during the Risings in north and west. And the flogging given to scholars caught having truck with magicians was severe, so that I too thought I was joking when I laughed back and said:

"Yes, and perhaps he'll tell my future too!"

On we went round corners, past drunkards mumbling in the ooze, and dim holes where rough men diced, and a warty old mother sitting with petticoats in the mire who shrieked with laughter at us. "Ey! What's this? Young gentry making like commons?"—so we hurried on with burning cheeks, wishing we'd muddied ourselves up better when we'd stopped in the woods to hide our scholar-cloaks. But then we were round another corner and into the bellowing jovial babble of the Fair itself, and we forgot our fears. *"Duds for the quarroms! Duds for the quarroms!"*—we were among higgledy-piggledy leather-walled booths, deafened by the barkers all ranting and pitching for the wares—clothes, food, drink, lovecharms, false remedies. Simon set his eye at a pretty farmer's lass in red lace and green kirtle who was trying on new yellow gloves; she disdained him, her pert nose up in the air like Milady of Muck; we laughed, and at an ale-stall put out a ha'penny for two pots;

then, dizzy, stuffing sweetmeats into our mouths, on past stock-pens where cattle bawled and kine squealed to a crowded green where folk danced to music and others laughed at a drunk wife calling down curses on Cranmer and Ridley.

"Rogues everywhere!" muttered Simon, unsteady on his feet as we pushed on through the joshing jostle, meaning to see the bear baiting, and he was right, for in this part the mob was thick with chapmen and queans, and tawny rascals swigging from their skins of bene bouse, and twisted poxy little rufflers looking for pockets to cut, and then a big man all unbuttoned came shoving and gasping past, he was chased from a tent by a screaming woman as undone as he: her bubs free and bouncing and black hair flying as she pursued him, a knife in one hand and a jug in the other, and as she went by us she paused to throw the jug, which shattered against the back of his head, stopping him, but with her knife at his back he staggered on, howling, until the crowd swallowed them from us.

Yes, rogues, and I had also begun to notice, here and there, a cunning man or woman going about their trade, safe in the mob—here, a man in shabby clerk's dress selling amulets of arsenic, quicksilver, dried toads; and there, a woman peddling bits of paper with magic writing she said would put out fires and keep lightning away—and here again, by a red-and-blue striped tent, a wizened old man who held a farmer's rough hand, studying it, and as we passed we heard him mutter hoarsely about "the harmoniacal correspondences of all parts of the body with the spheres above," but then we were gone, thinking no more of it, in fact thinking not at all, except to keep our hands on our pockets, for we were giddy with drink and the day.

But soon after, finding the bear-baiting was not yet, Simon turned to me with a strange light in his eyes.

"Well," he said. "That was your man."

"What man?" But I knew what he meant.

"That cunning man by the tent. Perhaps he'll tell the day you were born, and your future too!"

"They're all charlatans!" I said, most uneasy, with a laugh.

"Are you scared?" he demanded, his eyes too bright. And at that moment I almost hated him, and wished we hadn't come.

"I'll try it if you will!" I said angrily.

"But I know my birthday already!"

"Perhaps, but you do not know your fate!"

So we trapped each other into it. But when we returned to the red-and-blue tent, the man was gone. I felt great relief.

"That's that!" I said. "Now we should go!"

"Yes." Simon agreed.

But that very moment the cunning man hobbled out of the crowd and started across an open space before us. Simon gasped. The old man stopped, and stared at us, and we stared back, for how long I know not, for he was utterly ugly and ancient, hairless and toothless and wrinkled, in rags, with scabs and sores, and a cast in one eye, so it was his left eye alone that held us, entirely, until of a sudden he scratched himself, and giggled.

"What is this?" he whispered, spraying us with stink of raw onion. "Two young scholars out for what they cannot find in school? Would they dare their fate from one cursed with Knowledge?"

"My friend wants to know the day he was born," piped Simon in a quick, high-pitched voice, "and something of his fate to come, and I too would... like to know... for myself... if you truly can?"

The cunning man eyed me again, and I felt icy-cold.

"Two pennies," he hissed, "and Old Will will do your will!"

"Much too much!" I said angrily, "A farthing apiece is enough!"

"You rate your fate at a farthing?" The madman giggled, and held out his gnarly claw. "Give me your price, and your hand."

"We should go behind a booth in case we're seen," said Simon anxiously, but though I heard him I could not respond. I was in a dream, the Fair faded far away. I gave the old man my farthing, my right hand. He bent to study the lines, tracing them with his paper finger, and I stared, frozen, at his scabby skull. "You are of the ram," he muttered unexpectedly, "you were born the first week in April. And there is more! You will..."

"April, yes!" I said, suddenly rebelling, and tried to pull my hand away. "It's all I want to know!"

He held onto me. He looked up sharp. Again I was iced.

"You'll fly far," he said abruptly, "but fall short."

"What?" I was disbelieving. "How can I fall short?"

"It is the fate of all!" Again his horrid giggle, his withered gums. "Honest men must fall short, at least in their own reckoning. Those who claim they've reached their goal are fools or liars. You—you'll never be satisfied. You'll aim high, and fall short, yet open the door for others to follow."

"Yes!" My heart was pounding. "Now let me go!"

"No! There is more!" He clutched me tighter. I looked desperate at Simon, who was trying to look invisible. And then, with a fearful oath, the cunning man dropped my hand as if it suddenly burned him, and turned away, crossing himself as he did, which so alarmed me I snatched at his ragged sleeve to hold him back.

"What did you see? What was it, old man?"

"Not for me to say nor you to know!" He was terrified, and pulling away, but I held on furiously.

"I'll make you trouble if you don't say!" I hissed.

"Folk watch!" Simon said sharply, "Come away, now!"

I didn't care. I held on until the old man faced me again, his eyes bright with fear, of God, or the Law, more likely.

"If ever you go on the sea," he whispered in a voice so quiet only I could hear, "then it's from the sea you'll be seized and taken to your doom, and I cannot say by what, for it will be a power not of Christ and not of this world. Now let me go!"

"You must say more!" I was shrill. I shook him.

"I have said it! God save you! Let me go!"

"Humphrey! I see Parker! He'll see us! Run!"

Simon's warning reached me. I turned, and had the luck to see the praepostor the moment he turned and saw the pair of us with the wizard, who took his chance and broke my hold, and quickly vanished into the jeering crowd. But I could only stand and stare.

"Hurry!" Simon grabbed my shoulder. "Run!"

We did. It was useless. Back we went knowing what to expect. Simon took fifty stripes, and so did I, and a month later I took another fifty for refusing to say what the cunning man had told me. It was a long time before I could sit again, but the beatings hurt not as much as that devilish warning. *A power not of Christ?* Is that why the serpent had not bit me? I couldn't tell. I could not speak, and the cunning man was not caught. I never spoke of it till now. It happened as he foretold. Now it's done. I'm rid of him!

It's dark now, but calm, and the moon is up.

It's time to go out for a walk.

Of Golden Ships & the
First Map of America

Yes, you may well ask. I often do.

Why did I go to sea? If I believed a tenth what the cunning man told me, why did I not stay safe and sound at Limehurst with my family, why did I not grow into a fat and lazy old gallant?

Why? Because my dreams demanded better. The sight of the sea and the tales of the Unknown World inspired me continually where the wizard's warning but briefly depressed me: I preferred the inspiration, and so in time it all came to pass.

Yet dreams are easily destroyed. For months after the cunning man mine were in the balance. At Christmas of 1550, I lost Golden Ships—and found them again in the maps of adult purpose.

This was due to Uncle Philip's wit.

Uncle was a saturnine man, strict and studious, fair in his dealings, but sombre, and vexed by two growing boys without father or fear of the birch. Thrice a year we made his life difficult, for we had so little time from school, and such wildness to run out.

Now, as I said, Dartmouth men were famous pirates, and had been so for generations, the port a natural stronghold with its narrow deep channel and high rock walls, and chain across the harbour-mouth to keep out anyone unwanted, even kings of England. Often I heard how the French had attacked in the past, to be beaten off so fiercely they never tried again. Now we had a new enemy, and the rhyme went:

> Four-and-twenty Spaniards
> Mighty men of rank
> With their signoras
> Had to walk the plank.

Yes, Dartmouth men were lawless, always ready for a brawl, and when in wintertime they were all in port together the taverns and dens were like bearpits. Yet on the Quay was an inn called Saracen's Head, a man called Bidder the host, where I'd been welcome for a year or more. Often enough I'd gone in on a hot day, and Bidder would give me a cup of small beer: I'd sit in the smoky darkness, watching it all, and listening to the tales. Sometimes the sailors would twit me for my serious face, and pretend to treat me roughly, jostling me, or aping to threaten me with knife or fist. Bidder or Pysgie would stop that, but they were all glad when I met them in the eye, they would clap my back and try to get me drunk and tell me their tales. None of them ever hurt me, and Pysgie was my best friend there. He was called that because a pysgie is what he was like: a tiny man with a shock of hair and twinkling eyes, and wit to lead the sober astray. He'd been ten times over to the Banks, and done his share of plundering, and he told tales better than anyone else. It was Psygie who told me about the Golden Ships. He believed absolutely in his own stories, or so he claimed; he had a contempt for the commonplace; he fired me, and I was very sad when he died stupidly, being stabbed in a brawl a year or so after this.

Uncle Philip knew I went there, it was not a secret, but he made it a privilege conditional on my behaviour. At Whitsun of 1550 I was in disgrace because of the cunning man, and stayed pent up in the sombre house; then at Christmas found myself still under a cloud and forbidden to roam down to the Quayside at all.

I was angry at this, still confused by the cunning man and the fear he'd brought me. I needed the healing tales Pysgie could tell; I felt stifled in the dark house, and would not talk or smile, even to Adrian. I felt unruly, and so one night after Christmas, thinking everyone asleep, I slipped out by a downstairs window. It was a quiet night, and by the moon I took a path through the woods down to the point where the Anchor Stone sits in midwater, this being where the sailors sometimes stranded their disobedient wives. Then I followed the steep road down into Dartmouth, crept past the shipyards, along Fosse Street, through the Shambles, and so came without encounter to the back door of the Saracen's Head, and knocked.

When Bidder recognised me he shook his head.

"We're abed, lad! Squire Penkewell ud ave uz oop for . . ."

I interrupted him rudely, and said I had to see Pysgie, *please!*

My voice trembled. He took me in and sat me down and roused his wife and they both went out looking for Pysgie while I sat at their fire (they had a chimney) feeling like a wretched fool.

Pysgie came. That night he saw me all the way back up the road and near to Uncle's house. I couldn't tell him about the cunning man, but he sensed my distress, and all the way back as we walked he talked in his broad soft voice, telling me tales, including the Golden Ships, until I felt life flowing back.

He wished me luck then left me, and back to the window I went to find Uncle Philip waiting the other side.

"Come to my study," said Uncle in his most doleful voice.

In furious humour I followed him to his book-thick study, where he lit a lamp then sat, watching him in silence where I stood stiff.

"Humphrey, you have been to the Quay?" he asked sadly.

"Yes," I said, "So I have! And glad I did too!"

"Humphrey, don't drive me to tell your mother! She has burden enough at Hayes! What is the matter with you? Do you want to find yourself chained up like a dog like Sir Peter Carew was at school?"

"He broke his chains and ran away!"

"Don't be impertinent! Humphrey, there's no purpose in beating you. What is the matter with you? Why these escapades?"

"I'm almost twelve!" I burst out, "I must learn about the sea! How can I become a man if you keep me locked up when I'm here?"

Uncle sighed. He told me to sit down, which I did. I was bone-tired, but wide-awake, and shivering, though not with cold.

"Humphrey, you could have fallen in the river, or been waylaid and killed! You run off to drunken rogues who fill your head with nonsense and call this 'learning about the sea'?"

"They're my *friends!*" I insisted belligerently, "They wouldn't hurt me, and their stories are *not* nonsense!"

"What is your favourite story?" Uncle asked quietly.

"The Golden Ships," said I, and instantly regretted it.

"I want you to tell me this story of the Golden Ships."

I was furious. I felt I had betrayed a secret trust.

"Come, Humphrey. Tell me about the Golden Ships."

So there I sat and told him the tale of the Golden Ships. Now I remember that night well, if perhaps not word-for-word.

"Very long ago," I began unhappily, "Before the Flood, when folk lived for hundreds of years, and when many were very wise, the Golden Ships were conceived and built in the land we call Cathay. They were made of pure gold, for in that time there was so much gold on Earth that nobody had to hoard or steal it. Some say the gold first fell from the heavens, and that the rivers of the Indies sparkled and danced with it, and you only had to wade into the water to take as much as you wanted. And the rulers of those lands built temples of gold, and great palaces, and the roads were paved with it, so none who travelled those roads ever fell sick.

"And it came about that the wise men of Cathay received a purpose from Heaven, and they called for more gold than had ever been collected before, to build a fleet of Golden Ships. The gold was brought from many lands, and craftsmen and shipwrights were found, and the ships were built. More than a hundred were built, and each of them wider than the lagoon at Greenway, and so long from stem to stern it can hardly be imagined! They were made with many decks, and huge castles fore and aft, somewhat like those galleons that the Spaniards are imitating from the ship that Bressan made in Venice—but they were bigger, much bigger, as I say, and they had no masts or sails or rigging, if you can imagine it, nor any oars or rudder. For the gold was pure, and in those days the sea was pure, so that the gold and the sea could hardly bear to touch each other. The Golden Ships did not sail *in* the sea, they skimmed *on* it, being flat underneath, and given direction and power to move by the Pure Thought of the Wise Man who sailed as Master in each and every one of the beautiful ships!"

I paused then, suddenly crestfallen to hear myself grown so enthusiastic, Uncle Philip staring so mournfully at me from his shadows I could see he did not believe a word.

"Continue," said my Uncle, "Please."

"And as Christ hears me," I went on haltingly, "I swear these magi were not evil, though they lived long before our

Lord and could not know redemption. Should we blame them for that? Indeed, the man who told me this tale said that Noah did not build the Ark, as the Bible says, for the Ark itself was one of these Golden Ships, and ancient even then! For the Golden Ships had been sent all round the world, through every sea, to weave a web of light and inspire the hearts of men to righteousness!

"But the mission was not altogether a success, for not even these wise men of Cathay could counter the degeneration that brought the Flood. For even then it was after the Fall and the world was evil, so that God sent the Flood. Yet, before he sent it, he warned the wise men of Cathay, and told them to take one of the Golden Ships to Noah, which they did, and to take the rest to Peru, a land of high mountains lately seized by the Spaniards.

"So the Golden Ships sailed for the last time over the great sea that Magellan crossed, and which someday soon an Englishman will cross, and they were beached on the shores of Peru, where the wise men did as God had commanded. They dismantled the Golden Ships, and melted down the shining metal, and turned it into enough plate and ingots to fill a whole kingdom! Then they carried the gold—all of it!—high up into the mountains, where it was hidden in vast caves and secret cities that they built with their art. And thirty-two priests and thirty-two priestesses were left, to become a tribe that would guard the gold through the Flood, and keep alive the memory of what went before it.

"And so they did! They guarded the gold when the Flood came, and safely, for though the waters came up the mountains, mile after mile, those mountains were so high that the waters could not conquer the final mile!"

Uncle Philip interrupted then.

"But in the Bible does it not say that all the earth was covered, even the tops of the mountains?"

"Those who wrote the Bible knew nothing of the New World," I said excitedly, "They did not live there, they lived in the Holy Land, they were not able to cross the sea! How could they know?"

"Continue," said Uncle, with a look I did not like.

"Well," said I uncertainly, "Until lately the descendents of those ancient guardians, who now call themselves the Inca, have kept the gold secure. But they had no knowledge of Christ, and forgot their purpose, it's said, and now they have paid for it. A scant few years ago ill-luck struck them down at last. The Spaniard Pizarro came among them, and baptised them with fire and sword, and took all the gold in payment. Now the fleets bringing that gold to Europe make Spain richer every day, and Spain is Catholic, and soon must be our enemy, for they buy traitors among us to stir up trouble. And this is what happened to the Golden Ships, and this is the tale of it—though the man who told me the tale says he thinks there may be other places in the New World where the gold of other Golden Ships was melted down and stored, which Englishmen will find!"

"That is your tale, is it?" asked Uncle, his face so sad I thought he might weep.

"Yes." I felt wooden. "That is it."

"And who told you this . . . tale?"

"I cannot say! On my honour!"

"I know it was Pysgie," he said, nodding, without malice. "I heard it from him long ago, though it seems he has built on it over the years. Humphrey, do you believe this tale is a true history?"

"I feel in my heart it is somehow true," I said, "though my head cannot tell, for Pysgie admits that he is unsure of his authorities. He says he heard it from a scholar who found it in a book by Geoffrey of Monmouth, which was lost four hundred years ago."

"How convenient!" said Uncle, his voice droll. He turned and fetched down a heavy book from the shelf behind him. He gave me the book. "What is this?" he demanded.

"The Bible," I said.

"Correct." He pulled down another. "And this?"

"*De Mundo,* by Aristotle."

"Very good." And again. "And these three?"

"Marco Polo's *Travels.* The *Travels* of Odoric of Portenone. And the *Travels* of Sir John Mandeville."

My uncle steepled his fingers as he sat back.

"Humphrey, you will sit in this room and read these books until you find some mention of Golden Ships. You will enjoy Mandeville best, I expect, for he is full of nonsense such as dog-headed men; but I doubt you'll find your Golden Ships even in Mandeville. And when you've been faithfully through these books without finding one single word about them, I want you to study"—with sinking heart I watched him choose and pull down several more large volumes, and an unbound pamphlet of the sort that cost thruppence or fourpence, all of which he stacked up before me—"these works too. When you are through, you may be able to judge the matter more sensibly."

"More likely I'll be utterly befuddled," I said hopelessly.

"Then you'll understand very well how I feel in trying to deal with you and your brother," said Uncle as he got to his feet. "Now I'm going to leave you here, Humphrey. You may use this lantern to spare our eyes, I'll see breakfast is brought to you, and you may sleep at midday. In the afternoon you can go outside for half an hour, but otherwise you will stay here and search these books for your Golden Ships until it is time for bed tonight."

Then he left me.

The other books were Ptolemy's *Geography,* and *Imago Mundi* by Cardinal d'Ailly, the *Cosmographiae Introductio* by Martin Waldseemüller, and a treatise on geography by Strabo. The pamphlet, written in English by a Reverend Francis Judd of Lincoln, explained clearly how and why disobedient children would inevitably go to hell.

I had the choice, but I did not go out that afternoon, nor at all on the succeeding two days, which were the last before we went back to College.

To begin with I was furious and would not read a thing. I felt tricked and trapped. The worst of it was I knew I'd been fairly out-manoeuvered by Uncle, and must meet the challenge. But my pride was upset, and so an hour later I still sat stiff-backed and unseeing when Joan, who lived in and looked after us, came in without knocking and tumbled a bucket of burning coals into the grate with a sparky crash. She went out but quickly returned with a bowl of cold oatmeal, which she set before me with a thump. She was not pleased.

"Now you be listenin' to me! Oughter be ashamed, causing Mr. Penkewell such gashly trouble, and him sendin' me to ye wi' food and fire as ye don't deserve!"

Then she stamped out. I was impressed. Joan was a good woman. When she laughed, she laughed; when she shouted, she roared. She was about forty, red of face and grey of hair, and she wore a huge number of aprons and skirts even in summer. Why she and Uncle never married I don't know: they fit each other well, and sometimes shared bed as well as board, though pretending to all they were above or beyond or too old for such hanky-panky.

Yes, her anger shamed me, and so, though still grudging, I ate the food, trimmed the lamp, then picked up Sir John Mandeville and his book of spurious doings—and was quickly in deep, and found this famous book of lies remarkable, for it talked of sailing round the world before this was ever done, so that now Magellan had proved the lie true. But no Golden Ships, and so, with much of the morning gone, I turned to Odoric and Marco Polo. Their claims to have visited Cathay were true, and at first, glumly seeking Golden Ships, I found their true descriptions dull. Yet gradually I grew excited by their descriptions of Cathay's riches, and sense of passing time left me. All day I read, and never went out or grew tired, and only that night fell asleep, to dream of silks of Bambyce, and pepper and spice, and cloth of gold. And also I dreamed I had a ship of Devon men, and we found a new way to Cathay, slipping the blockades of Portugal and Spain, and that when we returned with great wealth to England I was knighted on the quarterdeck by King Edward.

I blush. King Edward never happened, it was Drake who did what I dreamed, and as for my knighthood, it came not for Discovery, but for killing Irishmen. But luckily then I knew little, even the cunning man seemed only a silly bogey, and on the next day I was early into Uncle's study. I turned first to the Ptolemy.

It was the splendidly thick and weighty Strassburg edition of 1513. Within it were the wood-cut maps of Waldseemüller.

The maps!

How can I tell this? Waldseemüller's maps seized me. They grabbed me by the scruff of the neck, shook me up, referenced my dreaming to a real world. Golden Ships? Until then I'd had no sense of scale. There was only beyond-the-horizon. I had never seen a proper map. I was young, and Navigation and Science were young arts, still thought occult. At Eton I'd seen only a wheel map, a *mappa-mundi*, with Jerusalem in the middle, saints and angels all choiring round the perimeter, and dragons rioting through imaginary symmetrical symbolic continents—as big a lie as Mandeville, and as true to its time. Apart from this, and a Portolan chart of the Atlantic coasts which Sir Gawen Carew showed me the year after my father died, I had seen only the rutters of the sea-captains—their pilot-books, with bearings, soundings, winds, descriptions of currents and ports.

But they were not *maps!*

New knowledge! New ways to see! Waldseemüller struck and lit me with increased sense of the world, of the vastness, of what we live to do, which in my opinion is to go beyond our limitations. With a shaky finger I traced the outline of the New World, and I felt my destiny snake over the globe, carried on this occult chart!

So, you say, a map is just a map, showing you how to get from *A* to *B*. Perhaps. Yet to me that day saw my initiation into a secret new language. *Secret,* for it demanded that the mind grasp it. And *new,* therefore imperfect, and subject to change, as I soon learned, when I came to compare the map in the *Ptolemy* with a later map by Waldseemüller, his last, in the *Cosmographiae Introductio*.

In his last map Waldseemüller abandons the past. He rejects Ptolemy and fifteen centuries of tradition. He accepts new measurement, reduces the longitude of Asia to near its true dimension—*and for the very first time the New World is named America!*

Yes! I first heard of *America* at Christmas of the year 1550! In my life it was conversion as dramatic as that of Saul on the road to Damascus! For those last two days before returning to Eton I sat entranced at Uncle's desk, drinking in the maps, the fire gusting or gone out, the lamplight flickering madly whenever the wet winter gale struck through the chinks. But I felt no chill. For hour after hour I sat, gaze moving back and forth between the maps, at last beginning to get my first adult measure of the world, of myself and my purpose. The New World! Discovery! Our awakening after centuries of sleep! Can you imagine how that astronomer felt two years ago when he discovered Persephone beyond Pluto? I'm sure I felt the same awed exaltation when I met the maps. Yes, and I felt fear at those empty spaces of the Unknown World, and the sense of imminent loss of a comfortable mothering past. *"A power not of Christ and not of this world?"* How could I drive it entirely from mind? Yet the awe and sense of purpose were greater. And that last night before return to Eton I fell asleep with my head on the crude, distorted, unfinished map of America, with all its north and west unknown. Uncle came in with my mother, and they found me there.

My mother was big again. We embraced, carefully.

"Have you found your Golden Ships?" she greeted me, laughing.

"Yes," I said, "I have. They're not made yet, but they will be!"

I was a humorless brat, but the maps inspired me. They ended my childhood. Now, I say, we need new maps, of new worlds.

⊷⊷❈[6]❈⊶⊷

How Humf Has Fought
for His Beliefs

Yes. In my life I met the maps forty years ago, but in the history of the world it is forty plus four hundred, and sometimes each of those hundreds is like a ton of lead on the neck. Now the physical world's no longer unknown, but fenced, staked, mapped, whipped, and bruised to its uttermost end! But I'll not start a rant. Two or so years ago in San Francisco for a time I ranted violently and often against everything. Once I nearly killed myself by kicking in a TV screen to stop the similar ranting of Thaddeus Carpenter, that lunatic who thieves a vast following of gullible souls in America with his *Plutonium Power for Christ* rot. "JESUS IS WITH AMERICA!" he was raving, flushed with rage, "WE NEED PLUTONIUM POWER FOR CHRIST TO KEEP THE GODDAMN COMMUNISTS AND ATHEISTS AT BAY, SO GET OFF YOUR FAT ASS AND SEND ME MONEY *NOW*, OR BY SWEET CHRIST I PROMISE YOU'LL BE LEFT OUTSIDE WHEN THE BIG ONE DROPS!" When I heard this I shouted furiously, I ran at him and kicked his face in. There was a flash, a shock that threw me back. That foul blight on humanity! It makes me shudder still to remember my youth, and all the fanatics who claimed Christ as their own—and how I have ranted too! That mottled man! As for the shock I got, it spurred me to self-examination, to begin awakening from the hate which had consumed me since Denver. The TV set was not mine, and cost three hundred bucks to replace. And ranting never did give me anything but a headache.

I'm nervous.

This wet gusty morning I went out walking and met the farmer from Gwernacca, a burly middleaged man called Griffith. It's he that owns and rents out this house, and two hundred acres of the land about are also his. No doubt he lived here before moving the family to the new house at Gwernacca. "He's a tight-mouthed old sod," Michael said. "You won't get much out of him."

I met him briefly the day we drove here, when Michael stopped at Gwernacca to say I'd be staying a while to write a book, but today is the first time we have talked. We came on each other round a bend and could not avoid it. I said something about the weather and he grunted, eyeing me with surly composure. I disarmed him only when I remembered a little Welsh. He shot a response, I managed reply, he laughed in surprise. "Well, now!" said he in his singsong so fast I could hardly follow. "You haff the words, like, but for a moment I did not know what you were saying at all! You haff the strangest accent I effer heard!" I laughed too. "It's a long time since I tried the tongue," I told him. He asked me to his house "for a little tot, like," driving us there in his Landrover, and in the parlour poured me a whiskey big enough to swim a goldfish in. I said "Iechyd Da!" His wife, a pleasant grey-haired woman, took off her apron and joined us, then one of his sons, a muscular lad, roared up in his car and clumped in, first removing his Wellington boots at the door. They questioned me indirectly, as the Welsh always did. "So your book's coming along well?" asked Griffith. "Well enough," I said. "You'll be from England, then?" asked Mrs. Griffith. "I was born there," I said. But the son eyed me challengingly. "Good to have folk in the old house," he said bluntly, "but a lot of folk hereabouts don't like us renting to foreigners." He looked hard at his father. "The man speaks a little Welsh," said Griffith, almost defensively. "Well, so he does!" replied the son, shrugging, and faced me again. "I've got nothing against the English, mind. We have to look after our own, see, and people are talking."

I thanked them and left.

So there's gossip. There always is, in such places. It goes on the wind. Very likely the lad spreads it about to cut a figure, to get at his father, or simply because there's nothing else to talk about. It makes me uneasy. There's nothing I want better than to be left alone, and I could be happy here, I could make my peace, for the house is friendly, the hills are even older than I am. It is wet, and wild, but that is comforting. The only thing I cannot live with is continual dread. The Dancer said the Fifth World approaches, but I know nothing of that, it's the day-to-day that concerns me.

How long can this last?

On my way back from Gwernacca I saw a hawk—Tari's bird, the falconhawk, Horus—hovering high above, watching; and I felt a thrill; and momentarily recalled the high stakes for which Tari said we fight. Then I recalled Denver, and the thrill faded into fear. If the Hawk watches, so might others. Michael, at Compton you harangued me for loose talk, but how many experts have we seen? Just one talking in his cups would be enough for rumour to reach the ears of those who can add and subtract. No doubt they know already, but don't care, thinking me no real danger to any vested interest. Yet what did your Chancellor say to you when we got back to Compton? Why did you pack me here so fast? *"Sail a tighter ship, Greene, or else!"* Was that it? Or am I merely maundering? The gossip worries me, but I haven't sensed any spies; nobody in this country cares if I have words to say against U.S. authorities, I upset no applecarts here, I'm no insurrectionary ranter! No! I was the Queen's Man!

Now what can I do but write? On with it! On with it!

My interest in finding Northwest Passage grew at Oxford. I was most studious there, but in my fourth year Mary's men burned bishops Latimer and Ridley outside my window. The stench is with me still, and the courage with which they died. I left that papist hotbed and, later that year of 1555, got preference to Hatfield as page to Princess Elizabeth. This came through my aunt, Kate Ashley, who was governess to the future Queen, and went through much for her.

"Mistress Ashley says you are full of new ideas," said the Princess when we first met. She had just come in dripping-wet from the hunt, tall and pale, red hair striking against russet cloak. She was nineteen, had been in the Tower already. "You have discretion too?"

Discretion. Yes. For three years it was the watchword. There were hunts, dances, masques—all of it—and much time spent studying with that venerable man Roger Ascham; but the main business she had was keeping her head connected with her body.

Her sister Mary was not vindictive, but suffered the witch-fire-conscience that springs from frustrated loins, being half-mad with sadness that no man really wanted her, particularly not her husband King Philip, who wanted only to bed England, not the woman.

But my Queen was canny, never passion's slave, using what used her, for by never marrying any man she gave herself to all, and so won our anxiety, attention, irritation, and love. As a child she knew the price, learned the act, of wearing the cloak of awful Majesty—and often at Hatfield I saw a tremendous distance on her, but then she'd laugh and make a jest. Her moods so switched it was impossible to predict or know her, as she chose. And if from these early days she listened sweetly to my dreams, she delayed twenty years before helping me to them. I could never charm her as Walter did—but he was generous, and made his good fortune mine as well.

In 1558 she was Queen at last, but in 1562 there was plot on her life, then she almost died of the smallpox. We all stared into the abyss again. She was pressed to marry, *now!* So her game began.

In 1563 I left Court and took up arms, giving as good as I got at Le Havre de Grace. For use of the port we defended Huguenots who did not want us and opened the gates to the besieging Catholic army. The French we held, but not the Plague, bringing it back to England, where it killed thousands.

But in Havre I first considered English *colonisation,* for there I heard of Jean Ribault's ill-fated voyage to settle Huguenots in Florida. The Spanish murdered them all. *We must try farther north*, I thought, *out of Spain's reach*. And back in London I joined the Merchant Adventurers: a Company revived by Sebastian Cabot's flight from Spain to England in 1547. He was a rogue, but already he had stimulated sea-searches by Chancellor then Willoughby for a Northeast Passage. It wasn't there, but Russian trade had opened up: London now buzzed with talk of Discovery and new opportunities. I took lodgings and set to work, inventing instruments and fervently arguing for the Northwest route. At the Adventurers I had every chance to hone my passion against skeptical men. "Yes, Gilbert," they'd laugh, "but why *should* this Northwest Passage exist?"

"Why not?" I'd reply emphatically. *"Quid non?"*—which over the years I had to say so often that in time I took it for my motto.

"Indeed?" they'd smile. "So where is your proof?"

Proof? I had it at my fintertips:

"Primus, America must be an island, as Atlantis was, for no Asian beasts have been found in America, nor any far-wandering Asian tribes such as Scythians, Tartarians, or Mongolians; and you'll find not one explorer, not in America nor in Cathay, who has found or heard least hint of land-bridge to the other continent; not Paulus Venetus, nor Coronado nor de Gomara nor John Baros nor any.

"Secundus, proof cosmographic: the motion of seas from east to west, following the diurnal motion of Primum Mobile, proves America to be an island with Passage to the north. Cartier says the current he followed continued strongly northwest of his furthest discovery; where else could such a current go but through the Passage?

"Tertius, the maps of Gemma Frisius, Petrus Martyr, Tramontanus, Hunterus, Gastaldus, and others, all indicate the likelihood that the Passage exists, and is navigable!"

And so on. But in 1566 I was assigned to Ireland as Captain of a Devon Company in Sidney's army, sent to suppress rebellion, and for the next four years I could not escape that hell! Ireland! Is it not amazing that now in 1990 the matter is still a madness?

Some say I acted hard there. I must speak of it.

One summer night in San Francisco three years ago I was in a dark bar on Mission Street, getting drunk enough to go to work—no, I'll not yet speak of *that,* save to say that I was in my mad ranting period, and with good reason—when a silver-haired old man turned to me from the neighbouring stool. He had a florid face full of broken veins, and he was as deep in his cups as I.

"Name's Butler," he said in a thick brogue, "William Yeats Butler. They thought I'd make a poet, but I'm sixty-three years old and never written a line. Did you ever hear of an Irishman with no poetry? Well, here he is, and who are you?"

I sighed. The night lay ahead.

"Gilbert. Humphrey Gilbert."

"Well! Cut your accent in half and there'd still be plenty left over! When did *you* leave England?"

I was depressed and irritable.

"Four hundred and four years ago!" I declared frostily.

(Absurd, but for a time in San Francisco this was my usual policy. By 1987 there were so many chrononuts all claiming to be DTIs stranded in the twentieth century by Project Vulcan that often I found truth my best disguise. Folk rarely turned a hair, and it was not unusual to find myself quite outdone:

"Gilbert. 1583. Pleased to meet you!"

"Mm. Napoleon. Put it there, pal."

Or:

"I'm Madoc. Sailed from Gwynedd in 1170, but . . .")

It didn't always work. On this occasion it did not work, for William Yeats Butler was not amused. He glared.

"Think I'm just another drunken paddy, don't you?"

"Sir," I said, rising, "I don't mean to offend you, but now I have to go to work. Perhaps another time."

I put it completely out of mind. But a week later I was in that same bar again, at the same time, when the face of William Yeats Butler loomed up before my whiskey eyes again.

"Oh! You, is it? *Sir Humphrey Gilbert!* You bastard!"

He was furious. I could hardly recall him.

"I'm sorry, sir, I don't know what you mean."

"Doesn't know what I mean? Liar! Bastard!"

I was taken aback, and felt my temper rising.

"Sir, I *demand* you tell me what you mean!"

The barman told us to quieten down. Butler paid no heed. He stared aggressively at me through the smoky dimness of the place.

"Did you not say your name is Humphrey Gilbert, and it's from four hundred years ago you are?"

"Yes . . . but . . ."

"I went to the library!" Butler declared. "I'm a poor old man with no work and not much wit but you stuck in my mind. I went to the library and read all about this man you claim to be! Butchering murderer! Lining the way to his tent in the English camp each night with the heads of the poor Irish women and children he'd killed! Why would any man call himself Humphrey Gilbert unless he was down on the Irish? Why?"

"Well . . ." I started.

"Well! Well what? Are you still claiming to be Gilbert?"

"Well . . ." I said again, at a loss, meeting his eyes.

"Well *nothing!*" Butler announced for all the room to hear, and I was glad there weren't too many people there. "If you are Gilbert or not matters not at all! It's the intention that counts! You said it's Gilbert you are, and I went to the library and read about the bastard. I know all about it. Listen! In 1562 the great chief Shan O'Neill (God bless him!) visited London to talk with that fine young queen Elizabeth. She tricked him and would not let him leave until she had extorted false allegiance from him. When he went back to Ireland with his men he raised right rebellion, so in July 1566 she sent Sir Henry Sidney to put our man down. Our young firebrand Gilbert was in Sidney's army, and he was just raring to cut off a few heads and prove himself a bold man . . ."

"I never wanted to go to Ireland!" I protested angrily, held by the man's mad eyes, "I did everything I could to get out of the . . ."

". . . And soon enough he was charging round Munster on his big black horse, waving his sword and putting hundreds of helpless starving Irish out of their misery, so they made him a colonel, and soon he had everything burned down, and all the people nice and quiet and dead or down to eating grass and carrion where they could find it. So what does he get up to next, in 1569, with Queen Lizzy's blessing, but bring in his roughneck Devon friends, Carew and Champernoun and St. Leger, to grab the wasted land and call it an English colony? And our people found spirit at this outrage to crawl out of their graves and fight again, under James Fitzmaurice and McCarthy More—bold men they were!—but our men had no food and no weapons and brave Sir Humphrey was equal to the task. At each castle he demanded immediate surrender, and if he didn't get it, why, he killed every man and woman and child. The English were very pleased with him, and so they made him a knight, at Drogheda, where that bloody man Cromwell murdered thousands more of us eighty years later—and may the Curse of the English be lifted from us some day soon!"

With people now watching and listening Butler paused for breath, his face burning and eyes glowing like devil's coals, and I think by then my own colour was quite on fire, for I felt not only infuriated by his rant, but unhinged by it, cast back in memory to that terrible, wretched, blackened desert of a land. As he shouted the image had come to me that again I was riding patrol in Munster, and it was void all round, with no buildings standing, and the graves opened so the poor might eat. This is what it was like, and not wholly the fault of the English, though true that Sidney's predecessor, Sussex, had left a terrible mess behind him.

But I restrained myself and said nothing, for behind me stood two men with pool cues. They'd stopped their game to listen, and for all I knew they were the bosom buddies of this lunatic.

"You're very quiet!" Butler affected astonishment. "Does this mean that you still claim to be this bastard Gilbert?"

"Sir," I said, almost in a whisper, my fists clenched at my side, "I acted in the interest and standards of my country and age, and I did my duty, though it was not to my pleasure, nor to my profit! I spent four years trying to get out of that hellhole, and paid the troops out of my own pocket, though I never got more than six hundred back of the thousands I was owed by the government!"

"Will you hear the man?" Butler appealed to all about, "it's not the killing of helpless folk that bothers him, it's the money!"

I almost struck him, but the pool cues suggested I might do better with words than with fists.

"Mr. Butler!" I said rapidly, "you blame it all on me and mine, but *your* family had been feuding with the Geraldines for years, taking heads and tearing the land apart! When I got there it was already a land of buzzards that the Irish made for themselves. As for myself, I was a soldier, sent to subdue rebels who were pirating English ships, blocking our way to the open sea, and welcoming papal troops come to invade us. I was told to restore order as quick and cheap as possible. I decided severity would be quickest and most merciful. So, as you say, I gave the option—surrender or die! Once they knew I meant it, twenty-six castles gave in without fight. Time, money, lives were saved. As to the heads outside my tent, the rebels were headhunters, and I gave them what they understood so they would not think me soft! In the event..."

Butler finished his whiskey and slammed down the glass.

"Ye fascist English bastard!" he shouted in my face.

"No trouble now, boys," said the bartender.

"In the event, I..."

"Look at the miserable man! Not an ounce of pity!"

"IN THE EVENT, I PUT THE FEAR OF GOD IN THEM, WHICH IS THE ONLY WAY TO RULE A REBEL AGAINST HIS WILL!" I bellowed, standing suddenly up. "WE WENT TO KEEP THE PEACE, WE..."

"RIGHT YE DID, *SORR!*" Butler bellowed back, spittling my face as he stood, saluting derisively, *"OUR* PIECE!"

That did it. It was a silly business, I was lucky to get out of it with no broken bones, I was laid up some days and could not work, the bruises stiffening so much I could not even crack a whip.

Yes, I was cruel in Ireland. I steeled myself to it, and did what I had to do, and was commended by all save the rebels. I did not hide from the enemy. At Knockfergus with but a hundred and fifty foot I withstood four thousand kerns and over sixty horsemen. At Kilkenny with thirteen men I charged twelve hundred, and we came through unscathed, though my horse was much hurt. At Kilmallock in September of sixty-nine I held a ford against over twenty men, covering the retreat of my men. Yes, I killed, and modern opinion condemns the cause I served, and what good did it do? As soon as I was gone they were up in fresh revolt, and now here we are four hundred years on, and nothing resolved. If I aided the growth of this tragedy, well, I am not proud of it, and was not proud of it then, despite the praise I got; I was sick of it, and unutterably relieved when at last I was let go from it. For years I was kept from my work. In all that time my only achievement was to complete the first version of my Discourse on the Northwest Passage, in 1566. I took it to the Queen that year when I found excuse to return to London with letters, hoping I'd not have to go back at all. She ignored both my hope and the Discourse, as did brother John when I sent him a copy asking for money to fund an expedition. He told me to give up my silly dreams, and so back I went to Ireland. But it passed, for myself, at any rate.

Bastard I may be, but I never yet stabbed any man in the back.

Now it's night again, and cold in here, and I'm hungry. Stoke up the stove, boil potatoes and carrots, unfreeze a slab of the white stuff that Michael called *fish*, fry it, and eat. And calm down.

I'm still worried. Gossip, the Hawk, my memories. This is

the fifth successive day on which I've written, and the twelfth that I've been here. There's a telephone, but so far Michael hasn't called me and I haven't called him. He agreed not to unless there is need.

I feel memories stirring of things I hoped I'd never have to call back to mind again.

7

Another Night
of Imp & Sprite

So to another night of imp and sprite. I could not sleep, I
burned, I tossed and turned, I was plagued by voices from the
past in every creak of house and blast of wind, and by succession of visions to match, very real to me. *"But Humphrey,
where will the money come from?"* my wife demanded, and
she was pregnant again; and then I heard a gruff Yorkshire
voice: *"Black muck!"* it muttered, *"No brass! No gold! Just
black muck!"* I looked, and saw that giant man Frobisher facing
me, bankrupt, back from his second voyage with his "golden
ore," later used as slag on London streets, and he was furious.
*"Northwest, tha said, Northwest! Gilbert, if tha'st such passion
for t' sea, why in Name of God art still on land?"* And now
a new ghost, bowing roguishly, offering me a copy of my own
Discourse, published by him, without my permission. George
Gascoigne! *"As your friend I had to do it, Humphrey. You're
too modest and meek to put yourself forward, and the world
should read this work. So I stole it from your library and got
it printed up, admitting my sin in the Introduction..."* But
suddenly a voice behind my shoulder and George is gone; I'm
looking up a glassy tube at a fiery rushing comet, in 1577, and
my heart is beating at the meaning of it. *"Jacta est alea!"* Her
Majesty declares grimly, *"So comets are not sublunary, the
glass makes it clear, nor exhalations of the atmosphere. The
die is cast. There is change in the heavens, the new star in
Cassiopeia proved that, and even if it means not the Last
Judgment as many say where will it take us? Where?"*

So there I lay with these voices and visions, not asleep and not awake, but in time I was asleep, it must be, because my dreaming was remarkable. And perhaps it was more than dreaming.

Deep in the night it seemed I was awakened, as happened the other night, by a pale light that glowed all through the room. The night seemed hushed and still, wrapped in a cocoon of motionless silence. The silvery glow came strongest from the doorway. Before going to bed I had shut the door, but now as I looked I saw a shining opening, and beyond it a corridor echoing away into milky misty distance. And standing either side of this brilliant gate, as though they had just come through it into the room, were two wraiths. Left of the gate was Mery-Isis, Tari, the Beloved of Isis, slim and small and dark, ghostily clad in the boots and jeans and denim shirt she wore that terrible day we were attacked in Denver. Her hair was a snow-white halo, her face somewhat hawkish and grave, yet I was glad to see her.

It was when I recognised the second shade that my heart missed a beat, or two or three. For this other, wearing black cap and his star-studded gown the colour of the midsummer clear night sky, was the shade of a man I once knew well—the magus, Doctor John Dee!

I gaped, and it was he who stepped forward, or rather glided, to the foot of my bed, where he stopped and floated all wan and pale and half-transparent like one of those spirits he was often accused of conjuring out of the netherworld. Yet when he spoke (in my mind, not aloud) he was as sardonic as ever he was in the flesh:

"I hear you found your Passage after all, Humfrey, though not what you expected, and time-consuming in the crossing."

"It is so," I answered drily, my heart stuttering. I looked past his shade to the clear blue spirit-glow of the Egyptian I loved, and still love. "How did you learn this? Did she tell you? Are you now among the spirits of the dead?"

"Yes and no," he said, his bright ghost-eyes giving me a sorry look. "Let me explain. Earlier this evening I was home at Mortlake, where you often visited me, packing boxes, because we are all off to Poland soon—Joan and myself and Kelly and his wife, and all the household too—when your brother Adrian and half-brother Sir Walter came suddenly to visit me. Hakluyt was also with them, and in a sad state, poor fellow. They brought the heavy news that last Sunday the *Golden Hind* returned alone to Falmouth from your Newfoundland expedition; and that Captain Hayes reports loss of the *Delight* with Parmenius and a hundred other souls, and worse, that two weeks ago you and the *Squirrel* were lost as well—lost, and almost certainly drowned. Yet none in the *Hind* actually saw your little boat sink in the storm, so your brothers and Hakluyt came asking me to use my art to learn if you might yet be alive, perhaps cast upon an isle of the Azores. It is a measure of his love for you that Hakluyt, who is devoutly of the Clergy, as you know, is willing to countenance such activity. At first I demurred, for such workings are not lightly undertaken, and I am busy, and Kelly is in a temper today. But they pressed me, saying privately the Queen also wishes to know, and your wife Anne. They asked if I were not your friend, so I said I am, and agreed to try it. *'It is for Great Britain,'* I said.

"Therefore I washed and anointed myself and went privately to my temple, and entranced myself through the shewstone, first gazing on a picture of you that your brother had brought. I journeyed, and cast an eye through the world, but found no sign of you alive. But neither did I meet any shroud or dark symbol to confirm your passing-over. This seemed strange, so I climbed higher up the Tree, holding your image in mind to attract any spirit that might help me. Soon I saw a flash of fish, a field of green blue, and heard a voice that spoke of 'a death, not any of the Seven Deaths, but on that same path.' I confess I was perplexed and most intrigued—what death is not among the Seven?—so I hastened to the relevant Path, the Twenty-Fourth, a Path of death and rebirth, between the spheres of Raphael and Haniel, where the Scorpion lurks in wait. For a time I wandered amid sombre brown fogs shot with lightning-bolts of vivid indigo, and skirted sighing chasms—then I sensed the silver flash of fish again, and took that key to the green blue way which is the higher arc of this Path, and there felt the presence of one I sought who sought me too. So I met this Priestess of Isis, your friend, and she has told me the remarkable tale of how you and she and many others from many ages have been cast, physically, without intervening death of the usual sorts, into manifestation at the end of this Age of the Fish.

"So, when I heard of your present strait, I agreed we must combine immediately to alert you before you forget everything important. But it has been most difficult to reach you! We almost had your attention several of your nights ago, but you became confused, and lost Mery-Isis into image of your mother, and lost your mother too, and instead of myself you heard your cunning man. But now you have rid yourself of him, so now we ask you to make a choice! Will you rise and step through this gateway with us?"

Now large in my vision loomed the crystalline glimmering of the transcending gate, and the misty passage with its hint of bitter emptiness beyond. My balls and brain both crinkled in fear.

"Where does it lead?" I demanded suspiciously.

"That's for you to find out."

"But why should I?"

"Humfrey, have you lost your British pluck?"

The Doctor, sounding puzzled, peered closer to me.

"He is now in a society that makes folk very defensive," came Tari's quick thought as she too approached. "He wants to *survive*."

"Oh?" Dee looked glum. "How sad. I never thought he was a coward." And he turned to Tari, his ghostly head nodding with concern. "Are you *sure* this man is *really* the Humfrey Gylberte I knew? I would hate to be in error. My professional repu . . ."

"I AM SIR HUMFREY GYLBERTE OF COMPTON!" I bellowed, starting up and stamping straight at the gate, quite forgetting how Dee always knew how to take advantage of my rash nature. "I'LL DO IT! WHY NOT?"

They did not stop me. I marched past them and into the shining doorway. There was a great wrench, everything turned inside out, instantly I was plunging through a universe ablaze, through the babble and mutter of a million voices and wars. I wailed, laughed, roared, wished myself elsewhere. There was another horrid jerk of dislocation, I was twisted back to front and landed where I'd started, in my room, facing the glowing, ghostly pair.

"What sort of Gate is *this?*"

I laughed incredulously but Tari faced me, stern.

"What did you see, my friend?"

"Vulcan," I told her, my teeth bared, *"Vulcan!"*

"Dear man, that is in the *past!* Why cling to it? The Gate

takes you where you most decide to go. You learned your purpose through the Hawk's eyes: why forget it now?"

"Purpose?" I was infuriated. "What purpose can exist now?" I cried. "History has fallen into Chaos; all Order and Hierarchy and Sovereignty are overthrown, the Chain is snapped into pieces!"

"These things are overthrown so that through struggle we may all come to live and work in the Light by choice!" Tari declared sharply, her eyes blazing bright. "These processes you speak of are but crutches of reality, not reality itself, and you cannot depend on them! Humfrey, imposed Order is only make-shift, and perpetuates its own weaknesses. Remember, now! My friend! We work so that there shall be no more priests and kings, save in that every man and woman is priest and king in themselves!"

"But without imposed Order," I protested, "you get madness and murder! Most folk cannot behave at all without Law im-posed: they are helpless children, ignorant and greedy! They need direction!"

"Speak for yourself!" she said pitilessly. "Humfrey, the chasm must be crossed. History has come to this, there's no going back. We can accept the challenge and try to live, or give up and go down with Black Osiris. That's our choice— and it is why the Eighty-Seven of us were brought from our times into this age!"

"What? To be locked up, tortured, and killed?"

"No! To bear witness! To unite the ages!"

"But the American Navy didn't mean that Vulcan should..."

"No! You forget. They were unwitting agents. They did not even realise they cast a net, far less what fish they'd catch!"

"But they did! How else would they have been so prepared with doctors and drugs and sterile chambers?"

"Yes, I must admit, I find this hard to understand myself," said the shade of Dee to Tari, "Do you mean to say that this 'accident' was organised on the Inner Planes?"

"More subtle yet," she replied, "Those on the Inner Planes knew of it, but would not stop it, being sworn never to interfere in human free will. Why? Because our purpose includes the aim that in time all people on Earth will know their true will, by connection with the source, and without need of imposed Order." She shot her look at me. "Humfrey, the revolutions in this age, however mad they seem, are a part of it—and they run deeper than the sphere of material cause and effect, which is all you are letting yourself see!"

"Did you die at Denver?" I demanded, in a sort of panic. "Are you alive on Earth now, or but a shade in my dreaming?"

She said nothing, but her expression said she thought my question a stupid evasion; her shade turned to the window as Dee approached.

"Hear what she says, Humfrey," said he sympathetically. "I have never heard it put in such a radical way, but there's wisdom in it. As for the Gate, well, let the lusty rage of your Lancelot give way to the Galahad-son within you! Let your child be father to the man! Stand up straight, and find the Middle Way, and..."

Then Tari turned back to us.

"I heard the cock crow!" she interrupted. "We must go!" Her eyes were like piercing jewels. "Humfrey, when you wake up you'll remember this! You'll see the Hawk again and know what to do!"

I was afraid, and hurriedly said to Doctor Dee:

"What will you tell my family, and my friends?"

"I must say that you are gone from us for good." His ghost nodded heavily. "It would not help to tell them anything else."

"You must tell my wife I'm sorry that..."

"Again!" Tari was impatient. "Doctor, we have to go!"

"One minute, one minute! Yes, Humfrey?"

"Tell Anne I'm sorry I never provided better for her and our children," I babbled. "I thought I had, but I was never good at business, and had so much on my mind with the expedition, and..."

"It crows a third time! Doctor, come now!"

"All right, all right! Humfrey, I'll do and say what I can. Bear yourself like a British gentleman! Now, farewell!"

Then the two of them turned and began to fade through the shining doorway, the Doctor still talking as in my dream the glowing light grew dim and I heard the wind outside. "Yes," he was telling Tari, "this has been most interesting, but distressing too, and I do not know what I'll tell Adrian and Sir Walter, let alone his wife the Lady Anne. One has to give such disagreeable news sometimes, and..."

They were gone.

I awoke, then or later, to the grey of dawn.

Now it is midday. When I went out earlier I saw the hawk, spiralling in the wind, and I shivered. To complete this work I'll have to go through the Vulcan-Gate again, the sooner the better, and leave my old life behind. But there are matters to wrap up first, never leave your laces untied when you start on a long journey. So, to Doctor Dee, my fatal expedition, Horsfield, the Hawk—yes, yes, in its time, soon, through that dreadful Gate—

For in 1578 I went to sea at last. . . .

8

"...You'll Be Richer Than Croesus!"

"Soon, my love, you'll be richer than Croesus!"

Yes, that is what I told my wife that day, the twenty-sixth of September in 1578, when at last, after many years of preparation and setback, I set out from Dartmouth with a strong ocean-going fleet. Despite every trouble which had beset us in the building of the fleet, I refused to doubt that soon I'd have success in my grasp. It had to be! The expedition had the backing of many friends of Discovery, but most importantly, Her Majesty was finally persuaded to support my dream. On the eleventh of June I had got my formal grant by letters-patent to colonise and govern in the name of England any "heathen and barbarous lands, countreys, and territories not actually possessed of any Christian prince or people," with rights extending to my heirs forever. I had drafted the document myself, months earlier, and it had been known to me for half a year or more that this time my plan would be approved. Four ships had been ready to sail by May, but enemies both elemental and human had obstructed us. Headwinds had held back several of my ships in the Thames for weeks; and worse, during the wait at Plymouth my second-in-command Knollys had deserted us, taking four ships with him. I'd put money it was Mendoza behind this treachery, for he had set spies and dissension among us at every chance, correctly suspecting that colonisation was not the chief intention of our well-armed fleet. Too sharp at his job by far: from a Spaniard viewpoint that old fox Philip had chosen his English ambassador well; but as far as I'm concerned it would have been no loss at all to have seen Bernardino de Mendoza strung up.

Early that day on which we first tried to leave it looked as if the weather might break at last. In the General's Cabin on my flagship, the *Anne Ager*, I took counsel with my Captains and Masters. Brothers Carew and Walter were there with me as commanders (it was a wonder the Queen had let Walter go), and an agent from Secretary Walsingham, and Ferdinando our pilot, and my good friend Miles Morgan, whose *Red Lion* carried "Now or Never" for its motto. That was my mood too, and it's a good thing we're not all cunning men who can see the future. As to that long-ago foretelling of my fate at sea, yes it had me tense, making men doubt me, but I could not ignore my chance. So, after much argument, I gave orders:

"There's been enough delay already," I said. "Yes, it's late in the year, but we are well-fitted, and God is with us if we are bold. We cannot stay here and brood on the treachery at Plymouth. We sail as soon as the winds permit."

And it was agreed, but two or three were dubious and remained behind to hear my further persuasion. I convinced them, and dispersed them to wait in readiness on their ships, but I was in a tight state when next my mother and wife and three oldest sons—John, Humphrey, and Otho, came aboard and were shown in by Walter. He was bright with enthusiasm to set out, it being his first sea-venture too, and he had no more mind than I for the business of Farewell and Godspeed. "Mother, I must go over into the *Falcon* now," he said soon in his perfect dapper way. "I am needed there, and it will spare you grief." And so diplomatically he abandoned me to deal with a scene that was not happy. They tried to hide it, but both wife and mother betrayed doubt of me. Side-by-side they sat on the mercy seat, all cloaked-up, and Anne in particular was full of *ifs* and *buts* and *whys*.

"But Humfrey, it's too late in the year! Our investment is too great to be risked on winter storms, and so are four hundred lives!"

"Too late? How can it be too late? I have waited all my life for this!" I paced up and down past them, head ducked to avoid the beams, my boys fidgeting, listening, told to sit down and not touch anything the moment they came in, and not by me. Anne's face had that look on it, that relentless dutiful patience, her shield against what she saw as my folly. *I know you won't listen to a word I say,* said her·look, *but I'll say it anyway!*

"If you have waited all your life, you can wait another six months, surely?" she objected.

"Her Majesty is eager for rapid return!" I was still pacing. "I cannot tell you everything, but I can promise that soon, my love, you'll be richer than Croesus! This fine vessel that bears your sweet name will carry us to our goal no matter how dire the storm, how bitter the cold, how . . ."

"Humfrey, sit down and relax!" Mother suddenly commanded. She was old now, but indomitable. She had rallied great support for this business, and her voice still carried strong. I stopped pacing but would not sit. "Humfrey, look at us! We may mean very little to you now, but for the sake of God don't make it so obvious you wish you were faraway! It is not flattering, any more than it is flattering that three of my sons should be quite so tightmouthed about what you're all up to! D'you take us for fools?"

"No, Mother, but . . . it's a matter of state . . ."

"But the Charter gives you rights for six years!" Anne jumped in. "Why does the Queen want you to go now? Why can't you wait till spring?"

"If we disperse now," I said, "we would lose too much."

"Matter of state!" muttered my mother, shaking her head.

"But already you lost four ships at Plymouth," Anne persisted. "What if there are more like Knollys to put a knife in your back?"

The clouds were lifting. A breeze was tugging at the waters. The boys listened wide-eyed, as impatient as I.

"Mendoza paid Knollys," I said, mustering my utmost control. "He has given me trouble at every turn. The sooner we're out of reach of him, the better!"

"But how can you be sure of your men?"

"I've got the bad apples out of the barrel!" I snapped. "We're much stronger now, the mood is good, we are ready, we will go!"

"Humfrey, you have worked miracles, and all admit it," Mother said quickly, "and if you must go now, you must go now. But . . . why do you take that Portuguese? Simon—what is it?—Fernandez? Ferdinando?" Her voice was soft. "I hear it's the Spanish mid-part of America he knows, not the Northwest."

"He comes for the . . . experience of new coasts," I said.

"My son," said Mother even more softly, "you're not made like Francis Drake. You think too much. I am proud of you, but I do ask you please to pay heed to your Captains and Masters, who have been at sea all their lives."

It was awkward, made worse when Anne started muttering against the Queen, accusing Her Majesty of driving me into making a "piratical bargain." I would not take this, we had a most improper scene, and by God I was glad when John caught my eye. "Father, you said you'd show us how to fire a cast piece," he complained, and Humphrey and Otho were immediately up in agreement, both talking at once, plucking my sleeve to lead me out. I met Anne's eyes and for once we agreed. How can you argue with your nearest and dearest at such an hour? Out we went into the stiffening wind, to the bustle on deck. Grey cloud scudded broken and low over the crags above the sheltered harbour; I steered my boys up to the fo'c's'le, to a good view of our seven ships and all the activity of final preparation: last-minute loadings from the quay and the rest of it. They were bright lads, seven and six and five now, and I was proud of them. I showed them how one of the big pieces was set and laid, then I told them the names of our ships—the *Falcon,* a Queen's Ship of a hundred tons, that Walter commanded, and the *Hope of Greenway,* of a hundred and sixty, under brother Carew, and the *Red Lion*—but as I tousled their heads a cunning voice whispered I might never see them again, and I stiffened.

"Miles Morgan captains the *Red Lion,* doesn't he, Father?"

John was oldest. He would have my height one day. Humphrey was six, with Anne's darker colouring. Otho already showed my brother John's taciturn humour, and watched, but rarely spoke.

"Yes, John, he . . ."

"Why did Mr. Knollys try to kill Mr. Morgan?"

"Mr. Knollys is a foolish, conceited man! Mr. Morgan would not obey his traitorous orders while I was away, and Knollys would have killed him—but I came back and put a stop to that!"

"But he ran away with four ships, Father! Can't you get them back to make you stronger at sea against the Spaniards?"

"How often must I tell you, John, we are not going against the Spaniards! We are going to the New World, to make a New England, which will bring us great wealth! Now, our smaller ships—that's the *Gallion* over by the harbourmouth, forty tons, and the *Swallow* next to it is the same, and that very little boat you see is my *Squirrel*, a stout little fellow, only eight tons but made of the best!"

"Father, how big is this ship?" asked Humphrey.

"Two hundred and fifty tons!" I told him.

"And how many cannon are there?" asked John.

"Two hundred cast pieces in all," I said.

"But what do you need them for," John asked, grinning slyly, the little devil, "if you're not going to fight Spaniards?"

It was then, to my great relief, that Mr. Pedley the Master of the *Anne Ager* came up to me.

"Zir Umfrey, uz can try it now. Du yu give the oarder?"

I felt a great surge of joy and apprehension.

"By all means, Mr. Pedley! By all means!"

For years it had looked as if I'd never get to sea at all, remaining a lubberly armchair sailor all my life.

In 1570, when I returned a knight from Ireland, my first attention was to marriage, which I soon contracted with Mistress Anne Ager of Otterden in Kent, whose father had been the last Marshal at Calais, dying there when we lost the port in 1558. Anne was a pretty, dark, spirited girl, and wealthy too, and she loved me greatly when we met, for in my early thirties I was not without looks and quality, being tall, wiry, active, and of a good colour. And yes, I loved her too, but soon enough she knew me too well, learning she would never wholly distract me from my fretful, constant fever to realise my dreams. I could never sit still with her long, and of course sometimes in my heat I ploughed other furrows, as she learned when that fraud Meadley the alchemist (well, he fooled Lord Burghley and the Earl of Leicester too) not only refused my advances but advertised them so that all knew my dual nature. Anne took this wearily but well, except that I had struck the knave: she was horrified I should stoop to strike. Yet by and large we got along for better and worse, and so in time she bore me six sons and a daughter that died, and myself I think perhaps she bore better than I deserved.

Those early years after Ireland were a confusion. I sat in the Commons as MP for Plymouth, and was insulted by old Wentworth the Dissenter (I mean Peter who died in the Tower, not his brother Paul). He called me names for supporting Her

Majesty's right to grant monopolies where she would, he accused me of reporting Commons business to her, and when I tried to speak in self-defense I was three times shouted down by the House. For this the Queen's reward was my appointment as Surveyor of Artillery in the realm, which got me some commission over the years, though not enough to replace what I had spent in Ireland. As for Parliament, I bid it farewell.

In 1572, that year of New Star and Huguenot Massacre, I was at arms again. The Queen sent me to Flanders with a rabble-army, to hold Flushing and wage what she called "underhand" war against the Spaniards of Alva's army. Walter was with me, it was his first campaign, and mad George Gascoigne too, but the campaign was a disaster. I am no good at Diplomacy and siege and patience, I like to rush and dash and charge. I raged in that mire for months before, disordered and beplagued as usual, we withdrew secretly back to England. There I "took the rap" of public reprimand to protect Her Majesty's interest, as we were not officially at war with Spain.

After all this I was glad for some quiet life, but not too quiet: I settled my growing family in a good large house at Limehurst, or Limehouse, as some even then called it. I have learned that later it became part of a slum in the city, but then it was out in the country, though conveniently close to the centre of all affairs in which I was involved. So, children were born, and summers were spent in Devon with family, on the water and in the woods, eagerly planning Discovery while playing; and winter nights in my Library at Limehurst I studied and wrote, revising my Discourse on the Northwest Passage in the light of new scholarship, but for the most part working on proposals for a new sort of school, to be called *Queen Elizabeth's Achademy*.

Yet at no time did I give up my hope of sailing west. Often I went into London to meet and talk with friends and with those who might help my designs. I was often at Court, and sometimes over to Mortlake to visit Doctor Dee and browse in his library, and meet with geographers there, like Ortelius; sometimes I met with Secretary Walsingham to discuss moneymaking schemes that might help me. I spoke boldly in many places about colonisation and the Northwest Passage, and now had the Muscovy Company (which had been the Merchant Adventurers) against me: they feared I might infringe what they considered their monopolies, and of them all I remained friendly only with Anthony Jenkinson, who'd travelled the length and breadth of the Russias. He was a man after my own heart, and so was the young cleric Richard Hakluyt, a map-enthusiast like myself.

Hakluyt was greatly unhappy when he could not come on my second voyage. Well for him and the world he did not. Parmenius went in his place and died: as I now learn Hakluyt lived to make a famous work out of the Narratives of English Discovery.

In fact it was Hakluyt they gave me to read in Florida, four hundred years later, to learn my own fate. It still disturbs me, this hindsight through recorded history of the ultimate fates of men whose lives I ran with until mine was translated. It is hard to reconcile my memory of Walter, for example, with a reading in history of how he met his fate on the block after years in jail and a last expedition as disastrous as mine. Such disconnection between living memory and recorded fact still bewilders me.

Yet then of course I knew none of it. I was a grown man, and zestful for my cause, and the cunning man was faraway. I had a dream to win. But most likely I'd never have got to sea at all if not for that scalawag genius, George Gascoigne, for he understood the value of what is now called *publicity*, where I did not . . . or would not.

George had a way with words and an even better way with trouble. He was kin to the sailor Martin Frobisher, which in part explains what he did. At the time I knew him as part of Leicester's glittering gang, but thought him a wholehearted man, no empty fool, no matter what many said. He had been with me in Flanders, and wrote one of the worst poems I ever read about that disaster, but some of his comedies were reckoned good.

He was one of those who care deeply while passing off everything lightly: the world condemns them for the surface frivolity.

One night early in 1576 I met him at a gathering of the Mermaid Tavern Goodfellows. In fact he had asked me there, for I did not much frequent the theatric circles. We met, and drank to this and that, and at length he said:

"Sir Humfrey, Doctor Dee tells me you have written a fine thing on the Northwest Way. When will you publish it?"

"Oh," I said, "I doubt I'll do that. Who'd read it?"

"I would," he said. "Can I call on you to read it?"

He visited a week or two after, and I took him into my library. In fact at that time I was more hot for my plans of education, so I sat him down with my proposals. "By these means," I said, stalking up and down as he read, "the youth of gentry will be some use to England instead of wasting their time running after hounds! They'll learn to serve and advance this great Nation! We must have *broad* education, not just book-learning, and . . ."

"My friend, your scheme is brilliant!" George announced. "So brilliant with all its grand new ideas that nobody will understand it for a minute." He put down my manuscript with a thump, then eyed me questingly. "Humfrey, it's your North-west thing I really want to study. D'ye mind if I borrow it for a week or two?"

"Oh, take it!" I said crossly.

He did. Three weeks later he came by and returned it, and with it he gave me a printed work at the title-page of which I stared with slowly-mounting horror:

A DISCOURSE
written by
SIR HUMFREY GYLBERTE, KNIGHT
To Prove a Passage by the Northwest to
CATAIA AND EAST INDIA

I stared at him in amazement. He gave me his fool's grin. "You are too modest," he said, "So I had to do it."

"But you . . . you . . ." I couldn't speak.

"Yes, I know," he said calmly, "I'm a rogue. That's what I'm for. Oh, and I wrote a little introduction explaining I've published it without your knowledge or permission, and that it's all my fault."

"How . . . how many of these . . . ?"

"Well, five hundred at first," said George, "but they were sold immediately, so we're printing another two thousand! You're famous, Humfrey! Look . . . back off!" he appealed as I advanced on him. "Sir Humfrey, if you truly want to get to sea, you have to come down to the practical level of things! This publication will win you much influence, which means money and support for expeditions! And while I'm about it, your *Achademy* scheme is all very well—but surely you realise the Queen will just put it away and forget it?"

He stopped me.

"In God's Name, what do you mean?" I demanded.

"Humfrey, m'boy, if you want to get her to help you, you have to come up with something more to her taste! Your schemes are all about *ideals!* Surely you know what she really wants?"

"No," I said. "What?"

"MONEY!" he said, "M-O-N-E-Y!!!"

He was right on all counts. The publication of my Discourse got me fame and helped persuade those who backed Frobisher's first voyage to the Northwest in search of the Passage. It did George no good, poor man, for he got sick and died the next year, in his early prime. As for myself, I grew crafty. I took his advice and tailored a treatise to the Queen's taste, on How to Annoy the King of Spain. I proposed covert attacks on Spain, among their Newfoundland fishers and in the West Indies. I said we should take those isles by force, striking Spain before Spain struck us. I said that Queen and Privy Council should disclaim all knowledge of such attacks, and afterwards imprison a scapegoat and seem to treat him harshly.

The time was ripe, for my stock was high. The Queen read what I had to say, and liked it.

That was in November 1577. Within a month I had secret sign from Walter that she would risk granting me a Charter of colonisation—if first I'd agree to try what Drake had already done in 1572.

"Quid pro quo, Humfrey," said she when we met privately to discuss it, "I have not much advantage to get from putting unruly malcontents in another land where the first thing they'll do is deny our Throne and Sovereignty. But of course you are only going to scout the land, and should you happen to . . . to veer a little southward, perhaps . . ." She made a gesture with her hand. "You understand me?"

"Yes, yes, Your Majesty," said I, bowing.

So to the months of preparation, hiring of men, victualling, purchase of ships and equipment and ordnance, and to the making of orders, open and secret, until at Plymouth I had eleven ships gathered. It was then that Knollys sailed off with four ships, leaving us seven, with which on the twenty-second of September we sailed to Dartmouth.

Four days later, as I said, we tried to set out.

The voyage was not a success.

First we were blown east to the Isle of Wight. A month later we tried again and were forced into Plymouth; and then again, and back to the Isle of Wight. At last on the twenty-ninth of November we sailed out and this time struggled to the open seas. We meant to make for the middle of America, and yes, we went looking for a fight. But it was too late in the year. The only fight we got during those dreadful weeks was with wind and sea. The storm never let up, and we were separated and driven apart, the *Red Lion* being lost, Miles and his crew with it. As for my command, it must be said I was too often angry, contradicting the better experience of others, insisting my dream *would* come true because it *must*. Even Walter got distressed with me, though he hid it, just as from myself I hid the fact that much of my petulance came through fear of the cunning man's prophecy.

But this time it was ruin I met, not the Power not of Christ. Each alone we limped back to the wreckage of my reputation and my wife's pocket. The investors got no return, I could not even pay the men, and the whole affair was wrapped in secrecy.

Yet I would not accept defeat. I was ready to try again and this time sail closer to my dream. But five years passed before I got a second chance. As soon as I returned Mendoza was at me. To tie me down he started new rebellion in Ireland, and brought a set of absurd charges against me, claiming I had thieved oranges from a Spanish ship in Walfled Bay, and sacked a monastery and village in Galicia!

I had to stay in London to answer all this and fight his agitation against me. He got my enemies in the Muscovy Company to persuade the Privy Council to order me not to leave the land; which was done, and also to revoke my Charter for colonisation, which briefly in October 1581 was also done. This put me in despair until the Queen restored me to my rights. Those rats! They lacked wit to see anything new! They saw to it that my ships were commandeered for the Irish fight; they made sure that I was bankrupted, discredited, cast from England's mind, reduced to selling the clothes from off my poor wife's back! It seemed impossible I would ever get anywhere again.

But in November 1580 Drake returned from his voyage round the world, his ship so heavy-laden with gold and silver of Peru it was a wonder it still floated. Golden Ship! Unlike me the Master Thief of the Unknown World was no dreamer; he went for gold and took it, returning his investors near five thousand times what they'd put in. The nation was overjoyed; the Queen too, for she knighted the bold little rascal on the deck of his ship while Mendoza and King Philip and all Spain howled for his blood. Yes, the pirate succeeded where the dreamer failed, not only in getting wealth but also in turning English thought more enthusiastically to the Unknown World. Profit of a million and a half had a lot to do with this, but truly, it was an epic voyage, firing the national imagination, and it helped me in my cause by improving the atmosphere for Discovery.

I met Drake after his return. He had knowledge that interested me, as you may imagine! While escaping the Spaniards he had sailed north up the coast of California, reaching that great Bay now overlooked by San Francisco (some claim now he landed in another Bay nearby, called Bodega, but from his description of it to me I think not). "I believe your Northwest Way is there," he told me. "The coast never turned west: I would have gone on to try it, but the men were tired and would not go any more north. So we came back via the Moluccas and Cape of Good Hope. But I think you're right!"

Hah! To know now I'm famous for advocating a Way that never was, that my argument influenced men for three hundred years! Well, I *was* right, there *is* a Northwest Passage . . . but none of us guessed how far America extended north, nor how frozen the Polar Sea. And had Drake tried it, he would probably have perished, and never have returned to stimulate the enthusiasm that got me to sea again.

Yes, for during this Drake hullaballoo I was busy trying to raise money and support for a new expedition, doing so by selling parts of the unknown American lands I owned by right of letters patent. To this end I had already concluded agreement with Doctor John Dee, making over to him the future royalties of all Discovery above the fiftieth parallel of latitude. Thus in September 1580 Doctor Dee became owner of the land of Labrador.

Dee! After the visit of his shade last night I have him much in mind, and also the night when he and I went to Cooke's house.

It's for tomorrow. My blood is chill from too much sitting.

9

How Doctor Dee
Founded the British Empire

Three times three!
  Three times three!
  Three times three I call John Dee!
  Here I sit, looking inward, and the mists are growing lighter.
I see a glimmering of light. I call John Dee!
  I hear a voice!
  "...for if there's no Intelligence in the Monad, how can
any exist in the parts and units? Whence comes Intelligence?"
  The light grows stronger. I see, I hear:
  "...How can we deny the Light that lets us deny? Humfrey,
this patch of sunlight that spills on the table and floor between
us—is its origin in the table and floor it lights, or elsewhere?"
  The table and floor. The table and floor—
  The light grows, and forms swim, and—
  I see him! We are in the full library of his house at Mortlake.
He stands the other side of a table which is strewn with books
and sheets of maps. He awaits my answer, his finely-chiselled
face austere, his tall slender form clad in his usual sombre
colours, with black skull-cap and white lace ruff less extrav-
agant than mine, the downward spear of his white beard prominent against the dull colour of his breast-cloth. As for myself,
I sit on a cushioned chair in my most bombastic doublet, the
black one, slashed with side-vents to show scarlet satin below,
and in my most inflated trunk-hose, with a thin gold chain
wound triply round my neck below my biggest ruff, and silver
earrings, and perfume in my beard, and the rapier with steel

lacework on the hilt. I am done up to the nines today. Also I
have a silver pomander, with many scents and spices, which'll
be important later on, as I'll tell. I know this day. It is September the tenth of 1580, and I am done up gorgeously because
I have a "product to sell," and wish to Impress, and because
I have notions for entertainment later tonight after Business is
done. Yes, I remember this day very well, and what came of
it! Yet this afternoon's a jewel, soft and mild with but a hint
of approaching autumn. The window's wide open with carpets
drawn back, the sparkling lawns slope gently down to the
willowy and placid Thames. I look out and see the swans glide
by, and the boats, and the wooded gardens of Richmond beyond; and the splashes and laughing of folk on the water drifts
in, and the scent of roses and heady murmurous bee-drowsing
pollen, mingling through this leather-dark room with its must
of books and binding-gum and strange incense. And the Sun!
It spills bright on the oak-plank floor and over my kid-booted
feet and climbs up clawed feet and legs to the top of the heavy
large table. It runs golden over the Gloucestershire sheet of
Saxton's new *National Atlas,* lights the numbers on opened
pages of nautical declination tables by Bourne of Gravesend,
and clarifies the heavy dark titling on the cover of Doctor Dee's
own *General and Rare Memorials pertaining to the Perfect Art
of Navigation.* It is early in the afternoon, after dinner, and we
await the arrival of my brother Sir John to witness our Labrador
agreement, and we are comfortably alone in the library. Doctor
Dee's second wife Joan is elsewhere about the house—I hear
her, singing somewhere upstairs—and the servants have been
dismissed to make the most of the lovely day. Best of all, both
Kelly and Barnabus Saul are somewhere else, thank God, for
in my opinion they poison this house with their backbiting and
treacherous, nervous excitements of jealousy and fear. But they
are not here today, and the Doctor himself is a reverend gentleman, about fifty years old now, Christian, but Celtic too, much
given to praying to Angels for Vision of God, and other dreamy
wayward practices which excite the suspicion of the ignorant,
so they call him Necromancer, which he is not—though I well
believe that Kelly may be: I heard he was pilloried in Lancashire
for digging up and using newly-buried corpses. The man is a
rogue, and violent, and Doctor Dee knows all this well, yet
insists he needs Kelly, or Saul, or whoever can scry for him,
which he cannot always do well. Yet it is not my business,

and the Doctor is a friend to Adventurers, and if his passion for the Unknown leads him astray sometimes, then I am the same.

And he waited, wanting my answer to his question about the origin of sunlight.

"Why," I said, "obviously not in the House of Man, but in the Sun, through the light and power of which the House of Man is built."

"So I should hope!" he answered, his voice jumping a little at the end in a way characteristic of him. He moved round the table and sat down on a chair in shadow on the other side of the sunlight, which now lay between us, with his hands folded in the lap of his gown, and eyed me with a gravity grown through years of difficulty. "Tell me, Sir Humfrey: how long have we known each other?"

"Near twenty-five years," I said, "As long as I've known the Queen. I came into her service just after she was released from the Tower, and met you likewise about the same time, when you came to see her after your own release."

"I was a young fool with a big mouth," he said thoughtfully, "and lucky not to be burned. I thought it was inevitable, when they dragged my cell-mate out to the stake."

He fell silent. He meant the time when he came back to England famous, with a European reputation as a mathematician, having at age twenty-three turned down the offer of a post as lecturer at the University of Paris. He drew up a chart of Queen Mary's stars, then went to Princess Elizabeth and did the same for her, and compared them too loudly, for which he was nearly executed.

"But the Queen did not forget you," I said.

"Without her protection I could never have stayed in England." He sighed, and almost smiled. "As it is, I can do what I can do."

"I'm grateful," I told him, "Your offer is a considerable help. I'll get to America yet! But do you think Cooke will help?"

"If you keep your temper and don't get high-handed."

"I? High-handed? I respect men as they respect me!"

"Precisely." He lifted one hand apologetically. "Excuse me, Sir Humfrey—surely you will know this for yourself—but many find it hard to deal with your quick impatient enthusiasm. They're attracted to you and your cause, but you make them uncertain, you bear too direct and make large demands without taking the temperament of others into account, and . . ."

"Large demands? It is a large matter! This thing to be founded, that you call the 'British' Empire! It is a large matter!"

"Yes." I see now he was patient, and that many tried to be patient with me. "But there are diplomatic ways of going about these things—which I hardly know, for I am an enthusiast like you, and often forget my common-sense—and I do think that with a man like Cooke you might . . ."

"Not diplomatic? I am not diplomatic?"

". . . try not to draw attention to his ancestry, nor compare it with your own, for he has the money, and you . . ."

"I'm not a fool. I will act honourably!"

"Money has little to do with honour. Sir Humfrey, I must be blunt! You have powerful enemies and few resources, your star is still occluded by your last effort to sea, you cannot be as rash and fiery as you please with men like Cooke. They are all too aware of their recent elevation, and apt to be sensitive about it, and I do suggest that this evening you try to contain your impetuosity, and let me speak for you, as much as possible."

I gazed hard at the pool of sunlight on the floor.

"True," I said rapidly, bitterly, "I have to go begging on every street-corner, and I'm in trouble again, with rumours flown sly about me, and Company wolves at the Privy Council to deny my rights—but still, I can speak for myself, though I know you mean well!"

"Sir Humfrey . . ." Doctor Dee began.

But then the doorbell clanged.

For the next hour or so I had to endure my brother's comments while he and his manservant Stoner formally witnessed my grant of rights to Discovery's royalties above the fiftieth parallel to Doctor John Dee of Mortlake. My brother Sir John and I never understood each other. He was phlegmatic, and shorter than I, and darker, and more thick-set, and he found as much to disapprove of in my life as I found to bore me in his. Yet by this time (we were both more than forty) we had learned a certain mutual tolerance. He had helped the funding of my 1578 expedition (though I suspect our mother had twisted his arm a little, for she had seen it very much as a family venture—not surprising, as three of her sons were commanders of the ships), and after my sad return he had defended me against the charges of piracy, and formally undertook to be answerable for me. Yet he did these things out of family duty, not for love of me: he still saw me as an irresponsible fool, avoiding family obligations to plan mad rushes across the seas; and the attitude he played on this afternoon of the tenth was very much that of Superior & Responsible Elder Brother. It was clear he thought both Dee and I fools, Dee for buying and I for selling a land we had not seen—land reported barren, moreover.

"Labrador? Haw-haw!" he boomed, exaggerating his voice, "a good un! Put 'er to the plough, will 'ee, Doctor?"

"Sir, I am a British gentleman," Dee replied icily, "and I mean to aid your brother in his patriotic and far-reaching scheme!"

"Iss, Doctor, vat be 'British Gentleman'?"

"Brother!" I interrupted sharply, "I'm grateful for your help, but you really don't have to play the bumpkin for us!"

This was just what he wanted to hear. It gave him excuse to stamp about, ostentatiously rustic in his jerkin and boots and slouch hat, booming about City decadence and calling me a snob while his man Stoner hovered behind a scarce-hid smile. It irked me, and I was relieved when the business was done. We parted frostily. Doubtless what he said about me was as harsh as what I said about him to Dee.

"Enough!" The Doctor cut off my mutterings. "We must prepare for Cooke's. First I have some work at the Table of Practice."

He meant his scrying and trances, which he did in an inner room that once he showed me. His "Table of Practice" carried a Shewstone on red silk cloth, and inscribed tablets of wax, a Solomon Seal being drawn on the face of the Table, and the Seven Names of God round the edge of it—all of it stuff I did not go with. So, while he was at it, I went down the lawn to the river's edge, and sat dreamily musing as the sun went down—then suddenly in the rippling water I saw a ship at sea, pitching in a fierce storm—and next I saw the scabby face of the cunning man! I shot to my feet, shaken, and uselessly scuffed the water with my boot to break the image, and in a pale state returned to the library to find Dee also disgruntled. He stared.

"You've seen something!" he said rapidly.

"In the water," I admitted, but refused any more.

"More than I did!" Up in the air went his arms. "Where's Kelly? I told him to be back for the Evening Working, but not a sign of him? Drunk, no doubt! How can I . . . oh, never mind! God's sake!"

"The sun's down!" I was fretful. "We should go!"

"Oh! Very well! Let me tell Joan!"

He vanished again, and I paced, but soon he was ready.

"Ned is harnessing the trap," he said. "Let us wait outside."

Dee's coachman Ned brought the trap round to the front, drawn by two roan geldings. It was a small affair, creaky and exposed and uncomfortable, and both Dee and myself were in poor mood as we took our seats. Ned, a small thin man buried under the bushiest beard and tallest hat I ever saw, hiyaa'd up the horses and started us away towards Chiswick Bridge and Wichcross Street, where Cooke lived. I was brooding on what I'd seen, and silent about it, but Dee wanted to talk. I said *yes* and *no* as I stared out over the soft twilit fields and parks, paying little attention, but he talked anyway, as he would, about anything and everything, about Anabaptists and the Family of Love, and Jean Bodin's absurd new book on witches, the *Démonomanie,* and how the conjunction of Jupiter and Saturn had caused such a popular scare the previous April and of a new perspective glass he had, "for the better grounding of true astronomy." And on and on until we were past Sheen and over the bridge and somewhere near Hammersmith, the sky near dark, with Venus bright and low and the first stars out, and he was still going on, about an infallible way of finding buried treasure while avoiding the guardian demons, and a new trigonometrical theorem for determining stellar paradox; then suddenly he was on about the Music of the Spheres; waxing ecstatic about Number and the "unit"—a word he invented— and before I could draw breath he'd jumped again, to the virtue of being "British." All the way to Chelsea he talked with perfect obsession how Walter and myself and others would found this "British Empire," and how British gentlemen would show the world "true Christian manners." Much though I agreed, he did go on till I was blue in the face, and my own thoughts about Cooke and the cunning man and where and with whom I'd rest that night in quite a spin. Yet I did not object: he needed to talk, and he was helping me, and his obsessions and mad tumblings of loquacity from subject to subject were all part of his genius. For he was a great explorer in many realms; he

knew more first-rate men and had more information than anyone else in Europe: information he made freely available to
any true seeker. He brought the globes of Gemma Frisius to
Cambridge, and knew Mercator well, and made many im-
provements to ships and navigation. As to his magic interests,
I have heard him rated with Agrippa and Paracelsus, and it is
true that he worked with the Moon, which Science has tried
to banish.

But that is that, for soon enough we were entering the
Borough of Chelsea, having gone steadily enough along the
West Road, it now being quite dark and still clear. The road
here was narrow through ill-lit streets that varied in their sort
between new-built houses of merchants and older buildings. It
had been raining heavy during the previous days, and despite
today's sunshine the way was still a mire. And soon enough
we got to the part where there were taverns and stews and a
playhouse, and much activity, with folk coming to and fro,
some wearing pattens, or stilted shoes, to keep their feet out
of the mud and shit of the streets. Now my mind turned quite
away from the Doctor to the loud bawdy all about, for here
and there I saw a pretty girl or boy, and thought again how I
might stop at a stew for the night on the way back. Then Doctor
Dee, coming down from his height to notice my wandering
eye, remarked:

"Well, Sir Humfrey, I hear the whoreshops here are reckoned of an altogether better class than those of Hoxton and
Clerkenwell."

I marked a handsome lad who lounged in a doorway and
met my eye boldly as he clattered by.

"It is true," I said. "They're mostly safe from the great pox
here, and I've been commended to the house of Mistress Hotbun, who apparently keeps a physician always to hand, ready
to treat the earliest sore with elixir of mercury." I turned to
him. "Perhaps later you will feel like a little sport?"

"It is not for me," the Doctor said. "I am lately married,
and content with what I have, in this regard at least. But tell
me, if you will," he went on, "or not if you will not: do your
tastes not distress your good lady wife, and do you not run
great risk? For the pox is virulent and epidemic!"

"My wife accepts that I am what I am," I said shortly.
"When my fire needs release, as it does when I am tense, then
I take what I find. As for the pox, this can be got as much by

common kiss of greeting as by fucking, so where's the odds?"

"It is most interesting," mused Dee. "I hear at the French Court it is so common a curse that any man of breeding who has not had it is generally considered 'ignobilis et rusticans,' beneath contempt."

"That's the French for you," I replied with a brief laugh. "They make virtues to be vices, and vice versa."

"I heard something interesting the other day from a doctor of Padua," Dee went on, "about the origin of this great pox."

"Yes. The sailors of Columbus brought it into Spain, who gave it to the French, who passed it on to everyone else."

"That's what I thought. But this doctor told me there is an African sickness called yaws, which was carried into Europe on the skin of slaves seized by the Spanish and Portuguese. He said that this yaws, taken into colder climate and affectionately nourished on bodies not naked but fully-clothed, has degenerated into the great pox that scourges us now. But I can find nothing of it in Frascatoro's *De Contagione et Contagiosis Morbis,* nor in his long poem *Syphilis sive Mobus Gallicus.*"

He turned to me with his bright-eyed, mordant look.

"Nonetheless, Sir Humfrey, please take care. Last year the surgeon Will Clowes told me that fifteen out of every twenty cases at St. Bart's are folk sick of the great pox, to say nothing of the smaller pox. As for boys, don't forget the law of 1563!"

I shrugged, my eyes roaming again.

"It's not enforced," I said. "Even that Papist scapegrace is not to be executed, though charged not only with buggery but also atheism and intent to murder the Earl of Leicester and Sir Philip Sidney."

"You mean the Earl of Oxford?"

"Yes, and of course there's that madman Marlowe."

"He'll not live long," said Dee thoughtfully. "I met him. He's too bright and fevered, he lives in a brawl, and..."

But then we were interrupted by a horrid shower from an upstairs window. And there is something now I wish to state plainly:

I felt no guilt for liking men. Yet I had the pain of contradictions in heart and soul, and the tension of a dream despised by most of the world. These contradictions, and this tension, I used to spur me harder in pursuit of my goal of America. It was my foolishness to hope America might lie beyond the tempestuous sphere of my human nature. Deep down I hoped for an imaginary land of Golden Ships! What a fool! Yes! And what a reward I got that night!

For as Ned took us along the narrow street, we came under a gabled house just as an upper window opened and a woman cried out *"'Ware below!"* But she didn't look, and didn't care, for as soon as she had shouted she heaved out the contents of her jake. There were laws against this, but many did it anyway. Dee and I were not directly struck by the filth, for the main load of it plummeted into the mire to one side of the coach, but in so doing it sent a fountain of nasty liquids in all directions, so that my cloak and the sleeve of my doublet were splattered, and the whole side of our carriage. Furious, I leapt out to make trouble for the lazy slattern, hammering at her door and shouting at her to come out while a crowd gathered to shout and heckle boisterously at the fuss I made. I think many of these low people had been soaked in the shit much worse than I, but none of them cared, they were used to it. I turned and commanded them to stop their comedy at my expense, but they would not, so that I became even more angry, particularly as the woman refused to open the door and show herself, which was most sensible of her—for I know not what I would have done! "Come out, you shitter!" I shouted, hammering, and could scarcely make myself heard above the clamour of catcalls and boos and vulgar advice. They were laughing at me! There was one big tow-haired fellow with a smith's apron and arms like gateposts, who came up and jabbed his thumb in my chest. "Ey, you, master," he demanded, "cannot the gentry take a dip in muck the same as honest folk?" And this was greeted by a great jeer of approval, so that I determined to make an example of this fellow, and would have drawn my blade—but then Doctor Dee intervened:

"SILENCE! I SEE A DREADFUL FATE IN STORE!"

At first I could not associate this gargantuan, vibrant bellow with Doctor Dee, for I had never heard such a shout from anyone before, not even in battle. Nor it seemed had anyone else, for the obedience was immediate and the silence complete, except I remember for shocked pigeons whirring out of the deafened eaves, and a cur that started howling mournfully seconds after the unnatural silence began. And we stood there, all of us, staring at the commanding figure of Doctor Dee, who had stood up from his seat, the carriage being stopped, and ordered us with his bellow. There were murmurs of awe. The

Doctor was tall and impressive in his black gown, his white-bearded visage as stern as an ancient druid's. Slowly, with everybody including myself standing frozen, he turned to me.

"Come, Sir Humfrey!" he said sharply. "We must leave. Our clothes will be cleaned at Cooke's house. What does a little shit matter with an empire to be won?"

I hesitated, being still angry, but then, with the cur still howling enough to madden a rock, I heard the little whisperings and mutterings of frightened but angry recognition starting up.

"'Ere, that's Doctor John Dee!"

"You mean the wizard what tells the Queen's own stars?"

"They say he fucks corpses and sprites at midnight!"

"My wife tole me ee cast a spell on . . ."

The Doctor's eyes were insistent. I agreed. I abandoned my quarrel and joined him in the carriage. Ned pulled us away through the slowly parting crowd, and not a word was spoken after us.

So we continued to Wichcross Street, stinking, pomanders to our noses, and I remained furious.

"That was a great shout, good Doctor! But we should not have left without recompense!"

"The other day," mused the Doctor, mild and philosophical again, and completely ignoring my anger, "I spoke with Sir John Harrington, who is justly famous for the high style of his low wit. He is concerned to find a practical answer to this great stench in our houses and streets. He says that a year ago he seriously considered hiring a gang to fire the whole city as the only solution. But this being, as he admitted, a trifle extreme, he has set himself instead to the invention of a device to solve the problem of jakes in modern overcrowded cities. He calls this device a 'water-closet,' and showed me his most ingenious scheme. 'But alas!' he said, 'folk so love and prefer their existing stench they'll not easily give it up and try something new. So, I must dedicate my life to creating an even greater stench, to end this stench, and I will do this with japes and jokes and sonnets on jakes, and on the Privy Council and such—and so I shall in time be remembered as a great public benefactor!'" The Doctor chuckled. "A most remarkable man!"

"As much a buffoon as Adrian, I hear," I muttered sourly. "Laughs at everyone and everything! As for this water-closet, the sooner the better! I could have killed somebody!"

"It would not have aided your fund-raising," said Dee, drily.

After that I kept silent. Soon, stinking, where I'd hoped to impress, we arrived at Cooke's imposing new house on Wichcross Street.

Cooke was a new man, a successful merchant, importing glass and Rhenish stoneware and porcelain and whatever else he could sell, for now many in England were getting rich, and there was a market for all sorts of luxuries that not even kings had required before. And it was difficult for me, to enter this large house, for to start with I was not pleased by the evidently false Coat of Family Arms which Cooke had erected on a shield above his front door. No doubt he had spent twenty pounds for it. Inside the considerable hallway, which was cluttered to the ceilings with monumental pieces of oak furniture, I was humiliated when the boy who took our cloaks could not resist a wrinkling of his nose at mine, though he quickly hid it when I looked at him. He led the Doctor and myself through a succession of anterooms, as though to audience with the Queen herself, and I suspect it was a roundabout route to impress us. But I was in no mood for it. It all seemed most vulgar, every room as cluttered as the hallway, crammed with embroideries and carpets, silverware and furniture, and pompous moralisms scribed in Italic above every door—"Waste Not Want Not," and so on.

"Coming to beg in such a state, and in such a place!" I muttered at Dee, so that he looked at me, warningly.

"The man gives to the poor, and supports Discovery!"

My temper was not improved when at last we were brought to the inner chamber where Cooke and his pretty wife awaited us by their well-laden supper-table, with a roaring fire behind them, because the moment Cooke smelled my doublet he broke into loud laughter.

"Judgement from on High!" he roared, his chins and belly wobbling as he advanced to offer kiss of greeting, apparently undisturbed by the stench. "Sirs, how unfortunate, it has happened to me, many many times, for shit sticks to me like flies to a . . ."

"John! Please!" cried his wife angrily, and came forward to us, most fetching in a red satin half-farthingale of the sort called the "bum-roll." "Doctor Dee! Sir Humfrey! Gentlemen, yes, this is indeed unfortunate, I don't know what you can think of our neighbourhood! Please, I will show you myself to our bathroom. Our servants will have your clothing clean and dry and as good as new by the time you leave, and for now I will find you robes from my husband's closet, if you will?"

We thanked her. She was pretty and dark and calm and never once wrinkled her nose, which impressed me, and arranged matters quickly, remembering Ned and the coach, so that shortly Dee and I were washed and properly scented (the Doctor having also been splattered, though not as severely as I), and dried, save for our hair and beards, and each drowned in one of Cooke's gargantuan fur-lined robes, of which we had choice from a closet containing somewhat over fifty. Doctor Dee chose a black-and-silver item, and I would have selected red, but Dee said, "Sir Humfrey, pray, wear green tonight, be pacific, put your martial temper aside!" And I listened to him.

Thus and in borrowed slippers (also much too big), we shuffled into supper and were quickly seated, with a chair for each of us, and the huge fire roaring. And the meal before us improved my temper greatly, for on Cooke's table that night was roast lamb and veal and boiled beef, soused pig, moorcock pie and baked calves' feet, a leg of mutton, chicken roasted with bacon, and bread, sauce, sops, and parsley, also dulcets and tarts, and ale, small beer, claret, and white wine. And amid all these steaming dishes I saw what looked very much like a numble pie, of the entrails of a deer, and so it proved to be! We dove in heartily, Cooke's wife leaving us to it, and if the wealth of his table, sparkling with silver and glass, contrasted too brightly with the dull pewter on my own table at Limehurst, well, I told myself that hungry beggars cannot be choosers, and put it out of mind for the time at least. And this was not too hard to do, at least not until Cooke, who was gobbling three mouthfuls for every one of mine, chewing and gnawing and drinking like a distempered demon with bottomless pit for a gut, began telling us through his eating of a miracle new purgative he got from Doctor Bell of Bermondsey, thinking not at all of our feelings and recent misfortune, but persisting, describing between each gulp and bite the size, number, and colour of stool it gave him.

"Sir!" I said stiffly. "Surely we can discuss another matter?"

"If I cannot rest easy on my bowels," boomed Cooke, "how may I think with my head?"

"This is very true," said Doctor Dee quickly, before I could speak, "and I have often wondered if there may not be some undiscovered equation to relate quantities and humours of foods to humours of particular bodies, thus inducing clarity of mind. You, sir," he said to Cooke, "are sanguine, given to much hot moist meat, as are many of us British, which amazes foreigners."

"It is known," came Cooke's voice through a mouthful of lamb, "the heat of English stomachs is of greater force . . . and we need more nourishment than folk in hotter regions."

"Perhaps," replied Dee. "It is also noted that diseases which plague us meat-eaters spare those who eat fruits and green vegetables."

"Green vegetables?" I laughed sharply. "Good Doctor, you'll have us drinking milk next! Vegetables are for the lower sort!"

"Then," said the Doctor, "rickets, and green sickness in young women, and the sore eyes you suffer must be exclusively for the upper classes, and constipation too. Clearly there is insufficient balance of humours in meat alone, as is known at sea, where on long voyages a supply of citrines is always needed against scurvy."

Cooke did not pick this up, to talk of the sea and my hopes. He continued his intestinal discourse until at length we pushed back our chairs and sat near the fire with full bellies and clouded brains. His wife came in to direct the clearing of the table, leaving behind the ale and the wine, then left us again.

I decided I must speak. I sat up, as firmly as I could.

"Mr. Cooke, I will be blunt, and hope not to offend you. My enemies wish to stop me sailing again. The Muscovy Company wants to steal my rights. I need your help, if you'll give it—because before God I mean this thing to succeed! I'll not be defeated in this!"

"You'll have my aid," said Cooke steadily, flatly.

I thanked him, and waited, but he did not specify.

"Never worry, Sir Humfrey," said Dee. "You'll reach America."

"Your scrying tells you that?" I felt suddenly glum.

"Please!" Cooke insisted quickly. "No such talk in my house! I have no wish to bring misfortune under my roof!"

"It is nothing of the sort," said Dee, going to the table to fill his glass: as he carried it back, full, it sparkled like ruby in the mellow lamplight. "Tell me," he asked Cooke, "this is one of Verzelini's glasses, is it not?"

"It is!" declared Cooke with great pleasure, "He is a master!"

"Yes," agreed the Doctor, and sat, facing me. I was between

the pair of them, gazing into the fire. "Sir Humfrey, you'll reach America because you're determined. And when Drake returns—I've heard Portuguese report of his rich approach—there'll be great enthusiasm for merchant adventuring, and you'll profit from it. You'll get your new chance," he said encouragingly.

I said nothing, did not look up from the fire. I thought I saw a burning ship. Dee inclined his austere face and regarded me thoughtfully as Cooke belched and went for more ale, I myself wanting no more drink. "Have you made other land-grants?" Dee asked me.

"Yes," I said stiffly. He knew very well. "Sir George Peckham wants one and a half million acres, Sir Philip Sidney says he wants three million, and Gerrard is also interested."

"I hear," boomed Cooke, thumping himself down again, "talk that Papists may be let out of England to settle the New World. Peckham and Gerrard are Papists, aren't they. Sir Humfrey, my advice is to have nothing to do with such a flaming issue. King Philip needs our Catholics here so he can accuse us of persecuting them. Mendoza will dog you if you get involved in such a scheme: the risk of you suffering Jean Ribault's fate will deter investors."

"Ribault tried too far south! I'll go north of Spain, to the Newfoundland, where English fishers have the upper hand."

"Still, the Spanish won't believe it," said Cooke. "Not after your last expedition. Also, you have the Queen's affection, and she's known to be worried by the tumult stirred up by Allen's sneaking Jesuit spies. What more natural than she'd welcome a plan to let the Papists go without persecution? It will be understood that she has secretly told Walsingham to secretly advise Peckham and Gerrard and others to support you." He sighed gustily. "This worries me. Association with Papists might harm my business." He eyed me, suddenly stern. "Any money I give must be in secret, between us three."

"Yes, I understand," said Doctor Dee.

"So do I," I said, "and I thank you, and so will the Queen." And I reflected in the fire again. "Though she doesn't want me to go. She wants me to stay close in England."

"She never wants to let anyone go." Cooke shrugged ponderously. "She's like a broody hen with no brood but the whole nation."

"You insult her!" I protested. "She is our Crown!"

"Your loyalty is what your friends like about you, if not your discretion," observed Dee acidly. "Cooke speaks sense, you want his money, but you rebuke him. Sir Humfrey, your last expedition still hangs over you, and Cooke here is trying to help!"

"Oh, nothing!" Cooke slapped his knee in good humour. "I'm a base man of money, Sir Humfrey is keen on high dreams. I understand!"

I breathed very deeply.

"I must hold to what I believe, or I'll get nowhere!"

"You'll get to America," Dee repeated. He stared into the sparkling wine-streaked cave of his glass. I ignored the chill I felt.

"I apologise," I said to Cooke, "But tell me: if you think that Walsingham spoke secretly to Peckham and Gerrard, did he also speak to Doctor Dee and yourself to make both of you support me?"

Cooke shrugged, and said nothing, and drank.

"There was no need." Dee's voice was sardonic. "I always wanted a land of my own, a *British* land, preferably barren and empty, so that in my old age I can sit on it without fear of a warm wife bringing me supper, or friends coming to visit from universities in Europe, or what-have-you. And if I tire of the solitude, well . . . I'll summon friends and we'll play, there on the rock and ice beneath the midnight sun." He looked up briefly, his smile pale, before his gaze returned into the glass. "How should we need Walsingham's persuasion?"

"You'll get very squeezed by the converging lines of longitude at the Pole," I joked uncomfortably with him, "and you may find yourself more magnetised than you care for."

Cooke farted loudly. I suppose it was meant as comment.

"Yes," mused Dee, "I've been thinking about longitude again . . ."

"You have?" I asked, and he nodded abstractedly, impressively.

"Yes. By spherical trigonometry I think I can find a formula to convert known longitude of departure into difference of longi . . ."

"Spherical *what?*" Cooke was grinning, but suspicious.

". . . of course, even with such a formula," Dee continued in the same distant voice, "accurate measure of ship-speed and distance sailed will be required, which cannot be done until someone makes an accurate seagoing clock ... which will come ... in time ... along with many other things beyond our present understanding and reach of mind...."

"No spirits!" Cooke repeated unhappily. "Please!"

"I think too much to raise spirits," said Dee remotely, "but when I'm tipsy I can see reflections in the bottom of beautiful goblets like this one ... I can see a flag made of England and Wales and Scotland together, flying in many lands, heralding an empire that'll rise and endure and decay ... and I see other shadows too...."

"I want not this influence!" Cooke insisted.

"It is but common sense distilled in wine and my fancy," Dee soothed him, tilting the glass in his hand. He looked at me. "For example, with my imagination set free like this, I can see that the work being done by your namesake William Gilbert will lead to great changes. He has coined a word, "electricity," for a natural power that he has isolated in his tests with magnets, and has also told me of the *Orbis Virtutis*, or field of power round the magnet, which I think is the power used by our wise druid ancestors, and those before them, who knew how to draw it out of the earth for use in healing and increase of wisdom. For Gilbert says that the whole earth is a magnet, and all matter magnetic, attractive and repulsive, which is why the moon goes round the earth, and the earth round the sun, and men and women round each other. It is why Darkness and Light do not exist without each other, being continually repelled in war but at the same time attracted in marriage of opposites. There is no Life without Death, no Purpose without Purposelessness! Male and female must marry magnetically to make the Divine Third without which there is no creative progression!—the Child, the Stone, the Elixir!—which is why I try to consort with Angels, to mate with Eternity and learn more."

And now his eyes caught me more strongly:

"Also it is why, Sir Humfrey, I cannot share your taste for your own sex. To match North with North or South with South brings chaos, not vision of God. So far as I see it can create nothing positive, but leads only to Via Dolorosa."

I was taken aback. "I'll wave my wand where I want!" I replied angrily. "What harm's in it? I'm a man, not an angel; there is variation in me just as in a compass! What life could there be if everything related perfectly to its opposite all the time? And by your own argument applied at another level, why therefore do you work not with women, but with male scryers?"

"I meant no personal criticism," said the Doctor. "I state only the principle of polarity that governs creation and progression. I take your points. We are all fools in some degree."

Then Cooke slapped his knee and started bellowing with laughter. I gazed at him in astonishment and some indignation. His red round face was a-beam at the new-fangled ceiling.

"I'm glad to be a fool!" he boomed. "I count my shit every morning and my pennies every night, and such idiocy has brought me the great pleasure of listening to wise fools like yourselves, Doctor John and Sir Humphrey. I understand not a word of this stuff!—principles and purposes and polarities!— and I suspect—his head dropped, he scanned us shrewdly— "that your high language is just my low language in disguise. I think despite these fine words you are really talking about God the Pound, God the Shilling, and God the Holy Pence. And as for our bodily tastes," he went on, giving me a broad grin to deflate my indignation at his scurrilous talk of the Almighty—"well! our tastes are as diverse as Nature allows: why should differences stop us making money together? I'm a merchant, a gross man, I admit it, and in a good mood tonight, having seen Lord Strange's Players this afternoon, and being entertained tonight by the—excuse me—comedy of your shit-stained arrival. Now I'm full of good food and drink and at last the Doctor has said something I can understand: that we are all fools in some degree. So, Sir Humfrey, I pledge you fifty pounds towards your venture!" He raised his tankard. "I expect no return, mind you, for you're one sort of fool, and I'm another, and the Doctor's a third. But what should I do with my wealth but take some chances with it?"

I was shocked by his attitude, but gratified too, his pledge being generous. So we drank to it, and I thanked the man, and thanked God too, and soon afterwards the Doctor and I took our leave in our clean dry clothes. I stopped in Chelsea for a night of it at Madam Hotbun's stew, spending a shilling for a girl and boy together, as I felt expansive and energetic. The Doctor went on home to Mortlake, to his wife and the madman Kelly, and where's the odds?

Twenty-one months later I set sail for Newfoundland.

10

Sir Humfrey Meets
the Power Not of Christ

Why am I scared even to write of it?

On the day I was taken, sailing the plunging *Squirrel* through
the awful storm, I shouted each time we neared the *Hind*: "We
are as near to heaven by sea as by land!" I was ready to die,
not out of morbid motive, but because my course had led me
into circumstance I would not deny. I believed as I wrote, in
the words that ended my Discourse, that: "He is not worthy to
live at all, that for fear, or danger of death, shunneth his country's service, and his own honour: seeing death is inevitable,
and the fame of virtue immortal. Wherefore in this behalf,
Multare vel timere sperno."

Who wrote that? Why am I so fearful?

June the eleventh of 1583 was a glorious day, fresh and
fair, with a good steady wind, and by sunrise there were many
small boats from Plymouth and roundabout, all come to give
my fleet of five ships a good send-off from Cawsand Bay.
Everything was ready, and once the business of family farewells
and last-minute provisioning was done, I was on the *Delight*
as quick as I could. Again I felt that anticipation mixed with
apprehension. This time I would take Newfoundland. Yes! But
what might yet go wrong? All was ready. Signals were exchanged. I gave the order. The roar of cannon boomed across
the Bay, and as our ships weighed anchor and started out there
was a great cheer from the many who'd gathered, and a crackling of small arms to speed us on our way. So we left England.
And all that day, until land was lost to sight behind us and

darkness came descending with rougher weather, I stayed on the fo'c's'le of the *Delight*, gazing west, refusing to look behind. And the truth is this was as much through fear of being ordered back at the last minute as it was through anticipation of winning my lifelong goal.

It seemed amazing, to have won free after all the years of trial. I stood, braced by the wind and by the spray that pearled in my hair and beard, hardly believing I truly breathed the ocean air again! After all the disappointments! Hah! *That* to Mendoza! *That* to the Muscovy wolves! Despite their every enemy effort I'd got the money and support I needed, though the Privy Council had made me take a ridiculous oath that I wouldn't go pirating. A Company of Adventurers had been formed of those who'd bought an interest in the profit of the venture: these included Lord Burghley, the Earls of Leicester, Warwick, and Sussex, Sir Henry Sidney, Philip Sidney, Doctor Dee, and others, including Sir George Peckham, who'd been most helpful even though the Catholic scheme had been dropped. Also Walsingham, who'd given fifty pounds of his own, had persuaded merchants of Southampton to support me in return for my grant to them of a monopoly on future supply of necessities from England to my colony. In all, I'd built more than five hundred and fifty pounds, a large sum, to equip my fleet. Most important, I'd received the Queen's leave to go.

I walked with her for the last time in the gardens at Hampton Court nearly twenty-eight years after I'd walked with her in the gardens of Hatfield. Her face was drawn. I know she was in great pain with toothache, and other complaints, but she was more a Queen now than ever I'd known her, and I told her this.

"Humfrey, your flattery always sounds awkward." Her smile was tight. "So, you're leaving me. Will you be back? I doubt it. I doubt you love me enough!"

"Your Majesty, I . . ."

She waved me aside.

"Thank your brother Raleigh. He's a rogue in some ways, I think less sincere than you, but it seems I cannot say nay to him. It's his persuasion that sets you off, not my pleasure. And I hear he gives you a new bark he designed himself. Two hundred tons. Considerable. He must love you well, Humfrey—as I do. You will promise now to leave me with a picture of you before you go."

"My Queen, with the greatest`. . .`"

"But what's this about the *Swallow?* Can you control those men? I hear they were jailed for pirating French in the Channel. Of course they agree to go with you for a pardon. But will they obey you and serve England when they reach the other side of the world? Who have you to captain over them? A good man?"

"Maurice Browne," I said. "He has considerable exper . . ."

"Yes, but I hear his hand is not so hard. Watch those ruffians, Humfrey." Her eye flashed on me. "And watch your own temper and discretion. Be impartial. Allow no favourites. Be not hot and hasty in command. Take no stupid risks to prove your courage where all good men already know and admire it. Now tell me: what are your other men and ships and captains? Tell me all about it."

I told her, that I was going as General in our Admiral-ship, the *Delight,* of a hundred and twenty tons, with William Winter, Captain, and Richard Clarke, Master. The *Bark Raleigh* had Mr. Butler for Captain and Robert Davis of Bristol, Master. I did not dare ask her to let Walter accompany us, I knew what her reply would be. There was my little *Squirrel,* eight tons, which alone survived from my former expedition. It started with William Andrews as Captain and a man called Cade the Master. The *Swallow* with its pirates was forty tons, and so was the *Golden Hind* (not Drake's ship), captained by its owner, Edward Hayes of Liverpool, with Cox of Limehouse for Master.

"I hear Hayes is a good man," she said, "but strange, is it not, that none who sailed with you before will sail with you again?"

I hurried over this and spoke glowingly to her of other strength, of our two hundred and sixty fine strong men; of our carpenters, shipwrights, masons, smiths, mineral men, and refiners; of the flags and course and watchwords and fleet orders I'd organised; of the music and toys and petty haberdashery wares we'd take to excite and win over the savage people peacefully. "And the scholar Parmenius from Hungary accompanies us," I went on. "He has been so excited by the work he has composed to celebrate this voyage that he insists on coming, to compose on return a great work that'll resound the glory of English Discovery! This can bring nothing but good to Your Majesty!"

"Yes," she said drily, "I have read some of it, Humfrey, and if your sailing proves as elegant as his Latin, then you'll return to us with cause for great celebration, and I'll not have cause to mourn the loss of another old friend."

So you can see why I feared recall, and did not look back, but only ahead, hoping misfortune was all behind.

It was not.

The first day was fair, but the first night there was fierce gale, and on the third night we were struck by a terrible blow. The *Bark Raleigh,* having signalled sickness on board, deserted us and turned precipitously back to England. I raged, accusing my enemies of it, of planning the desertion. There was never proof, but I still believe it. Such a blow! To lose our best and biggest ship, and so many men, and so much provision! It severely harmed us at the outset. Yet my rage was useless: we had to go on. And on we went. And the weather turned against us. As usual in my hurry I'd left too late. In April and May, with better winds, the voyage to Newfoundland often took no more than twenty-two days. It took us more than twice that.

To start with, thirteen days of fog and heavy winds drove us far south of our intended course, to the forty-first parallel, where I'd hoped to keep to the forty-sixth. Next, when we came about, we were driven too far north, to the fifty-first parallel, the mists persisting and causing us such confusion that on the twentieth of July we in the *Delight* and *Golden Hind* lost touch with the other two. We did not meet them again until we reached Newfoundland two weeks later, where we found that the rogues of the *Swallow* had already turned the fishermen of St. John against us.

The journey was long and incredibly tedious. Every night there was dice and cards and music and drink, and Parmenius with his Latin hexameters. The man simply could not keep quiet once he'd drunk a pot or two of English ale. Verses spilled out of him like piss out of anyone else, full of vision and prophecy of empire: fine stuff, in its way, but all in Latin, which I could understand, but few others. Still, he kept us diverted, and we needed every diversion we had.

On Saturday the twenty-seventh of July I saw from the fo'c's'le the castles of ice that Pysgie once told me of, and not long after we came out of the last of the fogs and over the Grand Banks where the fishermen go. We had about thirty fathom of water, and incredible numbers of gulls and other birds wheeling above and about, seeking and darting on the offal of fish thrown out by the fishermen. And it was three days later that we had first sight of the bare high Labrador coast.

I was glad indeed to see it. Hope began to outweigh my anxiety, I admitted to myself at last I'd been worrying about the cunning man. But now, surely, I was come to America, and triumph must be near, for now, with my own eyes, I had looked on America, and knew with my own reason where formerly I'd had to rely on others: America *did* exist.

So we started trending south, and the weather was fair and clear as we passed the isle called Penguin, which had French hunters on it. And thus at last we came to the Newfoundland. With utmost eagerness I scanned those beautiful forested hills and their every evidence of fertile wealth. And soon in the bay called Conception we found the Swallow again, but the meeting was not happy, for we learned that the rogues had robbed a Newlander, torturing its crew by tightening rope about their heads to get gear and provision from them. I was greatly angered, for thus my oath against piracy was broken, and it was little pleasure to learn that some had got their just desserts, being drowned on return to the *Swallow,* their cockboat overwhelmed in a heavy sea. Others, I was amazed to hear, had been rescued by the very men they'd just tortured and robbed. It seemed most foolishly Christian mercy.

"God has saved them!" I snapped. "Now we must curb them!"

"Then they'll mutiny and desert," Browne muttered wearily.

So I did nothing. As to the poor Newlander, I do not know what happened. We continued south along the rugged grand coast, I wondering how to control the villains, and somewhat morose, but soon we had cause for new excitement, for outside the magnificent harbour of St. John we found the *Squirrel* at anchor, and Captain Andrews came aboard.

"They woan't let uz in!" he complained. "'Arbour Admiral's English all right but calls us rogues cuz o' what the *Swallow* done! There be thirty-six sail in there an' all agreed against uz!"

"They'll change their tune!" I said. "We enter now!"

First I sent in a small boat to tell who I was. Then I directed the *Delight* into the run of the channel, which was half-a-mile of calm water between high rocky walls never less than two hundred yards apart. No problem, you'll agree, but my luck struck again, for we ran aground a long flat rock just under the water and scraped to a halt, stupidly stuck in sight of all the fishermen. Stranded within yards of the land I'd come to take for England! I was not pleased. Yet it turned out well. The English merchants rallied round and towed us off and we took safe anchor in the road, after which all came on board the *Delight* to see my documents from the Queen, which persuaded them that my commission was good and lawful.

French, Dutch, and Portuguese fished here as well as English, but English had predominated ever since Cabot, and the weekly Harbour Admiral was elected only from the English. Now I asked their help in repair and provision for my fleet, promising them privileges for such. They agreed to see this done. So, my captains drew up lists of our needs, the tax of these to be put on all ships in this and adjoining harbours, English as well as foreigners. It was clear to me that all must be equal under the Queen—and it must be said the fishers' change of heart was marvellous when they saw our strength and knew we came from Her Majesty! Soon we had all we needed and more. The Portuguese were particularly generous with delicacies beyond our demand—wine, biscuit, marmalade, oil, every kind of fish. And that day was Saturday the third of August. And when the sun went down behind the high wooded hills of America that night, I stood exultant on deck. *I'll not go ashore tonight,* I told myself, *I'll save that pleasure for the sunrise!* And I hugged myself! Success at last! I gazed at the rugged hills and deep green woods, and saw how the last of the light played in the quiet rippling water and in the restless tumble of greenery. The forest was primeval and grew down to the water save where steepness of rock prevented it, and was thick in birch and witch hazel, and lofty pines, and the bottle-darkness of spruce and fir. No houses or even huts had been built onshore yet. The fishermen lived on their boats, being here only a few months each year. The land still belonged to the birds and fish and wild beasts, there being no savage peoples in the region, or so the merchants said. Only a jetty, and a thin plume of smoke charring up to the sky from one of the crude fish-curing shelters.

It was ideal for my purpose. *No need to go farther south for now,* I thought. *Here is the place to lay down the law and take our formal possession.*

I had in mind exactly what the first three laws should be. One, the Church of England. Two, any rebellion here against the Queen of England to be adjudged high treason and punished as such. Three, any man speaking or jesting against the Queen to lose his ears, goods, and ship; and this because there were lying scandals about her affair with my brother. And, in general, all the laws of England, so soon as community should grow to make them appropriate.

So, gradually the sky turned deep dark starry blue over the forests and mountains and waters of this part of the New World, and I slept contented. And on the next day, the fourth, I went ashore with my company, and the English merchants showed us their walk to a place they called the Garden, where wild roses and raspberries grew in great profusion. That was Sunday, and on Monday the fifth, I raised the flag onshore, and in hearing of all declared this land to be England's, and also stated the laws which I had decided. Then we prayed, after which the assembly was dismissed, and we set to the repair of our ships, and exploration of the land as best we could. I had with me one Daniel the Saxon, a refiner, who went out looking for signs of precious metals. Yet the forests were so thick and tangled with fallen trees that we could not easily move through them. Parmenius suggested we should fire the woods, burn them all down to get easier access, but I said no, for fear that the seas would be made bitter by all the turpentine and resin flowing into the water from the burning trees, thus driving away the fish, which had happened elsewhere. And Daniel found ore, and said he would stake his life that it was silver, which pleased me greatly.

But there was little else to please me, after the first triumph. Sickness quickly came among us, with many dying and others made incapable; and others went and hid in the woods, disliking my command, while the rogues of the *Swallow* deserted altogether, seizing a ship at anchor in the next harbour southward and sailing off in it, so that within two weeks we were short of men and good spirits. The sick men were put on the *Swallow*, which started straight back to England, while the rest of us prepared to explore farther south before returning home. Captain Winter of the *Delight* being among the sick, I put Maurice Browne in his place; and as for myself, I took over command of the *Squirrel*, Andrews also being ill. And I prepared the *Squirrel* with nettings and guns, to give a show of strength if threat came against us, for I planned to sail the *Squirrel* into many small coves and rivermouths where the big ships could not go, the better to survey and learn the coast. And the ore found by Daniel the Saxon was loaded on the *Delight*.

In our three remaining ships we left St. John on Tuesday the twentieth of August, Hayes being recovered from his own sickness and still in command of his ship the *Golden Hind*. We were fully provisioned, and for the first nine days matters went well enough. But on Thursday the twenty-ninth, the wind rose, bringing rain and thick fog, the *Delight* being in our lead over shallow banks east of Cape Breton, and keeping such ill watch that she struck aground and was broken into pieces, so that her crew drowned, Browne and Parmenius too, and all the ore was lost.

After this dreadful loss we had little courage left, and the weather grew more severe, driving us round in circles out of sight of land, so that the men all begged me to give the order for return to England. I went on board the *Hind*, saying we'd learned enough and would return in the springtime. Hayes was reluctant, fearing the voyage to be unprofitable, but he agreed. So on the afternoon of Saturday the thirty-first, we changed course, and set for England, and even as we did, we saw a great sea-lion in the water, which bawled in such a horrible voice that many of the men grew fearful, calling it an ill omen. But I told them it was *Bonum Omen*, and pretended to be glad, saying I'd willingly fight such an enemy, even if it were the devil. So we started for England. The seas were dreadful, and more than once in our tiny frigate we were almost swallowed up.

Twice before my fate came on me I went on board the *Hind*, the first time to have the surgeon dress my foot, hurt when I trod on a nail, and the second time, when we were more than three hundred leagues on our way home, to make merry, for we were all feeling very low. I assured the company our success was such that the Queen would surely give us ten thousand pounds to equip a new effort in the next year, but it is true I said this chiefly to encourage them, and my own temper was very poor. In sight of Hayes and others I beat my cabin-boy in a rage, for before the *Delight* was lost I had sent him on board for my books and for the ore, but he had forgotten the ore, and now it was at the bottom of the sea, and I had no evidence of the wealth I thought we'd found. I complained greatly, and must have seemed half-mad, which for a little time I was. And they begged me to leave the *Squirrel* and come on board the *Hind* for my safety, which I would not do. "I'll not forsake my little company going homeward," I told them angrily, "with whom I have passed so many storms and perils!" Clearly they thought I was foolishly insisting on this to deny the reports that I was scared of the sea: Hayes said as much, and repeated this charge in the account of the voyage he later wrote for Hakluyt, which I have since read. But it is not true: I was not willing to abandon my few men on the *Squirrel,* nor willing to abandon the little boat itself. Yet I should have abandoned the nets and small artillery I had on the *Squirrel:* these overloaded it dangerously. It seemed to me that enough had been lost already and that we should try to get home with everything we still had intact. And no doubt I was stupid: I returned to the *Squirrel.*

So at length, on Monday the ninth of September, we were somewhat to the north and west of the Azores. Here we ran into the worst storm any of us ever knew. It rose continuously throughout the day, the wind attacking without cease from unpredictable and diverse quarters, so that the seas became outrageous, breaking short and rearing up high like pyramids. More than once during the afternoon it seemed inevitable that we in the *Squirrel* were about to be overwhelmed, with water continually breaking in, and direction all but impossible to hold. I spent much of the day abaft where the spray was not so fierce, sitting with Bible in hand, preparing myself to meet my Maker, if that should prove to be His Will, and praying that the cunning man's prophecy might not be altogether true. There was fear in me, which I hid, meaning to meet my end as befitted a Gilbert, so that I encouraged my men the best I could. And late in the afternoon the wind fell somewhat and we escaped immediate peril, so that, with the *Hind* again come several times within hailing-distance, I stood, bracing myself against the pitching and tossing of my groaning little boat, and cried out as loudly as I could (as I've said already): "We are as near to heaven by sea as by land!" I shouted this several times, so that Hayes and the others should know I was not afraid.

But I lied to myself, as my men understood very well, and it is a curious irony that I am famous in history not for anything else I did, but for this one phrase. My seven men, bailing desperately, thought me a stubborn fool for not abandoning the tiny *Squirrel* while the chance still existed. I'd heard them muttering that I was choosing my death and theirs deliberately, through misplaced pride, so that men should not call me a coward, and so that I should not have to return to England to live a second time with the ruin of my credit and reputation. And perhaps they were right, in part—I don't know. What had I achieved? I'd taken the Newfoundland for England, yes— but in all other aspects I had failed, and none of them thought I truly believed what I'd said; that the Queen would help me to a new expedition in the next year. Besides, my heart and mind had been under a black cloud ever since the loss of the *Delight,* and all knew it, despite my attempts at levity. Now they saw me apparently exultant in the very jaws of death: what could they think but that I wanted to die, and cared not if I sacrificed them too? And now I cannot blame them for thinking this, though I do not think they were altogether correct, for the motives that drove me were more complicated than even I could understand. Nonetheless, I lied: my good cheer was false, I did not feel it, and now I'm reminded of something that very peculiar Irishman, Oscar Wilde, said a hundred years ago, that "the basis of optimism is sheer terror."

So, as long as the dreary wind-wracked daylight persisted I sat abaft with my Bible, turning my spirit to God while Cade and the other men bailed for our lives, keeping the ship as best they could into whatever wind seemed most predominant. And when the light failed and the storm rose again, we rushed and pitched on into the bitter darkness, and I stood braced against the single mast, crying out prayers in a loud voice against the wind, exhorting my men to turn their thoughts to God. Then Cade on behalf of the others came and cursed me to my face for "wasting breath on God" when I would have been better employed fighting for the life of the ship and its men. So I went down among the men and rebuked them for such impiety, though now I see that the impiety was mine, for I abandoned my duty to them as Captain in thought of my own soul. They were very afraid, and I had no comfort to give but a sort they did not believe. For you should not think that skepticism about God is common only now. It was always common, and es-pecially in that time when the links with the past were being so thoroughly broken.

Soon enough it was only too sure that this night would be our last. The storm howled ever louder, and the black freezing seas came rushing over our half-deck so that we wallowed ever lower, with the lantern swinging so violently above us that we expected its extinction imminently. Then the evil blue fire of Castor and Pollux came crackling on the spars, which the men took as sure sign of their evil fate, and I confess that for a time I too despaired, and saw the cunning man's face in the darkness, and heard his voice telling me again of the *"power not of Christ and not of this world"* that would shortly take me and carry me to my doom. I felt dreadful fear, and wanted to scream madly to relieve it, but then made an effort, and got a grip on myself, reminding myself that I was of good family which had owned Devon land since before the Conquest, and that I had an example to give. So, with the strange fire now crackling with an electric blue brightness more intense than any of us had ever seen, and with the light from the *Hind* 's lantern ever more often eclipsed by the tremendous height of the waves that separated us and broke violently over the wallowing gunwales of the *Squirrel,* I fixed my mind entirely on the Redemption of Jesus Christ, calling out prayers for all of us in a voice louder than ever (though it could scarcely be heard at all, even by myself, the roar of the storm being so great), and trying to inspire my hope with dreams of the better world to come.

Yet had I known what was truly to come, I would have thrown away both Bible and prayers, I would have forgot my station and set to bailing as frantically as any of the men. And by the time I realised that the cunning man's prophecy was coming true, that something utterly devilish was happening, it was too late.

For in those last minutes that immediately preceded our Fate, our experience became strange and horrifying, the will-o'-the-wisp burning with an ever-greater brightness, casting an ugly light upon us and all over the boat, so that the boat and each of us gradually came to seem on fire, even there in the raging sea! The men stopped bailing in bewilderment and fear, and I heard one cry out, "The Devil has us!"—but no longer had the spirit or desire to rebuke him further, for doubt was on me again, I could not tell what was happening, I saw the cunning man, for the fire seemed to be burning now in my very bones! Our bodies glowed luminous in the rushing wet blackness of the night! I looked aghast at my hands, and found I could see right through the flesh to the shape of the bones beneath! It was then I truly wondered if God could be with us, or if He existed at all, and I do not care to write down any more of what I thought, nor what I believed I saw, the demonic shapes coiling in the night.

Then, when we were wallowing heavily, the wind suddenly broke, and hit us from a new quarter, catching us utterly by surprise, so that the *Squirrel* heeled hard over, and the sea poured in, and I knew that all was lost. I briefly saw the dancing flaming leaping skeletons of my crew in that instant before the ocean fell on me and sucked me into its commotion. After that, I do not know what. It was utter chaos, for the electric fire still crackled through me even as the waters took me, I did not feel the blow of the ocean at all. It was the pain of the fire that consumed me, and the glaring of its light, even in the blackness of the midnight sea! I could not tell what was happening. Surely I was drowning, or already dead, and these were visions not of heaven but of hell. For amid this madness my mind stayed with me, and next thing I knew I felt a terrible wrenching, as if some giant hand had seized me and turned me inside out. My eyes came open, there in the sea, and everything danced with flame, and then I was sure I was dead, for of a sudden my vision became brilliantly clear, and what I saw told me I could no longer be in the world I'd known, the world of earth and air and fire and water.

For the world was no longer there!

I seemed to be suspended in a universe of flame and strange distortions. I seemed to be looking down, down, down into an unfathomable abyss. And even as I was aware of looking down, I fell, spinning, so dizzily wrenched that all thought left me completely. I fell into the abyss, and it twisted me, and tore me apart.

And when it put me together, I was no longer the same man, and the world was not the same world.

That is all I can write now.

PART THE SECOND

11

The Nature of
the Vulcan Vortex

And so I missed the British Empire entirely.

"QUID NON? QUID NON? QUID NON?" This morning I awoke from dreaming that ended with a giant voice thundering this question over and over again. "WHY NOT? WHY NOT? WHY NOT?"

Yesterday I did not write but tried to rest. On the radio they said the government may fall and that there is threat of martial law if things get as bad as they did last summer. I was wondering what this has to do with me when the phone suddenly rang. Doubtfully I took it off its hook and said, "Yes?" There was no reply, only breathing, then a click. Ten minutes later it rang again. This time a cold voice said, "Englishman, go home!" I put it down without a word, and when it rang again I ignored it. At intervals throughout afternoon and evening it rang. Finally at midnight I picked it up and shouted "WHAT DO YOU WANT?" But it was Michael. He said he'd been trying to call for hours. I told him why I hadn't answered. He sounded worried. He says there is trouble he cannot speak about now, but hopes he can get here in a fortnight. "If you have to go anywhere," he said, "send word you-know-where."

Yes. I know where.

There have been no calls today, but when I went out I locked up the house, for the first time. I walked a long way, and met nobody. Yet something extraordinary happened when I was up at the old pagan stone on the hilltop. Three fighter aircraft followed by three more blasted out of cloud to the north and roared so low over my head that I was flattened and utterly deafened, and my heart just about jumped from my mouth.

Welcome to the twentieth century, Humf.

Project Vulcan!

How well they named it.

Part of me wants to walk away, to leave all this, to be anonymous and unknown again. I hate this sensation of trouble closing in, and I have no wish to be imprisoned again, or shot at again, simply for being who and what I am. But a stronger part says I must refuse to be intimidated. I have started this, I will finish it.

I noted down the dream I had last night. I'll get no closer at all to what it was like in the vortex of Vulcan. That event was too praeternatural to be caught with everyday words. My intellect cannot grasp it. Only my dream-self seems to know what it means.

In the dream I lay frozen in a fog. My eyes were open, but my gaze was fixed, there was only fog, and I seemed to be flat on my back. My hands were clasped upright in immovable prayer. My mind alone had motion, and I pushed angrily with it, and the fog lifted a little. Suddenly I knew where and what I was. A stone effigy! A cold memorial on its back on a raised slab in the dark corner of a derelict church in Devon! *In memoriam* Sir Humfrey Gylberte, 1539–1583, long lost at sea and forgotten! Petrified here in a lifeless place where nobody came anymore, where weeds pushed up, where the walls were all in ruin and the graveyard overgrown!

Only the moonlight moved.

Silver, it poured through a narrow stained-glass window high above me. When I saw it I knew the fog was dissipating and soon the light would reach me. It seemed odd that the stained glass had survived. I could not yet make out the design of the glass. Then I felt a strange, uncomfortable prickling. My toes! My feet! My ankles! The moonlight had reached me, was creeping up me. It came streaming through the stained-glass facets, highlighting the shape of a human figure looking down at me; a figure that was flat and transparent yet growing more definite as the cold flood swept closer to my heart, to my eyes and the seat of my intelligence. A slenderly robed figure I saw as the pale fire burned higher through me—then the edge of the full moon swam into my view, shortly to stand behind her, shining through her—and it was Tari who came down before me.

I breathed with a sudden gasp.

My body creaked as I tried to move.

But even as she flooded me with the light and perfume of her ancient ways I sensed another, darker presence behind me, unseen.

"Here lieth Sir Humfrey Gylberte, frozen in his past!" Her voice was sharp. "Humf, get up, now, please, this time come through!"

I creaked and groaned.

"How can stone possibly turn to flesh and blood?"

"Like this," she said, and lay down on me, kissing me on the lips so that her moonfire snaked all through the rock of me and stirred me to life, to my feet, tottering and dizzy with pins and needles and engorgement of blood. Yet still something lurked behind, and stayed behind, whichever way I turned.

"What's behind me? There's something behind me!"

"Never mind that. Come on! The moment will pass!"

The moon was already beginning to slip away from the window. *Why not?* I thought. *What's to lose?* So I left the crypt behind, and followed her through the window, through the gate, but the shadow was still on my tail.

There was an explosion.

I lost all my senses.

When I recovered, there was nothing.

I hung in a void, in emptiness and darkness.

"All is well!" spoke the calming voice within. *"Search steadily until you see a point of light. Will yourself towards it."*

So I did. I saw the point of light, and willed, and began a drift towards it, and it grew larger, became a flaming wheel in space, the heat of it reaching out through the abyss.

"On the physical plane this being is our sun! Hail Ra, whom you call Raphael!"

I was fascinated by the Glory. I wanted all of it.

"Not too close! Stop! Look about! Do you see those three spheres of lesser light? Mercury . . . Venus . . . and our Good Mother Earth! Turn to her now! Let her draw you close!"

It was hard to turn from the sun, but I did. I put my mind to earth, and moved to it, and found an urge for burial and incarnation growing as the world's gravity pulled more greatly on me, so that soon I was rushing down much too fast.

"Stop again! Stop and think! This is not the physical Earth, but an image of your state. Think before you choose. Who are you? Where are you? When are you? Choose carefully!"

So there above World I stopped with Tari and Shadow, suspended in the sublunary sphere, the beautiful Earth our Mother below me.

She was bathed in sparkling blue light that became an intense violet at the poles, where coronas of energy fountained, streaming and snaking up and down through the layers of her veils, her magnetic aura, that sparkled and danced in space all round and through me. Away to the west, wheeling out of night, the Americas were partly covered by white whirlpools of cloud that broke and shredded apart over the Atlantic, and below me most of Europe was likewise shrouded.

But the island-shape of Britain was remarkably clear, shining like a jewel. I felt both joy and grief when I saw it. Something dark and heavy came over me. Without thinking, I began a downward drift towards it. Even as I did, of a sudden there were hundreds of phantoms floating up to meet me, of all the people I ever knew, and of them all, the Queen was most immediate in my desire. Blind, I sought her so strongly that gardens and misty Hampton Court walks wavered on the edge of form, and I looked eagerly at her face.

I nearly screamed.

She was a hairless and discoloured skull, with no eyes, and black rotten teeth. The unseen shadows had caught me!

Then I fell.

I fell through water, fire, through inside-outness, through four hundred years, through the execution of kings and rebellion of colonies, through the rise of factories and revolutions, through terrible wars and incredible change. I fell through the Vulcan vortex. I knew none of it. I was torn apart.

Then I was one piece and one place again.

It is slightly over fifty-one months since 5:34 A.M., December twenty-seventh, 1983, when I "coincided" with the Sargasso Sea.

In the dream last night I recovered my wits to find myself staring, dazed, into the embers of a fire, in the night, on a cold wooded hillside under the moon and stars.

Sitting the other side of the dying fire, cross-legged and

wrapped in a blanket, was a dark, shadowy figure.

For a moment I was confused and fearful, but then I recognised the white halo of her hair, and remembered. Ragged and fugitive in Kentucky, months after our escape, we two alone still alive and free. Dogs had chased us up the hill. We were freezing and had nothing to eat. It was just before we met the rock'n'roll band KRONONUTZ, which changed everything.

"Are you awake?" asked Tari. "Are you *here?*"

"Yes-s-s," I agreed doubtfully.

"Then watch. Watch closely."

She produced a small mirror. It glinted in the moonlight. She flung it up into the night, towards the moon, and as I watched its arc became brilliant, enormous, slicing the night like a blazing knife. An awesome radiance flooded through in the wake of its passage, and I saw a great Hawk flying high in the heavens, and heard a giant voice that thundered: "EVEN THE GODS MUST CHANGE!" Then I saw the shining rainbow bridge described by the arc of the mirror; spanning from earth to heaven to earth through the ages; and I knew I must go up it, which I did, until once again I floated high above the forms of earth through time. Dizzily I looked down and saw a great isle in the Atlantic where the Azores are now, extending to south and west of them. And the isle was and was not, for there was a terrible flash of light invisible to the eyes, and a wind that shivered the very fabric of the bridge even as that island sank and ceased to be. And I saw a twisting, spiralling, ravening phallus of fire thrust violently up at the womb of the future; a thrust that tore many veils, a thrust that demanded reception; a thrust which in fact could not exist unless it *was* received... which it was, for I saw a finger that pressed a button; I saw a cave opening up that the lightning-flash shot into; a cave that swallowed the fire and completed the business; for as the bridge rocked and we all collapsed and were sucked to the negative pole of 1983 I saw how, for a twelve-thousand-year instant, the path of Distressed Temporal Immigration was not only open but demanded for all us poor fools who happened to be in the right place at the right time, or in the wrong place at the wrong time: look at it how you will. Some say Project Vulcan explains a disputed phenomenon called the Bermuda Triangle: I know not about that; all I know it was a great shock.

Then my dreaming went wild: I was on fire, I plunged, I

looked up, I fell through the cold pitted face of the moon, many faces and voices ran together in a great babbling of WHY? WHY? WHY? until at length, striving to wake out of this chaos, I came face-to-face with the head of a great brass hawk that thundered:

"QUID NON? QUID NON? QUID NON?"

⋯⋙{ 12 }⋘⋯

Swallowed by Leviathan
& the AMA

"Coincided." That's the word Norman Ernstein used when at Horsfield he tried to explain what we had done to earn the label of DTIs.

"You coincided with 1983 when we generated the energy-web."

Yes. As a condemned man *coincides* with his execution, no doubt, or as a falling body *coincides* with the ground. The Sophists would appreciate the use to which language is put today by these whelps of Faustus who seek to hide what they do even from themselves.

Enough. No ranting. If I start ranting I'm finished. I wish to God I had some whisky. Dreams are one thing, but what happened is another. How can I tell it? *Coincided!* Blight and Damnation! It is humiliating even to think of it. My pride and understanding have been in shreds ever since that hellish night. But hold straight, Humf! I cannot be dreaming these dreams for nothing. Tari is awake in me, though I cannot tell *what* she is. Memory? Dream-traveler? Spirit? A split-off part of my own soul? Doctor Jung speaks of the *anima*. Very good. He restates what was known before. Yet I have seen the Hawk, or a hawk, for three days running, and it is not *what* she is that matters to me, but whether her advice is good. In my dreaming she speaks of revolution towards a better state. Well, I have my doubts. All this talk of Pattern and Purpose and Progress sounds to me like wishful thinking. How can I believe otherwise since that hellish monster scooped me up out of the weed?

But why not? Quid Non? I am still Gilbert:

* * *

During that eternal instant I plunged four hundred years. Of course I knew nothing of that. When the fiery terror released me I knew nothing but darkness and pain. It took me time to remember who I was, and to realise that I was floating, naked, in a calm flat sea, my arms hooked instinctively over a broken spar. I felt as if a giant hand had pulled me apart and only approximately reassembled me. When something slimy brushed me and wrapped itself over my head I gasped and tore weakly at it, and discovered it was weed. For a long time it was dark. At last there was a greyness, but dawn came slow. Feebly I scanned about me. The ocean was weedy and stagnant, and I could not understand. What had happened? Where was the *Hind?* I saw other splintered timbers afloat. I thought I saw a dead man drifting, his head missing. The grey sky grinned at me like a skull. The light was strange, and the ocean too sullenly flat for the time of year, for the latitude, and for the morning after the wild storm of (as I thought) the night before. And all the weed! The only part I knew of that answered this description was that graveyard called Sargasso. Impossible! The Sargasso was a thousand miles away!

Then it struck me. The cunning man! *A power not of Christ and not of this world!* My God! I was forsaken! In the grip of black prophesied doom! Why cling to the spar any longer?

But I did. For hours I drifted amid the weed, beneath the ugly sky. Then in my body I felt a trembling, weak at first, that came from the depths below me. Quickly this trembling increased in its strength until I was all a-throb with it, and a swell arose to rock the weed, and then in horror I realised that some giant monster was rising up out of the depths to seize me.

Next I saw the Eye.

It appeared out of the water about fifty yards away, weed-festooned and standing atop a long black stalk. It was staring at me as it emerged, and it was plainly, dreadfully intelligent, and as soon as I saw it I was sure I knew it. The Eye of Leviathan! The Power not of Christ! In a state of awful fear I thrashed away from the spar, meaning to sink and drown before the satanic monster could take me. I could not see the monster's body through the turgid water, but the shaking throb of its breathing was very close below me as I tried to sink. I felt rather than saw the vast long dark shape as it rose up, and knew religious fear of an intensity I cannot express. The Serpent of Hell! It had me! I bubbled futile prayers to God and Jesus Christ His Son, but to no avail, for suddenly the surface of the sea was churned into huge commotion as first the snout of the beast—upsticking, black, smoothly enormous with its Eye atop the stalk above—broke water only yards from where I struggled helplessly, followed immediately by the entire great length of the giant. It burst up with a great roar and a *swoooosh!* Before I knew what had happened I was caught full and square on its cold hard carapace. Amid cascading water I was lifted high above the sea, and thrown hard at the snout, fetching up against it with such a thump that had I not been so limp I would have broken bones.

All motion ceased. The throbbing grew muted. There was only a slight rocking. More dead than alive I lay flat on the hide of Leviathan. The hide was hard and smooth, more like manufactured metal than skin of a beast. And it was incomprehensible, for now within inches of my eyes I saw writing on the black hide, writing in well-formed large red letters—and the words were in English!

"WARNING! EXPLOSIVE BOLTS! DO NOT RELEASE UNLESS . . ."

I could not take it in. I awaited destruction. Soon I heard scrapings and other sounds above me. Slowly, utterly weak, I looked up . . . and had to fight to accept what my eyes now saw.

Four white monsters with single huge eyes glared down at me from the top of the snout. Only the upper parts of their bodies could be seen, the lower parts seemingly within the snout, as if behind a low wall. I stared aghast. One of the monsters was pointing at me. Its arm seemed the same shape and size as a thick-clad human arm, with bulky fingers at the end. Gloves? Shuddering, breathing in painful gasps, I made myself look more carefully. Could these be men? Men in white garments that covered them completely, with oval glass windows to see through? But what men on earth dressed like this, and rode in such a monstrous vessel? Impossible! I gazed up hopelessly. The one that pointed saw that I watched, and opened its hand, clearly showing me its five gloved fingers. Then it bent away and briefly disappeared before turning back with a white object like a horn which it held up to its glassed-over face. At the same time another of the four aimed a black machine with a gleaming eye in it at me.

I crouched despairingly.

Then the voice erupted.

I'll never forget it—an echoing blare, like no human voice I had ever heard:

"BE NOT AFRAIDRAIDRAID! WE ARE HUMAN BEINGSEINGSEINGS! WE ARE FRIENDLYENDLYENDLY AMERICANCAN SEAMENEMENEMEN HERE TO HELPELPELP YOUYOUYOU! THIS IS ANUNDERUN-DERWATER SHIP CALLED SLOCUMOCUMOCUM! DO NOT BE ALARMEDARMEDARMED BY OUR APPEAR-EAREARANCE! OUR SUITSUITS ARE PROTECTIONEC-TIONECTION AGAINST DANGERANGERANGER OF MUTUALUTUAL INFECTIONFECTIONFECTIONION-ION . . ."

This idiot bellow overwhelmed me and proved conclusively that the huge monster was indeed the Serpent of Hell and these manlike creatures its slaves or servant-demons. I cowered against the hard black hide with hands over my eyes until I passed completely out.

When I awoke again, I was captive in the belly of the monster, and the monster was deep under the sea.

I'm a confused man. I went looking for America, and yes, I found it, or it found me. And I found Mad King Faustus on the throne.

The slash of a sword unriddled the Gordian Knot.

So cut clean! Dive in! I have read all about it.

On the nineteenth of November in 1983 the President of the U.S.A. shocked the world. In Congress he announced *"immediate go-ahead of a project to benefit all mankind."* Speaking of a *"new technique for harnessing natural electromagnetism,"* and claiming *"the full support of our allies,"* he explained that the Project *"though in the name of Peace"* had need of *military capability and security."* Also he declared that for the success of the project, the U.S.A. must *"temporarily borrow international waters"* in the area between 30° to 40° of latitude and 50° to 60° of longitude—an area including the Sargasso Sea. Further he warned all air and sea traffic to stay out of the region, or *"run risk of nonintentional destruction for which the U.S. Government, having given due warning, cannot take responsibility."*

The riot and outcry was immediate, global, and ineffective. The nay-saying Congressmen were canvassed one-by-one, and King Faustus won the democratic vote. The riot and outcry doubled, in every land against the U.S.A. and in the U.S.A. against the White House, the Pentagon, and the corporations said to be involved. There were predictions of Armageddon, of World War III, of magnetic pole reversal, and it was commonly assumed that a frightful new weapon was to be tested in this *"electromagnetically-anomalous"* region. But nobody, anywhere, was surprised! No! Such madness was taken for granted!

"We have needs to be met and by God we'll meet them!" declared the President on the eve of Christmas. *"With millions of mouths to be fed we can't just tiptoe through the tulips!"*

Warships laden with secret equipment took up position.

So the moment came. 5.34 AM, December twenty-seventh, 1983. Yes, I read about it. There are descriptions of a storm unlike any ever known, of wild lightning that flayed the sea, of an *"invisible flash"* of fire felt by observers, of a brief but severe fluctuation of the Earth's magnetic field. There is talk of *"success,"* of *"tremendously valuable gains in scientific knowledge."*

But there is no mention of Distressed Temporal Immigrants, nor of the distress of those who had to deal with us.

Weeks later, during my second "DTI Debriefing," having been brought to land, I saw the video-recording made of my welcome to the *Slocum.* I remember it. I was still sure I was in hell. My captors sat me down and tried to make me feel at ease, but relaxation was difficult. Because of the persistent danger of infection I had to wear, as they did, one of their white suits with the glass face.

"Mr. Gilbert, you are about to see the moving pictures we made of you when you came aboard the *Slocum.* Don't think it magic: it is simply a development of the *camera obscura."*

(They had a "psychohistorian" called Lubick at hand to explain everything to me: the poor fellow was scared to death of me, for I was his dead discipline come to life—and of him, more anon.)

So, I sat rigidly in my white-suit, breathing stale air, gazing at the moving pictures of myself being welcomed aboard.

I saw a naked wretch crouching like a trapped animal on

the black metal hide of the submarine, glaring helplessly up at the camera's eye. I heard the distorted mechanical blare of the horn again; saw the naked man crumpling, face contorted and hands clapped over his ears as he passed out in shock and terror. I heard Lubick apologise to me for the man who'd bellowed with the bullhorn, who apparently had been reprimanded for such lack of consideration. Next I was fascinated to see how three white-suited monsters put my unconscious body into a suit like theirs. A sling was lowered. I was hoisted up into the snout of the monster, and carried into its guts.

I was carried down levels and along passages to a bed in a tiny room with curving walls that were packed with machines and closets.

Still wearing their suits, they took me out of mine, then washed and shaved me, and attached me to wires and tubes connected with the machines, then drew blankets up to my neck and left me to sleep.

"You slept for forty-eight hours," the historian demon told me, "It shows next what happened when you woke up. Can you interpret what you see? Do you remember?" And he flinched at my glare.

Bright light brought me around, and sharp-smelling stuff.

No doubt this videofilm still exists, in some file, or coded in a computer—*DTI 15, GILBERT, H., SIR, M, CAUC., ENG., C16AD*, etc.

Memory? I gasped as the sharp odour went to my head, as the light pierced through my closed eyelids. I heard a man's voice:

"Lie—still. All—is—well. I—am—a—doctor."

Thus began my association with the American medical profession. What I saw on the video compounded the madness of my memory, which I had thought a dream. Cold, I saw the man in the bed shake his head wildly. His eyes opened wide, but immediately shut again to escape the light glaring from a spot in the low white ceiling. He began to struggle, his expression uncomprehending and terrified. One of the two white-suited doctors held him down with a firm hand. "Can—you—speak—English?" asked the other doctor, "Français? Español?"

"The light!" croaked the man, *"The light!"*

Those were my first words. The light was dimmed. The man opened his eyes and uneasily stared at the machines with their dials and multicoloured cables. He could not remember.

Surely it was but a dream . . . the fiery abyss, the sea-monster, the . . . throbbing of . . .

Then it struck him! The terrible truth!

"I'm in the monster! I'm buried under the sea!" Panic swept him. He tried to struggle out of the bed. Hands held him down. A needle pricked. They held him until his fear and rage went flat.

"You—are—safe," they said, "We—are—your—friends!"

"You are demons," I mumbled, "and this is hell."

In fact I was not the only scared one.

I did believe I'd been seized by demons. It seemed the only logical explanation. Now I know that most men on the *Slocum* were as reluctant to pluck us from the sea as we were to be plucked. It's not every day that living people from other ages, probably all carrying deadly diseases, start dropping out of nowhere. It's not every day you feel a tingling fire run through your body, nor every day that your officers order you into an area where you might suddenly vanish, where anything might happen. It's not every day you must open communication with a new category of Social Problem invented by your own error— the "Distressed Temporal Immigrant."

Yet was it an error as Tari claimed?

The response was so prompt and efficient. Within forty minutes of the invisible flash the *Slocum* and other submarines were moving into the danger-area, making for locations where large amounts of organic and inorganic materialisations were already reported.

So it is said, so it is denied. "An unfortunate accident," they always called it to my face. "We're very sorry."

Yes. But it is strange, how you saw us at all. And you could have left us to drown. And how wonderful, that by "accident" you had such thorough quarantine preparations on your vessels, so that we did not infect you and you did not infect us.

The crew of the *Slocum* nearly mutinied. They knew well what was happening and did not like it at all. I have proof of this.

One evening two years ago, before I went to Reno and hit the jackpot that bought me the Loomiss ID and my ticket to Heathrow, I was in Chaunticleer's, a bar on Polk Street in San Francisco, and my eye was caught by a thin dark man. He was staring at me from a nearby table. He seemed nervous and shocked. When I met his gaze he turned hurriedly away. I decided to find out what this was about, so got up and started towards him, coming on him quickly enough so that he could not leave. And there was sweat on his brow.

"You look at me as if you know me," I said, leaning close to him. "But I don't know you—do I?"

He leaned away from me, and gestured jerkily that I should sit down. "Yes!" he hissed quickly. "Yes, I've seen you. I was...on the *Slocum*. Don't be alarmed...I'm not going to..."

I relaxed a little. I got my Scotch, sat softly down.

"Who am I?" I met his eye. "What's my name?"

He licked his lips. There was a trace of desperation in his look.

"Don't know it," he muttered. "You only woke up once before we put you ashore, but later I heard you were the brother of somebody famous like Sir Walter Raleigh. You see..." —he met my glare with more determination—"...I couldn't ever forget you. I was the guy filming you when we fished you out of the sea! You're the same man for sure! But...I don't understand how...I mean, you..."

His voice trailed off. He was scared.

"Have a drink," I said. "What'll it be?"

"No," he said. "That's kind but, uh, I really got to be..."

"Pleasure's mine," said I, leaning closer at him.

"Listen!" he snapped, "Just, uh, DON'T BREATHE ON ME!"

I leaned back as one or two heads briefly turned. "Don't worry, cameraman," I told him quietly. "They stuffed us full of drugs and quarantined us for a year. Most of us died anyway. Several of us escaped with enough Interferon to buy a poor country. That was three years ago. Now I breathe the same air as you, and I haven't given anyone plague. What will you drink?"

Uneasily he accepted a whisky, but in fact he wished to talk, which he did, though nervously. I was curious. You can be lynched in many places if you don't sound right, but the Bay Area is different, full of so many chronic mystic come-to-naughts that all you have to do to be ignored is to gabble ridiculous theories loudly in public. But this man would not even give a name, and spoke as if he feared the FBI would pounce on him at any minute.

He told me that the *Slocum* and five other submarines had combed the flashpoint region for forty-eight hours.

". . . and there were these weird rumours even before we went in," he told me, his eyes darting about. "Before we knew anything for sure guys were talking about timeslips and the Triangle, and how Vulcan was a repetition of the Philadelphia Experiment the Navy did in World War II, when apparently they generated a magnetic field round a ship so strong that it vanished and reappeared somewhere else. A lot of men on that ship died, or burst into flame, or . . . just vanished. That's the story. We waited on the *Slocum* two days before we went in, and when we did we all felt . . . crazy and electric, like we had fire in our bones. By the time we started picking you people up we were close to hysteria. We were briefed that the web had been generated in the form of a Moebius Loop, but it had fucked up the continuum, but . . . well, we had these people on board, like doctors and stuff, who wouldn't say why they were there, so to most of us it looked like the whole thing was set up to grab the DTIs. We were scared as hell, and pissed that nobody would tell us the truth. And when we started locating you lot, boy!"—he shook his head—"that really did us!"

He said I was the second DTI picked up by the *Slocum*. The first was a furious Seminole brave who tried to spear the first of the white-suited monsters who approached him. After me they found two Phoenicians from Tyre, in the time of King Solomon, who carried an unknown strain of malaria. Then a black man from a slaveship, who had yellow fever and soon died, followed by three Japanese crewmen from a freighter, the *Raifaku Maru,* lost in January 1921.

"Those Japs got us really uptight," my informant told me. "They were almost modern. I guess that's when I realised the *personal* implications, if you understand me. Murder and abduction on the grand scale. Washington was gonna have to keep us all quiet!" He stared at me. "The DTIs weren't the only victims, you know!"

I know. I sympathise. There's prohibition on every tongue. "Accidents" have happened to those who wagged at home, while those who have spoken out from foreign lands have been denounced as alarmists, lunatics, communists, cultists, and frauds. I'm by no means the first to try telling this tale. And my faith in the truth of the cameraman's tale was fortified when, encouraged by another shot (myself too) he described the near-mutiny on the *Slocum* when an angry American rum-runner from 1931 was picked up.

"Guy's name was Herbie Pond," my nervous friend told me. "He'd been flying one of those old monoplanes, a Curtiss Robin, from Palm Beach to West End. He was loaded with booze when the Vulcan thing hit him. He said first the compass went crazy then the engine cut out, then it was like he was diving straight down into a sea of fire. He jumped, and pulled the ripcord, then blacked out. Next thing he knew he was in the sea all tangled in his chute and drowning. He got out from under the chute and found pieces of his plane afloat. He managed to hang on for over twenty-four hours until we got to him. We sent out three guys in a dinghy. They found him roaring tight and singing songs you'd never want your mother to hear. He'd salvaged some booze. He should have been jabbed righta-way but wasn't, our guys being so freaked when they got to him. The first thing they saw was this hand sticking apparently up out of the sea and waving a bottle. *"Hey you guys, have a drink."* They brought him in just as he was, reeling and mouth-ing off about, "Jeeze, the Maf laid a big one on me this time!" and "What kind of scientifiction shit is this anyway?" And I guess it was too much, him being American and almost one of us after all you—excuse me—crazies from crazy times; because some idiot goes and tells him the Big Truth we'd all been warned to keep tight—about it being 1983. And he went nuts. He believed it. He started gabbling how his kid's thirty years older than he is, it's an offence against God, he's gonna sue the Government. Then he caught on fast he wasn't about to sue anyone, or talk to anyone, or ever walk free again. He tried to grab a gun. He was jabbed to sleep pretty fast, but it got everyone real upset. A bunch of guys went to the Captain and said, *No more of this shit!* A lot of us wanted to throw you right back, you poor bastards. I did too!"

Now his eyes were fixed on mine, his face was flushed.

"It would certainly have solved our problems," I agreed. "How about you. You have . . . left the Navy?"

He went very tense. He bit his lip.

"Yeah, sure . . . and you, uh . . . you left where you were . . . too . . . ?"

"Nine of us," I said bleakly. "Herbie was one. I wouldn't be here today without what he did."

The memory still hurt. I tossed back my third shot.

"Guess you've had a hard time of it," said the cameraman.

"Most *interesting*," I said. "As in the Chinese curse." I stood. "Thank you. I must go now. Will you shake me by the hand?"

"Uh...um," muttered the man who'd filmed me from behind a white-suit, "you know how it is but, um, I can't take that risk, but maybe we could meet here, uh, later, and..."

I left. I never went back to Chaunticleer's. Eighteen months or so later, in York, on TV, I learned what became of that man.

⟨ 13 ⟩

In Which Sir Humfrey
Meets Psychohistory

If Ignorance were Bliss, then I was in a blessed state during those first weeks I spent in the modern world. Of course I was kept tranquillised, and any attempt to penetrate the haze as to where and when I was brought ashore in the U.S.A. is doomed to failure. Of my new life I first remember floating, like an uncaring infant, in bed in a sunny warm room, looking through tight-shut windows at a peach tree in blossom against the high brick walls of a courtyard outside.

This was at a Navy base in Florida. So they told me. It is where I went through "DTI Debriefing" before being transferred to Horsfield in New Jersey. It is where they told me I could never go home again and must stay locked up the rest of my life, for my own good. They were very apologetic and gentle, all of them, and all smelled most clean, with no hint of brimstone or sulphur about them at all. They watched me continually, videotaping my every move, and were concerned that I should think of them as good Christians, my true friends and not my imprisoners.

This I found truly remarkable.

For some time there is no clear picture. Faces come and go. It is a fog. But day by day the fog clears.

It was Chaplain Weil who broke the ice.

Vaguely I recall a diffident white-suited figure who sat quietly by my bed, waiting for me to notice him and speak. He sat with a Bible on his lap. It was bound in black with a large gilt cross on the cover, and the words in gilt, HOLY BIBLE. These were the words that attracted my attention, curiosity, suspicion, and fear. At last I must have mumbled something. Then. he spoke to me, slowly and very carefully and many times over until I understood. He said that the crew of the *Slocum* had plucked two other bodies, both dead, from the sea at the same time and place as myself. They had been my shipmates, he assumed. He wished me to know that he was a minister of Jesus Christ and that he'd prayed for their immortal souls. He asked if I had any Christian need he might satisfy, for he had heard I spoke English, and assumed I was Christian. Dreamily I told him to take off his suit and show me if he were man or devil. He said sadly he could not, because of the risk of sickness. In confusion I asked him what he was. He said he was John Weil, and Lutheran by denomination. He asked me my name, and where I was from. I told him, fearfully. His hooded head nodded, slowly. Then he asked me, his voice strained, what year I had sailed.

All this was videotaped. I did not know it then. I knew only that something was very wrong.

"... 1583 ... of course ..." I said hoarsely, and through the glass that covered his face I saw the nervous pity of his expression. I sat up with difficulty. I was weak. "... Sir ... if you are Christian, and not a demon ... you will help me to ... return to England!"

"Sir Humphrey"—his voice was quiet and unhappy—"this cannot be done. If you trust in Jesus Christ, then seek His strength now. You can never go back to the England you knew. It is lost to you forever. You have been ... taken by accident into ... another age. It is now nearly ... two thousand years ... since Christ was born ..."

I stared at the lunatic. The unseen camera stared at me.

"Ha-ha," I said unsteadily. "For hell this is merry humour!"

"Before God it is true! Sir Humphrey, you will not believe or understand me now, but you are in the United States of America, and today is the tenth day of this new Year of our Lord, 1984! Now hear me! When you fully understand, you may feel despair as great as Our Lord felt in the Wilderness! Yet essentially this is the same world that you knew. Men and women go through the same trials and temptations. Seek the help of Jesus Christ, Sir Humphrey! You can never go back. The shape of this world will be strange and alien to you, but Christ is common to every age! Let Him be your bridge and sanity!"

. . . the gulf . . . the fiery vortex . . . I was swept by angry lightheaded panic. The cameraman caught my terrified look with great clarity, as I later saw. "You demon!" I gasped. "You ape God's Word too well! Yet explain, if you can: how is it that when I was a boy the wizard told me that from the sea I'd be snatched to my doom by a *power not of Christ!* Explain it!"

He could not. Of course not. Soon afterwards he left, shaking his head, through the double doors that airlocked my sterile room. The doctors came with their efficient hands and stopped me worrying about it.

But the demon Weil left me his Bible.

It nearly drove me mad (or *more* mad) when I looked at it. It was the King James Authorised Version of 1611. On the flyleaf (such fine light paper) was this date: AD MDCXI! Also this date, of most recent printing: AD MCMLXXXIII! 1983! When I read this my hand trembled so much I tore the page. 1983? Impossible! Such infernal trickery! Such madness! I threw the Bible at the window but the glass was unbreakable. It was the beginning of my hate for much that masquerades as Christian now. When Weil came again I raved and tried to tear his helmet off. After that I did not see him, ever.

Now I thank you, Chaplain Weil. I think you did your best. For years I've associated you with the first great shock and horror. How could I see you but as a demon, my hypocritical enemy? But would I have done better, had our positions been reversed? You told me truth and tried to give me connection, though I wanted neither. You gave me sound advice, and if you served Caesar as well as God, well, that is reasonable.

You began my awakening. The doctors continued the process with their tubes and needles, their mush-food and the drugs they said kept me alive. These doctors now know as much of the body as the ancient Pharaohs knew of the soul. It's a pity so few can unite the spiritual with the empiric in their practise. They meant well and did well but they treated me as a *thing*, and they seemed like *things* to me, in their white-suits, with their gloved hands. Their gloved hands. This is all I recall of them. Big Hands and Small Hands—my two chief doctors. They tried to joke with me sometimes, but they were clearly nervous of my humanity, and did not know what to say. Yet every day I grew stronger and more clearheaded, though still I spent long hours floating or sleeping. The few dreams I had were dull.

They brought me books. Histories, the Plays of Shakespeare, the Constitution of the United States. It was too soon. I could read the words but my mind avoided the meaning. The same was true of the many minor miracles around me. Electric light. Zips. Plastics. The alcove with shower-stall and water-closet. It took me time to learn how to control the hot and cold water from the faucets. It was hard for me to comprehend the photographs of landscapes on the wall. In one of them a lot of men rode two-wheeled machines through rolling countryside. Big Hands said this was the *Tour de France*. He said the men chased each other a long way to see who had most strength and endurance. I asked him if he looked like these men under his white-suit. He said he did. I said I did not believe him. Next day a man came in wearing a transparent version of the white-suit. He was naked but for briefs. I asked sardonically if men still had prick and balls but he would not show me. I laughed, and later Small Hands, my woman doctor, said it was the first time I'd laughed, and that I was adapting "very well." For the first time I walked round the room without assistance. They gave me lightweight clothes that would have been comfortable but for their strange capacity to trap natural magnetism, and electricity, so that when I wore them I felt my skin was buzzing. They were made of "artificial fibre." I asked for linen. They gave me a shirt of linen and a cotton suit, also briefs for the privates, that I refused to wear, not wanting such construction. I demanded food fit for a man. They said my body would "reject" it, and that I must wait. And they brought me a copy of Hakluyt's *Voyages*.

With mounting horror I read Hayes' account of my Newfoundland expedition. I read his account of my death.

I think I was delirious for a long time. Later they said I'd had a "relapse." They said they'd miscalculated the speed of my "emotional reorientation." They apologised, and then enraged me back to life, to the present, by sending Frank Lubick to torment me.

Yes. He too is clear enough in my memory. One morning, without introduction or by-your-leave, this gawky young white-suit came in and sat down and started prattling at me. His speech was almost incomprehensible. He said he was a "psychohistorian." He said it was "truly incredible," "amazing," and "a great honour" to meet me. He would not let me speak, but went on and on and on, even when I sat up and glared at him. He seemed too much a puppy to be a demon. At length he began asking me stupid questions that I would not answer. Where did my wife's father die? Had I felt DRIVEN by DESTINY? Had I ever felt that *colonialism* might be *unjustified?* Finally I could take no more. "Your gabble's a disguise just like your white-suit!" I shouted at him. "You are ignorant and have no respect, you fool!"

That was when I heard the muffled laugh.

At first I thought it was the cunning man. I was still very confused. Then I realised it came from a watcher behind the dark glass-covered hatch which was set high up in one wall. I'd looked at the hatch before, and had sensed the watchers, but until this moment they'd meant nothing to me, for I'd been too much bound into the aches and pains of my mind, body, and numb confusion. Now for the first time, hearing that laugh, I paid attention. I glared up at the hatch through which they watched and videotaped me, and with my mind realised what my nerves knew already: that I was completely helpless and lost. I groaned, and slumped back, wanting to weep, to scream, to die inside. And I saw all this later, at the "Debriefing."

The Lubick had flinched at my outburst.

Now he said, with better respect and clarity:

"I'm sorry. I'm truly sorry. It was a terrible accident. But here you are . . . and you scare me, I guess, because I can't accept what you are any more than you can accept us. I've been talking nonsense. Please . . . let's start again. I'll answer *your* questions."

Thus began my modern education. I humoured him and occupied myself by asking questions. He came every day. Reluctantly, as detail built on detail, I began to accept my fatal transition. But one day I spoke of Devon, and wept bitterly, then grew furious at myself for such display of weakness. Lubick was alarmed. "Oh no, Mr. Gilbert!" he said quickly. "Don't be angry at yourself! We all cry sometimes, I do, and you have much more to cry about than most of us, so let it all out, please—you'll feel better for it!"

He was a curious young man. I grew quite fond of him. He insisted on calling me "Mr. Gilbert" because, he said, "Sir

Humphrey sticks in my craw." He said, "titles like that are elitist and redundant," language I could not understand at all. He explained. I was amazed.

"There is no longer an order of knighthood in England?"

"Yes. But many people think it should be abolished, along with all the other traditional titles of rank."

This was on the second day he came. I felt a terrible fear.

"But... there is still a... king... or a queen..."

"Yes. Queen Elizabeth the Second."

"Queen Elizabeth the Second??? Does she... does she... is she in good health? Is she a great monarch? Is England happy under her?"

"England is not exactly under her, and not exactly happy."

I felt I was drowning again. "Tell me the truth, man!"

He started to explain about democracy. I exploded.

"Democracy? But Plato proved that to be a low form of constitution that leads invariably to the worst sort of tyranny. Democracy means chaos, without order, every man fighting every other man!"

So it started. So it went. With great enthusiasm Lubick tried to bring modern light into my mind. He unleashed so many "facts" on me that if facts were gold I'd have quickly been richer than Midas. And despite myself I was fascinated. He drew charts innumerable to help my comprehension—family trees of revolutions, genealogies of four hundred years of change, and plotted these with steepening graph-curves to show me how much the speed of change, of everything, had increased. Industrial Revolution, American Revolution, French Revolution, Russian Revolution, Scientific Revolution, Transport Revolution, Communications Revolution! The balance and distribution of modern power! America, Russia, Third World, Middle East, Europe! And all the initials, used by people in a hurry—EEC, UAR, OPEC, UN, USSR, USA, Washington DC, LA, CBS, NASA, NBC, PBS, BBC, KGB, CIA, FBI, SAS, SALT, NATO, PLO, etc., etc., etc. It all sounded most cabalistic to me, a vast and bewildering mystery. I suffered frequent sweats and headaches, and a sense of panic sometimes. Then I think the doctors told Lubick to "cool it." For some days there were no more facts, graphs, dates. He brought me a book of crossword puzzles so I could "get into the way people think now." He played chess and chequers with me. Casually he discussed my sense of Order and Hierarchy that I'd brought from my time, and laughed through his suit, and said, "Well, yes, Mr. Gilbert, it's all hugely changed, but there are still four seasons, the earth still goes round the sun!" So my mind was eased somewhat. I asked for maps, and he brought me the *Reader's Digest World Atlas* . . . and I could hardly believe what I began to understand. The Unknown World, no more? All the wildernesses filled up with people, or known and fenced in such detail? Yet it seemed wonderful, too—the clarity, and scientific exactness now applied to Mercator's scheme! I pored over these maps for many, many hours, just as once I did with Waldseemüller's maps when I was a boy.

I pored over them with greedy fascination, tinged with fear. Maps of hell? Temptations of Satan?

How could I tell? What could I do but go along with it the best I could, bearing myself as well as I could?

So from the maps Lubick again tried to construct for me a picture of the world. He discussed the Constitution of the United States with me, and the Declaration of Independence, and told me something of the struggle of the Thirteen States against the English, two hundred years ago—two hundred years after my time. My emotions were mixed indeed, as anyone will understand, to begin to see this consequence of a dream of colonising America which I was the first man in England to try.

"But . . . you mean the Crown of England was rejected?"

"Mr. Gilbert, you were among the first to reject it!"

"That is not true! I was loyal to . . . I *am* loyal to . . ."

"Surely you were more loyal to what lay beyond the horizon!"

He had me there, and when he told me of England's history, I heard it with a strange mixture of pride, unhappiness, and apathy. He told me that the British Empire had been great, at one time embracing more than quarter of the world's population, but that now there was no longer an empire, England being drained and collapsed on herself, and the British Isles packed with sixty million people squabbling and enduring their way through a social revolution of a sort which, said Lubick, had been put off "for much too long." And when I heard this, I could only think of certain prophetic lines in the Ode that Parmenius wrote for my fatal voyage that was his fatal voyage too. Shakily, lost in myself, I murmured the lines in their Latin, and when Lubick asked me what I'd said, for some minutes I was too confused and distressed to answer. Then, in a low troubled voice, I told him my rough translation, and my voice sounded very strange and faraway to me, as faraway as Parmenius himself was now:

> *"O! Anglia, happy island, famed for the blessings of peace and war, the glory of the wide world, now rich in resources and thickly peopled, having won renown by thy deeds, and reared thy head on high throughout the world, careful of thy destiny, lest some day thy wide spread dominions should fall by their own weight . . ."*

Lubick was not impressed by the sentiment, and said so bluntly, but acknowledged the accurate prophecy. "What goes up must come down," he said, "but we still speak English here, Mr. Gilbert."

"Yes," I said, and asked him to leave me.

Another day he told me that Islam was resurgent, that the Papist Church remained united and powerful, but that over the centuries the Reformed Churches had divided so many times that now there were more sects and beliefs than could ever be counted, especially in America. Also he started to tell me about the "Moral Majority," and the "Electronic Church," and the "Christian Consensus" here in America—but here I stopped him and said I did not want to know. A peculiar distress overwhelmed me at talk of the Church. It reminded me of the demon Weil. It reminded me that, however things appeared, I was in the grip of *"the power not of Christ."* It made me hate myself as a traitor and weakling for talking at all with these white-suited men, or devils, or whatever they were. It brought back all of my lost life too strongly and bitterly, it reminded me that I could not be sure of anything I was told, it put me in knowledge of my desperate loneliness and confusion. No. I did not want to hear of it at all.

Lubick told me very little about himself. Such as I could see of his face through the glass told me he was fair-complexioned, perhaps blue-eyed, not very old, perhaps twenty-five. In fact later he told me he was forty. It took me a long time (once I was given faces to see) to get over my amazement at the youthful, unformed appearance of many American faces, especially those of the men. Lubick said he came from Salt Lake City. Once I tried to flirt with him, jokingly:

"I like the look of white-suited boys like you!"

"I'm not a faggot!" he said, stiffening with alarm.

Thereafter there was an uneasiness in his attitude to me, as if I had threatened him.

There were many mysteries. It was all a fog, a mystery, with continual insulting reminders of my helplessness.

One day the doctor with Big Hands said I could go outside and sit in the sunlight for a while—wearing a white-suit.

I said I would not under any circumstances wear a white-suit.

He asked me again the next day.

I said I would not under any circumstances wear a white-suit.

He asked me again the next day. A sunny day.

"Why must I wear a suit?"

"If you breathe our air right now you'll probably die. That's why we keep you in this sterile environment."

"Why? What's wrong with your air?"

"I told you before. About germs and viruses—remember? Your body has no defence against our diseases. They've changed since your time. Even the common cold would kill you. We're trying to build up your defences, but this will take a long time, and perhaps we'll never succeed completely. You must be patient. Do you want to go outside? In the suit?"

I shook my head . . . uncertainly.

He left the white-suit with me.

"If you want to go out, get into it, and buzz us."

I fought. I gave in. Slowly I got into the suit. It smelled strange. I could not put the helmet on. I pressed the buzzer.

Big Hands came in with Small Hands. Her hands were efficient and deft; his were more methodical. Their hands showed me how to zip and clip and shut up the suit so that no natural influence could reach in and kill me. With great effort I overcame my panic at being smothered. But the air in the suit felt hard to breathe, and it was difficult to walk, being so cut off.

They helped me out through the two doors, along a gleaming clean corridor, round a corner, through a door, and . . . into the sunlight!

It was terrible.

I sat on a chair in the suit in the sunlight that I could not feel at all. I sat in the walled courtyard, staring at the walls, and at the peach-blossom I could not smell. Very quickly I felt giddy, trapped, abused. I could not even feel irregularities in the paving-stones beneath my feet! I could not touch the earth! Gardens! Wild gardens, lost gardens, all snatched from me! I stared at the sun through the glass of the suit. Sickness rose in my gorge! I looked away, I saw red, I heard a rumbling in the sky, I saw a shining monstrous metal creature flying through the sky, bellowing! I began to pant with panic and rage. To be so cut off! To have life but not have it at all! To be so horribly *castrated* out of my own age! To be treated like a baby by these hidden people who would not show themselves, if people they were, and to be locked up in this place that had my body humming painfully with noise-waves and other unpleasant influences that surged from every direction—NO!

I stood. I nearly fell. I shook off the helping hands.

"What's the matter?" Hand, hands! "What's the matter?"

"I am Sir Humfrey Gylberte!" I panted dizzily. "On my honour I swear I'll never go out in one of these torture-suits again!"

Then I turned and walked unsteadily back to my room.

As it so happened, I did not keep my word. Later at Horsfield I learned to make the best of a bad business.

It went on for weeks. Still I had no idea I was not the only one, nor knew why the watchers watched me. While asleep I had dreams of being wheeled into a shining white room where the white-suited doctors did strange things to me with machines and instruments.

I grew stronger.

From mush I graduated to fruit and vegetables.

I asked for ale and got coloured bubbling water in a can. I asked for books and Lubick brought me *Moby Dick*, *Gulliver's Travels*, *The Grapes of Wrath*, and *Robinson Crusoe*. These were clever choices, though he had to explain to me what *novels* were *for*, as the nearest I had come to this kind of tale-telling was in Mandeville, Malory, and Geoffrey of Monmouth. Once I had the hang of it I plunged into these romances in the mesmerised way of a dreamer who doesn't want to wake up. In this fashion many days passed: I questioned Lubick on everything I read. Defoe I found resourceful; Swift at first delightful but finally much too true for pleasure; Melville, once I understood him, I found to be a high, high mountain—but it was Steinbeck who fascinated me the most, though the language was hard.

"But these Okies," I asked Lubick, "Where did they come from?"

"Where did *you* come from?" he responded, grinning.

After this he brought me newspapers. I met Doonesbury, Dow-Jones, football, the dramatic incantation of headlines— RUSSIANS ACCUSED OF WEATHER WAR—NEW OPEC ULTIMATUM—CREDIT CRUNCH RUINS MILLIONS— USAF IDAHO RADIATION DISASTER SUIT—SUPER-BOWL: FORTY-NINERS STRIKE GOLD!

It was too occult for me. I preferred the maps. When they brought me television I refused it because of the harmful rays. Lubick asked me what I meant. "I've already told you about the bad influences in and about this building!" I snapped. "If you are doctors, why do you allow them?"

He was puzzled. "What influences?" he wanted to know.

I pointed through the window. "From that direction," I said, "comes a power that races fiery, quick, and nervous through me. It is worse than the electricity and this television. What is it?"

"There's a microwave installation over there," he said, "but the radiation's below the harmful level."

"Not harmful?" I was amazed. "Can you not *feel* it in you?"

"No." He shook his encased head slowly. "Not a thing. Not consciously. Maybe you pick it up because you're not used to it, Mr. Gilbert. But . . . yes . . . some say microwaves *are* harmful."

Then I burst out in angry laughter.

"You're mad!" I shouted. "This is hell!"

Through his window I could see Lubick was embarrassed. "Not *altogether*," he said, "but you have a point!"

Yet they must have thought me ready. One evening Lubick came with Big Hands and Small Hands and they bundled me into a white-suit.

"You're going to meet Captain Pointer," said Lubick. "He runs this joint. He's got some important things to tell you."

They swept me through empty corridors to a carpeted region, to a door I thought was oak until Lubick knocked at it. False wood? Why not? I had begun to feel recalcitrant about hell.

Into a long low soft-lit room we went. The far end was a sort of study, with desk and machines and world-globe, and bookcases, and charts and diagrams on the wall. But the part we entered was meant for comfort. It was carpeted, furnished, with prints of sailing ships on the wall, with magazines on a table, and there was a sideboard stocked with many bottles. Captain Pointer stood at the sideboard.

When I saw him I gasped. I was stupefied, for he did not wear a white-suit. His face was uncovered, his body clad in U.S. Navy uniform. He was a tall straight man, his eyebrows bushy, his eyes keen grey, his hair thinning, his nose a great hook, his complexion that of a man who knew both wind and wave. And his gaze was level.

"Sir Humphrey Gilbert? I'm Captain James Pointer, U.S. Navy."

I stood motionless. He reached and took my gloved right hand firmly in his naked right hand. He shook my hand firmly.

"The handshake's how men in America greet each other, Sir Humphrey. All this must be confusing for you. I hope I can explain. I'm sorry about the suit. I know they're damned uncomfortable. But"—he gestured that I should turn round—"I thought perhaps you'd like to get a good look at us for once, instead of it always being the other way around."

I turned. My sense of shock was increased, for Lubick and Big Hands and Small Hands had all removed their helmets. They were people! Lubick was blushing as I scanned him. He was blond and curly-haired, not untoothsome, though a bit soft in the features, and he found it hard to meet my eyes. As for Big Hands, he had a curious, drooping face, with melancholy eyes and a drooping moustache. But it was Small Hands who astonished me.

"You . . . you are yellowskinned! You are American too?"

She was pretty, with almond eyes, and she laughed in a warm way at my consternation. In some confusion I turned to the Captain.

"Sir!" I barked. "Please be good enough to explain!"

We faced each other from deep soft chairs. I ignored my white-suited discomfort. Captain Pointer impressed me. Here at last was a man of sufficient authority and self-respect to acknowledge me directly. But he too was uneasy as he began to tell me what I did not want to hear. He licked his lips as he told me about "miscalculation" and "accident," and I became very unhappy.

"Sir, are you Christian?" I demanded.

"I'm not a great believer," he said honestly.

"Sir," I went on, "from what you say it seems that your government admits responsibility in the destruction of my vessel and crew, and in the forced transplanting of myself to . . . here . . . in America." I was finding it hard to breathe. "Plainly it is your duty to deliver me safely back to England, and also to make financial reparation for all the hardship I have been caused!"

His face was troubled. I ignored the others. In a grey voice the Captain declared his government unlikely to meet my demands.

"So!" I snapped. "You mean to hold me here and keep your blunder secret. Why did you not let me drown? Why go to all this trouble? I was ready for death, I'd prepared myself and made my peace—and you snatched me from it! How dare you! In the Name of Christ, how dare you! You have worked a science or magic on me that I cannot controvert, which you cannot or will not undo. At least you, sir, do not claim to be of Christ, you do not insult my intelligence! At least you tell me the bald truth, that I am a captive, alone, with no hope of redress or freedom. I thank you for that, anyway!"

There was a brief silence after my rant.

"Well, no," said the Captain slowly, "You are not quite alone. There are eighty-seven DTIs altogether."

"Deetee eyes? What are deetee eyes?"

He explained what the initials stood for.

"Distressed Temporal Immigrants? What does *that* mean?"

"Bureaucratic jargon. It means that, apart from yourself, eighty-six other people were brought into this time by the . . . accident."

I could not make sense of this.

"You tell me that . . . there are other men and women . . . from different ages . . . here . . . caught . . . like I'm caught?"

"Yes," the Captain agreed, looking more unhappy than ever. "Very soon I expect you'll be meeting some of them. I'm instructed to tell you that shortly you'll leave here and go to an institute in New Jersey, at a place called Horsfield. It is being prepared to take all of you. The U.S. Government acknowledges responsibility for what has happened, and as a matter of common humanity undertakes to look after your welfare and transhabilitate you as well as possible, so that you will be able to lead useful and meaningful lives . . . within the context of the situation . . . and taking the need for strict security and proper health precautions into account . . ."

"What does all *that* mean?" I demanded.

"I wish I knew," he said. "I'm very sorry, Sir Humphrey. Very sorry indeed."

His voice was perfectly wooden.

Thus began my Debriefing. Soon I was taken to Horsfield. Now I know exactly what he meant.

➺❴ 14 ❵➻

"Like a Million
Motel Rooms..."

Horsfield, Horsfield! That bitter place! If that was its real name
I know not, I never found it on a map, and doubtless the other
DTIs were taken elsewhere after we escaped, to avoid the
attention of reporters hot on the trail of the rumours. Perhaps
it was razed to the ground, or turned back into an insane asylum,
or ... how do I know? I recall it all too well, my first day
there, and how Tari made herself known, and how ... God!
I'll tell it all in one, if I can, without interruption, if that's
allowed, for it all floods back, oh yes—but how to disentangle
past from present? Where is the past found if not in the present?
Barely an hour ago something happened that shocked me anew
with sensation of the abyss that underlies our every sedative
hope of normality—and now before Horsfield I must tell of
it, though it may have been no more than my illusion, or wishful
thinking, or poor eyesight. I know I may be a fool lost in
darkness; my mind and memory may be weak—but if I see
some light, well, light is light, universal and healing, no one
man's property, enough for all, all we've got, sometimes found
in strange places—so I must leave no stone unturned. Remember the Hawk, Humfrey! The Day of Horus is—

But I babble. I'm still disturbed. I was almost back from
the village, walking through the woods, when—

No. From the beginning. Logically.

This morning I walked to the village, Brynafan, five miles
away. I needed supplies, fresh air, exercise, and also I needed
to face the local outside world. That anonymous call, though

not repeated, has preyed on my soul, and I will not languish in a fog of silly fear.

Hah!

Past Gwernacca and down the twisty narrow tarmacadam road I went, striding by sodden pastures and flinty dripping crags, and so came to Brynafan, a pretty little one-street place above a rushing river, not so far from Fairy Glen and Betws-y-Coed. And soon enough I knew that presently nobody can be very interested in the eccentric Englishman staying at Griffith of Gwernacca's old house. Brynafan must usually be placid enough, but in the general store it took me a good quarter-hour to get any service, for at the counter a crowd of folk were vociferously discussing the news. The government has fallen, there is renewed rioting in big English cities, and locally there are fears that the outlaw "Lorry People" are coming this way, set on havoc and rape. Of course I said nothing of my acquaintance a year ago with these modern gypsies, who are rough folk, it is true, but by no means as vicious as the cowardly self-righteous love to make out.

In the crowded little pub I stopped for a Scotch and found the same nervous excitement. There were a couple of questions, they knew about me, but nobody seemed to care. My mind is relieved on that score at least. The anonymous call was probably the work of a bored local prankster, no more, and I have no evidence it came from further afield. So, I had a drink or two, and listened to men arguing on what will happen if soldiers are sent to fire on rioters and Right-to-Work marchers, as happened last year. Nearly I told how I was shot and wounded when the troops met the marchers from Scotland in York last summer, for the buxom dark girl behind the bar gave me the eye. I was tempted to tell her, to impress her with my tale and my scar, but managed to hold my mouth. Yet I was attracted to her, and she to me, and before I left I got her name. A lusty lass: as I walked back with my load I contemplated how good it would be to plough her, first fierily, then sweetly and at good length ... and decided I'll call her to see if she'll meet me, for I've abstained too long, which is bad for the health.

But that's not important now.

For on the way back, nearly home, while tramping through dead bracken amid a bare wood, something made me look up past the trees to the top of the hill where the stone stands.

There was a woman up there, looking down at me.

It was Tari! It was Mery-Isis!

Impossible! But I swear I recognised her.

When I checked and looked again she was gone. With my heart beating hard I climbed the hill, but there was nobody there. Of course not! Of course not! Now I'm nervous again. What if my dreams are invading my waking? More fearful still: Tari once told me that a ghost can be solidly materialised by an intensity of prolonged concentration, and said she knew how to do this. Well, I know that anything is possible, and she did have remarkable powers, but... more likely I saw someone I mistook for Tari, someone who slipped away during the short time it took me to climb to the stone. Yet who else in the world looks like Tari? And where could they hide on those bare slopes? It's nonsense! As to the other possibility, that Tari herself... no! No no no! How can I even think it? Madness! No! It was an apparition, sprung from my wishful thinking and preoccupations, nothing more! My eyes are not good. I was still a little drunk. I fooled myself! It must be!

Yet I'm still puzzled. She was there! Our eyes met, I felt her presence so strongly. And there is one other thing, when I reached the top. For a moment, overcome no doubt by the effects of whiskey and the brisk climb, I fell into a dizziness, and had to clutch at the stone for support, and as I did I heard a voice in me, and it was *her* voice! *"Earth and Water are your friends!"* it whispered, *"Fire and Wind work on the hills! The elements are in you! We are your friends! No thought! No distraction! Act! Write! Remember! Testify! Fly with the Hawk! Awaken the divine neters within you: find your loving strength and responsibility!"*

Neters was her Egyptian word for *Gods* or *Powers*.

Well, I came trembling off that hill, hardly able to put one foot before the other, a fog on my eyes and her ghost in my mind, and feeling so wild and strange I began fearing that perhaps I never got away from Horsfield at all! *What if all my adventures have been but a spell or dream put in my mind by the doctors?* I thought madly.

Now I am here. I am real. I pinch myself. It hurts. Perhaps this visitation is no horror, but *Bonum Omen,* an encouragement!

Now I am ready for Horsfield.

I have no memory of the journey. One night at the Navy base I fell asleep. I dreamed I was in a vibrating, droning machine. When I awoke it was to find myself in bed in another room, another place, and outside the small square window it snowed. So I came to Horsfield.

For a year I existed in this room. It was like a million motel rooms. Carpet, TV, Bible, bathroom, bed too soft, all of it. And there was a spyhole, hidden in the air purification box.

Yes, that first morning at Horsfield I awoke dizzy in pale blue cotton pyjamas to find myself shaved again, completely, and immediately vowed to give these rogues no more respect than they gave me! A one-piece red garment awaited me on a chair, and white rubber sandals on the white nylon carpet. The room was too hot. I went to the window. The sight of the snow soothed me. It curled gently from a leaden sky into the huge inner courtyard my window overlooked—a square, a hundred yards deep each side, without break in the bleak grey walls save for an arched gateway halfway along the block to my right. Hundreds of windows were all about, electric lighting bright in some, but all steamed up so that I could not see through any of them. I realised my window was in the topmost tier, the fourth.

Standing on its own at the centre of the snowy quadrangle was an oblong building with pitched roof and space all about. I soon knew that this was the library-chapel. Alongside it I saw a row of large smooth metal objects half-hidden by snow. There was another such row along the wall either side of the gate. Even as I watched I saw the gate opening: a huge carriage emerged from the tunnel—a long, grey, snow-topped carriage, pushed or pulled by nothing but itself, with a dark window running the length of its upper part. It must be a *bus*, I realised, angrily curious, and those smaller things will be *cars*.

Lubick had told me about them. I had seen pictures.

Huddled human shapes got out of the bus and hurried inside. Like a child I stared. Who lived behind those misted windows? Other Deetee Eyes? Scientists and doctors devising schedules for us? I watched the bus being set parallel to the gatehouse wall. It left ribbed tracks. In time I saw people come out and get into it, and off through the gate it went. I didn't know it yet: what I saw was the change-about in the shifts of Institute workers. The bus came every day at eight AM, four PM, and midnight. But as yet I knew nothing. I was a lost man. I didn't know that this place had been an insane asylum, nor that folk outside thought this still the case. In a way it was. But the former inmates had been removed. There had been top-security appointments, reconstructions. Double airlock doors had been installed on many rooms, and the rooms converted into these sterilised imitation motel rooms. In fact the work of conversion was not yet complete, for as day succeeded day I saw many vehicles come and go, discharging stuff that was carried into the Institute.

Perhaps Tari was right. Perhaps they did not expect us. It certainly seemed that they were not quite ready for us. To begin with, life was much as it had been at the Navy base. There was no hint of the work and experiments to come. Yet I suspect this was deliberate, and part of our "Orientation Program." So. I read the books they gave me. I stared at the wall. I endured the bland food and the visits of "specialists" who "dropped by" to "chat" with me. I was taken to a dentist who cleaned, drilled, straightened, filled, capped, and crowned me. After this I hardly knew my mouth at all, and yes, I was amazed, as by much else. I even watched TV, sitting carefully to one side to avoid the harmful rays. I saw something called *The Burning Boy,* about a boy on fire who ran screaming from a house onto a busy city street. The passers-by stared at him as if they were watching TV, and let him burn to death. I felt the camera staring at me as I stared at the people who stared at the burning boy. Sick, I turned the TV off and did not watch it again. After that I spent many hours gazing through the window at the clouds. Without this evidence of weather I would have gone mad. Snatched from the mountains, forests, winds, oceans; from the natural world to this! I fought numbness by clinging to anger. I demanded to grow my hair and beard as I wished. They said there were medical reasons why I could not. "To hell with your medical reasons!" I shouted.

They said they were sorry. They did not look it. I could see their faces because here they all wore transparent helmets.

Norman Ernstein said this was done to reduce the "psychological stress" which the closed helmets had caused in many of us.

After a week or two this man Ernstein came to see me almost every day. His function was similar to that which Lubick had filled. (In fact Lubick had been transferred here, but I rarely saw him.) Ernstein was tall, with wavy black hair and horn-rimmed glasses that perched on his bony nose under the transparent helmet. He had studied history more sympathetically than Lubick and was less prone to foolish generalisation. He was Jewish, and said that usually he lived in New York City, but that for the duration of this appointment he had taken lodgings nearby. He showed me pictures of his wife and two children. He said that over ten million people live in or near New York. I was appalled. "That is more than lived in all England and France together in my . . . in my time," I said, and my slip pleased him. His eyes gleamed. "Do you now really believe and understand that you are actually in the year 1984?" he asked softly. "All I know is that I am falsely imprisoned and refused my beard!" I snapped.

Yet I asked him to tell me about the other DTIs.

He did.

I learned that fifty-seven of us came from the last two hundred years, when the volume of traffic through the region had been greatest; and nineteen of us from the three centuries before that; yet only eleven from the ages before the great Reconnaissance. With some hesitancy he told me that many more had come through dead or utterly demented and that, the further back in time we came from, the higher the casualty rate. As all the others did, he insisted the entire business was an accident. Also he said that nobody could explain how it was that I and some others had been snatched from outside the test region. "So far we can't explain the mechanics of selection either," he admitted, shrugging. "Millions of people have sailed or crossed that region, but it seems that only a few of you have been unlucky enough to strike the right combination of circumstances. We don't have the answer—but we're working on it."

But what shocked me most was his telling me that, in this very building, as solid as myself, were five people who had lived before the Birth of Christ.

At this my mouth went dry. Briefly I shared the fear in the gut surely felt by these people at what they've done. People . . . from . . . before . . . Christ? I asked about them, and yes, I trembled, and the palms of my hands were sweating.

He replied very carefully:

"There's a man we think came from ancient Ireland. We're finding it difficult to communicate with him, but his . . . language . . . appears to be a kind of Gaelic. There is a Greek called Dion who claims he was in the Athenian army with Socrates. Zakar-Addi from Tyre apparently worked on the building of Solomon's Temple in Jerusalem, almost a thousand years before Christ. We have a woman from Egypt, who hasn't said much but listens a lot, and we gather that she's from the time of Queen Hatshepsut . . . of the Eighteenth Dynasty . . . thirty-five hundred years ago . . ."—he paused, breathing deeply in his suit, in his own way as overcome by all this as I was, I believe—". . . and then . . . we have another man . . . a red man who will not speak to us, but . . . there are indications from material that came through with him that he's of an age much earlier still . . . seven thousand years ago . . . though the dating's very much in question. . . ."

I was utterly shocked. The Abyss! Holy Writ!

"That's impossible! The world's not that old!"

An expression I knew already came over his face. He was wondering how to break the news. I forced a very thin smile.

"So tell me!" I demanded, my mind in turmoil. "Affright me with the true age of the world according to modern scientific estimation! Ten thousand years? Twelve thousand? Thirteen?"

He gave me a number that meant nothing at all.

"About four and a half thousand million years," he said.

The cunning man! The Power not of Christ! Lies! Lies!

"Suppose this is true," said I as carelessly as I could, "then what of this man from seven thousand years ago: Is he rude and barbarian? Or like a Titan of the Golden Age when Saturn ruled?"

Norman Ernstein had humility and a good humour. I regret we had to treat him as we did when we got away.

"I feel like a child in his presence," he admitted soberly. "When he looks at me I feel that he sees right through me."

Escape? No, it was still faraway, not at all in my mind, as yet conceived of only by two of us . . . and this was the first I heard about Masanva the Dancer and Nefertari Mery-Isis. And though Ernstein's talk had me horrified and perplexed, when he told me of these ancient folk I thought briefly, for the first time since I'd come through Vulcan, of Golden Ships . . . of potential wonders and discoveries that need not all be completely hellish.

Such treacherous thinking I crushed, telling myself I did not really believe that other DTIs existed at all. Yet it was soon after this that Tari first made her presence known, most subtly; and that I met other DTIs. And I thank God that every society has its blind spots . . . for there are more ways to shake hands than with the hands alone. . . .

-»»❖[15]❖««-

Humf Takes a Dip
in the Ancient Nile

Tari's first communication was accidental. I thought it a sure sign I had gone mad. It came at night, some weeks after my arrival. The serious work had begun. I lay exhausted in bed after a long day of interrogation on speech-patterns in the sixteenth century. Ernstein and a linguist called Rogers had been at me all day with their nonsense, giving me passages from Shakespeare to read aloud, first in Devon dialect, then in polite courtly accent, then in the accents of folk from different parts. Next I'd had to read translations of these same passages in Latin, French, Dutch, Italian, and Spanish. They said I was enormously aiding their knowledge of the evolution of language. The passage I had to read most often came from that Scottish tragedy the name of which, I'm told, actors never mention:

> Tomorrow and tomorrow and tomorrow
> Creeps in this petty pace from day to day
> To the last syllable of recorded time . . .

I thought this a joke in very poor taste, but they said it was nothing of the sort. They had me repeat it endlessly, tape-recording my every variation until they were satisfied, and by the time they were finished with me I wished myself dumb, to be spared such lunacy.

Weeks later I learned I was lucky to be treated so lightly. When Tari's soundless shriek of outrage burst in my mind as I lay in bed that night, I had no idea what it was.

It shocked me bolt upright and wide awake.

It was an explosion in the head; a soundless shriek, a bright burst of blinding blue light; a sensation of vicious wounding that left me aching and afraid and unable to sleep.

It had similar effect on others too, including some of the surgeons. They had begun to drill a hole in her skull in order to slip an electrode into the left temporal lobe of her brain. They meant to stimulate her memory and language skills, so she could learn American English quickly and tell them everything they wanted to know about ancient Egypt. They had thought her drugged unconscious, believing that her very slow brain waves meant she was unaware of what they did.

"I gave them no excuse to try that again!" she told me much later. "When I knew what they wanted, then by Sothis I learned their tongue quickly! I told them they don't have to invade the human temple to grab this gold of the mind without asking. I had elements of the tongue already, so when they attacked me I screamed in my mind and awoke, and said, "DO NOT DO THAT!" Hah! It gave them white faces! They could not understand. They think their sort of understanding is the only sort. They call dream-travel superstition! They know nothing of Isis! Some of them were struck by my howl, but would not face it, and called it an *aberration!* You and Herbie and some others were struck too, and howled back, though you didn't know you did. Later I dream-walked with the Dancer and we agreed we could start the Circle without risk of them knowing it or spying on it—for how could they spy on what they refused to believe in? So, we began it!"

Three nights after that fearful howl I lay dizzy and sick after a drug-treatment meant "to boost the efficacy of the Interferon program." I could not sleep; I felt so blackly hopeless that for the first time in my life (save after Vulcan when I drifted in the sea) I considered the sin of suicide. The room was almost dark, with one dim bulb glowing from the ceiling, and a voice murmured from a grid in the wall—a voice so soft I could barely hear it: it crept in like a feather tickling the mind, as it did every night before I slept and (as I came to realise) during my sleep as well. *". . . and in 1969 the Apollo space program put the first men on the moon,"* it was murmuring, *"and in 1981, after successful unmanned American expeditions to the planets, the Space Shuttle Columbia was . . ."*

Poison? A rope? A knife? None of these were available. I floated in deadly fantasy of self-loathing. What point in fighting for an existence like this? Damned already, why persist? Midnight forever. No more dawns. No more sunrise. No more joys, adventures, tears or laughter, love and sport and mad flood of battle. No more Golden Ships. No more dreams, no more . . .

Golden Ships?

Borne on a subtle inner tide, they came stealing into my darkness so quietly that I did not even realise the dissolving of my wish to die until it was gone . . . and I saw them! The Golden Ships! Skimming a diamond sea in vast, silent, majestic array! And I was alive again, vision restored! With vision we can do anything! Without it we hate, we destroy, we bang our heads against the walls of the world, we work to make money, we can create nothing at all!

Yes! She radiated an optimism. She pressed nothing forcibly. I had no sense of another will involved in such profound and sudden uplifting of the spirit . . . until the next night, after another bad day, when I felt the subtle tide come again, and gladly let it in.

This night it was different.

I sensed the Golden Ships . . . and something else behind them.

For the briefest instant I saw a woman's face. She looked very intently at me. She had black hair, a copper face, deep dark eyes. Behind her I sensed desert, river, burning sky. I grew fearful, and the image faded. But . . . then came such a flood of sunny warmth that immediately I was ashamed of my fear. It felt as if a happy child wanted to play with me—and I a *man* afraid of a *child?*

I relaxed, and let the face and the landscape return.

In a sort of precisely detailed waking dream I entered that landscape. I seemed to stand in the shade of a strange fronded tree near a small baked-earth house, facing the smiling woman, and saw that she was young, perhaps no more than seventeen. She was slim, lithe, not tall, barefoot, wearing a simple white linen dress from neck to knees that left her arms also bare. Raven hair cut square across her brow fell to her shoulders, framing a coppery face with broad cheekbones, straight nose, a wide mouth. Her eyes held humour and gravity and the light of intelligence. When I smiled back at her she reached into a woven basket at her feet and from it gave me several small round sticky fruits, indicating the tree to tell me the fruits came from it. She ate, I ate, I found them good—they were dates, as I found later. She indicated the little house; somehow I knew it was where she grew up, with her brothers and sisters. Then her gaze travelled farther. I looked out over green growing fields to arid sandy hilltops that wrinkled the horizon. Then I looked down and saw the River! Down below us it flowed, brown and mighty and broad, swollen in fertile flood! And up above blazed the sun in a sky so bright it hurt!

She pointed, laughing, at the river, then began running down the dusty hill, past the irrigations, to the riverside rushes. I paused, then followed. I felt strong and young. At river's edge she stopped an instant to peel off her dress, then dived into the shallows. I was but seconds behind, and all sadness dissolved as I hit the water with a great S-P-L-A-S-H . . . then it all bubbled away, quite radiant, and I was Sir Humfrey again, in my dark room, with the sleep-talk whispering information about the Gross National Product.

I slept well that night. In the morning they said it must be the drugs, but I kept quiet, and later learned other DTIs had done likewise. The day was bearable, and that night, between waking and sleep, the strange tide came bubbling into me again.

This time we were going downriver in a large galley of antique design. It had a single bank of oars both sides and the square sail was furled. Many people of every sort were crowded in it, and goats and sheep, and somebody's chickens squawking about, and jars and parcels and baggage. Great urns and bales were roped down aft. There was laughing and chattering in language I did not understand, but this did not matter at all, for I saw every evidence, as we carried on so gently downstream beneath the hot sun, of a great and prosperous civilisation. And soon we came past a beautiful city which had many temples and large buildings. I saw a procession coming along a waterfront street, with priests and plumed horses and happy dancers. They were all coming to greet a beautiful barge that we passed as it slid towards the quay. It was slender, this barge, and rich with carved wood; jewelled ornaments gleamed on rich purple cloths; there were carved golden rams at prow and at stern, and a crowned golden falcon atop a golden sanctuary amidships. It was a Golden Ship indeed! The passengers on our ship and the crowds onshore were all cheering with excitement, and dancing, and pointing to the regal pair, the man and woman, who stood in the poop of that remarkable vessel.

So, on we went down that busy broad river, past the never-ending irrigations, until I saw, on the western bank, standing stark and clear and haloed against the setting sun, the three great pyramids.

Khem! The Two Lands! Egypt!

I felt shock that cleared my head, and turned to my guide, and found her changed! She looked older by some ten to fifteen years, her face grown sharper, with a greater clarity.

She put a finger to her lips and smiled.

Then the tide bubbled away again.

For some time I was unclear that these images originated beyond me. I was not even sure that other DTIs existed. I had met none, they were abstract to me, like space travel and New York City. Yes, I recalled Ernstein's talk of the Egyptian woman . . . but the truth is I did not want to think too hard about it. Thought of ancient Egypt conjured up images of matters of which I could hardly approve. I had read some of Herodotus, and once Doctor Dee loaned me *De Mysteriis Egyptorum* by Nostradamus . . . but such stuff made me most uneasy, I considering it all to do with black lore, or at least unchristian. In my time those mummies were brought into Europe ground up as medicine, or to mix with paint, some artists believing that mummy-powder would stop their paint cracking on the canvas; and then as now there was much belief in the strange powers of those ancient magicians.

Thus at first I preferred not to think too much about the source of these gently alarming pictures in my mind. And, as it turned out, for a while I forgot them . . . for life became active again. . . .

One bright morning, the sun shining through the east-facing window, after white-suits had brought the usual breakfast of orange juice, toast and jelly, and three pancakes saturated with Old Log Cabin maple syrup, Norman Ernstein entered carrying a suit. He told me the time had come to meet some other DTIs. He seemed cheerfully convinced I'd be delighted. I was not so sure, but I had to admit to curiosity, so I clambered into the monstrous garment and followed him out.

Through the double doors we went, and along an echoing bleak corridor to a door at the end. Unlocking this door, he led me down four zigzag flights of stairs to a cold stone lobby with a steel door at one end. Beside this, in a sort of kiosk, a black man in blue uniform sat in front of a board which had many switches and rows of holes, some containing plugs connected by coloured wires to plugs in other holes. "That's a *telephone switchboard,*" Ernstein said through his suit as we went outside. "I'll explain later."

Then I stood under the sky, staring.

Standing about on the hard black paving between our door and the library-chapel were a number of suited figures, in couples or in diffident groups. Each couple, like Ernstein and I, consisted of a DTI and an Institute staff-member. It was immediately clear which were which: every DTI was shaven bald and wore a red jumpsuit under transparent immunity-suit with air-container on the back.

I eyed them all most uncertainly.

"Come along, Sir Humphrey!" Ernstein took me by the elbow. "I want you to meet some people we hope you're going to like."

I didn't know it, but these introductions had been carefully assessed by computer, human common-sense being thought insufficient to avoid *faux pas* between strangers of so many different ages, races, cultures, colours, and religious beliefs. It had all been worked out most mathematically. Thus on this first day I met only Christian Europeans of the sixteenth to twentieth centuries. This was a sensible approach to a difficult situation—yet, as Ernstein propelled me out to my first meeting, I found the sky more interesting . . . or, at least, so I pretended, even to myself.

It was near the end of March. The clouds were high, fast, their bellies fleecy white, but their grey edges ragged and wind-blown. All about us the harsh high Institute walls, yet up there was the spring sky, and a bird swooping free on the wind, and I wished . . .

"Sir Humphrey!" Ernstein interrupted my nervous abstraction. "I want you to meet a fellow-countryman. He's not quite of *your* time; in fact he's quite *recent,* from 1948, but we think you'll both find a *lot* in common . . . Sir Humphrey, I'd like you to meet Air-Marshal Sir Arthur Coningham, who fought for England in the Second World War!"

So my gaze was torn from the clouds to Sir Arthur even as a similar introduction was given him by his Modern squire about myself.

Coningham regarded me calmly through the faceplate of his suit. He was a short, stocky, grizzled man of middle-age. "Gilbert, eh?" He extended a gloved hand and we shook, gingerly on my part. "Read about you in school, old chap. Raleigh's older brother and all that. Went to Newfoundland, didn't you? Glad to meet you, old chap!"

"Sir," I said, "you are an *Englishman*?"

"As English as old oak. Damn bad show, this. These *suits*." He shook his bald head disapprovingly. "Always thought the Yanks were funny johnnies. Too dashed frantic. Told 'em if I survived Rommel *and* the desert *and* that blasted Patton in 1942 then I can breathe their air now without this damn suit. But they won't listen."

I liked Sir Arthur immediately; he was a man of honour, and we spent much time talking together during the coming months. He had survived the Second World War only to be snatched by Vulcan in January 1948, being the only survivor of an airliner, the *Star Tiger*, that came crashing through the vortex. He told me of the war and I thought I understood . . . until later in Circle I experienced an air-battle through his eyes and memory.

The computer's next choice was less fortunate. I was faced with a thin, sour individual squired by my old acquaintance Frank Lubick, who seemed embarrassed to see me. This person was Howell Rees, a Methodist parson from Brecon in Wales, taken from 1763. He asked my religion immediately. When he heard I was Church of England he set his jaw, glowered, and announced: "I cannot speak with this man!"

"You are as bigoted as the Enthusiasts of my day!" I snapped, "and I have no wish to speak with you either!"

Lubick and Ernstein conferred, then Lubick took me aside. "Mr. Gilbert, don't take it personally," he said, "Howell refuses to talk to anyone who isn't Methodist, and we don't have any other Methodists here." And he shrugged helplessly.

"Then why does he talk to you? You're a Mormon!"

Forgetting he wore a suit, Lubick tried to rub his chin. "Well, uh, I've given him to understand he has a chance of converting me if he talks to me."

Next I met a burly Dutch merchant, Philius Van Roornevink, waylaid by Vulcan while returning to Holland from New Amsterdam in 1666. He told me immediately (with a roguish smile) that England and Holland had been at war; and that the Dutch fleet had sailed unopposed up the Thames and sacked our fleet. I started arguing, but Ernstein reminded him that the English had got their own back soon after his own departure, turning New Amsterdam into New York.

Ernstein was worried as he led me to my next introduction— a tall, proud-looking man who eyed me frostily as we approached. "Sir Humphrey, please restrain your nationalistic ardour! We're doing our best to find compatible people for you, but . . ."—he gestured helplessly—". . . since at one time or another everyone's been at war with everyone else, we'll get nowhere if you let emotion get the better with you all the time! Now . . ."—he glanced at the man we approached—". . . I want you to meet a man who was an explorer like you, in America—but there's one slight problem: he doesn't speak English, and as you speak Spanish, then perhaps . . ."

"*Spanish?*" I stopped dead. "I'll not speak with a . . ."

"Good *God*, man, England and Spain haven't been at war for . . ."

"To me it is but three months since I was at war with Spain!" I told him furiously. "What shall I do? Grow wings and fly? Love my enemies at a single moment's notice? Very well! Master! I am but a silly slave, and you are my Master! Command me, Master!"

"I am NOT your master! Sir Humphrey, you must . . ."

"You are a Jew, and you told me about the Nazis!" I snapped. "As a Jew, would you happily speak German to a Nazi?"

"SIR HUMPHREY, I *APOLOGISE*, GODDAMMIT!"

"Then lead me to this man! Lead me! I'll speak to him in his language, and clutch him to my bosom if you'll have it so, *Master!*"

Yes, and so I met Senor Bernardino de Oveido de Azurara.

He had been taken from 1547, before England and Spain were actively at war, so that he did not feel as badly about me as at first I did about him. But it was difficult. I nodded stiffly at the man, noting that he looked too much like that dog Mendoza for my liking, and as soon as we spoke I found him quite as arrogant as...well, as I was, I suppose. Yet I reined my feelings the best I could, and fortunately so. Ernstein was right: we had much in common. Azurara had marched north from Mexico in 1540 with Coronado, seeking the fabled golden cities of Cibola. He had much of interest to say. Yet he was a European coloniser, like myself, and later in Circle caused a crisis with all his boastful talk of *conquering the New World* and *bringing the savages to Christ*. Utak and others of Indio blood would not tolerate it: the resulting split caused Masanva to intervene.

At this first meeting he and I were coldly polite. It was a difficult day, but we agreed to talk further. *Mañana!*

⚔❲ 16 ❳⚔

Meetings with Distressed
Temporal Immigrants

The following weeks were a busy bewilderment. I had no time
for dreams of Egypt. For an hour or more each day I was
Outside, and met over thirty other "Baldies" computer-selected
for me in a gradually extended range of nationality, religion,
and era of origin. I didn't notice that none of the five from
Before Christ appeared: the thirty and more were enough to
deal with. We all found it very arduous, especially those more
ancient among us, and often I found it hard to keep my temper.
The continual one-to-one chaperonage was maintained for some
weeks, and relaxed only after the threat and frequency of physical assault and violent argument among us declined.

At first we were as sorry a bunch of refugees as could be
imagined. Shaved, suited, scanned, tricked and tested and op-
erated on—we were mostly as alien to ourselves as to each
other, with everything familiar gone, and hardly a chance to
speak unsupervised or without being photoscanned. Starvation
of soul and emotions while the drug-treatments and forced
education all dragged on—at first we had no common spirit:
it was impossible . . . and matters hardly improved after our red
jumpsuits were changed to green. God knows why they chose
red in the first place, though Ernstein said something about
"the first phase of transtemporal habilitation" involving the
"reawakening of your ego-image as a nucleus to attract and
integrate new experience." Whatever this means, apparently
red helped it, while *green,* he said, "assists the flowering of
your social and emotional responsiveness."

Very good. Dee once said something similar. Yet my "social and emotional responsiveness" was slow to flower. In those early days my temper was poor, my self-esteem zero, and my efforts at communication blighted by not knowing what on earth we were trying to discuss. It is perhaps as well that there were no other Englishmen of my era: no doubt we'd have formed an enterprising little clique. As it was, I found I had great need of Coningham's common-sense as a bridge.

With Azurara too I soon became, if not a fast friend, then a close acquaintance. Our positions were similar. Like myself, he needed a Modern DTI of his own race and tongue to help him. I doubt that he was as lucky as I was with Coningham in the choice the computer made for him. His initial introduction had been to Juan Battista Fernandez, an insufferably pompous Cuban landowner who'd fled from Castro straight into Vulcan: he advocated armed guards and starvation wages for workers as the best way to turn a good sugar-cane profit, and told Azurara sadly that not even the mighty U.S.A. had been able to stop "the foul tide of socialist revolution" from sweeping over his land.

Azurara was profoundly shocked by some of the changes in the world, and so at first was I. "Gilbert, they have abolished *Holy Mother Church* in some countries! And in others there are rogue priests who fight for this... this revolution of the people! I know you are not Catholic, Gilbert, but these people... they fight for unmentionable *blasphemy!* Priests of *Rome!*"

Coningham's advice to me was more deliberate. Before giving it he spoke first to John Kent, a Chicago banker from 1966, then to Jud Daraul, the black Vietnam veteran, and then to a Mexican called Rodrigo. He came to me on the lower floor of the library one day, where I sat trying to grasp Newton's Laws of Gravity, and said: "Hmmm. From what I gather, Humphrey, most of those priests deserve medals for carrying out their Christian duty among people being treated quite outrageously. I'm no socialist—born the right side of the fence, like you—but one has to draw the line somewhere."

The library, on two floors, occupied half the building that also housed the chapel. On the lower floor were the stacked shelves of Ancient and Modern books, and tables, and comfortable chairs, and writing materials. Ernstein introduced me to this haven during my second walkabout, and quickly, as soon as one-to-one chaperonage was suspended, it became my

practise to spend my hour or so of daily freedom in this downstairs section of the library, amongst the books.

I had been introduced to the upstairs section too, which was
an altogether different kettle of fish. It contained a computer
terminal that, said Ernstein casually, "can get you just about
any information you want from anywhere in the world in a
matter of seconds." It also contained the electronic games, such
as *Space Invaders*, and other games of more conventional sort
in which I sometimes indulged with Coningham, Azurara, or
Herbie Pond—chess, chequers, dominoes, also Monopoly,
Risk, and others of that sort. But the main business in the
upstairs section was education by computer.

Soon after being introduced to all this (and to the chapel,
with its daily "interdenominational services" that I would
not attend), I was visited in my room by suited experts in
disciplines innumerable. Did I want instruction in: Hatha Yoga,
Elementary Physics, American History, World History, Knit-
ting, Media Interpretation, Volleyball, Basketball, Football,
Musical Appreciation?—etc., etc., etc. Some of these courses
were to be taught by people; but also offered were many other
subjects—geology, astronomy, psychology, anthropology, bot-
any, neotony, and God knows what else—to be computer-
taught.

I found little interest in such a cold new-fangled method,
nor in the electronic games, though briefly I attended a small
weekly class in the downstairs section—*Philosophy Ancient
And Modern: An Epistemological Rapprochement*—given by
a self-delighted female Sophist called Strudwick who spoke
much on "the negation of the negation" and treated us as idiots.
Perhaps: I understood not a thing she said, but recognised the
type from my Oxford days, and quickly decamped.

Yet by May and June it was usual to see—crouching intently
in rows of red plastic chairs bolted to the floor both sides of
the computer housing—up to twenty DTIs all "interfacing" at
once, not with each other, but with keyboard and screen before
them. These were not only the Moderns among us. Our guardians were amazed at how many of us from the "pre-industrial
era" quickly "got into" worshipful relationship with High Tech-
nology, and some DTIs took up electronic academia with ob-
sessive abandon, preparing to spend the rest of their captive
lives working for Ph.D.'s in Esperanto or Romantic Poetry.
Of course we were under continual pressure to "do something

positive" of this sort; to "think Modern" and "relate."

Also, the flickering light of the screens of computer, electronic games, word-processing machines, and TV exercised hypnotic fascination over many of us. *Space Invaders* in particular came to obsess several people, especially Ketil Blund, a craggy Norse giant from eleventh-century Greenland, driven from his bleak steading and south into Vulcan by swift and drastic change in climate. I thought it an utter sad disgrace that such a man should have to turn from axe and plough to the dubious skill of shooting down advancing electronic blips that always get you in the end. "Good for hand-eye coordination," said Ernstein when I asked him the purpose of this depressing game—but to Blund it became Reason for Life itself. Swearing by Odin and Thor he'd stamp about, seizing Baldies by their suited shoulders, demanding, "Try beat Blund! Try beat Blund!" And nobody could better his score, not even Jud Daraul, until one summer day amid our common crisis Utak showed superior finesse. After this humiliation Blund grew morose, muttering about going berserk.

Utak was a short, strong, grim man from tenth-century Yucatan. *Space Invaders* he enjoyed as relaxation from his preoccupation with mathematics. He was skilled in manipulating symbol, having been an astronomer-priest among the Maya; Number being his sanity and madness too, as soon I'll tell. He did not mean to destroy Blund's only source of confidence, but it happened, and had sad consequences.

But all these things in their proper place, for the crisis I speak of came after Circle was founded.

Yes, great confusion, and much to learn, so that for some time I thought not at all of ancient Egypt, nor of the preChristian DTIs.

Then came the day when Jud and Herbie spoke of "timeprejudice," and Herbie alerted us by mentioning "weird dreams" he'd been having.

Herbie Pond was tall, lean, bony, blunt. When I first met him I was reminded immediately of the rogues who'd given me such trouble on the *Swallow*. He had swagger and insolent disrespect, infuriating me by calling me *Humf*. This I would not tolerate, and though several times after our introduction he approached me, I would not speak to him. But one day over the chessboard Coningham said: "Oh, by the way, there's a fellow—Herbie Pond's his name—who'd like to get to know you. Says he's sorry if he offended you. Only trying to be friendly. Has tiptop admiration for Francis Drake and yourself. Seems a solid sort to me."

"He must apologise to my face!" I insisted stiffly.

"Gilbert. Look, old chap, you must climb down a bit. I know the sort. Rough diamond. Good heart. Break you in."

So I let Herbie into my life, and a good thing I did.

"Listen, Humf," he drawled when I said I'd be his friend if only he'd stop calling me *Humf*, "Coningham's a regular guy, and you could get along pretty good yourself. But you need a guy like me to show you what gives these days. I mean I know the bottom line."

He said when he was young he'd wanted to live in my time, "when you didn't have none of this bureaucracy crap, and if you had the guts you could just sail off to America and go buccaneering." Nothing I said could persuade him that my time had as many clerks and laws as this present world, and that you could no more do what you liked then than now. "Man, you don't know what it's like," was his invariable response, which irritated me, but his stories about the U.S.A. in the 1920s so fascinated me, along with his own adventures, that I had to forgive him, often. Much of it seemed tumultuous and too tall for belief, but his wit never failed even in describing the Vulcan horror. "Thought it was a time-bomb, the *usual* sort," he said drily. "Got this warning not to fly the stuff, but I needed the dough real bad, and I was halfway there, and . . . shit!"

Herbie adopted me into a group of Moderns as low as himself, who idled much of their free time on the volleyball court between the library and East Block. As for volleyball, well, it is hard to be energetic and lithe in an immunity-suit. The nucleus of this group was Herbie, Jud Daraul, Connie Waters, Jim Gage, Jim Guerrero, Lucie Hopkins, and Clive Carlos.

Jud was about thirty, from Detroit, another lean man, who shocked me telling how he'd "fragged" one of his officers during the war in Vietnam, stalking the man to a latrine with a grenade, and . . . "Naw," he admitted, "I let the sonuvabitch live. Caught him there with his pants down and told him, *'You gotta wise up, man. Next time you take us out on a goddamn midnight headhunting trip someone's gonna blow yer mutha-fuckin head off!'* And he got the message, man, he got it."

Connie from 1973 had a freckled face and looked the sweetest thing you ever saw. I asked her what she did before Vulcan.

"With a rodeo," she said, grinning.

"Rodeo? What's a rodeo?"

"I got a lot of bread for climbing in a barrel and getting rolled about by real nasty Brahma bulls."

If Connie amazed me, at first I thought I understood Lucie Hopkins and her frivolity. Lucie was an industrial heiress lost to Vulcan during a yacht-cruise in 1926. She prattled on about black caviar with the Rockefellers at Pocantico Hills and how she spooned with F. Scott Fitzgerald before he was famous; she had a moony face and couldn't keep on the track of an idea for more than a second; and I thought her fluff, but events proved this an underestimation. As for Jim Gage, he was English, from Liverpool, lost at sea in 1941. He called himself a *Scouser,* and when he heard me talk he told me: "These days we string your sort up by the bloody neck, mate!"—then laughed and said he was joking. But I was not amused; he lacked Herbie's charm, though he was true to his lights. Jim Guerrero had been a stoker on the U.S.S. *Cyclops,* which in 1918 had left Barbados with a mad captain, a mutinous crew, and a heavy load of manganese. "We were going down even before it got us," he said. He was swarthy, usually silent, never without a pair of dice rolling between his gloved fingers. And Clive Carlos from 1956, half-Welsh and half-Mexican, had the loudest laugh I ever heard and never seemed to be downcast by anything, not even in this place.

For some time I was not at ease with these people, and they knew it, and knew why. "Problem with you, Humf," said Herbie, "is you're a goddamn snob. Think you're the Emperor, just like Lucie here thinks she's the goddamn Empress. Just wake up and see you ain't got no more clothes than the rest of us. Then you'll be a regular guy, just like us."

I found it hard to take this, but their friendship was genuine, and besides, whether I liked it or not, it was true, I too was now *of the lower sort.* So by May I came to spend fifteen or twenty minutes each day sitting with them in a circle by the volleyball court, out in the open where microphones weren't likely to pick us up, and speaking so that the cameras mounted on the walls wouldn't catch our lip-movements. "Why the hell should they know what we're talking about!" snapped Herbie. And though as yet we had nothing subversive to discuss, Ernstein and other nurses disapproved of this "flowering" of our "social and emotional responsiveness." Ernstein began to harass me, coming upon us to demand my presence at a therapy group, or in my room to be interrogated by some new expert in socioeconomic conditions during the Reformation, or whatever. At first I accepted this reduction of my free time philosophically— but Herbie and the rest of the gang were scandalised—and one day Herbie said:

"Humf, they screw around with all of us here, but if I were you I'd get really mad at all this goddamn time-prejudice!"

I asked him what exactly he meant.

"Like how Ernstein gives you a hard time for hanging out with us. See, the more Modern you are, the more so-called *privileges* you get, the less they bother you. They're not interested in us guys, they already *know* we don't know nothing they don't—or that's what they think. So we get to stay out here sunning ourselves in our suits while you're up there drugged and getting the sixteenth century dredged outa your brain! And who's seen any of those poor pre-Christian bastards? They're locked up tighter than gold at Fort Knox! I mean it's time we stopped cooperating, right?"

"Same old race shit too," Jud added, "What about the red folks here, and the orientals and latinos, and that Egyptian chick, and . . . ?"

"Yeah," muttered Herbie, "that's a dame I'd sure like to meet." He pursed his lips. "Hey, I keep getting these weird dreams when I'm not quite asleep. Keep seeing pharaohs and pyramids and . . ."

Then he sensed it, because he looked up and saw my face, and Jud's, and Lucie's, and Coningham was there too, and the expression through his faceplate was just as taken aback. We all looked at each other. The others stared at us, not understanding.

"Hey!" Herbie whistled softly. "You mean you guys . . ."

"We must not talk of it!" said I in a sharp low voice, eyeing the ground, spurred by a sudden strong sense of alarm. "Not here!"

"I agree." Coningham was quiet. "It would be sensible."

"Weird shit!" muttered Jud, *"Weee*ired shit!"

"You people crazy or what?" Clive Carlos demanded, and he and Connie and Jim Gage and Jim Guerrero all looked baffled. And Coningham realised a danger I failed to see.

"Something damned odd's going on," he told them squarely, disguising his mouth with his hand. "Until we know what it is, silence is best. You chaps understand?"

That was our first hint of the Circle forming.

"You must never try to force these things on people," Tari told me much later. "That is the black magic, and apart from the right or wrong of it, such attempts will often rebound on the perpetrator with increased and even fatal force. The Dancer and I agreed that you all had to realise the nature of my effort for yourselves. It was up to you to admit or refuse my sendings. You, Humf, you accepted my first sendings up to the point where they disturbed you. When you became anxious you refused to admit me anymore . . . until you realised that you were not the only one. . . ."

That evening in my room, after supper, during a wearisome interrogation about clothing fashions at Elizabeth's Court, I asked Ernstein why I received less time Outside than Modern DTIs, why none of the Before-Christ DTIs had been seen Outside, and when would we meet them?

Ernstein gave me a bleak eye.

"You shouldn't waste time with that crowd on the volleyball court, Sir Humphrey. I'm glad you're adapting so well to modern association, but perhaps you lack the discrimination to sort the wheat from the chaff, so to speak. As to your questions, the answer, both with regard to you and the pre-Christians, lies in functional and psychological necessity. We have an extremely interesting research program developing with you, but unfortunately it *is* time-consuming, so please bear with us. As to the pre-Christians, we hope that three of them at least can soon start to play an active role in our daily life here."

Two were already doing so, but he didn't know that, and I had scarcely more than an inkling of it. Nor did I know that Zakar-Addi the Phoenician had already followed his companion into death; nor that Othoon the Irishman would never be let out among us, for they judged him a dangerous fool who'd encourage us to resist them.

They were right. So he did.

That night, for the first time in more than a month, the golden tide came again, and I saw the woman's face again. She regarded me intently, and somehow her expression brought

to my mind what Herbie had said that afternoon, and our reaction, and the decision on silence. And at all this she
smiled . . . and distinctly *winked*. . . .

Then the apparition dissolved away, leaving me with hard-
beating heart, and much to consider. Still I wished to reject
such stuff, but I was no longer in my own world, my rules of
faith and conduct were all snapped, and I had to admit I was
glad to see that fine calm copper face again. And though still
it shook me to think that maybe this face and vision came from
one who'd lived over two thousand years before my own time,
now I was anxious, indeed eager, to meet the Egyptian woman,
and I wondered when this would happen.

The answer was, *soon*.

Yet before we met Masanva and Mery-Isis we met Dion
the Athenian, who first appeared Outside with Hyperia, a pale
and long-faced woman from Roman North Africa of the early
third century after Christ.

Hyperia's health was poor, but her spirit was strong: she
did not last the year, but worked hard towards our unity in
Circle, being a voice of reason and good humour, and I'll have
more to say about her.

Dion was a thin young man, demoralised and perpetually
dazed. Several times in the next few months I tried to speak
with him in his own tongue, but he refused reply. Perhaps my
Greek was poor, or perhaps he feared he'd be punished for not
speaking in broken American. In any case, he had no control
of his mind. I know not if this sad state came from Vulcan or
from what the doctors did: no doubt some of both, yet I suspect
he was not too bright to begin with. Yes, he said, he had seen
and heard Socrates: he had served in the Athenian army with
Socrates before deserting during the war against Sparta, which
act had apparently thrown him into a dreadful odyssey involving
enslavement, sale to a Carthaginian pirate captain, and three
thousand miles of ocean rowing ended only by Roman Vulcan's
American hammer cracking him from 426 BC to 1983 AD.
No wonder his wits were fled: he must have been deeply frus-
trating to the experts, for when I asked the poor wretch my
inevitable stupid Socrates question, he gave me a sallow grin
and nodded vigorously in his suit:

"Soc-rat-ees! Soc-rat-ees! Great—guy! Great—guy! He—

drink with us! He get—very drinked! He say—knowing is ... is ..."

"Knowing is *what*, Dion?"

He stared at the ground in crestfallen silence.

"I ... I not ... remember ..."

Dion, you are not the only one.

17

The Nine Dreams
of the Hawk

If seeing is believing, and nothing's done without belief, then
that day when we first met Masanva the Dancer and Nefertari
Mery-Isis in the flesh is the day that our Circle was sparked
into active life, being the point at which our vague dreaming
found a solid common base from which practical consequences
might be developed.

Now, reaching this point, remembering, with the wind
howling outside in yet another Welsh gale, I regain sense of
connection with the wellsprings, finding strength in recollec-
tion, feeling that finally I begin to rise again from the mire in
which I have stuck myself so long. Yes, trouble closes in, but
I'll do this, and then we'll see . . . for it is *how* we live that
counts, not how long.

The little group emerged from the West Block door one
sunny day in early June. Coningham, Herbie, and myself were
standing talking outside the library. The two DTIs were preceded by the birdlike figure of Director Piggot in his grey suit
and shirt and tie, and were followed by three white-suit guards.
When we saw them we wondered immediately at the guards
and at Piggot's unusual presence, and at the way in which,
before starting forward, Piggot stood measuring the quadrangle
suspiciously, as if afraid that somebody might jump from the
sky and abduct or kill his two prize specimens.

This done, he started a walk that took them out of our sight
behind the chapel and presumably round the back. We eyed
each other. We all thought the same: these two must be the

Egyptian woman and the mysterious man from ancient America. Certainly one of them was a small woman and the other a thickset man, and hopefully they'd be brought round this way. So, we lingered tensely where we were, and, as we waited, Azurara drifted up, eyeing the sky, and Jud Daraul, and Lucie Hopkins, smiling at nobody in particular; and lastly Utak came out of the Library, scowling, muttering to himself. But he shut up and joined us, his face suddenly intent, as Piggot's group came round the corner and approached us. And I saw Tari for the first time.

I had awaited this, and thought myself ready, but still I went weak at the knees when I recognised her from the visions.

Yes, they were both bald and caught under plastic and plexiglass just like the rest of us. What else? Yet in her case there was the raven-haired image to contend with. I had no difficulty recognising her. Her face was the same, with the same deep eyes, straight nose, wide mouth. There was no mistaking her, despite the incongruity between her image and her reality. I wondered why she used that image as her present signature, for unlike many of us she was not dehumanised or stereotyped by baldness or by the suit. She was small, not much more than five feet high, and the immunity-suit lay somewhat too baggy and crumpled about her. Yet, she approached us walking in a precise way which somehow suggested that the suit was irrelevant, or not there at all. This was heartening, and commanded immediate respect and affection from those of us who felt perpetually stifled and imprisoned in the suits, as I did.

The man who walked on her right side was also short, but massive and wide, with heavy jowls and a broad dark forehead. His skull was unusually large, with strong slopes and plates of bone tight beneath the gleaming skin. He could have been anywhere between thirty and seventy: his age was never made clear. His eyes were brilliant, and black as ink, and he walked not on his heels but on the balls of his feet. My gaze returned to his eyes... they were deep and very deep and deeper still. And where from the woman I felt a shining-forth of inner steadiness, a consistent unity with known purpose such as few of us have, of the man I could not tell what I sensed. It was not that he was a closed book, simply that I could not read his character at all. This is what I first learned of Masanva.

They both studied the not-so-casual group of us as Piggot, flicking a glance at us and holding his parchment-pale face slightly away, tried to steer them straight past us to the library door. At this the woman smiled very faintly, and stopped walking even as the man, Masanva, stopped too, despite the attempted onrushing-of-them by the three big strong young white-suit guards. Piggot turned impatiently even as one of the guards, a burly red-haired man, succeeded in delaying his own halt long enough to manage to bring his own foot down heavily on Masanva's left heel.

Masanva turned and looked at him without expression. The guard stared back for several seconds—then abruptly shook his head, and looked dazed as if he'd momentarily forgotten who he was, then stationed himself further back, biting his lip and confused.

Masanva said nothing.

"I want to speak with these people," the woman said. Her voice was low and her spoken American already as precise as her physical movements. Piggot looked annoyed, and glared at the crestfallen guard, but tossed a stiff hand and said, "Very well, go ahead!"

I could feel beside me Utak's attention on the massive black-eyed man as she, taking her time, met the eyes of each of us one-by-one. Her own expression was quite mobile and curious as she did this, with a sort of keen zest in it. And when her eyes met mine I felt a great cool clear rush, but there was something fierce there too, and very determined . . . and I felt the air between us charged with at least two levels of things: the apparent and not-so-apparent—the day and the night, the sun and the moon.

"My friends call me Tari," she said at last, smiling very warmly, then asked our names, which we gave, and even Azurara seemed impressed, for there was none of the usual haughteur in his self-announcement. Jud Daraul called her "ma'am," Lucie was flushed and slightly breathless, while even Coningham seemed a little awkward, and only Utak and Herbie Pond seemed quite unglamourised. For myself, I managed to say "Humphrey Gilbert," and leave it at that.

"Well, friends," she said to us, ignoring Piggot's scowl, and with some other DTIs drifted up from here and there, "How do you do?"

"Dunno." Herbie Pond grinned engagingly. "How *do* we do?"

"*Pond!*" snapped Piggot, "that's enough!"

I thought so too, and glowered at him, not then realising that he had asked a specific and necessary question, and at the time I felt quite jealous that she gave him such a slow, sweet, thoughtful smile.

"Well, if you relax," she said. "Not so well if you try too hard. Try to be like a bird, not like an ass with long ears."

"Now come along, please!" insisted Piggot, most uncomfortable at this. "We really don't have much time!"

Myself, I did not pick it up at all, and was amazed that she told Piggot so blunt and publicly what she thought of him. But later she said she phrased it as she did so he would take it solely as a personal insult, and not think to look under the surface, beyond himself.

"We'll meet again soon, I hope," Tari said to us, then turned to Piggot with a polite but distant nod. And Masanva remained massively silent, expressionless and not introduced, as Piggot chivvied them into the library to show them computers and Modern knowledge.

"That's one *regular* lady!" declared Herbie with awe in his voice as soon as they were gone. "And I mean *regular!*"

"*Regular?*" I snapped, scandalised, "You are a cheap man!"

"Humf, you're just jealous," he drawled, grinning.

"Gilbert, you must consider what she *meant!*" Coningham murmured softly, significantly. "About the you-know-what."

So I thought about it, and my stupid feeling faded.

As for Masanva, that massive man, only Utak had a firm impression.

"That man," he said in his rapidly improving American, "That man is in centre of . . . of . . . what is name for it?"

He made a whirling motion of both hands round each other.

"Storm?" hazarded Jud Daraul. "Cyclone? Tornado?"

Utak nodded sharply. "Yes. Cyclone. That man rides cyclone. Very strong man. He knows music of gods. Hears and knows."

With that for the day we had to be content. But then came the night, when many things began.

So we met Tari. Now is the time for her tale.

I'll tell it as I heard it from her, in her voice, the very best I can. Yet I must admit: it is true I never quite rid myself of the suspicion that her claim to a high Horus-mission in this age was but megalomaniac delusion, induced by the need to believe in some strong purpose after the frightful accident of Vulcan. Likewise I always doubted her claim that she (and Masanva, as she said, for he never said anything of himself) had sought the vortex deliberately. This seemed absurd and impossible. But so indeed she did claim, and who am I now to doubt it, with her ghost alive both within me and without me, as it seems? So here is her voice, as I know it and love it:

The Tale of Nefertari Mery-Isis:

Nature's creatures above are the stars of Nut. Below live men and beasts, plants and minerals, and every one with its signature, its divine nature and function, inscribed at birth by Thoth.

In every man and every age the scheme of things is writ down plain to see, as is known to every beast and bird, so why not to man? For every man has affinity with his special creature with whom he shares particular tendency—from whom at Dawn he learned his arts by imitation, whose nature at Noon he refines by human struggle, and whose destiny at Dusk he realises by ascent at last to the gods, or neters. When thus at last he joins himself with Divine Principle from which all comes forth, then the Nine Aspects of his Individuality are united; he is initiate, and may know his secret name, and knows why souls are bound in matter, and remembers what is to be.

My name on earth is Nefertari. My soul-name is Mery-Isis. My name in heaven I know not yet.

My service is with Great Isis, and with Osiris the Dead and Risen God, and with Horus their son—the Avenger, the Hawk, the Dawn, the New Age!—and my affinity is with the Hawk.

Who is Great Isis?

She is Mother of Earth and Mother of Heaven and Mother of Sorrows and her Star is Sothis, which disc she wears above her head. She contains all other goddesses and has power over the Father of the Gods, for she tricked him out of his secret name and forever holds it against him. She bore the Hope of the Future from the dead and dismembered body of Osiris, her Column goes from the depths to the heights, her ray is blue, her perfume is sweet;.she has her seat in every woman and in every man—and each may find it if they seek, and make alchemical marriage, and go through the tomb alive.

For also she is the Dark Queen. Why do men fear the Dark

Queen? The Black Isis leads through death to the Triumph of Beauty.

I have been instructed in the wisdom of Isis and Osiris, and it is through Vision of the Hawk that I am here.

The hawk-affinity was always clear. I knew it, and others saw it, for when I was young the hawks would hover over me, and once, when I played by the river, a hawk descended in a great rush of wings and landed on my shoulder. It took off again immediately, but my brothers and sisters were scared, and I was scared too, but for a different reason, for even then I knew it meant I was chosen. This may seem a wonderful thing, but it is fearful too. It meant I had much to learn and risk and endure, for when I was young I was not sensible, being rash and haughty by nature.

In time I went for training to the temple of Isis on the isle of Palak, which is shaped like a bird and lies in the River on the Nubian border. All to do with Isis and Osiris and their liberation in Horus was studied, taught, and practised there, and it was there I received the name Mery-Isis, meaning, The Beloved of Isis. It was my opinion that I should have a Hawk-name, but I was told that my opinion did not count, and that I must learn to obey, or else I would never develop the strength and purity to see beyond the shape of things.

Of my first training I will describe only this: After I passed the first examination I was taken through many inner courts and into a small temple which was the entrance to the underground crypts and hidden sanctuaries. The door was disguised by a statue of Isis, and flanked by two columns, one red and one black. The goddess was seated, and held a closed book in her lap, and her face was veiled, and beneath the statue was written, *"No mortal has lifted my veil."* Of the two columns, it was explained to me that the red one represented the ascension of the spirit into the light of Osiris, but that the black one referred to its imprisonment in matter, and to the threat of utter annihilation. It was made clear to me that whosoever would approach this science must risk everything; that were I weak or wicked I should find only madness or death through that door, and that many went in who never came out. I was told to consider it all most carefully, for there would be no turning back.

Well, in time I went through that door, and came out safe at another level, but it was only a beginning. There were other kinds of tests, and one of them I nearly failed. For it was outside the temple that I tamed two wild hawks, and was nearly tamed by a third.

No, "tamed" is not right, save in the third case. The two wild hawks came because of our affinity. They would stay quietly on my arms without a hood. This got me many odd looks, but nothing was said—until the third Hawk came.

There was a time when I was in rebellion against the rigour of the training, and tempted to believe it was all for nothing, a pack of lies and illusions. I suffered doubt and nightmare, but the only answer I ever got to my questions was *"Wait and work!"* And so I was in an angry condition when I met and was tested by the third Hawk.

He was a tall wanderer, admitting no other name but Hawk, who one summer was hired as a carpenter in the outer precincts. Soon enough he caught my eye, and I found him very handsome, and my regret at abandoning the outer world became more bitter than ever. We spoke together when we could, and came the night when he said he loved me and wished me to flee the temple with him.

For three nights I could not sleep. Which Hawk would I fly with, the neter or the man? Did I truly wish to work to be a Wâb priestess, seeking and finding and fulfilling my function and service in the god? Yet at length I made my decision, and went and told the man I would go not with him, but with the god. Then he looked at me gravely, and from his robe he took a knife, which he showed me.

"Had you answered otherwise," he said, "you would have married not a man, but Osiris. There is no turning back."

Only then I knew how close I had come to the abyss. After this I worked hard for a long time, and learned gradually, and was confirmed in certain things. At length I was sent to the other end of the Two Lands, to Per wadjet in the Delta, close by the isle of Chemmis where Horus is said to have been born.

Now, for a reason, I tell part of the popular tale:

Osiris was murdered by his evil brother Set, the Red One, who hoped to usurp his brother's high office, wishing also to prevent the birth of a son to Isis. Knowing of the magic skills of Isis, cunning Set cut up the body of Osiris and scattered the pieces in the Nile and all over the land. But Isis patiently sought and found the pieces of Osiris, and reassembled the body of the Listless One, and her power was such that she conceived! Yes, and some say that she found every part of the body but for the phallus, which had been swallowed by a crocodile, yet her Fertility was so great that *still* she conceived!

Then Osiris went down to the Underworld, to await revival by his son, who would bring him a new function. But Horus was not yet born, and in great danger. Isis fled and hid from Set in the Swamps, on this isle of Chemmis, which many call a floating isle, for the way it sits in a wide deep lake. So, Horus was born, and watched over by Sekhat-Hor, Nepthys, Nut, and Selkis, while Isis went about disguised as a beggar-woman. But the four of them had other things to do and had to go, so that often Isis had to leave the child alone. One day she returned to find Horus bitten and poisoned by a snake, which she said must be Set. But the doctor-woman who came to treat the child said it was but an ordinary serpent, for evil Set could not set foot on this holy isle. Yet the child was very sick, so Isis cried to the sky to stop the Boat of the Sun, and her cry was heard, and Thoth came down in a hurry, because the Boat of the Sun couldn't wait very long for him. He cured the child as quick as he could, so Horus lived, and grew up, and there were terrible quarrels between him and Set that seemed to go on forever. They fought, and Horus wrenched off Set's balls, and Set tore out the Hawk's left eye and threw it into the outer darkness, where Thoth found the pieces and made them into the full moon.

This is the popular tale, and in time Horus got the inheritance, the son prevailed over the uncle, so that what you call the "patrilineal principle" prevailed. And there was a reason for this that transcended any local motivation, just as there was reason for what was done in my time, during the reign of Hatshepsut, and for what was done during the reign of Akhenaton a century later, when the secret teaching of One God was briefly expressed in public. Yes, we knew of what was to come, and the popular tales were ways of preparing the people. The progression of things was already written, the new principle of monotheism which led in time to the Christ was ready to be expressed openly, and we worked so that it should take up its inheritance through Moses and the Jews, in due time and course.

* * *

The city of Per wadjet was known to the Greeks as Buto, and in time, as I have learned, there was also a temple of Apollo there.

Per wadjet was the metropolis of the nineteenth nome of Lower Khem, *Ammt,* and was divided into two districts, *Pe* and *Dep*. Every year, the people of each district fought each other ceremonially at the annual reerection of the *djed* column, this to signify and celebrate the rising of Osiris from the dead and the reflowering of the world. As the statue is in the block, so the Christian dispensation lay in our ways, and so now a new dispensation is ready to be born.

Per wadjet had many great temples but I went to serve the Oracle of Horus in the groves on Chemmis. And soon enough I had dreams making it clear I must embark on a very grave business.

The realisation was slow in coming, for I resisted it and tried to pretend it was not there. But one night Our Lady herself came and chided me for my cowardice, asking if I who aspired to the Hawk could not follow the beat and direction of his wings?

Still I doubted, and asked the Oracle, and was told:

"The lame sparrow is devoured by the cruel Hawk. The eager sparrow flies with the Dawn, and sees with the Eye."

In one of the nine dreams I had, the Hawk showed me the great temple that you call the Pyramid of Khufu, or Cheops. I had been in some of the lower passages and chambers for certain of the rites whereby we were taught to wake up or die. Part of the power in such places is that each obstacle overcome opens a door in the mind—so long as there were those who knew how to operate the intricacies of such strenuous initiations. As to the power in the temple itself, that waxed and waned, but was always strong, particularly in the secret higher passages and chambers, where the concentration was much greater. And I had climbed only so far, to such a point.

Yet in this dream the Hawk directed me to enter that temple again and seek a higher disclosure by closeting myself in one of the hidden higher chambers. This was a serious matter. Even when the currents of the land were at a low ebb, those who merged with the higher powers and lived were those who knew death already. Even so, the upper rooms were rarely empty. There were many purposes afoot behind the face of daily life and popular tales, what with the planning of ways and the planting of seed for the future. There was always a long waiting-list, and permission had to be sought from various levels of authority, and the purpose explained for approval or disapproval. Often you were told to return and ask again in five or ten years.

That is what I was told. I followed the Hawk, I sought permission, I was told my purpose must grow stronger. I came back ten years later and they said I was still not ready. Another five years went by, then I returned, and was told that the chamber was prepared.

I entered at the time of Sothis rising when the weather is hot and the floods ripe to come; I went in without lamp or food, wearing a light garment and carrying only a skin of water. I was led in blindfolded, and down for a long time, and then up, and up, and then through many crawling twists and turns, to the chamber, where I was shut up and left.

There it was done. The Servant of the Hawk arose on his wings and on the power of the place, and went on a long high lonely journey to a place she could not have attained without the power, for which of course a price was demanded.

I found what I sought, and safely returned, and stood up in my body and went out of that place after due closings and thanks were made. Then from Gizeh I went straight to Thebes, where I petitioned audience with the priestess-queen you call Hatshepsut.

Her influence was a great change in the rhythm of the Two Lands, and many argued what it meant, and where it would lead, and was it good or bad that a woman ruled, and would Thothmes depose her?

Many argued, few knew.

She called me to an inner chamber in the temple she built in the western cliff of the Theban mountain, the temple called Djeser-Djeseru, the Sublime of the Sublime. She asked my business. I told her the Hawk commanded me to go by sea to the Land of the Kas, in the quarter where Osiris dwells—in the direction that you call west.

She asked me, "Do you know the purpose?"

"The Hawk showed me a world where wings are thick in the air."

"What sort of wings are these?"

"Oddly stiff and rigid, with a strange grace, but not the

grace of birds, nor the grace of understanding of the sort we know."

"Then where was the Hawk?"

"Not in the sky, save in a few parts left to him. For the most part locked up, striving for new life like his father before him."

"What will he do if he comes to life, or is brought to life?"

"Catch fire again in the hearts of many who are oppressed by Set, who has perverted even the coming principle, so that there is much knowledge of one sort, but not enough of another."

"How far is this world? How many times will Osiris die?"

"Many times. It is at the end of our records, on the edge of a new sign. It seems that some of our ways soon to be forgotten will see light again, and marry with what's been learned through the new principle, so that another step will be made."

"You are sure of this?"

"I am sure of nothing save what the Hawk showed me."

"Has he shown how you will go to this new world?"

"It is not clear. I will take ship. Then there's confusion I could not understand, but after it I saw myself bald in a prison, trapped in very strange dress one can see through yet that covers head and body completely. I'll not be alone there, and an escape will be necessary for the work to begin. I do not know how all this will come about. I know only that I must take ship towards Osiris, and that the Hawk and his Mother wish me to submit this matter to your judgment."

"What is your own mind?"

"To serve the Hawk, and the Dawn."

"What is your own mind?"

"To take ship and go, if you'll have it."

"What is your own mind?"

"I have pictured the alternative," I said. "I could run away from this and from my vows and marry a man who stinks of garlic and onions, and get fat and old and watch my hair and teeth fall out. I think not. I ask you for ship and crew. But those who come as crew must know that very likely they'll go straight to Osiris at journey's end. It must be their own choice."

"You have the ship. If the purpose is good, you'll get your crew, and reach this place where they make you bald, and then—were you vouchsafed no vision at all beyond that?"

"Only that a lame sparrow will not survive," I said, "but that the eager little bird may fly high enough to witness new Dawn."

That is how I, Nefertari Mery-Isis, came to this world.

18

Circle Learns to See
What's Behind Its Nose

Yes, Tari and Masanva brought us purpose and strength, and
if I have little to say of the Dancer, this is not because he did
little, but because his activity among us was not of the sort
that is easily apparent. Utak assessed him accurately that first
day we met them, but thereafter, as Circle became conscious
and active, we became much split in our opinions of him, and
among our Moderns particularly we soon had insistence that
the Dancer should come off his shrouded Olympian heights to
sport with us ordinary mortals sometimes. But Tari always said
that his function demanded remoteness: that he was in pure
tune with energies he had channeled to her, without which she
would not have reached us with her visions at all. "So what
the hell are these energies?" Herbie demanded of her one day,
quite unguardedly. But she simply smiled at him, whereupon
later he asked me in a kind of rueful despair, "How can you
argue with her when she looks at you like that?"

Yet in time, amid our crisis, the Dancer unbent, showing
more than many of us cared to see, shocking us back towards
the unity we almost lost, demonstrating that he was as much
in harmony with his own function as Tari was with hers, come
to Dance the End of the Fourth World, as he called this age.

So, let me testify truthfully to these mysteries!

In regard to that first meeting with Tari and Masanva, each
of us was pointedly interrogated by our chaperones.

"What were Herbie and the Egyptian woman talking about?"

Ernstein demanded that evening. *"Birds, long-eared asses—are we the asses?"*

"I believe she was telling the Director that she dislikes him," I replied steadily, "I don't know. Ask *her,* not me."

Ernstein stared at me most unsympathetically.

"Let's get something straight, Sir Humphrey. Some resentment on your part is very understandable in this situation, but by now you should know—we're on your side. It would make things needlessly hard if any of you felt you had something to hide from us."

"Sir," I said, "what could we hide from you but little things?"

"I don't know," he replied. "That's what worries me."

It worried us too. It was that night we began to realise Circle by the making and receiving of pictures in the mind. Few of us knew what we were doing, or realised that the image-making was not an end in itself. Tari, Masanva, Utak, and Othoon had been trained to this skill in their societies (though their symbol-systems were not quite the same). The rest of us had to learn not only that such communication is possible, but that its development involves overcoming much disbelief, self-regard, and fear . . . and we all had problems, of which, in one form or another, self-regard was the chief. If you chatter to yourself all the time, of course you can't see or hear anyone else, and they won't want to see or hear you. *The Power not of Christ?* It was in me all along. MINE! ME! MYSELF!

"People communicate this way all the time," said Tari later, "but you have to be very quiet inside to realise it, and very calm to tell which are your own pictures and which come from someone or somewhere else. Moderns call it telepathy, and think it something unusual, but that's only because they talk and write and think and rush about so much they can't see what's behind their own noses."

Perhaps. Yet I think the bizarre severity of our situation had much to do with it. Apart from our deep need to find a private mode of communication, the fact is that we were utterly disoriented, cast out of our accustomed modes of thought, feeling, and experience; our self-structures cracked by Vulcan and the rest of it. We had no chance to retain habitual beliefs and complacent outlook. All that was destroyed. Without this destruction I believe that most of us (certainly myself) would have continued to "screen out" these subtle images, calling them illusions, and never realising what was going on in our very own minds.

It did not come easily. The first few nights I tried to do it consciously, knowing that others were doing likewise, I found images quickly forming, but had no way to tell if they were mine or if they came from someone else—except if they were from Tari. Likewise I found it hard to form and hold in mind any clear and *deliberate* image. I would make a picture—of myself, or some episode in my life—then forget it without realising, or lose the will to hold it, or find it squirming uncontrollably into something else. To relax and be like a bird, not like a long-eared ass? I soon grew frustrated, learning nothing from the relaxed mood of Tari's images—and those early nights she sent many: she was like a beacon, a point of reference, a steady strong light through our fogs. Yes, I got angry, and thought the answer lay in trying harder, and for several nights struggled and strained my brain until my mind rebelled and said it was all nonsense. Then I stopped trying, and next day I snapped at Ernstein, who decided I needed to be tranquillised to sleep, so that I was put out of action for nearly a week. But one night after that, near sleep, I lay idly picturing my boyhood days, and Devon land, and the tossing sea . . . then suddenly through me rushed a flood of images so real they had me in tears, to have lost so much. Silently I shouted with them, then fell quiet, feeling drained. And as soon as I was quiet, I saw Tari's signature-face—*with* the raven hair, which image she would not abandon; no doubt partly out of vanity (for she had her vanity); but also, as she explained, because this was her usual signature or seal in such communication, and she saw no reason to change it because of baldness imposed—anyway, I saw her image, and she winked and gave me a thumbs-up. Without realising what had happened I fell asleep, but next day during Walkabout she did the same, discreetly, and also Herbie came up and nudged me. "Okay, Humf, you've proved what I said, it was a helluva lot better in your time." So then I knew I'd put out pictures which she and he had received; and also Coningham, Azurara, Utak, Masanva, and others had picked up some of my sending, as I duly learned.

So I began to see that *emotion* is the root and fuel of such sending—not anger, but passionate feeling that drives forth, directed by the will from a mind relaxed and free of noisy argument.

"Enflame thyself with prayer!"—that's the principle.

Others among us were discovering the same thing, so that on the succeeding nights, relaxing, I began to pick up glimpses and flashes from DTIs other than Tari. At first these flashes were inconsistent and confusing, the sending being vague, and my mind still not clear or quiet enough to make much sense of them.

Yet finally one night came a strong reception, of images that were terrible and wonderful to me.

War. War of a sort I never knew, fought in a desert between huge metal behemoths that clank and wheel and fire big guns at each other and at running foot-soldiers. There are great explosions, gouts of flame, smoke and dust everywhere. Then abruptly I'm high in the air, swooping down out of the sky at terrifying speed in a flying machine, a propellor plane. My finger's pressed hard on a black button; hot streams of flaming bullets arc down from the wings of the plane into the battle below. I see them tracking over the sands, exploding amid a convoy of trucks as I go hurtling at dizzy low speed through the smoke and flame, the plane screaming as it pulls out of the dive. . . .

It was too much for me.

I shut out these pictures and sat up in bed, sweating and dizzy—yet not before glimpsing Coningham's face, and a blue cap on his head with wings on it, and a latin motto that loomed up close in Italic:

Per Ardua Ad Astra.

This experience greatly increased my respect for the man, and also increased my horror at the modern world, so that it was a night or two before I was willing to risk the Circle again. But once I returned, I found that some obstructive barrier in myself was gone, for from then on the images began coming from all quarters, mostly with identifiable signature-images. Thus gradually it became possible to make primitive image-conversation by this method . . . and almost every night during June and July the picture-tales of our lost familiar worlds came floating silently from each to others. So Circle grew . . . and at the same time, on most days, at library sessions and in suited groups in other Institute rooms, we were encouraged to tell our tales, and write them down, and get to know each other. It was difficult for those of us in Circle to disguise the true and increasing extent of our familiarity with each other, but we managed, and other DTIs who sensed something of what was going on said nothing, they being in Circle too, though in a vague, less specific way. It was a perpetual worry, that one of us in our sleep or in a drugged state might blurt out something suspicious. In Circle we learned to preface our sendings with the crossed-out image of a white-suit so that, should any of our captors be open-minded enough to pick up and recognise our hidden activity, our collective will blocked their reception. Yet Ernstein and some others *were* suspicious as to what we did in the late evenings, sitting in chair or lying in bed but not asleep, as apparently their instruments told them. *Meditating,* or *praying,* or *dreaming,* we told them, with which they had to be content. Because of the interest they had vested in their own beliefs and theories, they explored this occult "non-scientific" side of things only in a half-hearted way, as in October, when a team of "parapsychologists" came to test some of us. This was done by means of machines to find in us something called "biokinetic energy," and with objects hidden in boxes that we were supposed to guess, and so on. It was easy enough to fool them, for mostly they were of a mind to believe that if something cannot be weighed and measured, then it does not exist. They refused to look "behind their own noses" for what they *knew* was not possible . . . and of course this suited us very well.

Thus, night after night as summer became hot and sweltering outside the Institute and our immunity-suits, with trouble in the land and in the world that meant little to any of us yet, the picture-tales flowed ever more freely through and between us. At first it was all very innocent, devoid of dissension, and we got much delight through fooling our captors and learning about each other in this way. As our skill increased we became playful, even with Vulcan, as when Herbie pictured his final rum-smuggling flight with the comic image of what initially he thought had happened—he showed us a dirty duck in a big pond being blown skyhigh by a mobster tiptoeing up behind him and tossing a bomb attached to a big clock—and after this he used the Duck-in-a-Pond as his personal signature. Then

Lucie showed us Hollywood: a snow-capped mountain turning into a pyramid of white powder on a mirror, and the powder being sniffed through a rolled-up hundred-dollar bill into her nose, followed by a riot of images that I could not comprehend at all, but which apparently our Moderns found very funny. And Van Roornevink showed himself sitting, yawning with boredom, having his portrait painted by a warty-faced man he claimed was Rembrandt . . . and so on . . . yet of course many sendings were not so comic. Jud Daraul showed us childhood in ghetto streets; while John Kent the banker portrayed the good life of a wealthy American in the nineteen-sixties. Kent was another demoralised man: the system which had paid him so well had suddenly jumped on his back and shaved off his hair: he didn't know now whether to become religious or join the Peoples' Revolution. I could sympathise. Kazan Watanabe from 1921 and the *Raifuku Maru* sent delicately beautiful images of Japan; Ketil Blund showed us the last of the green on Greenland; through the eyes of Jean-Marie Leclerc we saw the storming of the Bastille in 1789; after which we met Ekapalon of the Yoruba in West Africa—another who was kept in his room for "medical reasons" and not allowed Outside. Through him we were seized by slavers and carried west in a stinking ship until Vulcan completed the horror: he was a fine man, and had no hate in him, which then I could not understand. We met Diarmaid, an Irish anchorite from fifteen hundred years ago, who had sailed west from his rocky Atlantic islet in search of greater solitude, only now to find himself packed in with us. He sent only once, telling us that our mind-pictures were disturbing his communion with God, and thereafter he wrapped a shield of silence about himself. And Howell Rees (named "Howell the Glower" by Herbie), at the edge of Circle and now somewhat unbent, sent enthusiastic images of his prayer-meetings in poor and rainy Mid-Wales. He also sent images caricaturing Frank Lubick, indicating that from now on he would talk to any non-Methodists as long as they weren't Mormons. And Hyperia: running away from home in the corn-fields of the Sahara when her father tried to marry her to a Roman senator's "greasy son"—she'd wanted to go to the Platonist school of Ammonius Saccas in Alexandria, but, as she said in the library one day: "I knew they'd look for me there, so I took the opposite road and in time reached Pretania. I had many strange adventures, and at last, seeking I know not what, I went with a man I loved on a ship of fools captained by a mad Gaul who swore he'd lead us to a land where *"there is no imperial taxman, slavemaster, or soldier to bind us."* Well, *hah!* to that!"

And so said all of us. But then, in August, crisis struck and nearly broke us all apart into warring, hateful factions.

19

The Conquistador
Who Acted like a Jerk

The trouble was triggered by a racial dispute between Utak and
Azurara. Had it not been this it would have been something
else, for by now, with the initial numbness of our strange
imprisonment somewhat worn off, many of us were so frustrated we were itching for a fight. Deplorable no doubt, but
there it is: of us all I think only Tari and Masanva were above
such stuff; and perhaps Hyperia, while Othoon (who had still
not yet decided to reveal himself in Circle) had the detachment
that came from laughing at everything and everyone equally,
himself included. In fact it was the fall-out of this crisis that
finally persuaded him to join us, briefly, as the Joker of our
lunacies . . . and his fate that turned us to escape.

One August afternoon in a pale blue room in the south block,
some nine or ten of us, including Utak and Azurara, were being
coaxed by our chaperones to tell our tales to tape-recorders and
each other.

As I said, this had been going on for weeks. I and many
others had already done our best, but some were recalcitrant
and surly, unable or unwilling to speak in daily words or nightly
Circle-images. These two had both been among the recalci-
trants . . . but on this afternoon Utak was at last persuaded by
his chaperone to tell how, over a thousand years ago, he'd
been a ruler-priest at the Mayan city of Tikal, and how a popular
revolt had forced him to flee . . . into Vulcan.

He was hard to understand, not only because of his guttural
tongue and alien notions, but also because the more he said

the more angry he got, standing and shouting at those of us with white skins.

Azurara understood none of it, for he held that Spanish was the only civilised language, and so refused to learn American. But he did not like Utak to begin with, associating the man with the Aztecs against whom he'd fought, considering him a bloodthirsty pagan cannibal. And after the group was over, with Utak hauled away still bellowing, the Spaniard approached me.

"Gilbert. Why is that fool so furious?"

"It seems," I said, "that when he fled the ruin of his society he set to sea looking for some White God who had once brought civilisation to the Maya, called Kukulcan, or Quetzal. . . ."

"Oh yes!" Azurara laughed harshly. "Quetzalcoatl! It is a very strange thing, but when Cortés first came among those savages in 1519 they all thought he must be this White God, because the year he landed was exactly the year prophesied for Quetzalcoatl's Return!" He shook his head. "Most peculiar, but it aided us greatly in our conquest, for because of this they were reluctant to resist us when we set out to destroy their demon ways in the Name of Christ! But—what exactly is this savage so angry about?"

"Well," I said, "he appears to be most disappointed that the White God he finds here and now falls so far short of what he had expected . . . and also . . ."—I coughed delicately—". . . having learned about the history of his people after his time he is angry at the way you Spaniards came and burned his holy books and, er, raped the land for the sake of gold."

Yes, there was still some feeling in me about these things. But Azurara ignored it. Again he laughed, his lip curling.

"The fool!" he exclaimed. "He lived five hundred years before we came to "his" shores at all! So what if we burned a few stupid books of primitive superstition? *They* did not keep to their tenets either! I *know* about this Quetzalcoatl of theirs! He told them to stop sacrificing human beings—but when we got there the Aztec were tearing out hearts by the thousand, saying it was all for religion when the truth is they wanted a good meal! Disgusting, Gilbert! What has *he* got to complain about? We *brought* them their White God! Christ!"

"Evidently he hoped for something better," I said.

"But we brought them Jesus Christ!"

"Yes . . . but perhaps it was . . . *our* Christ . . ."

"Gilbert, I don't understand you at all. You carry your English Dissent too far! Christ is Christ, and Mary his Mother . . . and if that Egyptian woman tells me once more that her Isis and Horus are the model for Mary and Jesus, I swear I'll take a crucifix and throttle her with the chain! As for these Moderns with their completely cynical atheism, the stake is not good enough for them. They are all very lost, Gilbert. It shows in their eyes—don't you think?"

"Bernardino," I said, "I think we are *all* very lost."

But he was not convinced, and that was only the start of it. For Utak's ire was well and truly aroused, and that night, for the first time, he burst into Circle with a storm of such vivid wild imagery that I was made utterly dizzy. It was by far the strongest sending any of us had yet put out or received, and its essence was the tale he'd told in group that afternoon:

Pyramid-temples, rain-soaked jungle, the fields in the clearings ablaze! There's blood on the stones and a great hue-and-cry, with men in bright bird-feather robes fleeing or desperately fighting a naked mob! Then abruptly, with sharp sword-like mind and sense of earlier time, I Utak stand by night atop a pyramid, on a small platform above the uppermost chamber, high above the great city of Tikal! I am agitated! For many *haab*-cycles now we have kept back the clamouring jungle, but for *how much longer?* We must know! I must calm myself! With feather-robe about me I study the stars and mark how the wanderers have moved since the moon last died, I move numbers in my mind and calculate, for every number has its own god-face; some benevolent, others not so, each demanding a different sacrifice so that balance is maintained. Some want fruit, others, reeking hearts, or virgins in the well. Of late, nothing but Bad Numbers; we have responded correctly and taken many prisoners, but the people tire of war and accuse us of taking the brains and best cuts for ourselves. Can't the fools understand? We must hold chaos at bay! We must build higher or fall into the terrible empty Zero! We must count, and calculate, or the Jungle will take us all again; Time will desert us and leave us frozen! Count! Measure Time by the wandering gods, find the Number for tonight! Count by *tzolkin* with 260 days, and by *haab* with 365, and by 52 *haabs* that combine the two and net us Time more tightly! And remember by the

Long Count! 4113 *haabs* since 4 Ahau 8 Cumhu when HE left our Big Head ancestors and returned east in the Time of the Wind-Sun! He brought Number and Proportion but only a few would listen, so he left, promising to return, promising destruction by wind for the fools that would not hear! And where are those Big-Heads now? Lost in the Jungle, little men who can't count, who can't remember anything—turned into monkeys as he promised! The wind blew them down into monkeys! Must this happen to us too? Will he return in time? The stars say nothing! Three-quarters through Sun of Fire, still a thousand *haabs* more—enough to finish us! The fools! Don't they see the danger? The reservoirs are dry, there are too many of us, the breadnuts bear no fruit, the ground's too tired for the second crop! Where are you? You with your beard and white skin, and the discs on your head, and your Numbers of Power— *where are you? Kukulcán! Huemac! Quetzalcoatl!* You Bringer of Flying Thought who unveiled the mind's subtle Serpent-Power to us—*where are you?* Must we lose everything? What did we do wrong? *Kukulcan!* Do you exist? Is our history a lie? Oh, not so, not so! Utak, a dark serpent in you thinks that! Cast it out! Out! But . . .

. . . riot, outcry, the city in flame, the people revolt! The mob rages through the streets, the temples, and the cries rise up! Kill the priests! Kill those who kill us with their wars and taxes, who keep the best for themselves! Yes! Yes! You fools, yes, do it! Break the Numbers! Let Time out! Destroy it all in one mad night! Now up the steps you surge to kill me, but the steps are steep, you slow down—and I plunge to meet you, and drive through you, and I break past you into the Jungle, with nowhere else to go! O Great Feathered Serpent, protect me from your little creeping brothers! The city flames bright behind me. Tikal the Glorious is dead—but Utak is not yet dead! I will not drop! There is a Perfect Number, yes, and I'll seek it in the east! Kukulcan, I will find you . . .

. . . so fugitive I came to the sea, and took a boat east past many isles until no isles were left, starving and thirsting and madly chasing the scent of the Perfect Number; the Number I had to find and speak aloud to call the White Saviour out of the Rising Sun before it was too late and the Maya forgot everything!—mad, mad, mad I was! The Number to answer all questions! On and on I went, numbers spinning incessant in me, faster and faster and round and round and on and on . . . into the explosion, the fire, the sea, the imprisoning by white devils in the deep... and now this hole in hell *(blackness, electric light, gibbering white-suit faces)*, these tortures and mad practises *(operating table, scalpels, masked faces, paper sheets of the letters of the American-English alphabet)*— they want explanation in this American language of what cannot be explained in it—they want me to bow to their gods, to study quantities without qualities, to master their fast-counting machines—they tell me my people are dead, my temples crumbled, my books long-destroyed by a "holy" white man called Landa! Hah! The "white god" who came and obliterated us now wants me to tell him what he destroyed! His history tells how he came and conquered with disease and the sword. White God! And I invoked you! Mad at sea I invoked you, and the Castillas came and killed us and married us, and the English came and killed us and killed us, and Time escaped, and I am seized and shaken through a thousand *haabs* to the end of Sun of Fire! But they do not acknowledge the ages! They despise what went before, and do not see that Number is of Spirit, not Quantity alone! Now I lie here and play with little numbers in their machines, and they think me demoralised into their ways— but *Number* I hold in my mind, and every night I calculate! I calculate! I know what Time this is! I know that the Nine Fifty-Two's are almost over! and the evil time is at an end! and the false white god in turn must bow! and I am a willing sacrifice on America's altar! for I sought this, though I knew not what I sought! and now I know I was in error, for Time cannot be chained! for nothing stops! and change is unceasing! and I am Utak! a fool who loves Number! a fool who sought to freeze Time for fear of being frozen! and here I am among you all! and is there not a great joke in it?

And when the flood of all this ceased there was a great stunned silence in Circle, for the power of the images that suggested all this had us quite overwhelmed. Almost all of us were ready to leave it there for the night—but Azurara was not. When Utak's flood poured over him he knew he must reply immediately for the sake of the dignity of Spain, the Holy Roman Empire, European Civilisation, and, not least, Himself, for he felt personally demeaned and insulted by what this Indio had to say against the White Race.

So, almost as soon as Utak was done, just as most of us

were preparing to slip out of Circle and into sleep, Azurara struck angrily back, surprising all of us, for he had never sent before.

His initial surge was violent, passionate, like a brutal bull butting at the half-closed gate of my mind. This uncouth approach irritated me, but I realised it was somebody new, and let in whoever-it-was. And in the next instant I was amazed by the grandiloquent appearance in my mind's-eye of his name, all of it—SEÑOR BERNARDINO DE OVEIDO DE AZUR-ARA—spelled out in large golden letters, the gold rimmed with ruby-red against an azure background, the whole being framed by elaborate green-and-brown foliated scrollwork. It was not so much the haughty self-insistence that amazed me as the artistry involved in this imagining! Clearly our conquistador had hidden talents! I was amused, but wary, sensing the approach of trouble—and trouble was what we got.

After this introduction his first image was neutral enough. Our proud Castilla showed himself in shining light armour, astride a fine black stallion on a hilltop, hand shading eyes against the setting sun as he surveyed the deserts and mountains and forests he'd come to claim for Spain. But then his anger took over. His subsequent images were confused, blurred— but clear enough for his purpose. In rapid succession he sent pictures of ugly stunted naked redmen hacking dead bodies to pieces which they roasted and ate; of pyramids with miles of captives lined up awaiting the tearing-out of their still-beating hearts by priests who all had Utak's face; of huge piles of skulls in city squares; of Spaniards crossing themselves in disgust; of defeated savages bowing to the Cross and . . .

Of a sudden his sending was interrupted and overwhelmed. With a fierce and furious blast Utak blotted Azurara out of us and imposed his reply; he sent an image of Azurara crucified upside-down on a bloody cross; he sent pictures of cruel Spaniards raping Indian women, disembowelling children, burning men alive . . . and within a few seconds Circle was in chaos, with angry protest flying in all directions . . . until without warning Tari used her greater power, showing us all a knife that sliced through all this, telling us to shut up.

We did. We slept, uneasily.

Next day the crisis got worse.

In the afternoon the same group of nine or ten of us was brought together in the same South Block room as the day before. The tension was apparent to our baffled chaperones from the moment they ushered us in, Utak and Azurara glaring at each other, and Coningham, Herbie, Hyperia, Fernandez the Cuban, myself, and Jim Guerrero all obviously unhappy. Only Tari seemed her usual calm self. And before we could even sit down round the table, before anyone could turn on the tape-recorder or get a word in, Azurara was loudly demanding his chance to tell the tale which thus far he had refused to give— and, turning to me, he insisted that I and not Fernandez should be his interpreter. I saw disaster ahead and began trying to argue him out of it. Ernstein, learning what was demanded from Azurara's Spanish-speaking chaperone, told me bluntly to "do it and stop wasting our valuable time." I would have argued with him too, but Tari caught my eye and nodded very slightly. Later she said it was a risk we had to take: the more openly our spleen came out, the less reason our captors would have to suspect that much of this ugly passion had arisen in a manner unknown to them.

So, glumly, avoiding Utak's glare, I set about the unpleasant business of translation as Azurara angrily told his tale:

"I am Bernardino de Oveido de Azurara!" he began, standing, staring about as though we were *all* his enemies, so impatient that he gave me hardly any time at all to tell what he said. "My blood is of Castile, my emperor Charles, my salvation Holy Church, my profession soldier! My first action was in the Year of our Lord 1527, when I went with the Imperial Army to ensure Rome's continued allegiance! After this I went out to join the armies of Cortés in Mexico, the pacification of those Aztec heathen being not yet complete! And I can tell you our work was cut out, to destroy their bloody demonism and teach them the Mercy of the Lamb. During those years I saw the most frightful sights! I saw towers made of uncountable numbers of skulls cemented in lime, and piles of skulls in the plaza of Xocotlan numbering over one hundred thousand, and racks of skulls in Tenochtitlán numbering one hundred and thirty-six thousand! *One hundred and thirty-six thousand!* Yes! Yes! As counted, skull by skull, by Tápia and Gonzalo de Umbria! What were we to do but rid the land of such abomination? Yes! And we..."

It was then that Utak, understanding the drift if not all the words, abruptly stood and interrupted my stumbling translation:

"Bearded 'white god' was *not* Kukulcan!" he snapped across the table in Azurara's reddening face. "Just greedy white man with gun! Now he says he is good, we are bad; he wants Utak to want Ph.D. in Pure Mathematic! Wants Utak in immunity-suit! We all prisoner here! *Your* doing, Spaniard Castilla—and yours, English!"

I tried my best. Stiffly I inclined my head. "It is *possible,*" I began, "that we may have been ignorant and selfish . . ." But I got no further: Azurara knew he was attacked though not understanding what Utak said; he interrupted and shouted me down. "You savages," he bellowed at Utak, "that we called *In-dios,* Children of God, are children still, but not of God, for I have seen on television how your descendents have joined this satanic 'Revolution of the People'! You are all scum, sons and daughters of whores!"

Utak frowned at me amid the horrible silence.

"English, what that man say?"

"Oh," I muttered, "he is somewhat disturbed."

"English, *what he say?*"

I looked to Tari, Herbie, Ernstein, but got no help. Slowly I told the Mayan what Azurara had said . . . and Utak, with a surprising calm, eyed Azurara with contempt before turning away and sitting down.

"Poor white god not remember truth," said he, softly.

Azurara turned to me, shaking with fury.

"Gilbert, WHAT DID THAT SAVAGE SAY ABOUT ME?"

I didn't know what to do. I was never skilled at the politic lie, the soothing gesture. I sat dumbly, then Coningham said, "Look, er, Bernardino, old chap, don't you think you'd better sit down?"—this accompanied by a distinctly officious downward motion of his hand which only enraged Azurara the more. "TELL THAT STINKING SAVAGE I WANT TO FIGHT HIM!" he roared, so that Utak glared and half-rose to his feet again; all of us stiffened; the white-suit guards at the door started forward with hypodermics at the ready; our chaperones eyed each other, nodding sagely as they made notes; and I gazed despairingly at Tari, seeing Circle finished before even truly begun.

But Tari was expressionless. She did not move at all.

That was when Hyperia stood up and said something in Latin, her voice gentle, but rising and insistent in a way that somehow caught and undid the ugly knot of the moment. Everyone looked at her, taken aback—then looked to me for the translation. But I did not have to give it. In her stumbling American she spoke:

"All forget when birth," she said. "Some more, others . . . not so more. But how remember anything if all behave like childs?"

Utak smiled grimly when he understood this, and even Azurara was briefly shamed by the gentle rebuke. Hyperia . . . this was one of the last times we saw her . . . she was a fine woman, quiet and true, and if her remark was soon forgotten, well, it was not her fault.

Yet at least we got through the rest of Azurara's tale without more dispute, though of course that incorrigible man had learned nothing at all from the scene he was glad to have created.

"Well, so," he continued when we had quieted down, myself still wearily translating. "Where was I before this . . . interruption? Yes! By 1533 all was calm in Mexico: I elected to stay in the land and seek further afield. Pizarro had already gone to Peru to find his greatness there; so in the year 1540—in February, it was—I joined with Francisco Vásquez de Coronado, and a great company of us went north over the Rio Grande in search of the seven golden cities of Cíbola. Well, we were much disappointed, for all we found were the rude adobe villages of a people called Zuni. We showed them the power of Spain so they should not misunderstand us; and while there we heard of more villages a hundred miles further north. So Francisco despatched Pedro de Tovar with myself and a friar called Juan de Padilla, and some others on horse and foot, to learn if these northern villages might be the golden ones. We heard they belonged to a tribe called Hopi, that called themselves 'People of Peace.'

"So we went, until late one day, near sunset, across the barren land we saw a village atop a mesa. We got there after dark and made camp at the foot. In the morning these Hopi came down from their village and tried to impress us with heathenish ritual, throwing cornmeal across the trail that went up to their stronghold. We were not impressed, and decided to teach them better, so, refusing to talk, we rode at them— and one of them had the effrontery to strike a horse on the bridle! *'Why are we here?'* cried Padilla the friar, exhorting us, so that we sounded our battle-cry—*'Santiago!'*—and charged with lance and sword, driving these savages up to their village, where most sensibly they surrendered and gave us presents. But then all their chiefs came and made a ceremony out of begging! They drew four lines of cornmeal on the ground, and one of them stepped up to the lines with his hand held out, palm up. *'Give him something!'* said de Tovar. So one of our men dropped a trinket into that begging hand. The savages looked most disappointed, and all began muttering and mumbling! What did they expect? That we'd give them gold?

"After that they fed and quartered us, but only so they could tell us absurdities; that we were brothers, and they had awaited our coming for many years, and we must join Christ with their wretched superstitions, and accept *their* correction of *our* laws! They were completely mad, and had no gold, so we went away and told Francisco there was nothing there. It was a great disappointment. Soon after that I started back over the ocean to Castile . . . and now here I am . . . forced to live like a pig with pigs!"

"Jeeze!" Herbie muttered as we filed out at the end of the group. "What a jerk! Humf, how in hell can you talk to a guy like that?"

"You do not understand!" I said stiffly, obscurely feeling my time was attacked. "One age's meat is another . . ."

"Oh, I understand! A jerk is a jerk, right? Doesn't matter when he comes from—that guy is a jerk!"

That night Circle was a boiling pot of personality clashes all caused by this Utak-Azurara dispute. I'll not go into the names we called each other by image that night or in words next day, but it was clear we'd all been ready for it. At first it seemed all between the men: the women agreed they disapproved and told us so; within a day we men agreed we disliked the women as well as each other. Yes, absurd—but *because of the suits we could not even touch each other!* Like plague the bad mood quickly infected everyone, including our Institute guardians. No fucking in that place—abstention puts folk brittle and on edge: the velvet glove came off, and next, I don't know, Lucie shrilly denounced Tari as a "pagan bitch" on the volleyball court and we were all in a battle of pagan-catholic-protestant-banker-commie-jew-red-black-and-white dimension. Back on Square One, with fights breaking out on Walkabout so that our captors struck us with *treatment* and the solitary lock-up, and in Circle our rage denied reason. We ignored Tari, who waited. God! A loveless time!

But after Blund's tragedy the Dancer stepped in.

⸺❄❪ 20 ❫❄⸺

Why Othoon Laughed Himself
to Death

We were almost all of us in such a state at that time that it is
hard now to recall the precise sequence of events. Yet I think
it was probably the day after Azurara told his tale that Utak
took on Ketil Blund at *Space Invaders* and quite casually bet-
tered the obsessed Greenlander's highest score; and during the
next two or three days that Blund brooded on this humiliation,
muttering about going berserk. Had the rest of us been in better
order we might have paid some attention to his wounded pride,
but as it was, we were all too full of our own resentments. So
it came that one afternoon upstairs in the library he attacked
Jud Daraul.

I was distractedly playing chess with Coningham when it
happened; about fifteen other Baldies were at the computer-
screens. Blund was hulking at the *Space Invaders* machine,
persuaded back to it by his two huge blond friends from tenth-
century Norway, Brynjof and Thord. He must have been at it
for over an hour, painfully trying to regain his touch and improve on Utak's score—and for at least half that time Jud
Daraul had been pacing back and forth, impatiently awaiting
his turn at the machine which Blund would not give up—and
Coningham had just taken one of my bishops when Jud, unable
to wait any longer, suddenly stopped dead in the middle of the
floor and shouted: "This is all jerkoff bullshit, man, playing
with these goddamn stupid toys while these bastards slowly
kill us!"

Blund's American wasn't good, but he reacted to the angry

tone, he must have thought himself insulted, for he turned, his
face contorted, he roared and rushed at Daraul, knocking the
black man down. Amid the wailing of the alarm he tore Jud's
helmet off and had him almost throttled before the four white-
suit guards in the room all converged to drag Blund off and
needle him through his suit with a drug that immediately knocked
him out. Brynjof and Thord threatened to attack as well, but
held off as the rest of us stared and Daraul stood weakly,
helmetless and breathing Modern air (though to him it was only
a few years more modern).

"See?" he panted, waving a finger at his naked head, "This
is all complete *bullshit!* Trapped like dummies in these suits
and fighting each other which is just like they want it!"

Then the guards dealt with him too, and none of us did a
thing about it as both of them were taken away for *treatment*.

Jud was back in two weeks. They dealt not too harshly with
him, putting him on a course of lithium and another drug called
atropine methyl nitrate . . . but when Blund finally reappeared
among us in late November he was no longer the same man,
no more than a stirk is a bull. Not his balls but his brain had
been castrated, an electrical pacifier having been placed in that
part of it called the amygdala.

They didn't tell us this, and Blund couldn't. We learned it
in Circle . . . for by then, through vision and tragedy, we'd
found some unity, and our plans were well-advanced.

This sad event in the library was a turning-point, for it was
that evening Masanva at last communicated.

The Dancer had been part of us but not part of us; he had
never sent images, never spoken to anyone in library or quadrangle or group, though often enough we'd seen him standing
or walking alone, massive arms folded, an expressionless mystery who'd soon gained a number of nicknames privately among
us—"Sphinx," "Big Daddy," "Ancient of Daze," and so on.
Some had tried talking to him, but without response. He would
simply look at the importuner until he found himself left alone
again, and so thus he had remained as great a mystery to us
as to our captors. I suspect they made no headway with him
at all.

So, that evening in Circle we had horrid chaos for the fourth
or fifth night in a row, with quarrels over what had happened
to Blund and Jud Daraul, and Azurara again attacking Utak,

who was sending sneering images of stupid white asses, and
Herbie attacking Azurara, and myself attacking Herbie, lashing
out, finding dark pleasure in it, using my friend to unburden
myself of all my pent-up hate—for on one or another of these
mad days he'd given me excuse for it by infuriating me with
comment he'd made about Mery-Isis. "Wow, Humf, I'd really
like to grab me a piece of that juicy ass!" he'd said with
disgusting relish, watching her walk. "I mean just the thought
of it keeps me going!" I had glared at him. "LEARN SOME
RESPECT, YOU LOW MAN!—AND STOP CALLING ME
HUMF!" And he'd punched me on the shoulder, complaining,
"Aw, c'mon, Humf! Holy-schmoly, they like to doodle as
much as we do, and *she* doesn't pretend she's a plaster saint,
so why should you?"—Which left me speechless but vowing
revenge, so that on this night I speak of I sent the low man a
low image of a cock like a worm, crawling through the mud,
with his face on the front of it and duck-feathers sticking out
of the back; and in reply he sent image back of myself as a
large stone prick permanently frozen upright—and this amid
a visual concatenation of the same futile sort between many of
us, when, suddenly . . .

Jove's Thunderbolt is the nearest I can think of.

Either that or the Electric Shock Treatment.

Like a bolt of lightning it struck through us all and shut us
up with such effectiveness that for over a minute there was no
response.

Then Masanva showed his face.

It was glowering, with hands clapped over ears.

Next he showed a dozen of us jabbering at each other, all
with distorted faces and ears of asses. He showed Utak with a
monkey's face, running desperately after a vague White God,
then Azurara with drooling moron's countenance topped by
dunce's cap as he drops a trinket into the offered red hand.

Then all this dissolved into a thick darkness. There was not
a breath of protest from any of us—though I did, strangely,
seem to hear the distant echo of a ghostly laugh which at the
time I thought came from Masanva. Then it too was gone, and
there was nothing.

I waited, suspended in that illimitable darkness imaged by
Masanva, imaged so strong I no longer knew myself.

In time, in distance, I sensed a dull red haze. It seemed to be coalescing from the abyss, to be thickening now into a circular form, spinning like a whirlpool as it grew brighter into crimson. Then above it another field of light appeared, and this slowly coalesced into a spin whose heart was emerald green—then above this, a third, that was golden yellow; then a fourth, again above, so that all these whirling fields described a vertical axis—and the fourth became a dazzling violet—and finally, so bright that I could sense it only as a field of indescribable incandescence that lit the entire universe and banished all darkness, the fifth leapt into creation.

Then I saw the Man whose spine these whirling circles of light defined. He bestrode the living, shifting, suddenly animate cosmos—yet even as, dazzled, I looked again, I saw, no, not Man, but Woman, and then—no, not Woman alone, not Man alone, but both, and more!

What happened next is beyond my words: there was a mighty turbulence, a tremendous dance of energy, the sense of simultaneous vision in many dimensions at once, a Making and Shaping and Shifting, a Song being sung in every register—then vision stabilised.

I saw the earth, our earth.

It was bright like a jewel, all colours, with people on it made from it and from the spirit breathed into it, their heads haloed by the light pouring through the open door in their crown, the Song and the spinning spheres full and rich and harmonious in them.

But something went wrong. Darkness infiltrated the people, then fire gouted, and I saw that beautiful world destroyed.

Yet the planet swam out of the catastrophe, renewed and fair, if not quite so bright as before—and the new people on it were not quite so bright either. This time I saw them killing animals and each other and so delighting in the cleverness of their hands alone that they forgot to look up, and their halo grew dull, the darkness came again, and a second catastrophe, for the earth lost its spin and wobbled, and rolled over twice like a drunk, then fell through space and froze into ice. And only those with a hint of the Song in their hearts had taken underground refuge with the ants in time.

So came a third world, a world in sharper focus now, with harder edges and the light more locked-up and shaped into things made by hands; I saw the survivors multiply and build great cities; but the door atop their heads by now was almost completely closed; they knew they'd lost something but couldn't remember what, or denied it had ever been; many worshipped the behaviour of beasts and rushed about in flying machines from which they attacked each other's cities—

There was a flash of that terrible invisible light.

The rains came, and Flood covered the lands.

Next, suddenly, I found myself amid a crowd of many and we were bobbing on the ocean, and our craft were not golden ships, but rafts of reed, and when at last the clouds cleared and the sun set behind us, there was still no land in sight. We sent off swallows that brought report of beautiful islands which soon we passed, but of each isle a voice in us whispered, *"No, not this one, go on, go on!"* And we were of every race who heard this voice—red, black, yellow, and white, and every admixture; all united on this great odyssey.

On and on we went towards the rising sun. At length we came to a land of high mountains that marched north and south without a break, so we could find no place to land. Then the voice in us whispered: *"Remember the door in the crown of your heads!"* We stopped paddling, and relaxed, to let our vision-faculties work. Thus, with the aid of that inner eye which knows what outer sensation cannot, we found an opening in the giant cliffs, and through the narrow neck we went, and entered a great shining bay.

Gladly we put ashore onto this hard new fourth world, but immediately sensed a giant before us, and heard a thunderous voice:

"Who are you?"

We knew who this was! He whose pride had wrecked the third world, who had been cast down into Death for it! But the One Who Made us had decided to give him (and us) another chance to learn the Song we can sing and the Dance we can dance, of our own will, so that All Things may come alive in spirit and splendour as the Plan intends!

So with the greatest respect we asked the giant spirit in us if we might stay in this land, and the Caretaker (for so he was) rumbled, "Yes, but before you can settle to seek the Plan you must prove yourselves able to concentrate and remember. You must go about the land to every corner, north and south and east and west, to learn the shape of things and find your proper homes. But if on the way you forget what you are doing, there you will stop and freeze into grotesque forms and beliefs that will bring only unhappiness.

"Now," continued the thunder-voice, "I have a tablet here that I break into many pieces, and to each of you in your groups and families I give a piece of the broken tablet to carry with you on your separate ways: to you, black man, this piece; red man, this is yours; yellow man, here is the map of your direction; and white man, you take this piece."

Then in each of us the great voice spoke with instruction according to our individualities, preparing us to set forth and in time to return with knowledge, to join the tablet together again. And we were shown ways to remember these things down through the ages of the fourth world, so that when we met again we should recollect our brotherhood and work together with what we had all learned.

"May we meet again!" we called to each other as we departed on our different ways through the long generations.

So we made many journeys, and I know of them all, for we all try for the same, and in time I saw that some of us found our way back, but others forgot and founded stone cities, or wandered off their way, or partly remembered but got interested in something else. And so many were late returning, and many who did return were bitterly wounded though calling themselves whole. And many had blood on their hands.

But some who remembered made the great circuit and found their home in a power-place of bare desert lands, where all their strength of the open door was needed for the evocation of rain. And through the centuries they waited there for the return of their brothers.

So, now it comes to pass that I stand on a mesa-top and I dance, for I know the time is due, and past due, yet my dance is full of foreboding, for White Brother in particular is late in returning, having got himself into all sorts of trouble along the way.

Yet I dance, feathered staff in hand, I dance to the wind and the earth, the fire and the rain, but still the horizon's empty.

No, look!

Clouds of dust arising from the four quarters!

I hear a rumbling that is not a sound I ever wanted to hear, and now I see great hosts approaching, converging, appearing out of the dust in all their flashing might and pride, with marching bands and millions in rank, their weapons gleaming and their generals prancing in front, and behind them a great sea of sweating weary enslaved hordes who carry piles of broken things, their eyes blank and fearful, and I see some so mad at their imprisonment that they break out completely, setting up other poor states in which nobody must be any different from anyone else, By Order! And my dance grows more despondent still, for the forgetting of the Few is a curse on the Many, and the slaves who are left are herded against possible breakout by ranting preachers and dog police and flying machines that spray black poison behind them, forcing them ever onwards, nullifying every effort to create and remember, for even amid the madness of these hosts there are brave attempts to open up the door again.

In accordance with the plan I go down and lay out the sacred cornmeal in welcome.

I stand and await their leader with my hand held out. The one they call leader comes forward, and his face seems young but his eyes have night of death in them and his door is completely shut; and he has forgotten everything but the mirror in which he admires himself, for he does not shake my hand at all but, with guns pointed at me by his guards behind, he *gives me a trinket!*

Chaos! Bloodlust! The red haze throbs! Machines digging up the land! My dance is grown frantic! We dance to strange songs! I see lightning-visions of falling forests, broken hoops, deformed children, blue men striding the flashing thunder-sky— turbulence, confusion, again that terrible invisible white light; the tremendous dance of energy as things are returned to their matrix for remoulding.

Darkness overwhelms everything.

Amid the night in the wake of this my vision I undertake a journey far to the east, to another sea; I paddle out through mud-choked waters to a sea of weed where I await what dream has showed me, and it comes and seizes me in its whirlpool, into a madness—

Now the dust clears, slowly, and as it lifts I find myself here in an indeterminate place, my soul a coiling redness, but all around me the forms of folk approaching—I see Utak, Azurara, Herbie, Tari, all of us, without our suits, as we are already if only we'd look up; and I see light flowing up the axis of five whirling spheres, from crimson to emerald, gold, violet and beyond into incandescence: I see Utak and Azurara meeting again, this time shaking hands; losing moronface and monkeyface and becoming fully human, bright and light with open doors, and hear a voice: *"Falling fools may arise wise!"*

And now a long journey, to learn how to dance all this.

Later I return to Humf, at Horsfield, amazed.

We had no more argument that night. Next day Director Piggot called us all into the chapel and gave us a lecture on how we must behave or all be shut up in solitude. The sheepish meekness of our conduct in the next few days no doubt persuaded him that we were impressed by his threat. In fact we were in a kind of shock. After Masanva's vision those of us in Circle were like dazed children partly awoken from a squabble. The rest, who did not directly share in the image-making, picked the new mood up from us. But our distemper was not automatically banished. Still we had no idea what Masanva was doing, nor Tari; there was lingering resentment at Big Daddy's blast, particularly among our Moderns; and it was almost a week before Utak and Azurara actually did shake hands, the peace-formula being that Utak admitted he'd expected too much and Azurara admitted he'd seen too little.

It was Othoon and his fate that completed the process of binding us. For, with daily degradation of suits and untouchability continuing, even as Hyperia fell sick and we remained low with no ulterior purpose for Circle yet introduced, the Irishman decided to join us—and just in time. Masanva's vision was potent but hardly optimistic.

But Othoon found our situation laughable.

Came the night his mad humour burst brilliantly through us, as if out of nowhere. Yes, there'd been that ghost of a laugh at Masanva's high vision, and once or twice, when casting about at the edge of Circle, I'd felt a . . . tickle of . . . someone slyly watching and laughing, and others had felt the same, and we had wondered about the Gael.

I had asked Ernstein, and he had frankly said:

"I'm afraid you won't meet him. He's in no fit state."

So, we met him in Circle. At first I found his images incomprehensible. They were an endless interplay that tumbled grotesquely with each other, making no apparent sense at all. But soon, finding his rhythm, as it were, we began to realise the deliberate nature of his tomfoolery and madcap poetry. I cannot hope to represent it well, but here's something of what it summoned up in me:

> I am Othoon of the Dobharan Folk
> Child of Danu, warrior of my people
> Poet and fool, I have seen everything
> The invisible ones were on my side
> I had free entry to the faery-mounds
> I have seen ages in the glass
> I have been with Abraham and Cuchulain
> I have been born many times in many lands
> I have been a boar, a buck, a bird, a fish
> I have been a boy, I have been a girl—
> I have been black and white and both together
> And I have been up and down and in between
> There is no where or shape I have not been
> There is no taste I have not tasted
> No weariness I have not known
> No passing stone I left unturned
> No passing wench I left untupped
> No passing coin I did not spin
> No skill I could not master
> For Mighty Lugh gave me a hundred hands
> Great Manannan gave me many shapes of mist
> Beautiful Brigit gave me charm and beauty
> For I am Othoon the Poet, the Bard
> I have joked a million jokes
> I have riddled a million riddles
> I have cast a million spells of words
> And turned a million sober tables
> When the King of Munster insulted me
> I raised foul boils upon his face
> When Ulster's Queen refused to pay me
> Her lovers' staffs all crumpled
> When rogues of Leinster scorned me
> They lost their wits and babbled
> And laughed until they cried instead
> And begged me, let them die for peace!
> And called me bard without compare!
> But their crawling did not please me
> I stole a cheese and a sweet young girl
> When the Hawthorn month was done
> I took to sea to find new jokes

Being bored with what I knew
I cast a spell of words before me
To set a wind upon my sail
To take us fair and far away
To the Isles of Earthly Paradise
To the Isles that stand on legs
To the Isles where nothing dies
Where all is music, mirth and mead
Ah!—I knew I'd find them, Manannan helped!
For first the fog and then the storm
Then the fire that burned the sea
Then the abyss of burning nothing
In which I raved and flamed and roared
And laughed and heard the Gods all laugh
Then sea again, I was laughing still
The monster took me, I joked its jaws
The Americans have me, I laugh—haha!
They want me to speak, I laugh—haha!
I sit in this room and laugh at myself
And I laugh at your arguments every night
For your fears are foolish and your ferment is flat
And every day I see you stumbling Outside
Like fish out of water, gasping and goggling
I giggle and gobble at your gasping and goggling
And I gaggle and gasp when the doctors come in
I roll my eyes and grunt and groan—haha!
I gibble and gobble and gaggle and gasp!

I can do no justice to the wildness of his laughing, which grew wilder as the doctors tried ever more desperately to get some of old Ireland out of him and into their dissertations. He would not help. On and on he laughed and gabbled in some unknown Goidelic dialect; they could make no more sense of him than they could of Masanva. They tried to persuade Diarmaid to speak with him, but Diarmaid would not. They tried to hypnotise him, but he raved on—I don't know what they didn't try: they regarded the poor man as a "challenge," and would not leave him alone. The pressure was increased: the mad luxuriance of his imagery increased likewise as his condition became ever more desperate. We tried to help, to send him our images, but he thought us as absurd as the doctors and himself and all the world, he gabbled on ever more wildly until he gabbled his way into a fatal fit, and though at the end his raving seemed to be but raving, some of his final images struck and have lain in my mind ever since—

> . . . there's no way from misery if you're in a fuddy-bluddyblackymuddy. They've got you by the bawls all gut-tied and trounced! Life's a short abort but we blackbrain buoys bob up, bob up, bob up! Even if Mymannan with his Big Mac Leer pineals us all to his whatevery bedlocks in the fourgatten cities fool fathom deep on the tyresome sidon the mind, we bob up, bob up, bob up and keep on laughing—hahahahaha! Morriganmorrigan! Brrrrrr! Why fear the Dark Queen? She'll help me break walls! I'll go to her laughing while you fools groan and I'll bob up, bob up, for I'm her child and I'll be born again!

So suddenly he died amid a fit they could not stop or treat, and next day Hyperia went too, wasted away. We were all utterly low, and dared not mention Othoon's name aloud, nor that we knew he was dead—for they did not tell us. We moped aimlessly. But then the day that Hyperia died Masanva broke silence and announced his purpose to some of us on the volleyball-court. Without preamble he came and said:

"I am the Dancer. I have come to dance the Unmasking. When the Brightness shines too bright, the Dance will be danced and the Mask removed and the Gourd will be filled with ashes. When the world is quiet again, the ashes will be spread on the ruined fields and barren deserts. There will be a new fertility, for Life cannot be stopped!"

Only hours later, that night, having pondered all this without understanding any of it, I was in my room reading in *Time* magazine about what had happened at Damascus, Arkansas, when Tari, who'd been unobtrusive for weeks, surprised all Circle with a new image:

ESCAPE! ESCAPE! ESCAPE!

--➤➤[21]◀◀--

How Common Ground
Planned Escape

Yes, and we so decided, and wove spells over the minds of
our captors, and nine of us left Horsfield during the early
minutes of Christmas Day, 1984. Four of us left on a flying
carpet, and the other five on the back of a giant bird.

No, not quite.

The scheme we developed was utterly prosaic, though it did
involve persuading the Institute staff that we were deeply and
laudably immersed in the creation of a new religion appropriate
to our situation. Principally we depended on planning, decep-
tion, precise timing and coordination, and a large measure of
that essential quality which, in Common Ground terminology,
we coded as *Seven*—though I preferred then, and still in many
ways prefer now, to call it *Luck*.

We were in September by this time. The entire business
took us three months. On the surface life went on during these
months much as it had before, with our daily routines of eating
and sleeping and being tested, treated, and questioned continually, with cameras on us and microphones to hear what we
said to each other in our suits—but from here on I speak of
Institute life only where it touches on our escape, for there's
much still to tell, and in my thinking now I'm anxious to be
out of Horsfield as quick as possible, to marry past with present
and bring it through the best I can.

ESCAPE? I hadn't even thought of it. The image startled

me when it came. It was of bars being bent, a wall bulging out and collapsing, dim figures running off unseen on a dark and moonless night—and it was signed by the raven-haired face of Mery-Isis.

Yes, a sad day, with Hyperia and Othoon both gone—but odd, too, with Masanva speaking his piece as casually as another might speak of the weather. His unfathomable eyes had gleamed on each of us, then he'd turned away, leaving us staring, not knowing what to think or say. In fact none of us spoke: what *could* you say? What did he mean by the Brightness shining too bright, by the Mask being removed and the Gourd being filled with ashes? Ernstein wondered too: as I ate supper in my room he'd entered and asked what Masanva had said. I shrugged. "He told us he's a dancer," I said through a mouthful of half-cooked potato, "and that there's going to be a new world."

"Oh. Is that all?"

"I didn't understand what he meant."

Ernstein gave me a suspicious look, but said no more. After he left I had a bath, then sat down to read *Time* magazine. We were encouraged to read *Time, Newsweek,* and the rest of them, which I did infrequently, for they made little sense to me. On the cover of this *Time* was a lurid mushroom-cloud, and below it, in bold black letters, the legend: DAMASCUS, ARKANSAS. I scanned the articles within. They were all about the recent "Broken Arrow" nuclear disaster in Damascus, Arkansas. Many people were dead and more were expected to die. It made no sense: I put the magazine aside as the sleep-voice began its evening drone, telling me how Russian interventionism in the western hemisphere had to be ... when suddenly, this image of ESCAPE!

It surprised all of us, except Mery-Isis and Masanva.

I breathed deep, turned down the light, composed myself as if for sleep in bed. My heart beat hard. Escape? How? To what? Damascus, Arkansas? The entire Circle was similarly excited. Question-images swirled so raggedly I couldn't tell which were mine and which came from others. Then out of the confusion came a detailed, sarcastic image, evidently from a Modern, for it had a clear picture of the Outside world. It showed three obvious DTI fugitives—shaven, in jumpsuits and immunity-suits, blundering in flight along a city street past people ignoring them, policemen looking the other way, soldiers shooting each other instead. Then a (???)—and *Duck-in-a-Pond*.

Tari replied with this even more startling proposition:

Three DTIs *take off* their immunity-suits and jumpsuits. They don Modern clothes and breathe unsterilised air.

This caused some consternation.

I sent image of these unprotected DTIs Outside; reeling, choking, collapsing. I added signature: my hand on gleaming brass astrolabe.

Reaction came from several people at once:

Scales, a Balance, a Weighing-of-Risks: Coningham.

Running naked and free on a moonlit beach: ***LUCIE***

Disdainful wave of a hand: a So-What from Utak.

A (???) followed by ass-ears listening. Conspiratorial image of Tari studying unrolled PLAN OF ESCAPE with other DTIs all gathered round. (???) again, followed by *Duck-in-a-Pond*.

That was the start. Coningham came up with an idea involving the midnight shift of Institute workers; Masanva pictured his scheme for Common Ground and its code. It became clear that he and Tari had worked on this for some time. I found it hard to sleep that night. For how was it possible? Even if we could develop the code and all else that Masanva suggested, even if some of us could escape, what was the point? How long could we live Outside, and to what purpose?

In fact for some nights I and others thought it no more than a ploy produced by Tari and the Dancer to persuade our minds out of depression, and I could hardly take it seriously. But then, about a week later, I caught pneumonia, and nearly died.

I *would* have died if not for Circle. I was in a coma. The doctors tried to plant something in me. A THING. I don't know what it was, but I have strange and horrid dream-memories. The Circle drove this THING away even as I was about to give in to it. I seemed to be drowning. They took me on a boat to an isle with a garden and a well. They gave me pure water to drink. I slept, and awoke recovered . . . and after that I was very ardent for escape! Where there's life there's hope, in *any* sort of world . . . and a slim chance is better than none.

Ernstein was diffident with me after my recovery.

As soon as we knew that some of us were in earnest, the problems began. Circle was in ferment for the next two months.

Who wanted to go? Who *dared* go? Should Moderns get precedence because of greater immunity? Who outside Circle should be told of it via code? Who should be told nothing at all? How to be sure of each other and ourselves, that we were truly ready to risk it, and unlikely to panic at the critical moment? If anyone talked because of drugs, hypnosis, sickness or force, how should the others react? What about clothes, money, accents, baldness, medical supplies, information about Outside? *Time* and television didn't tell us what lay immediately beyond the gates. Checkpoints? Electronic scanners? Searches of the outgoing bus? Details of the surrounding countryside?

Little by little we learned what we needed to know, mostly by asking innocent questions. Much of what we learned did not cheer us, and some who had at first been enthusiastic grew depressed as the realities of the situation became apparent.

Yet by the end of October it was clear that at least six were set on it, with another half-dozen willing to try it. The spirit grew, and would not be stopped. The specific plan developed. The pie was put in the oven. And on Christmas Eve we brought it out. And this is how it tasted:

Christmas Eve was dark and windy. Nine of us were ready— Carlos, Daraul, Gage, Gilbert, Hopkins, Masanva, Mery-Isis, Pond, and Utak.

Coningham was sick and had to withdraw, which saddened us, but opened a place to one of the reserve three—Azurara, Carlos, and Waters. None of them really wanted to go. Each gallantly insisted the other two should decide, making the rest of us very nervous. In time they tossed for it, and Clive Carlos won. That still left a problem. Using the code, Tari and Herbie questioned him to be sure he understood thoroughly and was really willing to risk it.

"Well, now," he said, "you've got me hooked, haven't you? I was never one for the chapel, but the way you put it there's nothing else, is there? It'll do my soul no good at all to stay stuck in Four, will it? You show me how to get to One, and I'll do my very best!"

We used number-system for code to avoid squabbling over god-names. It was not absolutely accurate to the inner meaning of Number but it worked well enough. Each number had an exoteric meaning as a Common Ground principle for the benefit of the Horsfield staff, and a hidden meaning for our benefit, so that we could talk freely of escape while seeming to discuss Common Ground doctrine. The open meanings had been worked out in great detail at many seminars attended by interested Institute staff and outside experts who were all delighted that we should show such positive response to our situation . . . though, when in October we had first approached Piggot to tell him we wished to develop common religious ground amongst ourselves, with the aim of holding our first Common Ground service in the chapel on Christmas Eve, he had been somewhat shocked, demanding to know what was wrong with existing chapel services. Coningham had exploded most effectively at this, invoking the First Amendment, calling the Institute's Christian-only services "a damned disgrace," and telling the Director that "there's as much spirit in that place as you'll find in a bottle of Glenfiddich the morning after Hogmanay!"

All of which had been true. We had got our way. Now, on Christmas Eve, we were ready to celebrate the first Common Ground service. After it, also in the chapel, we would stage an entertainment, *Impressions of 1984*, which we very much hoped our invited guests from the Horsfield staff would attend and enjoy.

A midnight movie show was also arranged, in the library.

The code, in brief, as a matter of interest:
One in Common Ground meant *God*, secretly *escape*. *Two* was *Duality*, secretly *Diversion*. *Three*, *Common Ground*, secretly *Circle*. *Four*, the *Material World*, alias *Horsfield*. *Five*, *Human Beings*, or *DTIs* to us. *Six*, *Perfected Mind*, equalling *Coordination of Escape Plan*. *Seven* we explained to the experts as *Fate*, *Luck*, *Chance*, or *Divine Guidance*, depending how you looked at it, while among us it referred to these things but also to *Invoked Circumstance*, meaning certain ritual workings carried out on behalf of all by Mery-Isis and Masanva, in which not all of us had belief, as I have said. But Luck *was* with us, as events soon proved. *Eight* referred openly to *Worldly Circumstance*, alias *Horsfield Security;* while *Nine*, being of course those of us who were making the attempt, was explained as *The Aspects of the Soul*.

The preceding days and hours were a blur to me then and remain so now. Only particular events stand out. When Coningham fell sick I got permission to visit him in his room. This was rarely allowed, but we were known to be friends, and he was not well. We said little, yet I was glad we could say our (coded) farewell and godspeed face-to-face. He was a fine man, and made no complaints about his fate.

Also I recall our efforts to prepare the chapel for the service and the entertainment after, and the last-minute argument we had with Piggot about the Modern clothes we said we needed for *Impressions of 1984*. Lucie won that tussle for us, telling Piggot maybe it *was* ridiculous, putting Modern dress on over immunity-suit and helmet so she could play her twin role of Las Vegas hooker and Washington wife, but it would be even *more* ridiculous without it, and goddammit, what sort of creep was he that wouldn't let a girl dress up at Christmas?

Yes, Lucie was a surprise to many of us, by no means a fluffyhead as I'd assumed, and in fact had done something which none of the rest of us ever managed to do—she made Masanva laugh. When we started planning seriously, Masanva began coming down from heaven more often to join us in Circle—so one night Lucie had put out a cartoon of grumpy Big Daddy on his mountainpeak smelling something good and coming running to join in the feast. This had created an expectant chill among us . . . but it had turned out well, improving our spirit.

And as for Masanva, by the time all was finally prepared, none of us were any longer in doubt of his strength and stability.

I remember eating the evening meal in my sterile room for the last time, both hoping and fearing. I remember staring through the window at the cold overlapping pools of flood-lighting on the quadrangle, wondering how our ramshackle plan could possibly work, and realising how, even if we did get out, in a few short hours we might be done for, struck down by bullets or by the rapid onset of some virulent Modern disease. I remember in my nervousness I turned on the television, feeling some need to identify with what we were going out to join, but the quiz-show I saw began to make me doubt if One was really worth it, so I turned the thing off. I sat down instead, and relaxed as we joined in Circle calm, quietly to confirm in each other that now was no longer the time for mental pictures, but for physical action. Then, at precisely half past eight, we put on our immunity-suits, and called to be let out and taken to the chapel. The timing was most important. The tanks held four hours of air, but recently we had won agreement that we should never have to go more than three hours, or three and a half at most, without recharge.

It all depended on the timing.

(I forgot: Jim Gage was in Circle by then. There had nearly been trouble with Jud and Herbie's friends who knew about it but who felt left out because they could not send or get the images. We had asked them into One, Tari making more of her apparently irrelevant remarks until they picked up the code. The interesting thing is this: once they no longer felt excluded, Clive and Connie and Jim Gage and Jim Guerrero each began to send and receive, just a little, and likewise Brynjof and Thord when they were brought in to help with Two. Tari's *sympathy* was remarkable, it awoke the best in people. Yes, I loved that woman, and I was not alone.)

That night the chapel was candlelit, beautiful, mysterious.

By day it was a plain little hall, about forty feet by thirty, with white plaster walls and uninteresting windows, and a screen of artificial wood behind the altar covering the dividing wall between chapel and library. There was an electric organ and a small stainless steel pulpit, both slightly in front of the communion rail and raised altar dais. The floor was of varnished wooden bricks; and the seating unfixed, consisting of collapsible wooden chairs. Of the three plain doors, the main one was at the south end, facing and about thirty yards from the main gateway. The others were to the left of the altar, one opening to the library, and the second, adjacent and close to the first, giving access to the east side of the quadrangle.

We had wrought change.

Over the windows were hangings on which we had painted golden circles with equal-armed crosses in each. The arms of the crosses were citrine, olive, russet, and black. The hangings were opaque.

Similarly painted cloth screens on wooden frames stood on either side of the altar, creating a backstage area for the entertainment. One of these screens hid the two doors from the audience.

Our request for incense—patchouli and sandalwood—had utterly mystified Piggot. ("But you can't smell it in your *suits!*"—

and Tari told him, "It is not primarily that *we* should smell it.")

Now, as I entered the chapel among a group of others all converging, thin rich spirals of smoke curled up from shoulder-high three-legged wooden stands set in the corners and midway along the walls. Clusters of candles were also set and lit on these stands: the waftings of incense we could not smell coiled up through the soft warm tents of light and vanished into raf-tered darkness above: going we hoped to the nostrils of what we called Seven.

The Christian altar and cross had not been covered over, but were as and where they usually were as we each took chairs and sat down wherever we would. We did not speak to each other, we waited very quietly, until, by nine o'clock, some forty-eight DTIs were gathered together in there: this being the entire number of us then in social circulation and considered "sane and rational within the context," as I once heard it put. (Of others we never saw, like Othoon and Ekapalon, Circle had searched, and found that by mid-December sixty-one DTIs were alive, and that most of those kept locked up were in fact seriously crippled, in mind, body, or both. Othoon's case I could understand, but why Ekapalon and two others who seemed sane and sound (another Japanese and another red man) were never let out I found hard to comprehend, though Jud called it "the same old shit.") And of the forty-eight now gathered, twenty-eight knew the inside meaning of One. Fifteen, like Dion, and now, sadly, Ketil Blund, didn't really know what anything meant. That left five we couldn't trust. Juan Battista Fernandez was one of these. Herbie said he was a "stoolie," and for tonight Azurara had promised to keep him out of our way, while the other four also had "companions" for the eve-ning.

As we waited I caught Azurara's eye. He nodded, very slightly. I wondered if he or I had made the right decision. I think nothing he had seen at Horsfield had suggested to him that Outside would be any better. He seemed happy to stay behind. Like John Kent and Jim Guerrero and Howell Rees, he was however willing to help us all he could. Others like Diarmaid weren't interested even in helping, but neither were they interested in making trouble for us.

Just after nine, Director Piggot and a number of staff came

in and sat at the back. We were ready to begin. There was a silence.

Then, one-by-one, whoever among us felt the urge stood up, and spoke their simple *Word of Beginning,* giving it to Common Ground:

> *In the beginning,* said Azurara, *God created the Earth.*
> *In the beginning,* said Mery-Isis, *Atum spilled his seed.*
> *In the beginning,* said Masanva, *Void in the Mind of Taiowa.*
> *In beginning,* said Brynjof, *Ice. Snow. Cold. No life.*
> *In the beginning,* said Jud, *One helluva Big Bang!*
> *In the beginning?* asked Lucie. *How can anyone know that?*
> *In the beginning,* said Watanabe, *Illuminating Essence!*
> *In the beginning,* said Gilbert, *Was the Word.*
> *In the beginning,* said Pond, *ONE!*

When this was done, Piggot and the staff left until later, save for a few discreet guards and observers at the back. Now began the succession of things. In that quiet dark place the atmosphere was strong between us. For the first and last time we were almost all together. Common Ground was no fraud. Outer veil masked inner purpose, yes, but that purpose depended on our unity now.

We cleared the chairs back and made a circle, gloved hands linked, and there we stood, for some time utterly silent, reflecting on all that had happened. Somebody began sobbing quietly, and somebody else too, and first we let this mood spread through us, all having much to lament. Some of us wept, and some stood quietly alone, and others embraced through the suits—we did each as we felt like, calling on our own lost gods if we wanted, all on Common Ground, briefly united in our differences, in our sorrow, from our ages. There was no dogma, yet there was a purpose, and the purpose was served, for our tension was eased, in those of us staying, and those of us going.

Slowly we rose from that mood to another, carried on our own wings and on the quiet river of sound that Jud now coaxed from the organ. At first it was gentle and faraway, but gradually the river ran more rapidly and became rhythmically compelling, with urgent variations of pace and flow to it that alerted the mind and body, so that some of us began beating time, to

dance—but Masanva stood without moving—and it was then
that Utak started a wild and wordless chant or ululation ("Like
the howler monkeys," he said later) in counterpoint to the
organ, so that we found our energy, and started dancing and
jumping about, with whooping and windmilling arms, myself
too, though as I did so I thought how unutterably strange this
would have seemed to me but a year of my life before, for
what we danced was certainly no galliard or pavane, though
perhaps it had some Pan-spirit of Mayday in it, save for the
physical restriction of the immunity-suits—

The physical restriction of the immunity-suits—
In less than three hours from now . . .

Yes, we broke out of despair with wild emotion and increasing passion, until through the Circle ran the deep sure
current of Masanva quietly noting that too much of this would
excite and alarm our captors where tonight we wanted to soothe
them, lullaby them, and let them know that our spirit was
entirely pacific. So the raving organ struck braking backbeats
and slowed, and Tari came in with a chant which slid in cool
like silver, which Utak acknowledged, and thus we came off
Utak's burning height and went down a moonlit river instead.

After some time we were all silent and still again. Then
some words were spoken about the meaning of the Numbers.
We thought about this, then closing words were spoken among
us.

We sat again in silence.

It was nearly ten o'clock.

We divided into five groups to prepare the chapel for the
Entertainment and *Impressions of 1984*.

The first group, in many ways the most important, was the
one that did nothing at all, and did not know it was a group.
Azurara and Jim Guerrero and John Kent were among these
people for us, making sure they continued to do nothing at all,
but at the right times.

Of the others, amid the bustle, one group curtained off the
altar and set up lighting and in general managed the stage. The
second lot got busy blowing up balloons and hanging coloured
paper streamers all over the place, to add to festive relaxation.
Several others went with two guards to the North Block to get
the laundry bags which had a selection of discarded Modern
clothes which Piggot had so reluctantly acquired for us, ap-

parently from a Salvation Army Thrift Store. And the fourth group, also with two guards, went to the Institute canteen to pick up trays of prepared sandwiches, soft drinks, beer and other goodies for our guests, plus some tubes of squirtfood-and-drink for our own suited selves. All this was set up on trestle tables covered by white linen, and also there were bowls of flowers from Florida. It was not a feast that would have satisfied Falstaff, but the best we could get out of Piggot having told him it was for himself and the Institute staff.

The clothing arrived. The Entertainment players were most eager to turn from setting up the stage and see what Piggot had provided. Lucie, Herbie, Tari, Jud, Connie, Clive, and yours truly—we were quick to open up those laundry bags. We had asked for wigs, but there were none, as we found, yet the rest of the clothing was sufficient for nine at least. Some of it was almost new, though the variety and mixture of styles was amazing.

We wished to begin at ten-thirty, and there was no time to waste. We were all somewhat nervous, save for Tari, as calm as ever, and also Masanva, who sat doing nothing more conspicuously than anyone else, on a chair amid all the bustle and flurry with hands on knees and feet apart and back straight and eyes fixed straight ahead. We pushed and pulled Modern clothes over our immunity-suits, some being too baggy about the body to permit such an operation with ease. Yet we did it, and had to laugh at each other. Wearing a business-suit with shirt and tie that ballooned over the contours of immunity-suit beneath, and a porkpie hat taped to the top of my helmet at a jaunty angle, I looked no more ridiculous than some of the others. Yet my nervous hilarity was mixed with doubt as I went to check on several matters, according to my agreed responsibilities. Six guards supervised us—five men, one woman; four whites, two blacks—all in their thirties or forties, in grey uniforms, not wearing white-suits, their guns concealed. They were relaxed and not suspicious, for my appearance amused them. This was satisfactory. I entered the library. I found Kazan Watanabe on the lower floor, setting up screen and equipment for the musical extravaganza to be shown at midnight, a movie called *Mary Poppins*. He eyed me in shock at my disguise, then bent over in a fit of the giggles, silent save for a *"sssszz-sssszz"* that escaped him. "Sir," I said with what dignity I could muster, "we met well on Common Ground, and may Seven make this evening happy for us all! Is everything ready here?"

"Gilbert-san . . . sorry I laugh . . . but you . . ."

He went off into another fit of "*sssszz-sssszz*-ing," before managing to inform me that he had his responsibilities under control, at which point I was able to laugh with him. I returned to the chapel. All seemed ready. Masanva's eye caught me and held me for an instant, and I felt steadied as I went to the south door near which stood Brynjof and Thord. Blund was there too, but he had the eyes of a heifer.

"Ah! Englishman!" barked Brynjof, blue eyes fixing me from his leather face, "Modern this night, eh? You look that you walk on breaked glass!"

"I am ready for play. And you, Norseman?"

"Yes! Yes! I like to play!" He took both my shoulders in his meatloaf hands and squeezed, and even through his suit and mine I felt it. "Not to fear, Englishman! We know how to play!"

Then, with dry mouth, I told one of the guards that we were ready to begin. The time was twenty-five minutes to eleven.

"...The Japanese
Never Made Nothing!"

Impressions of 1984 was not a success. We stumbled through
our silly sketches, forgetting our lines, unable to concentrate
on the business of making people laugh. Our audience out there
in the dark between the candlelight clusters were politely amused
to begin with, but soon the increasingly cold silences told us
we would never hold the attention of our Institute guests until
eleven-fifteen, as we had planned. The joke of Modern clothes
over immunity-suits quickly wore thin, while Lucie's saga of
the progress from Las Vegas to Washington of a lady of easy
virtue seemed to cause more embarrassment than amusement.
We held a backstage council-of-war, then abandoned the programme, and Tari called for impromptu tricks and turns from
DTIs and staff alike. Then followed an uncomfortable ten minutes. Herbie told bad jokes, then John Kent recited a poem
called "The Wreck of the Hesperus," but the audience was very
restive. It was Norman Ernstein who saved us, for suddenly
he came up on stage, grinning, and asked for an assistant, and
with his parlour-magic carried us through the next fifteen minutes in a good mood.

Poor man, by doing this he sealed his own fate. For, approximately at the right time, we brought it to a close, and set
the crucial phase in motion. With the special midnight movie-
show coming up next, clearly we had to refill our air-tanks—
an operation which could only be done ten at a time.

Now it was a matter of timing, and not merely our own.

* * *

The first group of ten went at eleven-seventeen. None of the Nine were in this group, though Azurara and Kent were with it, having steered several of its members into answering the preliminary call. While they went, nearly eighty DTIs and Institute staff mingled in shifting groups. We played the social game for all we were worth. I spoke with Ernstein, who was flushed from his success on stage. He was drinking a bottle of Budweiser beer rapidly. He said he hoped there were no hard feelings between us, but that now he had to go and take a shower before catching the midnight bus. He went, and then it was eleven-twenty-six, and the second group went, with two guards, none of our nine being with them. I found myself listening to Piggot amid the crowd. I nodded and smiled and I cannot remember a word he said. Then it was time for the third group to go, Jim Gage and Herbie among them. This left the chapel noticeably less crowded, not all the first two groups yet being returned inside. I felt extremely tense. No more than twenty minutes remained. People were drifting in and out of the main south door, and some of the staff were leaving. We wanted to keep them longer. Somebody exploded a balloon, and some were dancing as Jud began to play the organ again. I escaped Piggot, and Lucie talked with him instead. The mood of the staff and the guards appeared to be quite relaxed as Watanabe called out that the movie would start soon. It was quarter to midnight, and the fourth group was called, and went, including Masanva.

It was time to act. Discarded Modern clothes had been put back into the laundry bags. Jud and I still wore our costumes. Carlos and Van Roornevink were waiting by the screen next to the side door. I scanned about, then gave them the all-clear. They carried the bags outside and left them in shadow against the wall, then they came back inside without having been noticed.

The clock said eleven-fifty-two. My heart was beating very hard as I went to the main door. Just outside it, Brynjof and Thord and Jim Guerrero, all of whom had been in the second group, were starting a loud but good-natured argument in front of several other DTIs and some amused guards and staff. "Yes, big animals live in sky!" Thord was insisting. "Live in sky with stars!" Tari was there. She caught my eye. I felt encouragement flow from her.

Then we heard what we awaited.

The roar of the bus. The gates of black steel opened. In came the midnight shift. I turned away from the glare of the headlights. The bus backed into its usual space by the wall. We breathed again as the workers disembarked, as the driver got out too.

The fifth group was called by a guard.

It was five minutes to midnight.

We gathered quickly. There were but eight of us in this last group—Carlos, Daraul, Gilbert, Hopkins, Mery-Isis, Utak, Waters, and Van Roornevink. We all had specific functions to perform.

With one guard in front and the second behind, we crossed the quadrangle to the door of the West Block. *There's too much light!* I kept thinking. All the lit windows, and the floodlighting in round overlapping pools on the quadrangle. I looked back at the bus. Its metal gleamed, I could see every inch! Mad to think we might get away with it! A mad dream!—yet my mind was more sharp and awake than it had been at any time since that moment three hundred and sixty-two nights and nineteen hours ago when Vulcan had seized us.

The door into our block was open, the black man at the switchboard was cleaning his nails with a little knife. As we went in, Masanva came unhurriedly down the stairs, on his own, with fresh air, and the black man, who was called Joe, didn't even look up, far less make Masanva wait for either of the guards who had escorted his group up the stairs. There was no hint that anyone suspected anything.

We climbed the stairs, step by step. It seemed to take forever. Tari and Utak were in front of me. I wondered if they were ready, if their stomachs were as knotted as mine.

We reached the second floor and went thirty yards along a bare passage to the green door, and started into the long low room with its cupboards, closets, and ten tank-changing stalls. The last two DTIs of the fourth group were emerging with their guards even as we got there. The guards of the two groups stopped to talk for a moment, and one of the DTIs, Howell Rees, gave us a good-luck wink. I felt stifled by nervousness and impatience.

Then the chatter was over and the last of the fourth group were gone and we were in the changing-room. All of us.

"Right, guys!" The guard who spoke was a big man, slightly

paunchy. The other was short but solid. "You know the rout..."

He stopped talking. His eyes widened. He stiffened, and his mouth fell open, and the moment had arrived.

The moment we were all inside, unseen by the casual guards, Tari and Utak made the moves we had pictured and feared so often. They had released some of the clasps already. Now they removed their helmets at the same moment and each tapped a guard on the arm and then confronted him naked-eye-to-naked-eye.

For about two seconds both men were too amazed to move. It was enough. In that time, Lucie shut the door, Jud removed the length of wood that he had hidden under his Modern overcoat and fiercely coshed the guard whose eye was held by Tari, while Utak struck his man in the adam's-apple with his left fist, kicked him viciously in the groin, then rabbit-punched him.

And it was done. Both guards collapsed, unconscious.

We stood, staring at each other. For several seconds there was neither motion nor sound save for Utak's harsh breathing. I knew what I had to do, but I couldn't move. My eyes were fixed on the face of Mery-Isis. For an instant, as I gazed at her, there flashed in my mind an image of that door she had described, with the statue of Isis and flanked by the red and black columns. That door which, once entered, allowed no turning-back.

She nodded sharply at me.

I took a deep breath. I unclasped and removed the helmet. I breathed unsterilised Modern air. There was no obvious difference. The thudding of my heart was painful. I breathed out... and in... and out... and in, deeply... and then the spell was broken.

We knew our parts. Everything happened quickly. Jud had taken off his helmet at the same time as I had. Both of us climbed out of Modern clothes and immunity-suits and jumpsuits as Van Roornevink and Carlos stripped the guards of their uniforms. Carlos tossed a chain of keys to Mery-Isis. She and Utak put their helmets back on and slipped out of the door of the room after checking to be sure that the coast was clear. Jud and I pulled on the uniforms. Grey trousers, metal-buttoned jacket, shirt, tie, black shoes. Everything fit more-or-less but for the shoes. Discarding jumpsuits, we struggled back into the transparent immunity-suits, then pulled the disguising Modern clothes back on top, then helmets again, and taped-on hats. We pocketed the guards' guns as the two men were bound, gagged, and heaved into two of the closets which held empty white-suits. Carlos and Van Roornevink shut the sliding doors on the unlucky pair, then joined Lucie and Connie Waters to recharge their tanks as usual. Jud and I did not. We eyed each other. Jud winked. I tried to smile, but it was hard. I wondered what horrible Modern germs were already crawling round my lungs. It was all right for Jud, he was Modern already. I put these thoughts away as Tari and Utak returned. Tari carried a plastic bag containing drugs from a store along the corridor. She had looted them quickly from shelves and cabinets, which later she told me she had seen through somebody else's eyes, which made me feel most strange.

Jud took the plastic bag and it too went under his overcoat.

Mery-Isis nodded and gestured. It was time to go. But first, each of us embraced Connie Waters and Philius Van Roornevink, saying farewell and thank you. They had agreed to linger behind as long as possible, as if with the guards, to delay the alarm.

Then we left that room, in ones and twos.

Tari and Jud went first, then Lucie. I followed Lucie— along the corridor, down the stairs, step by step. I cannot describe what I felt, but it was hard to put one foot in front of the other without making any mistakes. At the bottom, Joe at the switchboard stared sadly at us. Lucie stumbled and nearly fell as she passed him. He reached out and caught her by the arm, holding her up. She mumbled thanks and hurried out. He met my helmeted eye as I came up.

"I'm real sorry about all this," he said. "What's happening to you all. I want you to know that we're not all dogs. I'm here cos I need the bread and if I cop out I'll never get another job." He shrugged helplessly. "You're not the only poor dumb bastards. Just want you to know that tonight."

I said something to him as Clive Carlos and Utak came down behind me. "Hey, Joe," said Clive, "the others'll be a minute or two yet. They're having a little trouble with Connie's suit, see?"

Then I went out into the quadrangle again.

* * *

The lights were harsh. The night above was black, with no stars. I looked over by the chapel, and saw many people, DTIs and Institute staff, gathered between the south door and the main gate, near the front of the bus. I heard voices raised in argument and laughter. Other smaller groups and a few individuals were standing or walking about here and there. The clock said three minutes after midnight. It was Christmas! We had taken eight minutes.

In front of me, Jud and Tari, then Lucie, were going to the library, as if for the movie. I saw Herbie stroll past them, apparently on his way to the large group at the chapel's south door. Briefly Tari showed him three fingers spread against her thigh. *Three minutes! Give us three minutes exactly!* He showed no sign of seeing this, but instead veered briefly in my direction, beckoning.

"Hey, Humf! That you? How you doin? Coming down this end to see what the fun's about?"

"I . . . think I'll try the movie," I called back.

I realised I was very glad that Herbie was with us.

One by one we entered the library. It was dark, and almost empty. *Mary Poppins* had already begun. The movie was at the other end of the room. I followed the others through the darkness behind the beam of the projector to the side door into the chapel. Faint candlelight spilled through. The screen was still in place, and there was nobody to see us as one-by-one we slipped quickly through that door and then through the other one adjacent to it which led out of the chapel.

I joined Jud, Lucie, Tari, Jim Gage, Masanva, and the laundry bags. We were deep in shadow. "You ready?" Jud muttered. I nodded. Then he and I took off our helmets again.

The wind! I gasped.

I'd forgotten what wind felt like!

It was cold, with a hint of snow and the north. Instinctively I breathed deeply. It rushed like ice into my lungs, and I had to bend double to suppress a fit of coughing that threatened— yet as I straightened up again I felt life rushing through me, a flood of it! I had to restrain the desire to whoop for joy, and Jud did too, and we had to punch each other on the arms instead, in mute jubilation. No matter if it killed us! I was so exhilarated I almost forgot our business, but Tari tapped my arm as Clive and Utak joined us safely.

We had to be quick.

Jud and I stripped down to the uniforms. Jud gave me a guard's cap. He'd carried two of them under his coat. These went on our bald heads. Masanva pushed a pair of canvas shoes against my already-cold feet: our immunity-suits and Modern clothes went into the laundry bags, and I scrambled to tie up the shoelaces even as the shouting erupted.

The timing was excellent.

The eight of us moved, Jud first, myself last, but all of us close together, in an arc that took us for the most part through shadow to the back of the bus about forty yards away. We covered that distance in about seven seconds! We went straight past the rowdy shouting crowd all gathered round the squalling fight started by Brynjof, Thord, and Jim Guerrero. I heard Brynjof bellowing amid the uproar: "Solstice is *not* December twenty-fifth, Modern fool!"—and Jim shouting back, "It's *symbolic*, you mindless Viking idiot!"

The fight was brief, and was being broken up even as we reached our goal. Nobody had been looking in our direction but, as to the photoscanner eyes, we could not tell. And where was Herbie? With hearts in our mouths and in single file we crept up the narrow dark alleyway formed by the proximity and neat parallel of the bus to the South Block wall. Then, crowding each other, we dropped to hands and knees and waited anxiously as Jud carefully tried the baggage compartment door. If it was locked...

It wasn't.

Observation had told us it would not be locked, but nonetheless it was a relief to hear that slow faint rattling of our open sesame.

One by one, and as quickly as possible, those in front of me crawled into the dark cold space. *But where was Herbie?* I was cold, my teeth were chattering, I knew that anyone coming out of the gatehouse or passing in front of the bus might or might not see the dark moving shapes of us, and I was starting to clamber in last of all when without warning something solid slithered into me from beneath the bus. My breath hissed out... then I realised it was Herbie.

We joined the others in the baggage compartment even as the last of the shouting died away. The space was crowded, the ceiling low, the feet of Institute staff climbing aboard reverberating just inches above our heads as we arranged our-

selves in cramped squatting positions. As soon as Herbie and
I were in, Jud carefully lowered the door without closing it.
We'd considered this in Circle. If there were no inside handle
we'd have to keep the door slightly open or be trapped. "Nope,"
whispered Jud. He laid a thick wad of cloth over the locking
port in the deck, then let the door sit on it. It left a crack about
an inch high all along the bottom.

The next few minutes were dreadful. Over five minutes had
passed since we'd left the changing-room. It was impossible
to tell whether or not tonight there would be any large parcels
or baggage to be carried out. We squatted there in the blackness,
waiting for a sudden rattling-up of the doors, waiting to be
discovered as the Institute staff clumped and stamped into the
bus above us. Jud and I were both shivering violently. The
compartment was freezing cold, and smelled of oil, metal, and
gum. I feared I might be sick, but controlled myself. The
seconds ticked on . . . and on . . . and on. We dared not speak
or hope, or even think what would happen next, if we got out.

The engine started up!

It revved, throbbed, roared!

There was a slight jolt. We began to move . . . in reverse.
Then, an agonising thirty seconds as the driver shunted into
position for the narrow gateway. We moved forward. Next,
increased booming and reverberation told us we were in the
covered passage that burrowed through the South Block to the
world beyond.

From our questionings and Circle searches we knew there
was an outer perimeter wall with a gatehouse, then several
miles of semirural land, with two country stops, before a small
town. There were cities to south, east, and west, and a complex
of freeways to the immediate north. To stay at large at all
meant we would have to get out of the entire area very quickly.
It was a tall order.

In fact it was this apparent impossibility which had dis-
couraged many of us who might otherwise have been interested
in trying the escape, even though Mery-Isis had remained continually confident that Seven, or her Hawk, would see us through.

But first things first. We were almost discovered. At what
must have been the outer gate the bus slowed down. There
were shouts:

"G'night! See you tomorrow!"

"Happy Christmas, Sam!"

"Yeah, man, you too—*hey, hold on!*"

"What's the problem?"

"One of your baggage doors...I'll give it a slam."

Our hearts froze. We saw our castles melting.

"Naw, don't bother, there's nothing in there."

"It's no trouble, I'll just..."

"Forget it, you'll freeze your balls off. Just stay in there where it's nice and warm and I'll shut it when I get home. See ya tomorrow. Okay, man? See ya."

The bus picked up speed and we breathed again. A bad few moments, but it looked as if Seven was with us...so far....

Now we had to work quickly again. We had reached another crucial point, another door that opened one way only.

An electric flashlight came on, and then another, and I saw pale faces, gleaming helmets and suits, the eldritch circle of us crouching in this rattling metal witch-cave! Now! Time for those who'd not yet removed their helmets to do so. The suits could wait, there was no room to change in this cramped space— but it was agreed that we must at least all see each other's naked human faces before we separated into the two groups.

Tari and Utak easily removed their helmets for the second time. Then Jud, who held one of the flashlights, played its beam on Masanva, who was next to me. Masanva took off his helmet, and I was fascinated to see that great-headed man plain for the very first time. His eyes gleamed in the light like blackberries washed by rain, he wrinkled his face very slightly and pursed his lips as he laid the helmet down, and yet again I found myself trying to guess his age.

He looked at me, as expressionless as ever, and still I could see no bottom to those eyes, and he looked at each of us in turn as Herbie said, "Ready or not, here I go," and removed *his* helmet, followed almost all at once by Lucie, Jim, and Clive—and then we were all looking at each other, all breathing the air of 1984 as the bus rumbled away from Horsfield. And again, as in the changing-room, there were several seconds during which time seemed frozen, none of us knowing quite how to react or respond. Then Masanva opened his mouth and spoke for the second and last time.

"We have found common ground," he said. "This is very good, for the Dance will be danced before many more years are gone, and after it, those who live will find common ground as we do now, and make a new race out of all the peoples who have lived in this Fourth World. There will be war, and then there will be peace, and the peace will be good for as long as it lasts, and many new things will grow."

Then Masanva smiled.

It was a brilliant, joyous smile, there in the metal catacomb, and he reached forward and embraced Mery-Isis, who reached forward to meet him. And then, and only for a little while, but it was long enough, we looked on each other, and knew each other, and scrambled to hug and kiss and let the tears mingle. DTIs no longer, we were human beings again, and it was all worth it, no matter what happened after all this! We had found common ground, we had overcome the differences and the suits and the isolation imposed on us, and we were out of Horsfield. It was wonderful!

But the bus went rattling and rolling on.

"Good friends!" said Tari softly. "We must get ready now, the first stop is near, it is sad that we have to say goodbye so soon after hullo, but we must remember now what we're about."

The plan was that Jud, Lucie, Clive, and Jim would roll out at the first stop, and the rest of us at the second. Somehow we organised matters. Packages of bread and meat and drink had been diverted into the laundry bags: now these and the drugs and the clothes were divided equally into two of the bags amid a sudden tension. The joy was gone, now it was practicality again—and even so the first stop took us by surprise, for suddenly the bus was gearing down. The four getting out first scrambled into position, I got a foot in the face and Jim Gage panted an apology as Jud and Herbie snapped off the flashlights. Jud rolled the door up two feet, I reached out to take the wad of cloth he thrust at me: we had agreed on this. I took it and crouched, ready to take over the door as the bus came to a stop.

"Now! Go!" hissed Tari, and muttered something more in her own tongue that sounded like blessing as Jud, Lucie, Clive, and last of all, Jim, rolled out onto the dark road and wriggled away into the night even as the engine roared again and the bus picked up speed, so that in seconds these four were utterly disappeared, and not even time for farewells. And I have never known what happened to them.

Yet at least we had the chance to meet each other first.

That left Tari, Utak, Herbie, Masanva, and myself.

I laid the wad of cloth over the locking-port and carefully drew down the door. Light came on again. We stared at each other's wan and ghostly faces. Masanva was withdrawn into himself again. Utak's teeth were bared, his face clenched against the cold. Herbie looked gaunt, his cheeks pale and hollow. Tari's nostrils were flared, she was breathing deeply. Without the helmet her face seemed sharper. Yes...there was something of the fierce bird, the Hawk....

"Listen, you guys," said Herbie abruptly, "I'm the only Modern here...you know...I'll do my best...."

I liked him for that, and also for the fact that he'd cast in his lot with Utak and Tari and myself—for I think we all knew that Masanva would go on his own...*if* we got clear. We were not yet ten minutes out of Horsfield, but surely by now they had found out?

Our stop came. We were ready for it. Herbie took the bag and slid out first, then Tari, Utak, Masanva, and lastly myself. I left the door rolled up and wriggled after the others as the bus began to grind away into the night. We crouched at the verge of the road.

Behind us there was still no sight or sound of pursuit.

One passenger had been dropped. We heard tuneless whistling floating through the darkness as whoever-it-was waited. And even as the lights of the bus receded, the approaching beam of a car's headlights speared through the bare winter branches of trees above.

We were at a crossroads. The car approached at right-angles to the road by the side of which we waited. Herbie whispered a suggestion. We crouched, ready, as the car drew up. Then we did it.

Four of us rushed out of the night and seized both passenger and driver before the passenger was fully into the car.

The passenger was Ernstein. The driver was a slim dark woman, presumably his wife.

"Oh my *God!*" exclaimed Ernstein when he realised who we were.

"Never mind that!" snapped Herbie as he slung the laundry bag in the back of the car and gestured at the woman to get out and let him in behind the wheel. "Now both of you be smart and get in the back and don't make no trouble or we'll all be dead in a ditch pretty quick. Humf, you've got the gun, get in the back and keep 'em covered. Utak, if he won't get in, push him in. That's it. Get in the front. You too, Tari. And . . . hey . . . where's the old man?"

That's when three of us realised that Masanva had gone. While we had rushed the car, the Dancer had slipped away into the night, following his own direction. Tari knew. And gradually, as I got gingerly into the back of the strange machine, I realised that I had known as well. And Utak and Herbie, for none of us spoke of it further.

"Okay," said Herbie, checking the controls. "Shift-stick. Gears. Brakes. Lights. Good. I think I can handle this. Now, let's see if they make 'em like they used to!"

Apparently they did, for with a mighty jerk and clashing of gears he started us off again, with Tari and Utak beside him as perplexed as fish out of water, and myself hardly less so. I felt very unsure of myself as I waved the gun menacingly at our two terrified captives.

"Who are they? Norman, *who are they?*"

"Oh my God!" Ernstein repeated, in numb misery.

I introduced myself and the others as courteously as my shivering allowed, and apologised for the inconvenience.

"You fools!" Ernstein whispered hoarsely. "You'll die without . . ."

"Shut . . . mouth!" Utak demanded, a nervous angry tremor in his voice as he swung round. "You hear, Modern? Be . . . quiet!"

Ernstein heard. He and his wife were silent as Herbie clashed through the gears again and threw us from one side of the road to the other as the back-lights of the bus loomed in front. We went past it at such dizzy speed that I felt sick. I saw more lights ahead, hard bright globes in the night, but did not realise they were the lights of a town. Nor did I understand the orange glow in the sky to the west. But I *did* understand the meaning of the hideous wailing that started up suddenly through the night behind us. My fingers tightened reflexively at this evidence that our escape was discovered, and accidentally I fired the gun. It made a tremendous noise in the enclosed space. Luckily nobody was hurt or killed, for the bullet went through the roof, and Herbie, though from the shock of it he swerved almost off the road into a huge lit-up sign that said EXXON, recovered control amid the general confusion and shrieking of Utak, Ernstein, and Ernstein's wife, and started cursing me as he drove us rapidly through a small town without the slightest diminishment of speed. Red lights loomed before us, and other cars, but Herbie only drove faster, swerving wildly amid horrible sounds of mechanical screeching on every side. Dazed by this introduction to the U.S.A., I looked back and saw faces staring, someone running, and two cars which had apparently crashed into each other in our wake. Ernstein's wife was sobbing, Utak was shouting, I was mumbling about the cunning man, and only Tari was silent, for Ernstein was muttering "Oh my God ... oh my God ... oh my God!" over and over again, while Herbie wouldn't stop cursing me, calling me Humf-this and Humf-that, until I could take no more and roared to him TO STOP CALLING ME HUMF! "Okay, Humf!" he snapped back. "You want to get out? It's an awful long walk back to the sixteenth century. Just don't shoot that thing off in here again! I thought you had guns in your time."

"WHO ARE THESE LUNATICS?" wailed Ernstein's wife. "NORMAN, ARE THEY SOMETHING ... TO DO WITH YOUR WORK?"

It was not in fact very droll, though I represent it as such. It was insane. Ernstein wouldn't speak to his wife, though I could feel him shivering too, and next thing I knew, we were rushing up a curling concrete ramp that took us high in the air at dizzy speed to a vast roadway past another huge lit-up sign at our point of entry. The sign said: US84—WEST. I was stupefied by the size of this road, and at the speed we were traveling, and Utak gasped too, while by the lights over the road I could see the tight line of Tari's jaw: she hadn't spoken a word since we'd left the bus, though she seemed in better control of herself than any of the rest of us. As for Herbie, he appeared to be enjoying himself, for he chuckled, and smacked his lips, and leaned forward over the steering wheel. "Hey, this must be one of them freeways I heard about!" he shouted appreciatively as he swerved past two cars and a truck in a manoeuvre that made me feel sick to the pit of my stomach yet again. "Beats any roads I ever saw. Guess now we'll really see what this pile of junk can do! Hey, Ernstein, this thing's real easy to drive! What the fuck is it anyway? Ford? Chrysler? A European job?"

"Herbie," said Ernstein carefully, "you're doing ... ninety-seven mph, and ..."

"I asked you who the fuck makes it!" screamed Herbie.

"Oh my God," muttered Ernstein, casting a fearful glance

at me and the gun, which now I held pointed to the floor. And it was his wife who answered Herbie, her voice fearful, but unexpectedly angry and determined.

"Toyota. It's Japanese. And you don't have to shout!"

"Japanese? The fucking Japanese make *cars?* What in hell are you talking about? The Japanese never made *nothing!"*

"Herbie!" said Mery-Isis in a sudden sharp voice. "Be in control of yourself! Please!" And the dim front-seat shape of her turned to Ernstein's wife. "Woman, you must be amazed by this. You must think we are mad. I think your husband has told you nothing about his work or who we are. I assume that he *is* your husband? My name is Tari, as my friend Humfrey told you. What is your name, please?"

"Sandra!" said Ernstein's wife with an angry sigh, and would say not another word to Mery-Isis, but turned instead on Ernstein, and started to relieve her feelings by scolding him, accusing him of telling her nothing, threatening him with divorce *if* they got out of this alive, telling him (and us) exactly what sort of no-good excuse for a man he was, and refusing to believe a word of the truthful explanation about us that he reluctantly told her.

So we escaped Horsfield and roared into the night, into the United States of America.

PART THE THIRD

·❦[23]❦·

In Which Humf
Grows Very Thin

Soon I'll be gone from this place too.

It's well into April now. Yesterday I thought to celebrate my birthday and this reliving of the leaving of Horsfield with some rest and play. So I brought ill-luck on myself, by twice making use of that device, the telephone. The fiendish thing! Its disembodied voices make me tremble; I like to see folk when I speak to them!

Yet bodily needs denied my intellectual judgment. Hesitantly I called the pub in Brynafan and spoke to the girl at the bar who gave me the eye when I was in there a week ago. Her name is Grace. She said she would call back, and did. We mumbled for a minute or so, then she mentioned she had the evening off. I asked her here for supper. She said Yes, then No, then Yes, then No, but finally agreed to come, and to bring some supplies that I needed.

She arrived after dark in a battered old car. We got down to it quick, without misunderstanding or false modesty, and pleasured each other well. Afterwards she was regretful that she had to go.

"Keep quiet about this!" she insisted. I watched her, happily sad as she covered up her voluptuous form. "I'm glad I came, but I can't risk it again. Folk talk about me as it is, and about you too." She eyed me boldly. "You're a puzzle, and no mistake, with all your scars, and your talk of war . . . I just don't know. . . ."

I'd spun her my usual yarn of leaving Britain twenty years

225

ago as a mercenary soldier, to end up a drifter in America before coming back. Of the last two years I told more-or-less the truth, about the Lorry People, and how I was shot in York, and what I'm doing here.

"You don't believe a word I've said, do you?" I demanded.

"Doesn't matter what I believe, does it?" She shrugged. "It's no business of mine. But why won't you let me see what you've been writing?"

"I don't want anyone to read it until it's done."

"When will that be?"

"Soon. Very soon."

"What will you do then?"

"I have no idea," I told her truthfully.

"Well, you're an odd one," she said, putting on her coat, and then added, with apparent inconsequence: "The Lorry People are up the road in Betws-y-Coed. About sixty of them, with trucks and carts and caravans and big motorbikes, putting the fear of God in folk, though all they're doing is waiting."

I couldn't hide my interest.

"What are they waiting for?"

"Joe Thomas who knows them says they'll go on to Liverpool to join folk behind the barricades if the troops are sent in again—the riots, you know. Says they're talking of civil war."

When she went away she left me thinking hard. I decided to call Michael. He hasn't been in touch, and the month is almost up. So I got myself into the first of two bad surprises. I called York, but the phone was answered by Michael's married son, John, who usually stays in London. His voice turned ugly when he realised who it was:

"You, is it? Listen, Sir Humphrey Fraud or whoever you are, we don't want to hear from you ever again! My father's in the hospital because of all the strain you've caused him, and..."

"What?" I was greatly shocked. "But what happ..."

"None of your business! Well, I suppose it is. He lost his job, and his heart...he...he needs rest! Don't you dare bother him again! Understand? We want you out of that house and out of our lives! NOW!"

Then SLAM went the phone.

My God! I thought. Poor man. *If* it's true. He did sound

tired when we last talked, and it would explain why I haven't heard from him. Heart-attack? What should I do? I sat with many thoughts buzzing. I have almost no money, and if my association with Michael is to end so abruptly, then what am I doing here, writing all this? I should be out on the road already. But it's hard to abandon a task once begun. I decided I must finish all this, and get it at least to the alternative address we agreed upon. I *did* give my word!

Then the second surprise was sprung. As I thought on all this, a car drove up. I thought it was Grace back for something she'd forgotten. But no. There was a hammering on the kitchen door. Before I could speak a word, the door flew open, and in stumped Griffith's hostile son with two surly-looking friends.

"So you've been having fun with our amazing Grace!" he declared with pugnacious sarcasm as I stood up. "It won't do, boyo!"

"My friend, I..."

"Be quiet, now! Saw her drive past our house. Time we had a little talk, like. When will you be moving on?"

The way these things happen! I restrained myself.

"When I've done my work," I said, facing him.

One of his friends started forward with a brandished fist.

"You'll go right now, or else!"

"Hold back, Tom," said Griffith's son, then to me again: "How soon are you going to be done?"

"A week," I said flatly, holding his eye until he nodded.

"Right. A week it is. We'll be back to see you out. And you leave that girl alone or we'll break your legs. Okay, boys."

Very well! Very well! So I'm a fool. Now I've got six days to lay the ghosts that remain. I was furious for a while after they left last night, but soon cooled down, and at midnight walked up to the pagan stone. There's a finger of fate in all this: I must shed my husks and start out again. It was a clear starry night, very beautiful. I talked with Tari's ghost again, like the madman I probably am, and sensed the Hawk hovering like a shadow against the heavens. These are potent times, all know it, and yes, soon I'll take up the reins again, as she said I would.

Humf isn't finished, not by a long chalk! My mind grows clear, now that I sift through these memories.

So, to complete this task:

* * *

Thanks to Seven, and to Herbie's driving, we got away.

Between midnight and dawn of that Christmas Day he drove us from Horsfield to the shores of Lake Ontario. We used sideroads for the most part once beyond the city of Scranton, myself navigating with the aid of flashlight and maps in the car. Twice we stopped for gas from self-service machines, Herbie operating the pump and paying with money taken from Norman Ernstein while I held the gun on our captives. Utak and Tari wore hats to hide their baldness, and Herbie had a wool cap pulled over his head.

It was a strange and monstrous night. Towns and cities glowed in the dark like vast vague orange mushrooms: several times police cars wailed past us, Herbie having been persuaded to slow down to the legal speed. At first we couldn't understand why we weren't stopped. Both Herbie and I wanted to be rid of this machine as fast as possible, for surely by now it was known that Norman and Sandra Ernstein weren't at home, and as a matter of routine security the number of their car would be known to the Institute authorities? We argued this, but Tari insisted: "No! The Hawk protects us! He brought us this machine, we must use it to the utmost!" When we still argued, she said she intuited that the Institute files had a different type and number of car registered in Ernstein's name. At this Ernstein gasped, and in a low voice admitted to his wife that he'd forgotten to "update" his file with regard to this fine new car they'd recently bought.

So, Seven was certainly with us, yet we knew we must not push it. We were exhausted, and had to find somewhere to lie low. Crossing over into Canada was considered, but that presented too many unknowns, so we abandoned the idea. Also we knew that we could not let Norman and Sandra Ernstein go. They knew it too.

It was just as dawn rose, bleak and grey, that we reached Lake Ontario, passing through the tiny town of Albion, between Rochester and Niagara Falls. We explored small lakeside roads and, before day was fully upon us, found and broke into a locked-up summerhouse hid invisibly near the shore in a wood of willow-scrub, alder, and wind-twisted pine. There was farmland about: the nearest occupied building was about a mile away, and once again it was Tari's intuition that helped us, for it was she who saw the narrow track and persuaded Herbie to try it. As for Herbie, what he had done that night was prodigious, but his work wasn't yet over: he had to gather up his will and courage again and go alone in the car, taking all the money the Ernsteins had (about a hundred dollars, as I recall), to a nearby town (but not the nearest) where he successfully bought the food we needed, then returned to us safely and unseen.

We hid there a month. It was a miserable time. We hardly dared go outside, and had to watch the Ernsteins continually. The two-room cabin was freezing. There were blankets there, but little else, and we could risk a fire in the iron stove only at night. We told Ernstein how we'd escaped, though not about Circle: those left behind might still have need of our secrecy in that. And something else we discovered: the faculty for exchanging mind-pictures seemed to have died or gone dormant in us, perhaps because the circumstances of Horsfield no longer prevailed—now we could talk face-to-face with no need to hide what we said.

After two weeks a great blizzard came roaring off the lake, and in the middle of it Utak fell sick.

Of the four of us, he had found it hardest from the start, and had remained in a sort of bewilderment. Now he got pneumonia. The drugs did not help, though, as Ernstein sullenly confirmed, Tari had managed to loot a small fortune in Interferon. Utak sank quickly, having little will to fight, though Tari attended him constantly, and at one point seemed to have him on a road to recovery, for he sat up and began to take soup.

One night, storm howling outside, we all sat round the stove, wrapped in blankets, Utak in the warmest place. He was a little delirious, and began speaking of Kukulcan as though forgetting we were there. Then Tari, her face soft in the glow of the oil-lamp which was all the light we allowed ourselves at night, said:

"Utak, my friend, I have something to tell you. This *Kukulcan* of whom you speak—it was from the Two Lands he came. His name in our tongue was Naram-sin, and he was son of that Menes who united the Upper and Lower Lands and founded the First Dynasty. It is known that he sailed to the Land of the Setting Sun, and returned when his father died. It was he who brought your Big-Heads their knowledge of Number and Proportion—and that is how your people came to build the pyramid-temples much as we built ours, and for much the same cause."

Utak believed this; I was fascinated to hear them discuss the properties of these pyramids—how the shaping of their inner chambers could banish fatigue, and much other strange stuff which Norman Ernstein could not bear. Harshly he interrupted to say all such talk was rubbish and lies. Mery-Isis said nothing to this, but I could not resist reminding him that once *he* had told me *facts* which I had found incomprehensible, such as the age of the earth and the height of the towers in New York City. He fell silent at this, and his wife was silent too, for she had a horror of all of us, and was convinced we could not let either of them live. I do not think she was ever convinced by us. Whatever we or her husband said, she thought us to be but some exotic new kind of lunatics appropriate to lunatic times. Yes, Sandra Ernstein was my first meeting with that great disbelief which, ever since Vulcan, has afflicted so many, marching hand-in-hand with the equally irrational credulity of so many others. So, most people find naked truth intolerable and insist on clothing it with masks of their own preference. So, the circle is round. Why describe the way things are, Gilbert? Who wants to know what everyone knows? To Sandra it was irrelevant what time we came from. To her we were but four menacing bizarre bald people escaped from the Institute who talked funny, held her captive, and threatened her life. (As for the baldness, our scalps and the beards of the men were slowly sprouting with new growth . . . but Tari's fuzz was snowy-white, not raven-black, which was the only sign upon her of that horror of Vulcan or Set which she claimed to have met deliberately.)

No, I never got to know Sandra Ernstein very well, she maintained a spirited resistance to us, and to her husband as well, blaming him for getting her into this. I'm sure they could have escaped us had they chosen to work together, but they did not, being divided by their own opinions of each other where unity would have served them better, as it had served us. Perhaps she could even have got away on her own, but she never tried it, preferring to wait for us to act positively.

After a month we had to do this.

Utak walked out to his death, Sandra Ernstein fell sick, Norman Ernstein attacked Herbie, accusing Herbie of "trying it on" with his wife and infecting her. If there is any truth in this I don't know: certainly Herbie is the only one among us she liked at all. She could bring herself to speak to me with difficulty, but Utak and Mery-Isis she would not acknowledge at all, except in a vague and offhand way.

For Utak's fever returned. Deep one night as we all slept (I was supposed to be awake, but had nodded off) his sudden shouting awoke us all. I sat up in the dark, heard a confused moving, and Utak raving in his own tongue. I lit the light. We saw Utak on his feet, sweating and shaking all over, his eyes like hot coals in his congested face. But with the light he grew calm, and recognised us.

"I have had a dream in which I awoke from a dream," he told us with a curious tenderness, with reflective wonderment even as the breath rattled in him. "Now it is time for Utak to go, and seek the Perfect Number... in another land... more likely to... express it."

Then, with a slow, concentrated steadiness, dropping the blankets so that he went wearing no more than jeans and a shirt, he walked to the door, and out into the bitter weather. Yet first he met each of us in the eyes as he went, so that we knew we must not protest. And in the morning, when the storm was done and the sun up sharp and pale on the waters, we found him seated upright and crosslegged, looking east. He was stone cold, covered in snow, and quite dead. Tari spoke for his soul, and we took him down from the rock even as we saw a boat far out on the lake, and feared we were seen. We buried Utak as well as we could. Then we found that Sandra Ernstein was sick, and Norman launched his desperate attack which Herbie fended off with difficulty, and our food was almost gone, and the three of us knew we must go, whatever the risk, while we still had our own health.

So we did. We took the car and drove it south-west to industrial wastelands, where we quickly abandoned it, knowing that Ernstein would raise hue-and-cry against us. We had left them only lightly bound, so as to give ourselves two hours or three at most in which to get clear. None of us wanted to do them any worse harm. I hope that Sandra Ernstein got better.

The next few months are a blur of hardship and hunger. Both Tari and I depended on Herbie. He had the measure of this time where as yet we did not, and seemed to find conditions very similar to those in his own era, sixty years before. After we abandoned the car, he took the gun and left us in hiding. We waited while he went and robbed a store and stole another car. For a day and a night he drove and drove and drove. Tari was silent, and I could make no sense of anything I saw, and could not see what hope there was for us, and could not believe all Tari had said about her Horus-mission. I hated the endless roads, and the enormous cities which we avoided, and the need to avoid people for fear that our speech and appearance would betray us. We listened continually on the radio as we drove aimlessly about through Ohio, Indiana, Illinois, but heard nothing about us, nothing about the stolen car. Instead we heard about the perilous condition of the country, about the "Raydee" refugee problem, about the unemployment, the Crime Wave, the National Guard being called out to quell riots in this place and that. The forces of law had their hands full. One more stolen car was not important, nor robberies of corner stores in small towns. And of course we heard nothing at all about escaped DTIs. We were lucky.

Lucky?

Depression settled on Herbie and myself after too many days and nights of aimlessness and fear. Bickering and argument became more frequent between us, and Tari could not help: she remained calm, but we snapped at her too. And then Herbie fell sick. We had depended too much on him, he had taken too much upon himself, insisting on his personal responsibility to us, as though trying to take all the burden of America's Vulcan-guilt onto his own shoulders. One night in March he left us in a wood while he went off in the car, looking for another store to rob. We waited all that night and most of the next day, wet and cold. I complained and stamped about, and Tari endured it calmly, as she seemed to endure everything calmly, which only irritated me the more. At length Herbie returned, on foot, exhausted and sick and emptyhanded. He'd almost been caught, had only just got away. We were desperate. The weather was still severe; without food and warmth and shelter we had little hope of living. It seemed impossible that we could continue to survive and escape notice—especially given our ragged clothes and Tari's appearance—her striking face and the snowy sprouting of her hair.

Of course, what we did not take into account, being ignorant and concerned with our own problems, was that we were in effect no more than another three bums—drifters and vaga-

bonds and refugees—of whom at that time thousands were
about and abroad in the land due to economic policy, nuclear
disaster, and great social confusion. And if there was a special
call out for us in particular, we never met any evidence of it.

Yet our situation was poor. And Herbie went mad. Something in his mind had snapped. He raved at Tari and myself
as we trudged south at dawn along a deserted and sludgy country road. We approached a freeway, slicing across the flat
landscape. When he saw it he laughed and shouted at us that
now he'd show us "ancient creeps" how to deal with modern
America. Before we could stop him he ran ahead of us and up
onto the freeway, and he was killed. He ran out in front of a
car and straight under the wheels of a Coca-Cola truck. We
stared in horror as brakes screeched too late, as traffic began
to back up. Then Tari took me firmly by the arm. "Come,"
she said, "we can do nothing for him now but stay alive ourselves."

We survived. We slept in ditches, thickets, wherever we
could. We stole clothes from washing lines and ate whatever
we found. We kept moving, avoiding people, fearing dogs,
daring not to open our mouths to anyone we did meet. We
dosed ourselves with the drugs and remained alive. I had been
sick already, at Horsfield, and perhaps this helped. But Tari's
health was a wonder to me. She said that Horus and Isis within
her would not let her go to Osiris until she had done what she
came to this land to do. I learned to say nothing of this, perhaps
because I feared to believe it rather than because I could not.
Her strength and inner conviction never failed her, while on
many a morning I felt I could not get up and go on again. I
had dreams and fantasies not only about my former life but
also about the comforts of Horsfield. Yet she persuaded me to
keep going, and so we did, heading south. We grew thin and
hard, and my hate for this modern world grew into a terrible
loathing. Even the sight of a metal roof glinting in sunlit distance the other side of a valley, or of an electricity pylon
stamping on the land, was enough to enrage me. More nights
than not I had nothing to eat but this hate. I thought it sustained
me. Now I see it harmed and nearly destroyed my spirit, for
Hate is of the Devil, and gobbles up Life.

Often Tari tried to talk me out of it. She had no need of
hate. Even now she retained her zest and humour, inhabiting

a serene deep, an apparently illimitable reservoir of patience. When we hid deep in the Kentucky woods as springtime blossomed, she saw delight everywhere. While my mind brooded and gut grumbled, she *would* keep going on! Look at the curl of this petal! Smell it! See those beady little eyes that watch us! Listen to the song of the birds! Yes, this spirit was part of her health, but I hardly appreciated it, and often snapped at her, asking why couldn't she be realistic. Yet now I see she was. She was matter-of-fact about Vulcan, Horsfield, the U.S.A.; about her knowledge and needs and desires; and sometimes chided me for seeking in her something she said she was not.

"I'm not your mother, nor the Queen you lost, but a woman called Tari," she said sharply one cold night. "Why look in me for what you already have? Why your guilt and self-deprecation? Did your Christian Church do this to you? Is it what Christ intended? These Churches are as bad as the Priesthood of Amun became! *'Only through us!'* they cry. *'Dare not speak with the God yourself!'* "

"But we should not *presume!*" I snapped.

"No, never presume, but *become!* The neters work through us even if we do not will it, but that does not mean we have to freeze into statues! You don't have to be cold as the grave because life is not perfect! Please, stop this gallant rigid false respect you have for me, give up your hate, come and give some warmth and love!"

"How can I love amid this?" I demanded. "How should I *not* hate these people for what they have done to us?"

"Do you hate a blind man who denies sight? As for love, that is up to you and whether you can remove your Protestant armour that insists on being *offended* by the world. Why blame folk you never met for what's in yourself? Did you hate Norman Ernstein?"

"No . . . no . . . but the men responsible . . . the tyrants . . ."

"They'll get what fate they deserve. The Judges are not concerned with your hate, save so far as it clouds your own mind. Why hate? Leave it! Look up at the stars! We are on a path!"

Yes, I remember that night. We had been chased by two mastiffs who gave us up only after one of them tasted my leg and found it too scrawny for his liking. We were up a hill with trees looming about; we sat at a tiny fire that hardly warmed me at all, and I could see no practicality in what she said.

"What path?" I demanded angrily. "It looks downhill to me!"

But she was looking up in the starry sky.

"Look," she said, very quietly. "Look up there!"

I did, reluctantly, and for a moment thought I saw the silhouette of a great bird hovering high above, occluding the stars. Then it was gone, or I saw it no more—and it is of this night that lately I dreamed she showed me the rainbow bridge through Time.

"We will reach a gate soon," she said then. "The Hawk has promised it."

--►►{ 24 }◄◄--

With KRONONUTZ
in St. Louis

So we did. We met KRONONUTZ.

Early one morning Tari shook me awake. I opened my eyes to find her urgent face only inches away. There was excitement in her eyes.

"Get up quickly! There's a road twenty minutes away. We have a chance to meet people who'll help us! Come on! Now's the time!"

I stared. "What people? What do you mean?"

"I don't know yet. I saw a picture. It came and went, but I caught it. Now, get up!"

So down we went through the cold foggy woods as the sun hinted rosily behind eastern slopes, I following her brisk thin form with great doubt, but in twenty minutes or less we struck a narrow, winding road. Only a minute or so later we heard a vehicle approaching.

"These are the ones," said Tari, and without hesitation she stood out in the middle of the road, only yards from and facing a sharp bend. And I remembered what had happened to Herbie.

"They won't see you! They'll run right into you!"

"No, they won't. Come. Join me, Humfrey!"

I did, not knowing why, and only seconds later the vehicle— later I heard it was called a "minibus"—came round the corner at some speed. The driver saw us and gaped, and frantically hit his brakes. The brightly painted vehicle shuddered and screeched to a halt halfway off the road and to one side of us.

KRONONUTZ, read the flaming-lettered legend on the side

of the bus. Faces stared at us as the driver leaned out furiously.

"WHADDAFUCKYATHINKYADOIN? ICOULDAKIL-LEDYASTOOPIDBASTARDS!"

Tari eyed him in that interested way she had. The anger went out of his eyes. Puzzlement replaced it. He was a burly young man, bearded, wearing a green tee-shirt with the full moon on it.

"Good morning," said Tari calmly. "I am sorry we gave you such a fright but we had to be sure you would stop. We came out of the woods to meet you. My friend here is Humfrey, and I am Tari."

Her accent and the look of us took him aback as much as what she said. He turned and spoke to the other four people who sat beside and behind him. They all seemed quite young. He shrugged. Then he turned back to us and asked, in a much milder voice:

"Who in hell are you? And where are you from?"

"I am from Egypt," said Tari, "and Humfrey from England. We ask your help. We have not eaten, we have no place to stay, we do not know who to trust—but something told me you were coming and that you'll not do us harm. What is your name, please?"

"Jesus H. Christ! No! My name's Dan!"

"Hullo, Dan. What are KRONONUTZ?"

"We're a band—you know—rock'n'roll—listen—just hold it a minute. . . ."

He turned and talked again with his friends. I was confused and uneasy, like a suspicious wild animal. Tari's glance told me to hold my peace. I did not like the smell of oil and rubber, nor the way that shafts of rising sunlight through the trees gleamed so brightly on the painted metal. KRONONUTZ? Rock'n'roll?

"Hey." Dan turned back to us. "We're going to Saint Lou. Got a gig there tonight. If you wanna come along you're wel-come."

A door slid open and they made space for us. Very stiffly I followed Tari into the back of the vehicle, where we crammed ourselves down amid stacks of black boxes, odd-shaped cases, and other strange stuff. Five faces stared at us—four men and one woman. I cannot blame them; we must have been a sight, both of us filthy and ragged: I heavily bearded now in old coat and bib overalls and sneakers all covered in sticky burrs and falling apart; Tari in jeans and boots and torn sheepskin jacket over a tee-shirt we'd found somewhere that said: *I AM A MUSHROOM—They Keep Me in the Dark and Feed Me Bullshit!*—and her bone white hair, sprouting like a halo from her coppery head above those wide dark pensive eyes. And I think probably both of us smelled rather strong too, but our new hosts were polite enough not to mention this as the driver, Dan, started us off again. But they did stare, until Tari politely introduced herself again, and nudged me to do likewise, which I did with some difficulty.

Then they followed suit:

"I'm Chris," said the powerfully built young man from the front seat next to the driver. He had a bony nose, blue eyes, and a shock of blond hair. "I'm the drummer."

"I'm Sylvia." The woman, on the bench-seat behind the driver, was dark and had an intense face and her eyes were fixed unremittingly on Mery-Isis. "My folks came from Greece."

"Vic," said the gangling black youth next to her, his curious gaze flickering from myself to Tari. "Glad to meet you."

The fifth, sitting almost on my knees, courageously gave me his hand to shake. I took it carefully. His face was surly, his hair a mess, he looked exactly the sort whom once I'd have dismissed as a bumpkin. "I am called Johan," he said in a guttural voice. "I play the synthesiser. In Atlanta last night they throw rotten fruit at me. It is okay in New York but here they do not like the new music. I am from Europe too. How is it in England?"

"I . . . don't know," I said haltingly. "It is a long time . . . since I was in England."

"Ah." Johan nodded sagely. "Many people leave England now and come here. It is the same in Germany, where I come from. They are fascists everywhere in Europe now except where they are communists. Everybody wants to put everybody else down. Here there is more room and the people do not like to be told what to do. I play in England last year. There they throw stones, not fruit, and shout that I am elitist because I do not shout their slogans. Yes, many shitheads are here too, but some good people, and for me it is better."

"Where are you from in England?" asked the woman, Sylvia.

"I was . . . born in Devon," I managed to say, dizzily.

"Devon? Great! I was there two years ago. . . ."

"Hey, man," interrupted Vic—but he addressed Tari, not me, which confused me, "where you from in Egypt?"

Tari smiled. "I lived near . . . Alexandria. . . ."

"What're you doin' over here?"

"I have come looking for a new expression of what some would call the Life-Force," she declared slowly, her eyes bright. "There are many possibilities in this land, though it will take much remembrance of the purpose behind the foundation of these United States before the Force can know itself, before enough people find the will and courage to make a difference. Now tell me—what does KRONONUTZ mean?"

They looked at each other. Then Vic demanded:

"You mean you ain't heard about *chrononuts?*"

"No," said Nefertari Mery-Isis.

"Man, you really *have* been in the woods. You haven't heard about Project Vulcan and all those guys from other times that the government keeps shut up somewhere?"

Tari and I looked quickly at each other.

"Yes," said Tari, "we heard about that."

"Okay. *Chrononuts* are people who can't stand the way their lives are going, so they make out they're from other times and got kidnapped here by Vulcan. And that's like how *we* feel sometimes, like we don't belong here. So we're KRONO-NUTZ. I mean, we started out in skull-masks and stuff as THE DEAD ZONE—you know, that story by Stephen King—but we get a lot more bookings since we changed to KRONO-NUTZ. Guess it relates better."

"We wanted to call ourselves the DTIs," said Sylvia, still gazing at Tari, "but there's another New York band calling itself that."

"Right," Vic went on, "and we got this act on stage, we're all decked out in weird gear from different times and cultures. I come on like an Ashanti warrior and I've got this rap about how the white slavers grabbed me but I got away. Dan there makes like Daniel Boone, coonskin cap and all. Chris is a Viking. Syl does a Minoan priestess bit when we play big cities on the coasts where you can get away with bare tits and stuff, but out here in the sticks she has to cover up. And Johan's just Johan, like mad scientist in silver suit. We wanted him to wear Nazi gear for his big Raydee number, but he won't have none of that."

"I am a musician!" protested Johan, "not a goddamn clown!"

"Listen," said Sylvia. "Don't want to offend either of you, but I get this really strange feeling about you. What exactly did you mean"—she addressed Tari—"when you said you came out of the woods *to meet* us. That sounds like you *expected* us."

"Yeah," said Vic, "you said something *told* you we were coming."

"Sometimes I'm right about these things," said Tari, "and sometimes not. This time, I am glad to say, I was right."

"You mean, like *precognition?*" said Sylvia.

Tari looked blank. "I don't know that word."

"Seeing the future," said Sylvia.

Tari shrugged, still smiling.

"I saw a picture of you in my mind. I was sitting very quietly, and just for a moment I saw you coming." She eyed me for a moment before going on. "We would like to go to Saint Lou with you. We have no money to pay our way, but . . ."

"Forget it!" Dan called back over his shoulder.

". . . but we have a drug which I'm told is valuable," she continued, bringing one of the carefully wrapped bottles of Interferon out of her jacket. "Perhaps you know where we can sell it? We were in danger of sickness, but now I think we will be all right, and . . ."

"What is that?" demanded Johan. "Liquid speed?"

"No, I think it is called Interferon."

"Interferon?" Sylvia's eyes widened. I sensed a strong current between her and Tari. Later Tari said it was Sylvia's mind she had picked up that morning in the woods; and also how she thought that Sylvia had indeed once lived in Minoan Crete, about the same time as Tari had lived in Egypt, but that Sylvia had no recall of it. "Where did you get *that?*" Sylvia went on. "If it's not spoiled it's worth a fortune." And she grew more puzzled still as she stared into Tari's eyes. She tried to joke. "Just *when* do you come from anyway?"

"I think," said Tari, gazing straight back, "that possibly you and I were born within a few years of each other."

In this remark was a resonance that nobody cared to pursue so early in the day. And so we met KRONONUTZ, and went to St. Louis.

We reached St. Louis in midafternoon. I slept much of the way, save when we stopped in a dusty one-street town for food and a stretch of the legs. I was worried at the suspicious looks we got, but Vic told me to ignore them. Soon enough we were back on the road again, and I sinking teeth into the first De Luxe Hamburger of my life, and so hungry that I had no heed for beard, manners, or digestion. This I regretted later, somewhat, but at the time I was refreshed, and sat up energetically. I asked about this event to which we were going. In reply Sylvia unrolled and showed me a large broadsheet, or poster. At the top of it, in a row, were a number of ugly monkeyfaces, some in military uniform. Others, I was told, were the faces of prominent politicians and leaders of great corporations. Under these faces, in large red letters, ran a message something like this:

THE LIFE ALLIANCE DEMANDS AN END TO THE WARS IN GUATEMALA AND PAKISTAN! WE DEMAND THE TRUTH ABOUT VULCAN AND DAMASCUS, ARKANSAS! WE DEMAND FEDS OUT OF NATIVE AMERICAN LANDS AND ALASKA! WE DEMAND THE RESTORATION OF SOCIAL PROGRAMS AND CUTS! WE DEMAND AN END TO MILITARY INVOLVEMENT IN THE SPACE SHUTTLE PROGRAM! WE DEMAND AN END TO PENTAGON CRIMINALITY, AN END TO HARASSMENT OF MINORITIES, AN END TO NUCLEAR PROLIFERATION!!! JOIN US NATIONWIDE TO FIGHT FASCISM AT RALLIES IN NEW YORK, WASHINGTON, NEW ORLEANS, ATLANTA, ST. LOUIS, CHICAGO, DENVER, PHOENIX, LOS ANGELES, SAN FRANCISCO, PORTLAND AND SEATTLE ON 23 MAY 1985!!! JOIN US IN THE FIGHT FOR LIFE!!!

During the next few months I was to see many such posters, and to become much involved in all this, but at the time, of course, it made little sense, so as we drove along Sylvia and Vic tried to tell us what was happening in the land. They said that U.S. Government and corporate policies in many areas were arousing huge opposition at home and abroad, and that KRONONUTZ would be just one of many bands playing in the rally at St. Louis, and that also there would be many speakers for a great variety of causes. On the other side of the poster was a list of the names of participating groups who funded and supported this "Life Alliance." There were over seventy of them on the list. We were told that there would be many different racial groups protesting discrimination, and Gay Rights groups, and Women's Rights groups, and young men resisting the Draft, and many teachers, doctors, and administrators fighting the abolition of public services, and others fighting agribusiness, and nuclear policy, and chemical companies, and oil companies, and . . . on and on it went. "There's a whole lot going on that's been building up over the last five years," said Sylvia in an urgent voice, "and just lately it's got really mad what with the Slump, and Vulcan, and the Idaho Leak, and Damascus, and the Feds going into Indian lands for coal and uranium, and troops up in Alaska protecting the oil pipeline from secessionists, and the war in Guatemala, and eyeball-to-eyeball shit with the Russians in Pakistan. I guess there'll be some Raydees there tonight as well: the military deny responsibility for the Damascus ICBM and won't pay compensation; they say it was enemy sabotage; and the AEC insist that the Idaho leak and a dozen others aren't really that bad, even though people are dropping with cancer everywhere—I mean, it just goes on and on and on!"

But then my eye was caught by the enormous bridge we crossed over a great wide brown river. I gaped as we entered the city of St. Louis past a huge gleaming silvery arch that stood hundreds of feet high in the thick brown hot city air. Soon we were among buildings that dazed me with their size, with the severity of their glass-and-steel construction. But Tari did not seem impressed. "They have the proportion," she said later, "of monuments built by men more concerned with the size of their pricks than with healthy harmony."

Nor were the others interested in what so amazed me.

"Right," said Chris, continuing what Sylvia had been saying, "and what with the religious nuts going full blast it's a wonder anyone manages to stay sane at all. It can't go on. The Monster's gobbling itself up. Pretty soon it'll all blow up and we'll have to start again." He sounded almost cheerful about it. "The Hopi have prophecies about that, and Nostradamus too, I guess."

"Nostradamus?" I cried, as Tari gripped my hand warningly. "He was very famous in . . ." I was about to say, *"my time,"* but checked myself before the words came out.

In fact it didn't matter, for soon I would inadvertently take a drug called LSD, get up on stage, and babble out the history of Vulcan and Horsfield in front of one hundred thousand people.

* * *

One hundred thousand human beings, shoulder-to-shoulder? Nothing in my former life—not even the coronation procession of Her Majesty on the seventeenth of November 1558—had prepared me for such a spectacle.

The sun was low when at last we reached Forest Park and began our crawl through miles of parked cars, Dan flashing a Performer Pass at the stewards who waved him through the seething crowds and the great blare from the stage. I was amazed and nervous, and Tari was bemused at first too, but our hosts were too excited to note this as finally we reached the backstage area and found a place to park. They jumped out and started removing equipment as Tari and I eyed each other.

"You two staying here?" Chris asked, bright-eyed.

"Until we're used to it," said Tari, breathing deep.

"Sure thing. Hang about. You're with us, if anyone asks."

Fortunately there was no rock'n'roll band playing as we arrived there. Had there been, I think I might have turned tail and run all the way back to New Jersey without stopping for breath. It was bad enough as it was, with a vast amplified voice booming through the late afternoon. The words throbbed and echoed, reminding me of my welcome to the *Slocum*. It was as hard to understand them as it was to breathe the hot and sticky air, which smelled foul, and worried me. "There must be many... germs and... viruses here to which we are susceptible," I said to Tari in a low voice. "I think we should take some of the physic." Tight-mouthed she looked at me, then nodded in swift agreement. So, with crowds of people surging about, some of them rough-dressed and others dandified in bizarre ways, we sat in the minibus and swallowed several pills apiece, and also wet our thumbs with solution from one of the Interferon bottles, and licked. Johan saw us doing this as he came to pull out a long flat case.

"You are sure that is not liquid speed?" he asked suspiciously. "Why do you need Interferon? What illness do you fear?"

"Aw, leave them alone," said Sylvia, pulling him away as the giant voice rolled and thundered from the stage:

"*...The FBI act like Nazis on our reservations! Nothing has changed! You people ever hear of the Treaty of Guadelupe Hidalgo made in 1848? Promises, promises, promises were made, but...*"

"Who is this man who speaks?" Tari asked Sylvia, not shouting, but pitching her voice very sharp in order to be heard.

"Navaho guy, I think." Sylvia still stared intensely at Tari. "Biggest and richest tribe in the Southwest. Lately the army moved in on their land because of coal and uranium, and they . . ."

Her voice was suddenly drowned by a tremendous burst of cheering; and when the cheering died the angry voice roared on:

"Remember the words of our brother Russell Means! 'Rationality is a curse since it can cause humans to forget the natural order of things. A wolf never forgets his or her place in the natural order. Europeans do.' Yes! And so does the Washington President!"

For this the cheering was even greater. Sylvia left us, and I turned to Tari. I was shaking and afraid.

"What *is* this? What sort of world have we . . ."

But I stopped, because her eyes were very bright, her whole face was shining, and I could feel the power radiating from her.

"Can't you feel it?" she demanded, "This is why we came!"

I was taken aback by the speed of her adjustment to this mayhem.

"It may be why *you* came," I stuttered, "but leave me out of it!"

"This is where our work starts," she said in an intent voice that chilled me. "There's Hawk-energy here, but all divided, without focus, not knowing itself. Surely you can feel it!"

"It's madness!" I cried, near panic. "How can people live amid a tumult like this?"

She shrugged. "Of course it is different to what you knew, and to what I knew. Now"—she eased herself out of the minibus onto the grassy ground—"I am going to look about. Are you coming?"

I wavered, caught between fear of discovery and fear of loss of face, then realised that sooner or later I must step into this wild new world. So I followed Tari into the crowd. We were both still filthy and ragged but, as we pressed our way round the side of the huge covered stage, I found out that this hardly mattered; many other people looked just as tattered—though closer inspection soon showed me that most of them were not tattered at all, their "rags" in many cases being artfully made to give the *impression* of poverty. This I could understand no better than false wood and the rest of it, but later Sylvia told me it was part of a recurrent craze for well-off folk to spend a lot of money in order to look poor. "Guilt is part of it," she said, "and *looking* poor helps to avoid being mugged by the *real* poor. It's a crazy world."

Before leaving us, Sylvia had given us ten dollars. "I'm very thirsty," I shouted at Tari. "Perhaps we can buy an ale, or a Coke."

She didn't hear me, but pressed on. I struggled after her, giddy already, pushed on every side, taken aback by the near-nakedness not only of many men but women too, feeling attacked by the booming from the stage, by the shouting of hundreds of people, by the pandemonic blare of loud dance-music from radios at close-quarters. I passed bright-coloured stalls and kiosks from which wafted the aroma of hot dog, hamburger, fried chicken, and then, with Tari somewhere in front of me, I found myself in front of the stage, looking out over the vast audience seated or standing on the natural grass amphitheatre. Here for a moment I stood, trying to collect my wits, and saw a big man with a spadelike beard, a hairy chest, and a leather apron over blue jeans. He carried a big red plastic bucket and a stack of paper cups, and he was giving cupfuls of the bubbly drink in the bucket to anyone who wanted one, winking at them as he did. I licked my dusty dry lips, and he saw me watching him. "Hey," he said, casting an eye about as he did. "You like some pepsi, man? You know, real special, like way back when—none of that Jim Jones shit."

"Thank you," I said. "That is very kind of you."

"Sure thing." He gave me a cupful. "Have a good one!"

I drank it down quickly. It did very little for my thirst. Grimacing, I looked for Tari.

I couldn't see her.

The crowd had swallowed her up.

I had sufficient presence of mind to mark where the KRON-ONUTZ bus was. Then, feeling I must press on into this amazing new world, I did so.

It must have been about an hour later, with the sun setting in a muddy blaze of ochre-tinged reds and yellows, about the time when KRONONUTZ came on stage after a succession of angry speakers, loud announcements, and continual tumult, that I began to feel very strange indeed.

* * *

In the first place, as will be clear, the monstrously loud rock'n'roll was an experience as initially terrifying in its way as anything I ever encountered, including war, including Vulcan, including the night of our escape from Horsfield. Nothing in my life had prepared me for it—and I was right in front of one of the banks of loudspeakers when it began. Yes, at Horsfield I'd heard a little of the modern music, and had not much liked it, I whose experience was limited to a gentle galliard, a stately pavane or frisky almain. I could play the lute with some proficiency, and had tried viols, flutes, and sackbuts, and even the harp. Dowland was popular in England in my time; Batchelor and Bulman and Cutting also had their following—and I used to enjoy a merry rush around the Maypole as much as anyone else—but of course none of this was any preparation for the insane assault that my gentle KRONONUTZ acquaintances unleashed upon me.

Nor of course had I any experience of this drug, LSD, all those drugs administered to us at Horsfield being of other sorts altogether. And even before KRONONUTZ began to play I knew I was feeling most odd. I stood amid the multitude as I first sensed, apparently from the back of my skull, dizzy upward-surging waves of some force or power released in me, distorting all my senses and giving rise to a combination in me of terror and glee combined. Then I think I began to wander about, not clearly knowing who or where I was.

Then . . . it began:

"OKAY, OKAY PEOPLE . . . FROM NEW YORK . . . KRONONUTZ!!!"

The first onslaught of electric shrieking struck me with Vulcan force, and threw me into the Vortex, falling, falling, spinning round and round, buffeted by the howling of fiends. I tried to face the source of this attack, I saw figures on the stage, and did not know them, nor knew it was a stage. I saw a Viking beating drums, a black warrior fingering an instrument that put out deep throbbing sound, a burly bearded man in buckskin with fringes who had a smaller instrument, coloured red, that screamed and wailed under his fingers. I saw a woman of Mediterranean type clapping her hands and swaying, and a surly gnome on a stool bent over an instrument from which he tore a wavering, curdling sound that was surely Satan screaming! Then, as I gazed flabbergasted and stripped of sense amid the Vortex, with the waves of power still pulsing ever-stronger through me, the woman stepped forward to an upright stick with a black ball atop it; she gripped the stick and put her mouth to the black ball, and started wailing words to the intolerably loud and rapid rhythm. Of course I made no sense of it then, but it was a piece I heard often enough in later weeks and months, and I read the words as well:

> *Damascus Arkansas*
> *Damascus Arkansas*
> *Whatcha wanna do that for?*
> *Blow us up and melt our bones*
> *Make us sterile and wreck our homes*
> *Now I piss plutonium every day*
> *My teeth fell out and my hair turned grey*
> *So I went for compensation but*
> *You know what they say?*
> *They say:*
> *Whatcha wanna come here for?*
> *Whatcha wanna fall down for?*
> *You gotta walk on your own two feet*
> *So join those others on the street*
> *And if you're dying, don't do it here*
> *Go on home, boy, just get on home*
> *To Damascus Arkansas!*
> *To Damascus Arkansas!*

And I was suddenly sure I was in Bedlam, amid the babbling insane, and I thought I saw the cunning man leering at me from a dozen, from a hundred shifting faces in the swaying crowd that shouted and screamed and danced all round me; and I was screaming too, at the prancing figures on the stage which, lit by flashing colours, was a parlour of demons. For their noise split sanity like an axe splits wood. What happened next? How can I say? I was falling forever through seas of flame, in the grip of the Power not of Christ, locked on the operating table, pressed deep by THE THING—then of a sudden, amid many other potent images passing so fast I could not catch any, I seemed to sense the Circle and, without knowing it (but later recollecting) I was split into the Circle, into images of those I remembered—I was Utak, the giant noise drilling holes in my skull and eating my brain, *chomp-chomp*, the howler monkeys chasing me through the jungle, the people burning the city; and Senor Bernardino de Oveido de Azurara, screaming in Spanish (later they said I did this when I burst onto the stage), and Coningham, amid the bombs bursting, the bullets screaming; and Blund berserk with an axe, amuck and seeing red—red, red, it was all red—and the only restraint was an image of Tari, her face calm and thoughtful, contemplating this madness with a dispassionate interest, considering what it meant and what its function might be in the progressions and setbacks of Evolution in Eternity—only this image had any power to restrain me as, without reflecting on it, I pushed closer and closer to the source of the utter disruption, to the devil's kitchen where brew was cooking to wipe out the world, where the meat of the mind was being boiled down to the bones. It was repulsively attractive in a terrible way that I could not resist, as if my bones were doing all my moving for me. Then KRONONUTZ came to the end of *Damascus Arkansas,* which was greeted by a great roar—then almost immediately they were off into a new piece I also came to hear often enough, about Vulcan:

> *Someone pressed a little button*
> *And history fell through Vulcan's hole . . .*

And while this began and continued, this subject of their song, now as mad as a hundred hatters, pressed on through the mob, and some things I saw were unbelievable even without the drug, the noise, the situation—I saw a man walking about whose *skull-cap* was lifted up, hinged at the back, showing the brains beneath, they being covered by some sort of plastic membrane—he was cool as you please, and I could not believe it, but later learned this to be a new cult activity; the notion being one of public exposure and self-advertisement—"coming out of the closet for intellectuals," as Dan contemptuously called it. He said that these Freebrain Cultists were numerous on the West Coast, as I was to discover for myself; their rationalisation being that Modern Man's brain has grown too fast for skull capacity, thus being compressed and reduced in efficiency; this elevation of the top part of the skull apparently promoting oxygenation, stimulation, and lucidity. They claim that in the past some people used to drill holes in the skull for these same reasons; and also say that the world is mad now because too few people have holes in the head.

This was a surprising thing to see. So too was the sight that met me next as (all unknown to my normal self) I came up

against the guarded approach to the stage and found myself
confronted by a riot-prepared policeman. This being was dressed
all in black leather, with helmet over his head, and visor mask-
ing his face, and so many weapons and paraphernalia slung
from his bulky body it seemed a wonder that he could even
stand up. I stared at him; he snapped something unfriendly, so
I continued my dazed wandering, looking for I knew not what
as the noise continued to crash and roar. And how I got onto
the stage I have no memory at all, but later Sylvia said she
had seen me, and sent someone to bring me up—though what
gave her this idea she could not tell—and neither did she know
why, as I appeared onstage at the end of a KRONONUTZ
number, she led me to the microphone and told me to say
whatever came into my mind.

It was then that Tari, deep in the crowd, saw me and realised
that the Hawk was at work. She dismissed her contemplations
immediately and came to the stage as quick as she could, where
at a gate she flashed a piece of paper the colour of a Performer
Pass, and went straight through before the policemen there
could really see it.

By then I was already babbling full-blast.

First when I held the microphone I said into it:

"HORSFIELD! HORSFIELD! THEY KILL US AT HORS-
FIELD!"

I didn't speak loud, but the sound of my voice jumped back
at me with huge power, and split my mind again, and what I
said after that, as later I heard from the tape, was a demented
babble:

"AT SEA! AT SEA! THE QUEEN WILL GIVE US TEN
THOUSAND POUNDS! I'LL NOT FORSAKE MY LITTLE
COMPANY! WE ARE AS NEAR TO HEAVEN BY SEA AS
BY LAND! THE POWER NOT OF CHRIST HAS US! BAIL,
YOU BLACKGUARDS! BAIL BEFORE WE'RE SWAMPED!
THE FIRE! THE FIRE! THE CUNNING MAN PREDICTED
IT TO ME! THE MONSTER SLOCUM SNATCHED US
FROM THE SEA! SNATCHED US FROM TIKAL AND
BUTO AND DEVON AND CARTHAGE AND TYRE AND
THE HORN OF AFRICA! SNATCHED US FROM CEN-
TURIES AND TIMES AND SHUT US UP IN WHITE-SUITS
AND CALLED US DTI'S! AT HORSFIELD!—"

There was more, much more, but at some point Tari reached
the stage and caught Sylvia's eye, calling her over and quickly

telling her half the truth of the matter: that we were fugitives, not for doing evil, but from evildoers. She said they had to get me off the stage and both of us away before we were seized. Sylvia came and spoke to me but I was in full flood and would not hear her, so she pulled the plug on the microphone. I was shocked as my giant voice suddenly vanished. So was the crowd; its displeasure sounded like surf crashing onto shingle as, rapidly, I know not how, I was bundled offstage and into a car, Tari following me, she having already told KRONO-NUTZ that if questioned they should deny all knowledge of us.

This must have left them as bewildered as I was, but even as the car moved off, with two people in front whom we did not know, the music started again.

We were taken to a discreet place outside the city as guests of friends of KRONONUTZ, who joined us there later, saying they were sure they hadn't been followed. I was still babbling, and that night Tari told Sylvia the truth, setting her hands on the girl's head and showing her mind-pictures that persuaded her. The men in the band were not so easily convinced, yet were curious. When I mentioned the drink in the red plastic bucket they explained about LSD, which a week later Tari tried for herself. After sitting quietly for hours she said that it is an Opener of the Ways, if not the best guide for one with no previous experience of the perilous secret levels.

"Well, Humfrey," she said after my strange experience, "you made up my mind for me, about telling Sylvia who we are."

"Not I," I said, "but the drink in that cursed red bucket!"

"The Hawk was in it, and in Sylvia!" She eyed me steadily. "Now these people know about us. Whether or not they believe it, they'll protect us, so the seed begins to sprout. Our work is begun!"

"*Our* work?" I demanded angrily. I was exhausted, and bemused by all that had happened since that morning in the Kentucky woods.

"Yes, Humfrey! *Our* work! Are you still thinking in terms of *accident?* Can you *still* believe we were brought here for nothing?"

"It's madness!" I snapped. "What do we do to awaken this Horus you speak of? What if it's work of the Devil?"

"I know what I serve!" I had never seen her angry before.

She was tired too. "How do you think we gained the spirit and purpose to escape Horsfield? The Gate is open, we must go through it! We have our work, as the Dancer has his! No more of this weak talk!"

"And how do you know that Masanva still lives?"

"He is! We have dream-walked! He will not slip!"

"Well, so when will we see the sense of this lunacy?"

"If you will not see it now, then you will see it later!"

"Good!" I sneered, perplexed and fearful. "Proof of the pudding's in the eating! When I see your wondrous Hawk aloft in the sky, and the kings and princes of this mad world bowing down before him, then I'll believe it, and not before!"

"Look in your heart, man!" she flared. "The Hawk's no tyrant, but a fire of wings that'll beat in your heart and burn away your dead ideas and bring you strength—if you want it!"

And to this I had no answer but weary silence.

·····{ 25 }·····

How Set Struck
the Hawk in Denver

Seven months her mission lasted, and I at loggerheads with it all the way, clinging to patterns in which Humfrey Gylberte had been formed, afraid to take that leap into the abyss which any true fool can and must take before any progression can be won.

For two weeks, until we were sure that no ill might arise out of my public rant, we stayed in the house of Ron and Eileen.

These are not their true names.

During the first week we were secluded, recovering from our long ordeal. Days passed before I began to grow calm. We ate and slept and bathed, and heard talk of what went on in the land. During the second week people began coming to meet us, Tari telling our hosts we were ready for this. They were friends of KRONONUTZ to begin with, but soon we had spoken with such a variety of odd individuals that I was utterly out of my depth. Doctor Dee would doubtless have enjoyed himself with these students of hidden things, and of course Tari was quickly active, guiding meditative groups of people on long inner journeys. This she did by way of triggering words and symbols that struck in their hearts and created in them resonant images of ways of thought long alien to western culture. I had little to do with these group adventures, preferring to closet myself privately with books.

At first it had seemed that Sylvia alone accepted our tale, by some inner prompting that she trusted. Nonetheless, though

many others would not believe us so easily, most seemed open
to the possibility that we told the truth. We learned that there
had been a great public furore about Vulcan, and many strange
rumours about the DTIs, which had been utterly denied by
Government and Pentagon. Such utter denial was taken by
millions as sure indication that DTIs did exist; a cynicism that
seemed remarkable to me. Moreover, in the early days of 1984
several people involved in Vulcan had published their lucra-
tively disapproving accounts of the ugly affair, and official
papers had been leaked, "... *until the 'accidents' began*," said
Syl drily one night, "*and since then people have kept quiet*."

And soon (though it seems to stand against us) I realised
how many folk in times like these have need to believe in stuff
of dreams, some even substituting their fantasies for the un-
bearable truth. Well, folk always did that, but now it is a great
industry, what with television and the movies, and games such
as *Dungeons and Dragons*—and of course it is claimed that
"Chrononut Cultism" is but an extension of such; and that
chrononuts do but project their inner mythic dramas onto the
unpleasant outside world. No doubt in many cases this is so;
I have met such people, who believe a mystic word will feed
them better than a solid meal, who try to foist their untutored
wishful thinking onto others as the truth. Yes, quite a few of
those who approached Tari and sometimes myself were lost
souls seeking approval for their particular schemes of belief.
They wanted to know about pyramid prophecies, spacemen
from Sirius, the nuts and bolts of the spirit-world. Often enough
they offered a bargain:

*I'll believe in you if you believe in me. I'll believe your tale
if you'll give me a sign and tell me what to do.*

This always horrified me. I'm a simple soul, and never
learned how to deal with it. "My good fellow!" I'd bluster.
"Why should I know any better than you what to do?" At which,
though some would thank me for honesty, more often I'd be
shot a look of hate.

Tari knew how to deal with them.

She never said much, she'd sit and consider the guru-seeker
dispassionately, then give him or her some task to perform.
Many of her "tasks" seemed absurd—"Learn to walk on your
hands, and do so every day for at least five minutes until six
months are up. Then you'll know what you are and act of that
knowledge."

"But what *is* this nonsense?" I expostulated once after hearing her tell an infatuated woman to learn to walk a hundred yards every day for a year with an orange balanced on her head. "What has this to do with your rebirth of Horus?"

"Humfrey, you want everything to be obvious and measurable!"

"It is true! I appreciate clarity in thought and deed!"

"The man who sweats to walk on his hands will learn the value and benefit of good balance on his feet. The woman with an orange on her head will start seeing through the rubbish she presently believes because she has to hold her head still—*if* she does as I say. Humfrey, mystic belief is positively destructive if used only to flee a world we've made unpleasant through general ignorance. We're here on Earth to bring the powers of the mind into harmonious manifestation, and fantasy has its place in this—but how can anyone do anything worthwhile without learning balance and self-control?"

"Oh, come!" I said. "What would you have *me* do?"

She regarded me frankly, with the trace of a smile.

"Take up the sport called hang-gliding," she said. "Learn to soar, forget your night and seek the Dawn!"

After St. Louis we began passage through many cities, hosted by an ever-broadening network of friends of friends of friends. Now I am glad we were not in Europe, where too many people have known too much for too long to believe in anything new, where the suspicion is deeply rooted that the future must prove even worse than the recent past with its two world wars. There are many idiotic beliefs in the U.S.A., but the other side of the coin is this: Where many people need to believe that the impossible will soon be possible, then *some* of the impossibilities become first of all possible, then probable, then realised fact. And before I die I would like to walk on the Moon. *Quid Non?*

Yet the cities troubled me. It was not so much their size and foul atmospheres as their continual *shivering*. Tari also felt the strain of these jungles. "Their designers were ignorant of the best shape of things," she said. "A well-made city is a temple, like the body, in which vitality increases. These cities have vampire-souls. They *drain* people. Yes, Red Set is in the counting-house, the Hawk is still in jail. I smell it everywhere. But it will not last."

The truth is that less and less I believed her Horus-talk. Her qualities and power which in Horsfield had so impressed me now had me irritated, the more so as they seemed to impress others. Increasingly I assumed the role of devil's advocate, often publicly contesting whatever she said, thus as I thought preserving something of my pride, identity, and sense of independence. I did not realise nor admit to myself how in the eyes of others I must have cut an angry, stiff, somewhat ridiculous figure, upholding beliefs and principles many of which are now suspect, condemned, or disregarded and forgotten. I remained trapped in the dramas and assumptions of my own time and culture; Mery-Isis looked underneath the surface to principle and function, and was thus more rapidly "modern" than I. She did not feel personally threatened and insulted by the United States as I did, and each person she met, she met as she would have met anyone in any time, directly, with humour either gentle or sharp according to the situation. But I quickly forgot the Circle and began asserting Gilbert's old arrogance as a mask for my uncertainty. Now I see I must have been difficult to deal with. Yet whatever gaucheries I committed, I was well treated by many who had no obligation to be friendly, though often I found my loud opinions severely tested, and had difficulty restraining my temper. In fact, I lost most of the tolerance I had learned at Horsfield, and soon I was keeping at quite a distance from Tari and her work—most particularly when she was closeted with people versed in occult or esoteric disciplines. At times we moved in different circles for several days without meeting. She accepted that I did not regard the work of the Hawk as being my work, and did not press me. For politeness' sake I would ask her what she had been up to; she would say quietly that things were going well here, or not so well, and that a new channel had been opened up, or that in this place the way was seriously blocked. It was all too vague for me, but I demanded it that way; and somehow managed not to observe that I was living amid a most energetic and well-managed state of affairs. We were moved steadily and smoothly from one location and group to another without any apparent difficulty. This did not last, but while it did I had some perverse need to diminish it.

What did Gilbert do while Tari pursued her work which many seemed to recognise as valuable? Well, Gilbert was busy turning into Humf the Idiot, taking pleasure where it was offered and despising it when it was over, continually comparing the present unfavourably with the past, clinging to the night. It was remarkable how many women, and some men, wished to sleep with this man who claimed to have been the brother of Sir Walter Raleigh and to have personally known Good Queen Bess—and remarkable too how much advantage I took of all this while getting so little pleasure from it. It was remarkable how much I ate, drank, and slept, and how little attention I paid to what was going on. It's not good enough to claim I was still in shock. Perhaps, but in that case we might all claim that the shock of being born is enough to excuse us whatever we do in our lives. For months there were friendly strangers in two dozen cities to take care of my needs. Many people took risks and put themselves out for us, and even if some wished almost to deify Tari *(ancient Egyptian priestess! strong magic, man!)*, most knew what I had forgotten and only now begin to remember—appearance is not what counts. They were willing to admit the worst as well as to claim the best about their energetic and self-obsessed culture. How can *I* fault them? Americans are good enough at faulting themselves, in many cases, and are often alive to the problems of their imperial power. No one nation or system holds a monopoly on wickedness or righteousness, and most of the people I met forgave me my arrogant disdain, my disbelief in their belief.

So, I played the fool while Tari worked, disregarding what she did, while at the same time (without admitting it) depending on her for my balance, having no real assurance of myself.

Soon enough I found this out.

The tragedy began in Chicago.

We spent Christmas week as guests of a poet and his strikingly beautiful wife who was involved with Wicca, this being a modern inheritance of the Old Religion which in my day was known, denounced, and persecuted as witchcraft. Now, I found, though witches are no longer burned, they are often the butt of those kind of jokes which men like to level against women. Whether or not this is preferable depends on the urgency of your desire for martyrdom. At any rate, during these months I learned, despite myself, of the hidden tradition of knowledge which has run through the centuries from long before Tari's time to this: a lunar way, not opposed to solar masculine science and reason, but aspecting it with intuition and dream—and much of Tari's work was and is involved with this urgently necessary Marriage of Sun and Moon. But, as I say, I avoided all this, and, like Doubting Thomas, believed only what I wished to believe, which was not much, and this because I was afraid. I have heard it said how in the Country of the Blind the One-Eyed Man is King: well, I fear that for too long I chose to be among the blind.

I'll call our hosts John and Jane. It was not their fault. The snowball had grown too large.

One evening just after Christmas and a year since our escape, over fifty people gathered to meet us. It was not an open house, but by no means everyone knew everyone else. Some of those present were well-known: there was a famous pianist, a best-selling writer, a high-energy physicist whose work had led him in an occult direction. Sylvia of KRONONUTZ was there too: we were glad to see her.

The evening began well enough, yet I had trouble with a supercilious academic who grilled me to learn if my "racist imperialist" attitudes had changed now that I had tasted my own medicine; with a man who couldn't believe that I'd never met Shakespeare or Marlowe; with a woman who wanted to know what I was doing afterwards—and so on, and on, until soon enough I joined the larger group round Tari.

She was splendid that night in a long blue dress. Her snowy hair had grown out considerably, contrasting with the coppery highlights of her sharp, animated face. She wore no jewelry or emblems, and needed none, for her eyes were jewels enough, as I had to admit despite the reserve I'd developed. There was something almost transfigured about her that night; a quality attracting people like moths to a flame. All afternoon she had been closeted with a group, leading them on a mythic journey through their own brains to what she called "The Seat of Isis in the Temple," which as I understand had something to do with the pituitary gland, and the teaching of self-control of hormonal secretion—all of it beyond me, as I demanded.

Now, still fresh and enthusiastic, she was speaking in her low quiet voice of the need in a healthy society for understanding of how the mythic sphere of mind works in the everyday, and of how in the world today there is generally poor recognition of such things even when transparently clear, as in the recent *"long live the king; the king must die"* spectacle of President Richard Nixon; a crippled tyrant who (as I heard) confused himself with his office to such ill effect that his sacrifice was demanded and consummated by the people.

"Some tell me," she said (for I remember it plainly now, as if I am in that room again and listening to her now), "that Americans and Russians and so on no longer have kings and such. Not so! Changing the title and means of accession does not do away with the function, though it endangers understanding of what's involved. Kings and presidents are *representatives* on earth of the inner organisation of individuals: society and ruler reflect one another. This has not changed much. Over three thousand years separate my time from this, but what is that? We are all in the boat of millions of years: do you really think your basic needs and capacities so different from those who went before you? If so, why permit presidents and rulers? Why is the predominant understanding so Roman, with spirit denied and material power elevated above all else? Why are the blind exalted to confirm the blind in the virtues of blindness? Where is the spirit of your Constitution, which was set out by initiates? Why is the secret wisdom still secret, disregarded by many as fabrication and fantasy, unknown to most? *None of these things must be hidden anymore!* Is this a new message? No! It is two thousand years old! Christ proclaimed it, that from henceforth initiation was open to all, that divinity is revealed in humanity, that religions which deny each other or which refuse to explain themselves are not religions at all, but imposture! Did he not make it plain? And did not the institutions sprung up in his Name then proceed to hide it all over again? Yes, I hear the Churches have brought some good, but for the most part what have they done but wear the outer garment while persecuting the heart, damning and demonising those very traditions from which the Christ emerged? And how do I know these things, I from so long ago? By reading in books? Certainly—I have learned much since the Hawk brought me here—but there are other sorts of books that were written long ago, and not in words. Words are but the outer seal of truth that awaits progressive fulfillment through the ages. True prophets are true scientists who see the shape of things eternal that descend into human embodiment to work their passage through into what is realised on earth.

"Now, in this age, much has been realised and mastered in

the physical world by development of intellect and individual capacity. This is good and necessary—but the price is heavy: other things have been forgotten, distorted, cast down. Now it is time for us to recollect our denied faculties, to pursue a general establishment of that Inner Light which the persistence of gravity and ignorance will always drag down into selfish darkness if not firmly opposed. There is no easy victory. Only fools without sense of history can even hope for it. The Boat has far to go yet: this age is but a particular note in the progression. History spirals between what we perceive as opposed extremes: the pendulum now is at a critical point, for the unconscious and untrained creativity of the species has materialised demons on the earth. But there is a new principle that beckons, demanding recognition, for Light is born out of Dark. The doors are opening again, and if we refuse to go through them, then much will be lost. The technological Modern is not to be cast away, but it must seek balance through the rediscovery of most Ancient wisdom in heart and mind. Individualism and Socialism are curses without the balance of each other; so too are men and women! The Female Principle will be restored! *Women's Rights* are not enough; they do but ape male error. *Initiation* is what is required! A new Child is manifesting! The birth may come about in chaos or in reverence— the choice exists: everyone must decide. History is a vast alchemy of transfiguration: we are the alchemists; our Work is ourselves and the raising of Nature. Why are we here, if not to learn to carry out functions that the eternal and ethereal Principles alone cannot express?

"Some speak of History as *accident!* They deny Intelligence to that which grants it in us. How absurd! How irresponsible! If you put your hand in the fire and get burned, is that *accident?* If a stone is thrown in a pond, are the ripples *accident?* If ignorant Caesar hungry for power presses a Vulcan button and gets a result he did not expect, is that *accident?*"

"And you," she went on in the same quiet intense voice, turning to a man leaning on the wall behind her, "is it *accident* that you are here with that transmitter disguised as a pen in your jacket pocket?"

She caught us all by surprise, but most of all she took aback the man to whom she'd turned. He was tall, saturnine, dressed in brown corduroy. He was the man who couldn't believe that I'd never met Shakespeare or Marlowe. Now, unexpectedly at the centre of attention, he stiffened and stared back, his nostrils flaring as he breathed in deeply from the sudden shock of it.

"Accident!" she murmured with soft emphasis, her eyes unwavering on him. "No, no *accident!* Does anyone here know this man?"

It turned out that nobody did.

He was trying to break her gaze, but could not.

"Take out your *pen,"* she said, "and show it to us."

His struggle was obvious. His face grew flushed, he began to shake all over. Yet his unwilling hand crept slowly to the inside pocket of his jacket and drew out what looked like a black fountain pen. Somebody took it from him. The top was unscrewed, and to our consternation it was found to be a radio gadget which would have transmitted her every word . . . except that it was broken, the components fused together, melted as if by great heat.

"Your masters will be wondering why they haven't heard from you," Tari told him. "You can go and tell them why . . . in a little while . . . *if* you can remember what you were doing and where you were."

Then she put him out of mind and turned to the rest of us, and he stood there dazed, apparently frozen, as she told us we must all leave at once in case the house was raided.

She and I were driven in different cars to someone's house near Indianapolis. We stayed there a week, including New Year.

The sudden threat unbent me towards her again. I was confused and felt no power in me to deal with this nemesis closing in. How could we fight it? I felt there was nothing under my feet at all.

One night I lay abed, and suddenly felt that old familiar golden bubbling in the mind . . . then I saw her, raven-haired. She regarded me for a moment . . . then her face dissolved and abruptly I felt myself *pulled,* out of myself, and next . . . I was high in the sky, soaring like a great bird, looking down on a world of tumult and change, the west all dark, but the glow of a rising sun in the east.

I felt horrid vertigo and resisted this, and so just as abruptly crashed down, back into myself, utterly shaken.

Disturbed, I went to her room. She sat cross-legged on the carpet. Her face was grave. I paced. She asked me to sit down.

"Humfrey," she said, "you still deny it, but the Hawk flies in you. You must live with it, for soon you'll be on your own."

I was shocked. "What do you mean?"

"Take my hands," she said, extending them, and I did, though reluctantly. But her cool dry hold calmed me. "Now listen," she said quietly, "my time here is almost up. I don't want you to worry about it, for it happens to everyone, and I have already been through the Gate of Fear." And she went on before I could speak. "The seed *is* sown, my friend, and the chasm *will* be crossed, though not easily. Many will not learn. They'll die in terror, and the souls of some may be extinguished—but it *will* be crossed. Do you understand?"

In confusion I fell back on the faith I doubted.

"But why should their souls be extinguished? Christ made that unnecessary! He died for us all!"

She smiled. "You are not responsible for your own soul? What nonsense! If one-tenth of these Christian churches were truly of Christ there would be much less confusion now! Humfrey, you and others have made yourselves the victims of ridiculous dogmas created by men who hid the inner truth to ensure their own power on earth!"

"What ridiculous dogmas?"

"Vicarious Atonement, for one—that Christ will save you no matter what you do so long as you say you believe. So, a murderer can be forgiven—but can the effect of the act be obliterated? What's the value of forgiveness if nothing's learned from it?"

I thought on all my sins and I was frightened.

"If so, then I *am* damned forever," I said dully.

"Rubbish! You're human! You pay for whatever you do that goes against the flow of things—if not in one life, then in the next!"

"Oh! You preach Pythagoras and metempsychosis!"

"Did not Christ rise from the dead?"

"Yes, but He was special! He—"

"If he was special then is not every human son and daughter special? What did he do but *demonstrate* what every Son and Daughter of God can become and do? Oh, Humfrey, that fear in men which killed him kills him still! It will be a long time before all learn to take responsibility for themselves and make their own inner marriage without need of mediation. A *long* time."

"Then what?" I demanded. "When this fine marriage is made and we all govern ourselves without need of priests and presidents?"

I felt angry. Now I see it was anger at myself.

"I cannot say," she said. "I don't know it all. Humfrey, you don't have to worry about the future. Deal with the present."

"Well, so what did the Dancer mean about the end of the Fourth World? What is to happen—in the present?"

"I told you," she said patiently. "We work towards self-responsibility so that the need of hidden elite groups is reduced!"

"Spiritual socialism?" I asked bitterly.

"More precisely, it is *an-archy*, meaning *'without a ruler,'* or perhaps I should say, *'without* earthly *ruler,'* for it's impossible to gain such a state without *some* common sense of things within and beyond, through which we are, in fact and always, united."

"Oh! The Golden Age! A myth! A fantasy! A dream!"

"What else did you ever live for?" she demanded drily.

"I would have been content with political governorship and material gold in the New World!"

"No! You would not! It would have brought you no satisfaction! You would have gone on hunting this dream you now seem to despise!"

"I do not despise it," I told her sullenly, my eyes downcast. "It is simply that I no longer believe it possible to attain. The world now is a madness worse than anything I knew before. Good God, they have wonderful plumbing now, they can go nowhere very fast and say nothing to each other over great distances, and look where it gets them! Oh, they have made marvellous inventions, but . . ."

"Humfrey, Humfrey!" Quite sharply she let go my hands. "Why do you insist on the dark side alone? Because you dream of better you see all that's wrong with the world, but you don't look far enough! Old structures grow rigid and crack apart so that new forms can be born, but they are all impermanent. Only the Great One is eternal and perfect—and *That* is beyond all the logic, reason, religion, science, and human experience that arises from It!"

"So why are we here?" I demanded, stymied. "Tell me again!"

"You don't want to tell yourself? We are seedbearers, witnesses of history. In this age all ages merge and knowledge from all times is made known, so that men can make a choice, to proceed and manifest the Light on Earth at a higher level of civilised harmony than before—or commit mass suicide in despair. So, speak what you know the best you know, and go through your doors when you come to them! There's no going back, so remember it, for soon I'll be gone, and I cannot tell you again, and it is not my business to do so!"

This sent a chill down my spine.

"But . . . can't you avoid this . . . this . . ."

"Only by deviating from the path I'm on."

"Well, then you should . . ." But I stopped, belatedly remembering the bold words I myself had spoken in better days. I felt lost, and stupidly asked her if she knew when? or how? She shook her head, unsmiling, but I felt her great love and encouragement.

"Humfrey, whatever happens, you will learn in time, and if the Hawk acts through you in ways that bring you hurt and confusion, then recall how once you were willing to risk everything for what you believed worth winning. You are not the fool you like to think and make yourself. You will take up the reins again."

I cannot and will not speak of it at length, but it happened like this: the next day we were taken to Omaha, all movements being carefully considered in advance. Tari dyed her hair black, but it made no difference: I think she did it only to convince others that she had a sense of caution, so they should not worry quite so much.

After three days in Omaha we went on to Denver, to a suburban house owned by people recommended as devoted and discreet. Tari seemed quite her usual self, though more silent than usual, but my nerves were not good. We came safely to the house after nightfall, and after washing we sat down to supper with our two hosts in an upstairs room, when from below came a sudden tumult, followed by the sound of feet pounding rapidly up the stairs. We had scarcely time to stand before the door burst open and two masked men wearing dark suits rushed in. They aimed large automatic pistols at us and opened fire. Dreadful pain exploded in my head and I lost consciousness.

And that was that.

⊸⊱{ 26 }⊰⊷

Visions of Rose,
Mud of the Road

It was not the end of the world, nor even of Gilbert.

At four o'clock one chill March morning fifteen months later, I sat in the coffee-shop at the Greyhound bus station in Salt Lake City, nursing the cup of lukewarm brown stuff my last dollar had bought. I stared numbly at the flashing lights of advertising displays. I was ragged, half-mad, without prospect, caught in a dream of frozen anger—and I was about to meet Bobby Fiorelli.

Two things have happened here.

One, last night Ursula Greene rang Mr. Griffith, asking him to turn me out. This morning through the fog he came, most embarrassed. He spent five minutes muttering about the weather and such before managing to say it. Evidently he too wants me on my way: he may or may not know of his son's visit and threats, but I'm sure he feels the mounting pressure of family and local disapproval. So, I should never have called Grace at all, but to hell with that! I'm glad I did, and what odds does it make?

"We got a call from the Professor's wife last night," he said, looking away, "wondering how long you'll be here. See what I mean? Somebody else wanting the place at the weekend, like."

A lie, I thought, and asked:

"You didn't personally speak to Professor Greene yourself?"

"She said he's very poorly." He darted a quick shrewd

glance at me. "You'll know about that, won't you?" And his glance said that Ursula managed to imply my guilt for Michael's illness.

"I've heard," I said in a flat voice. "I'm very sorry about it. As for myself, I plan to be gone by the weekend anyway."

He eyed me sharply, saw no guile, then nodded in quick and surprised relief that I made no fuss. He nearly smiled, but caught it, then muttered something about, "Well, then, I have to be up on the top pasture," and with his black-and-white dog barking loudly he took off over the field in his landrover, lumping and splashing away through puddles into the fog. Well, he has to make a living.

He was surprised at my calm. I was not.

The fear is gone.

Last night, driving myself to write of Denver, it was painful until I surmounted it and it was done, whereupon a great soft sadness welled through me like a pearly grey cloud. With this came a lethargy and peacefulness at last, as of something letting go. With tears in my eyes I turned off the lights and pulled an easy chair into the warmth of the stove, and must have been quickly asleep—for the next thing I knew I was sitting up and looking round, and there was Tari!

She stood, misty and faint, and had a bloody wound on her breast, and behind her was the shining door with the passage beyond. She was so wraithlike I could scarcely make out her face as she pointed at the floor between myself and the gate.

"Humfrey, look!" Her voice was a far-off winter wind from the north. It chilled me. "Look what we have here!"

I looked and saw, and shot to my feet, then froze colder still. "In the Name of God!" I hissed. "I'm a dead man!" For there on the floor before me I saw the ghost of myself, stretched out, a corpse, head torn by a ghastly wound. At that horrid sight I had no feeling at all but for the throbbing of the scar at my hairline; I could not take my eyes from it until diverted by another voice:

"So what you gonna do about it, Humf? Just stare?"

I swung, violently. It was Herbie.

He was a mess too, but he grinned, and shrugged.

"No big deal, Humf. Happens to us all. So how about it?"

I simply goggled and could find nothing to say at all.

"The gate," came Tari's grave whisper. "Humf, come through!"

They said no more, but turned and went through. Somehow I followed, over my dead body. It seemed the best thing to do.

I found no footing, there was a wrenching-apart. I fell a great way, losing consciousness. I fell all the way back to the coma I was in for days after Denver, to what happened when I was nearly gone—which I had not remembered at all until now!

I seemed to be in an open coffin or sarcophagus with the chill of death on me. There was only a pale blue light, barely sufficient to hint at stone sphinxes supporting the columns of the crypt where I lay. And as I lay I saw the scenes of my life flit before me in rapid phantom succession, until at last I saw the masked men burst into that room and shoot us. At this, all dissolved and fell apart. I lost all connection with my body, not knowing who or where I was. Yet it was strangely serene, there seemed to be music, and then there was a shining point of light. This swiftly grew larger into a flashing five-pointed star with rainbow-colours streaming from it. The heart of this star was incandescent, a pure whiteness too dazzling for any form to exist in it until at length it began to fade, to be replaced by a flower that formed in it, or from it. And the flower was a scintillant white rose that unfolded with utter tremorous delicacy. Yet soon it too began to evaporate, sending out a marvellous perfume as it did, and assuming many transient forms which I could not understand nor clearly see until, from the condensation of its subtle coilings of light, a human figure took shape, of a woman, smiling and radiant, slender form shining through the layers of the veils of light upon her. This was Mery-Isis, yes, and more: a veritable visitation of that Great One she served that shone through her! Most beautiful and tender and awesome! And her perfume breathed knowledge and great lightness of spirit through me as she came and showed me the book—the one with blank pages and my name on it that she showed me before I began all this a month ago. Now there was writing in it, but still blank pages, many of them! And she said:

"I am your sister and your soul, and here is a life. You are not yet at the end of that road you began so long ago, so record it all, good and bad, then be done with it and start out again. There are new doors to open and pass, and one day, at the end of your journey on the boat of millions of years, you'll come to know them all."

So, this morning I awoke, and found the fear gone . . . well, almost.

After Denver was a man who forgot everything and felt little for a long time, except for the frigid angry impulse to keep going.

Again the first memory's of swimming back to the world in a bed. Very far away through a window like a tunnel I saw snow-boughed pines, great white mountains, an infinite pale blue sky.

It was only after a week or so that the elderly couple who had agreed to look after me told me about it. I had been unconscious nine days since the shooting and emergency operation. They said the gunmen had killed Tari and one of our hosts, critically wounded our other host and myself, then got away, unidentified. Well, we knew, but it was too late now. And, ugly irony, the cost of surgery and shut mouths was met out of the sale of the Interferon Tari had carried all those months. The rest of the profit, over three thousand dollars, had been turned over to these two folk for the risk and cost of looking after me.

They never touched a penny. When I said I must go they insisted I take it, and when I refused, they outwitted me. They were a fine couple, very strong in themselves, and I wish I'd been in better state to appreciate their kindness and who they were, for both had lived adventurous lives of the politically radical sort, the old man being a great populist orator of his time. So, I'll say no more of the who and where, for these are no times to be loose with names.

I was abed a long time, in shock and weak, bandaged in terrible dreams, unable to read or do anything but hazily wonder why I was still alive. The bullet had ploughed into the top of my skull, making a great mess while destroying no critical part of the brain. But I remembered nothing before Denver, and for a time it was also feared my left side might be paralysed. Yet gradually motion came back, and more memory than I wanted. By late February 1986 I was out of bed for short spells, listening to the old man's tales of Wobblies and McCarthy and the Murmansk Run in World War Two, and towards the end of March I was taking brief walks outside. We were still cut off from the outside world by snow (I heard I'd been brought up the mountainside in a machine called a Snocat), and I think the mountain air must have been as great a tonic as the silence up there. Yet I felt and smelled nothing at all, until in April I was taken by an increasingly impatient urge to leave, to wander, to forget and be forgotten and swallowed completely in the world. So, though my head still ached, I told them I must go.

They asked me, Where? I said I had no idea. They said, Please stay, you are under no obligation. "Thank you," I said, "but I must go, my legs demand it!" They accepted it sadly, and when the snows were melted they drove me to the bus station in a town called Golden. I had refused the three thousand, but they prevailed on me to take five hundred at least. Later that day, on a bus going west, I found the other twenty-five hundred rolled up in a sock in my pack . . . and I think my rueful smile was the first since Denver.

That first night I stayed in a motel. It was strange. I could make no sense of anything, but at least when I left in the morning I had the money divided into three rolls—one in my left boot, the second taped to my thigh, and the third, never more than a hundred bucks a time in small bills, in a wallet in my jacket pocket. This precaution was to prove intelligent.

I don't know what was on my mind. All I wanted to do was walk and walk and walk, and so I did, all summer, another drifter on the roads. I remember little, but I know I never told anyone who I was and where I'd been. I slept out as often as I could, saving money, avoiding company, half-starving myself, gazing at the distant stars and mountaintops, walking northwest until one day I was in sight of the Grand Tetons in Wyoming, high on the Continental Divide. There on the road I met a wanderer who told me to turn back, because of the Idaho Leak and the ugly mood of people there against strangers. Without asking myself what I was doing I turned south, and in time came to New Mexico. By then winter approached. I thought of trying Mexico, but had no papers, and feared the desert crossing, so that in due course, still aimless, I found myself in Arizona. One cold night I sought shelter with a hobo desert camp. They were suspicious at first, but shared their food and fire . . . and after the sparse meal I heard a man speaking of the Hopi, the People of Peace!

I remembered Masanva, Azurara, Utak! I felt a sudden painful flood of hope! Perhaps the Dancer was with the Hopi!

Fired with what I told myself was a sense of purpose, on through the desert I went until I came to the Hopi reservation.

Perhaps Masanva could tell me what I should do! I came to a village called Oraibi that sat on the lip of a mesa, and found federal troops guarding it against any attempted reoccupation by its inhabitants. They had been driven out to make way for a mining consortium. In a fever I went on to the villages of Moencopi and Shongopovi, asking for the Dancer, but the wrinkled old men with their names like Macdonald and Adamson just stared silently at me in my madness, and the children chased me until their mothers called them away, laughing.

That killed my false hope. Driven by anger I did not even know as such I wandered on. Sometimes I'd stop and say, "I am Humfrey Gylberte!"—but it meant nothing, and I could not quite believe the past any more than the present. With little money left I went south to Flagstaff, and in hotels asked for work washing dishes. Yes, I know about the bum's rush. Somehow I got through that winter. For a time I was with some other down-and-outs: one night near the Grand Canyon a man beat and robbed me while others stood by. So I went on by myself, in any direction, stiff and thin, until with my last bucks I took a Trailways bus from somewhere to elsewhere. Thus I found myself in Salt Lake City in the early hours of a March morning in 1987.

There was no coffee-shop at the Trailways terminal. I walked down the street to the Greyhound station. So I met Fiorelli.

I had grown suspicious of people, wise in ways I hadn't known before, but he fooled me. I let him take me. I had exhausted all options, and from the moment he saw me he knew me as a particular sort of angry man for whom he could find an angry use.

Simply put, he came and sat at the table where I moodily stirred sugar into coffee, and he started talking. He was slim, bearded, about thirty, sharply dressed in a suit of crushed black velvet. He told me he was waiting for the San Francisco bus, and that I looked an interesting sort of guy, and that he wanted to talk, if I didn't mind. "Talk all you like!" I said, glaring. He warned me not to go out on the Salt Lake City streets. "This place is just incredible, man," he said in his slow drawl. "You know every morning at dawn they bring out teams of convicted juvenile delinquents and make 'em lick the sidewalks round the Temple clean? Hawhaw. Only joking. But it's weird here. Weird graffiti too. WOMAN IS THE WORK OF SATAN, shit like that. Makes me shudder. Hey, don't mind my asking, but you look down on your luck. Where you headed?"

Quickly he learned what he had already guessed: that I was a desperate man. He smiled, and bought me a good breakfast.

"Hey, I like you," he said, "and maybe I can help you out. Why don't you come along with me to San Francisco?"

I shrugged.

"Why not?" I said.

27

What Humf Did
in the Steamhouse

Every paradise has its ugly side, and San Francisco is no exception. My benefactor turned out to be a procurer for a most unpleasant trade. What he meant by saying he could help me out was that, in return for allowing myself to abuse and be abused by insane and violent individuals on a regular nightly basis, he would find me a place to stay and pay me four hundred dollars a week, no questions asked.

I knew none of it until we reached San Francisco. I gaped when at last our bus came over the Bay Bridge into the city. The towers were ablaze with the light of the sun setting out to sea beyond the Golden Gate Bridge. It was a beautiful sight, and vaguely I knew it as such. It hurt me, and I hated it for being beautiful.

"Listen, Humf," said Fiorelli when we reached the terminal at last, "I can see you're pretty whacked out, and we'll get you some food and a bed, but first I wanna show you something."

He made a call. Soon a black car driven by a black man wearing black leather with silver chain wrapped tight round his body came and picked us up. He also wore a black peaked cap which from my modern education I recognised as a Nazi cap. Even in my dull state I found this all most fascinating.

"Why this uniform?" I mumbled.

"Hold it, Humf," said Fiorelli. "You'll find out."

In silence we were driven through a bleak industrial part of the city to a dirty alley, to a door in the alley. The door had a barred grill over it. Mr. Black Leather unlocked grill and door, and into the dim red light of a musty interior we went.

Fiorelli wrapped an arm round my shoulder and steered me past a scarred black leather curtain into a room from which came grunts and groaning male voices. And when I saw what was going on, I stopped dead. Even in my numb state I was quite astounded. For some seconds I gazed at the uncouth activities without taking in what they were doing to each other. I looked up and met the eyes of a hooded man hanging upside down in chains, naked. He winked at me. Opening and closing my mouth, I looked about again. "Interesting, eh, Humf?" said Fiorelli, guiding me on through busy torture chambers that would not have disgraced Torquemada, past racks and Iron Maidens and other gear. "We get guys here who'd be out on the streets hittin' on innocent passers-by if they couldn't get it off here. We're legit, we pay our taxes, y'know, First Amendment, just like the churches." And so saying he led me into a small room that was bare but for a whipping-post. "The moment I saw you," he said conversationally as he started removing his clothes, "I thought, 'Now there's an angry guy that hates just about everything he sees. He'd like to beat the shit outa someone.' Right? Well, here's your chance!"

Must I say more? Supervised, so that my rage might not fly fatally out of control, I passed that test splendidly, and Fiorelli, grunting with pain, hired me on the spot. And I went with it. How could I sink so low? I have heard of karma. Perhaps that's what it was. Once in my enthusiasm I willingly sold the clothes off my wife's back. Now for the sake of survival I sold the skin off my own, and not willingly! I drew the line at some of the games Fiorelli suggested might double my pay, and the details of such often deadly pursuits as fist-fucking may, I think, be left out of this account with no loss to anyone. When he suggested it I threatened him with a fist in the face! "Hey, Humf," he said cordially, not in the least put out, "take a tip. You could retire in a year if you used your assets right. A lot of the trade really got this thing for you. It's that classy accent, and the Man-of-Mystery bit, and the impression you put over that you really despise 'em. Gets 'em hot. Just aim to *despise* a bit more and you'll be Big Time!"

The club, called the *Steamhouse*, was situated in the dangerous South of Market district. Scores of winos and bums lived and died on the streets about, life was cheap, and though

nightly I took a bus from my one-room apartment on Valencia
Street, still I had to walk several of the roughest blocks in
town. My built-up rage was astonishing even to me; it was in
these months I often let ranting hate overwhelm me, and met
William Yeats Butler, and kicked in a TV-set when I heard
Thaddeus Carpenter preach his *Plutonium Power for Christ*
insanity. It was too much to bear, it drained me, soon I could
not be sure I was still human, and reaction set in. I saved
money, and it was with unutterable relief that finally, in July,
I began to cut down the number of hours I spent in that foul
place. A long time had passed since I had allowed myself any
feelings at all, but now at last I began to feel I must mend my
ways. Enough is enough! I began to explore this most energetic
and beautiful of cities, taking ferry-trips out to Angel Island
in the Bay, visiting the parks, walking briskly up Twin Peaks
from the top of which the view of all the hilly districts is so
superb. I began spending time in the Public Library, thinking
of Vulcan again, finding out what I could about it from back-
issues of newspapers and magazines. I went to movies, and to
art-galleries, and sat in coffee-houses, eavesdropping and learning all I could, and sometimes talking with people almost like
a normal human being.

Yet I was still not completely free of Fiorelli and the money
he paid me that I needed; the dreams I had were frequently
dreadful, and I was almost always in a state of dull fear that
those who had imprisoned me and shot me might catch up with
me again—and of the advice which Mery-Isis had given me I
remembered nothing at all. I kept her completely out of my
mind. But perhaps, though I had forgotten the Hawk, the Hawk
had not forgotten me, for before the coming of autumn my
luck changed again.

One bright September day, dressed in style and with neat
beard, yet depressed and thinking of jumping off Golden Gate
Bridge, I was sitting in the Japanese Tea Garden in Golden
Gate Park, eating the little cookies they have there, when I
saw a handsome blond woman eyeing me from a neighbouring
table.

She was on her own and had the bold bearing of many
women in this city where women are in competition with men
for men, and where it is commonly believed that to miss the
moment is to lose eternity. I quite liked the look of her, and

nodded an invitation for her to join me, which she did.

Within five minutes I knew that her name was Marianne Lofgren, that she was separated from her husband, had a twelve-year-old son called Colin, an apartment on Sanchez Street, and a job in the Bank of America at Twenty-fourth and Castro. She wasted no time at all. She said she knew she liked me, and asked me what I did. I told her bluntly, to which she answered that she didn't care, but did I think it was healthy, and was I strictly gay, or was I bi?—and if the latter could I go for her and would I like to go home with her *right now*?

And what did Gilbert say to this?

You have it! *Quid Non?*

So we went to her apartment with its wonderful view, and soon enough she was in a position to see all my scars, which disturbed her. "Aren't a lot of people killed doing this S&M stuff?" she demanded. "I don't mean to be judgemental but you could get something a lot better going for you. You've got real style, you just don't have to get into that sort of shit, and I could do with a man around the house, and I've got this real deep feeling we're just naturally going to hit it off and probably fall in love and maybe get married. So I suggest you call this Fiorelli guy and tell him to stuff his dick up his own ass because you're quitting and moving in here, and apart from anything else that'll be a real help to me, because of Colin, you know. I have to go out at some pretty weird hours and I sorta get worried about my boy. He's sharp for his age but I don't like the way he goes running out with those Chicano kids looking for gays to beat up in Dolores Park. I mean that's not a good leisure activity at any age but for twelve it's too much. He could use some positive male influence, and I know he'll really take to you, because you've got like an air of authority, and as far as I'm concerned you fuck real good too. So how about it? If you don't feel like being a house-husband, for a trial period or something, just tell me now, and no offence given or taken, we'll shake hands and walk out of each other's lives. But that would really make me sad because I have this real deep feeling about you and me. So how about it?"

San Francisco! Yes, a truly amazing city!

And yet again I smiled and said: "Why not?"

"Great!" she said. "Feel like another line?"

* * *

Thus I became a "house-husband," and for some time all went well, except that, unfortunately, her son Colin and I loathed each other at first sight. He resented my sleeping with his mother, and had quite a talent for "accidentally" treading on my toes, and so on. To call him precocious is a huge understatement. I am glad only that, when he wasn't out on the street, he was usually closeted in his room smoking pot and playing Atari video-games with any one of an endless succession of preteen girlfriends whom he squired with all the aplomb of which a young California Romeo is capable. I tried to communicate with him, but the best compromise we could reach after a few weeks of war was to ignore each other as much as possible.

Marianne hardly noticed. She didn't want to notice. She was determined to lead her own life, and didn't want Colin in her hair. So, she persisted in pretending that he and I were the best of friends.

As I said, she worked in a bank, as a Banking Services Officer. She was also a dealer in cocaine. For the most part she supplied executives at the bank, and other professional people. "I like to keep it clean, with a real good class of people," she said. This activity explained what she had meant about having "to go out at some pretty weird hours," while her own consumption of the drug had much to do with her high-strung, nonstop character. She never did her dealing at home— "I don't want my boy to get the wrong ideas"—but always elsewhere. As for myself, I had no grounds to be critical: cocaine has its attractions, but I had already learned that it makes me greedy and much too argumentative, so I could take it or leave it, preferring the soothing qualities of marijuana when I wished for anything of the sort.

So for some months, despite problems with Colin and a few other minor irritations, things went well enough. I was more than grateful for the haven, and found her attractive, as she found me, our fires being well-matched despite the many great differences between us. At weekends we would drive into the countryside, to Mount Tamalpais or Muir Woods or Stinson Beach, or further afield, to the wine country of Sonoma, south to the cliffs and forests of Big Sur, and once we even spent a week camping high in the Sierra. For a while I relaxed and found some happiness, as far as this was possible.

For of course there was the problem of my past.

Early in our affair I'd told her the tale I'd invented soon after my arrival in the city: that I was English, and that I had come to the States having lost my job in Britain, which she had accepted, knowing from the news what a state Britain is in. Also I had told her I was in the States illegally, that I had been shot and nearly killed in a mugging eighteen months earlier, losing my passport, credit, identification, and some of my memory. This she wished to accept, and my tale of memory-loss eased her mind with regard to my ignorance of many little things about the modern world known to any child of five. Nonetheless, there was much about me that distressed her, such as redundancies in my speech, and some of my political and social attitudes, which she called "neo-fascist," and my "paranoid" behaviour in company with her friends—for after William Yeats Butler I was no longer so willing to play the double game of *pretending* to be a DTI, or chrononut. On Hallowe'en Night that year we went to a party where I met a man who claimed to have *met* two DTIs: as he went on I realised to my horror that he was describing a meeting with Mery-Isis and myself! He had encountered us in Buffalo during the months of her mission! Fortunately he did not recognise me, having apparently paid me little attention, being more fascinated by Tari, as most of them were. "She changed my life!" he said. I should have kept quiet, but I could not bear it, to be reminded of her, and lost my temper, calling him a liar and fool to believe such rubbish! There was an ugly scene: it was two days before Marianne would speak to me again, and only after that I realised I must try to be cool-minded about such situations.

Yet the strain of duplicity grew immense, and so came the night I tried to tell Marianne the truth.

This arose out of another upset. Marianne was an addict of historical movies of a sort which naturally upset me, which she could not understand. One night near Christmas she insisted on going to see a new movie called *The Virgin Virago*, in which Jane Fonda portrayed my Queen Elizabeth as a misunderstood radical feminist ahead of her time. Halfway through this abomination I stood and exploded with such loud anger and contempt that we were both told to leave, so that on the street outside we had a violent argument. "I'm beginning to think we made a mistake!" Marianne snapped. "I can do without that sort of childishness! What's the matter with you?"

There and then I knew I'd had enough.

I told her, simply and directly, as we confronted each other on California Street, who I am and how I came to America.

"My God!" she said, still angry, but taking it quite in her stride. "And I thought you were a reformed gay crept back into the straight and comfortable house-husband fold! Why didn't you tell me? Closet chrononut! I should have guessed!"

Yes, no doubt I should have left her then, but I did not, for despite every difficulty I was comfortable enough, and she still wanted me in her bed. So we stayed together, I humouring her while she thought she was humouring me, and I spent many hours walking or in the Library while she worked in the bank. Then it was 1988, and I met the *Slocum* cameraman in Chaunticleer's, which renewed my fears, and life grew problematic, for rioting broke out in the Mission district just down the hill from us. The riots were caused in part by U.S. military suppression of popular movements in Central America, but more by white developers raising rents to levels which the predominantly poor latino population could not afford. There was arson and looting and killing. Amid it all an earthquake rattled every building in the city, and one night Marianne came home and said:

"I need a break. Let's go to Reno for the weekend."

"What about Colin?"

"He's okay. He'll wreck the place while we're gone and have a great time. Humf, I damn well *deserve* this!"

We drove to Reno with threats of world war on the radio, and checked into a motel, and I found that KRONONUTZ were playing just down the street. I did not go to see them. The thought of them, of Tari, of my half-buried past—no, it was still too painful. So, we entered a noisy bright casino where people wasted money in frantic efforts to pretend the rest of the world did not exist. Marianne showed me how to work the machines, and gave me a silver dollar. I fed it in, pulled the lever . . . and met the Janus-face of Fate again:

6*6*6*6*6

Luck. Fate. Fortuna. I stood there and watched those sixes click into a row, each in turn against all the odds, and the bell went off, and Marianne shrieked with disbelief as the other gamblers all came crowding round, some of them telling me they'd been trying and failing for years to do what I'd just done first time. And that is how it was with Vulcan. We Eighty-Seven were the *lucky* winners of the Vulcan jackpot. Why? Well, why not?

Yet perhaps—just perhaps—the Hawk had something to do with it. For once again my life was changed. We returned to the city richer by $102,000, and on the way back through the mountain night, after a long silence, I said to Marianne:

"I want to go to England. I need a U.S. passport. Do you know anyone who might be able to arrange it?"

She braked hard and stopped at the side of the road.

"Say that again," she said in a nervous voice.

I repeated what I had said, very carefully.

Then she suggested something I had not expected.

"Why don't we all go together?"

Impossible! I thought quickly, and said nothing. The money was already in an account which of course was in her name—all but for $10,000 in cash for spending. Yes, I kept quiet.

"Humf, I want to go with you," she said in that nervous voice, "and Colin too. I'm not blind. He's turning into a brat and it may be his last chance. We all need something new. England may not be great, but we could go to Scotland, or Scandinavia. Now listen! I *might* know people who could fix the passport, but we'll have to pay whatever's asked, or they'll cop out and turn us in and take both ways. It happens all the time. You'll have to trust me. I still don't know who you are or what you're running from, but I'm in hot water too, with this coke thing, and I want out—with you. It was your luck, but my dollar, right? I mean you're not exactly Jesus Christ, but we get along, don't we . . . Humf?"

I'm not proud of it. I let her assume what she would until one night she brough the Loomiss papers and said that the $30,000 asked had been paid. Also she showed me three air tickets, $20,000 in traveler's cheques, and a new tweed outfit she'd got herself, for the English weather. She said that next day we would all go to the British Consulate for our visas, and that in a week we would fly to London. "I've put the rest into a short-term government loan," she went on, "so it'll work for us while we're away."

That night, with Colin in his room locked up in drugs and

stereo headphones, I paced for hours before deciding. $7,000 was left of the $10,000 spending money. I gathered it from its corners, packed a bag, made sure I had the Loomiss papers, then with difficulty awoke her from her Valium sleep, knowing I could not just sneak away.

"I am going now," I told her unhappily. "I am going alone. It's the only way. You don't believe what I told you, and I would bring you no happiness at all. It's just a dream you have that we could last together. You have still got the money and the tickets, and you can still go to Britain with Colin, and I hope you find someone who'll treat you better than I can. I'm sorry that I deceived you, but we must stop pretending now. It really is better this way!"

We argued bitterly, then I left quickly, calling for a cab to the airport from a street-phone, knowing that she would not try to stop me because of what I knew about her cocaine dealings. It was necessary, but ugly, and I hated myself for it, for bad leads to worse when folk treat each other like that. I know it very well, and I hope very much that she has found some peace in her life.

Thus again I tried return to England from America. This time, four hundred and five years after my first attempt, I was successful.

The nonstop flight to London took just eleven hours. Arguing myself out of the depression caused by my act, I found the experience at first most frightening, then exhilarating, with the vast gleaming ice-capped curve of the planet to the north. Day came, and fled fast, and it was night again already when the old 747 came down the length of Britain from the Hebrides to London. I watched, and saw how the lights of cities and towns seemed never to end, as if no countryside at all were left. For the first time it came home to me: *sixty million* people crammed into this one little isle! What was I doing? A return to England had seemed to be my obvious necessity, the desire springing to mind as soon as the jackpot was won. Yet it was not a matter of reason, but of deep emotion, and perhaps treacherous. And as the plane heavily lowered itself down to the Heathrow runway, I was wondering if I had made a dreadful mistake.

28

A Pint in the
Sir Walter Raleigh

Well, and so I found a land foreign to me. The weight of the first shock was such that pride alone stopped me turning tail in immediate flight back to California. Only after a few days I realised that California was quickly coming to seem as unreal to me as the England I'd left behind, though less painful to remember.

For immediately, in the tumult of this overcrowded and angrily haunted city, modern London, I met continual disturbing half-reminders of my past before Vulcan. For several days, caught in a "culture-shock" that had me in utter spin, I tortured myself by seeking out the ghosts. My Queen was the first of these! After two days and nights I sought solace in a visit to Hampton Court Palace. Unable to bear the *Slocum*-claustrophobia of the Underground, I braved the bus system instead, and got utterly lost. At last I got there, and knew immediately the visit would be worse than the journey.

The Palace was well-preserved; *too* well-preserved. In agitation I hurried through familiar chambers, hardly seeing the crowds and clumps of tourists at all: the ghosts were much more real. At length I came to a particular audience-room where I broke down like a child, seeing myself and Walter and Walsingham there in animated talk with Her Majesty. Smitten, I stumbled blindly to an embroidered chair in a roped-off alcove, and a uniformed attendant was quick to pounce.

"'Ere, mate, that chair's fer lookin' at, not sittin' on," he declared. "You can sit in the cafeteria but not 'ere."

A little old lady was more sympathetic, giving me a Kleenex and asking me the matter, but I could not speak, and rushed away.

That should have been enough, but I was fevered, feeling my pain to be no more than my duty to past loyalty. Next day I had my nose pressed up against the railings of Buckingham Palace. *Queen Elizabeth II!* My Queen's namesake and four-centuries-distant successor!

"So, you're leaving me. Will you be back? I doubt it. I doubt you love me enough."

Over and over at Hampton Court I'd heard her words of farewell, sardonically whispered, and now here again at the Changing of the Guard, amid the bus-parties. I felt a fury rising. "Well, I *am* back!" I snapped aloud, not caring who heard, "But four hundred years late! This is not England, and this Queen Elizabeth is not my monarch! What am I now but Humf, a common man, and proud of it, and nothing to do with the likes of this!"

Only then I realised that a Japanese party around me had drawn back; that one of them was photographing me amid my rant—and that their armed Securicor tour-guides were eyeing me most suspiciously. But in my fever I felt no alarm. "Fools!" I shouted, striding through them and away from that place. "How can you live like ghosts here? Why such shadowy faded half-life? Where is that exuberant glory that was England? How was it lost?"

I ran through the traffic, nearly getting killed, and ran madly on through Green Park, only coming to some measure of sanity again amid the hordes on Piccadilly.

Exactly one year after this I was on the great march south with my friend Red Robbie. It was a most strange year.

As for the rest of it—the trouble I had with Immigration to get a four-week visa; the way I was cheated by the cabbie who took me from Heathrow to an absurdly expensive Chelsea hotel; my initial shock at London's noise and enormity; the anti-Americanism I found; my visit to Eton College just after the bomb was planted there; and my futile search through a decayed industrial wasteland for the site of my old house at Limehurst—let it pass. Enough. A week of London was more than my emotions and finances could bear. On the night before I left, I sat in the hotel bar, voicing my complaints to a neighbour as drunk as I—a commercial traveler, so he said.

"Yes, I have been away from England for a long time!" I told him stridently. "And I must say I am utterly bewildered to find that even *enthusiasm* is a crime! The apathy! The lack of spirit for any cause that is not an angry one! The horrible way so many people demand that everyone else should be buried as deep in the shit as they are!"

"That's socialism for you," he said, giving me a bleary eye.

"Socialism, sir? No, it is nothing of the sort!"

"Then it must be the immigrants!"

Of course I had to take him seriously.

"Sir, I think not! They may be the only hope of this jaded isle! I have been back only a week, but to my eyes the old Anglo-Saxon stock is utterly exhausted! If anything *good* happened here, sir, people would immediately tear it apart to find something *bad!* The new blood is the only hope of a zestful future!"

"Y'don't understand, old boy," my companion slurred, "Dunkirk Spirit! Dunkirk Spirit!"

"Dunkirk Spirit?" He had me. I thought as quick as I could. Dunkirk Spirit? Someone—Coningham?—once told me of it. But what was it? Of soul, or of bottle? For the life of me I couldn't remember. Did it matter? "Yes, exactly!" I went on recklessly, "All the drink and drugs, and defeatism and immorality and television! The moral fibre of your Anglo-Saxon has gone rotten, sir!"

The commercial traveler winged the grizzled barman a wink that I caught as he turned to me. He grinned as he said:

"Not the same since we lost the Empire, is it?"

At this a sobering shock ran through me, to remember Dee's prophecy of the empire that would rise, then decay and fall. Excusing myself I left, and spent a restless night daring to hope I might find better outside the city, and that under this frigid modern English exterior some fire might remain. Yes, it took me time to understand.

In the morning, with a dread on me, I took train to Devon.

Well, well. Much nasty business here.

A telephone call, a would-be lynch mob, and for myself, I do believe, departure tomorrow, meaning work between now and then.

An hour ago Grace rang me from Brynafan with a warning:

"Mr. Loomiss? John? There's a bunch of the boys coming out to see you." By the sound of her voice she was almost in tears. "Their mood's ugly. You should go, now! If you like I'll meet you somewhere and drive you clear of the area."

I found myself calm, and not surprised.

"What do they want with me?"

"It . . . it got about . . . you know . . . about . . ."

"I know!" I felt a fire stirring in me. "I've had visitors already! I thought it was straightened out! I'm truly very sorry to be such trouble to you, but . . . what's the matter now?"

"They're scared and angry," she said simply.

"Good God! What about?"

"Everything! What do you think? The Lorry People, and that Rex Fisher taking over the country, and the soldiers . . ."

"Rex *Who?*"

"Don't you listen to the News, man?"

"Haven't had the time," I said.

"Well, you'd better wake up! You're a mystery, they don't like you, they want to think you raped me! Do you want me to meet you and drive you out? You *must* decide now!"

I marvelled at the good-hearted lass. I said:

"Grace, you're very brave, but you're in enough mess already. I won't run. I'll meet them here."

"But they'll tear you apart!"

"No, they won't. I'll be all right."

She heard the assurance in my voice. I thanked her, then went out into the yard and waited, arms folded and feet well-planted.

Several minutes later four cars came lurching through the gate. They stopped in a row in front of me where I stood and disgorged twelve angry men. Griffith's son (I still don't know his name) was there with his two friends from the other night, but it was another man, balding and powerful in middle-age, built like a wrestler, who took the initiative against me. Stamping up through the mire of last night's rain he stuck his choleric face in mine.

"We've had enough of you," he growled, "It's time you learned a lesson! Okay, boys?"

"Twelve against one," I said quietly as they ringed me, my arms still folded. "Good odds, for brave men!" It stopped them a bit, and I turned to Griffith's son. "I gave my word I'd be gone by the weekend," I said, "and so I will be. And you agreed to that."

"Well, so I was wrong!" His anger hid a sheepishness. "Taking up with our girls and causing trouble and making everyone nervous with this work you won't speak about! What are you doing here?"

"He's on the run!" said another man. "You can see it in his eyes! He's hiding from something!"

They were about to seize me. A beating I could probably take, but I did not want them finding and destroying this work. Time to throw caution to the winds! "Yes," I said quickly, but still quiet and not moving, "you're right! I'm on the run, and have been, for five years, and through no fault of mine. And what I am doing here is seeking peace to write the story of my life and the ills done against me so that I might hope for some human justice at last!"

Yes, my voice was quiet, but had some fire in it. They looked at each other, and the wrestler-type cocked his head.

"Well, and what sort of story is it?"

I met him in the eyes.

"You will have heard of Project Vulcan," I said. "You will have heard of the DTIs. I am one of them. My name is Humfrey Gylberte. I was born in the year 1539, and snatched from the year 1583. It is two years since I got here from America, where I escaped the place they held us."

Griffith's son started laughing, but his laugh broke off into a silence. They stared at me as the wrestler-type backed off, giving me that cautious look the caretaker at Compton gave me when I went there with Michael. "Bloody loony!" he muttered, looking away, but I did not care, I waited confidently with folded arms as the seconds passed with nobody making a move, so their uneasiness increased and their gumption drained out. I knew it had to.

"Listen now, we don't care who you are, but you'd best be gone quick!" Griffith's son blurted at length, a sort of desperation in the rising note of his voice. "I'm not one who likes breaking his word, but for your own safety, see?"

"Thank you," I said. "I am also anxious to be gone. Come by this time tomorrow and you'll not find me here, or anywhere near."

"Well, and we hope not!" he said fiercely, suddenly turning

on his heel back to his car, where he stopped and faced his friends. "I don't know about you lot, but I'm going!"

And that was it, because, though with much shaking of heads and angry looks, they followed him, even the wrestler-type. I was a hair tense as they reversed their cars about me where I stood, but it was only to get out of the gate, they did nothing to me. And as I watched them drive away, something made me look up, and I saw the hawk, high on the wind. And back inside I came with a confidence I have not known since my youth! The fire's in the heart again! New gates, new doors! Tomorrow in good faith I start on the road again—but first, now, to be done and reconciled with the past, to tie the final knot so I may cut it and be free to set out!

So. With my traveler's cheques and Loomiss papers and a guidebook to Devon, I returned at last to the land of my birth. I expected nothing, but I had to walk that earth again. Walk it? Why, at one point I got down on my hands and knees and *ate* it.

At Exeter I was heartened by the Cathedral and by the greater calm of the local folk. I took bus to Dartmouth, where I took the shocks and discrepancies as they struck me, but as quick as possible I walked out past housing projects on the road to Greenway.

The house where I grew up was gone. The woods were much reduced, the river lower and of different colour than I remembered—only the shape of the land was the same, for which I thanked God, and soon I turned away through the woods towards Compton, finding trouble with barbed wire and electric cattle-fences. When at last I reached the well-restored Castle and found I would have to pay, I did not go in. Instead I turned aside and spent time at the place where once I buried my soul . . . and it was an hour or so later, in pensive melancholy, that I walked a winding sunset road until I came to an inn called, inevitably, the *Sir Walter Raleigh*. I quaffed two pints of ale, ate a slice of shepherd's pie, and guardedly questioned the folk in there. Rich Devon lingered in their accent, though much diminished. They assumed me to be some strange American cousin, assured me that Walter had lived at Greenway, and though the woman at the bar had heard of contemporary local Gilberts, when I asked her what she knew of Sir Humfrey, Raleigh's half-brother, she said, "Oh, he was the one that got drowned." And when it came to pay five pound thirty for my fare, I found that I was almost out of cash, and asked her if she would take a traveler's cheque.

"No, sir," she said firmly, "afraid I can't do that!"

"But it's American Express! Very reliable!"

"Sorry, sir, you'll have to leave your bag here and go to the bank in Dartmouth tomorrow. Or, if you prefer, you can wash up here and save me the bother. But we can't cash dollar cheques here. Brewery policy. Sorry sir, but that's the regulation."

After washing dishes in the *Sir Walter Raleigh* I set grim foot to road that night (it is a joke *now,* yes), and so down to Dartmouth again, where I spent a night and day on the rocks, gazing out to sea just as did that child who dreamed of Golden Ships. Late in the afternoon as I watched the tide go out, a boy aged eight or nine came along the pools with a shrimp-net, and apparently found me odd.

"Hey, mister! Wotcher doin'?"

"Golden Ships," I murmured, in my melancholic reverie.

"Yer *wot?*"

"Golden Ships," I said more loudly, looking up, "Don't you ever dream of other worlds, of . . . Golden . . . *Starships,* maybe?"

"Golden—bleedin'—starships?" His face screwed up and he pronounced each word as if he were picking up worms with his fingers. "Yer *daft,* mister! Out of yer nut!" And he turned and ran away.

In town I bought a tent and supplies. In sad fury I walked north, feeling no rest until I was deep on Dartmoor, far from anyone. For a week I camped before moving deeper into the wilds. Thus for three months I lived, wanting nothing to do with the human race. Sea, sky, the moors—not so changed I could find no comfort in them. But I was changed, and by night I gazed at the stars, trying to remember the Egyptian names for them which Tari had told me—and I could not. My memory was blank. I could not even clearly picture her face, far less recall what she'd told me. It was all gone, as was memory of Herbie, Utak, Coningham, and the rest. Denver was a blur, San Francisco a strange fantasy, my American journeys like a distant dream. On Dartmoor it were as if none of it had ever happened, and that if it had, it hardly mattered.

For a while I found some peace in this, but it was a fragile, cowardly peace, and so in time I broke it, and moved on, back into the human world.

That is how I met a group of the so-called Lorry People.

⸺⟨ 29 ⟩⸺

"...No Blame:
You Must Go On..."

It must have been late September or early October, for the leaves had begun to fall and the damp cold nights were affecting my teeth and bones, when I met the tribe of traveling folk on the banks of the River Tavy.

They numbered over forty, being of all ages, with children and old folk, and dogs and chickens and a few goats. They had several battered old trucks, and half-a-dozen powerful motorbikes, and three dilapidated but brightly painted caravans. Also, erected in a clearing in the open woodland near the road, they had eight high-poled tents of the sort called tipis that the red people once used.

At first from my distance up on the moor I thought what I saw must be some sort of apparition caused by my tiredness. I hadn't realised that anyone in Britain chose to live like this.

I wavered, wondering if I should pass them by, but I saw faces turned up towards me, and curiosity as well as loneliness drew me closer. Dogs came barking out at me as I thrashed through the golden bracken; voices called them off as diffidently I approached these rough weatherbeaten folk and their encampment. Slowly I walked into the circle made by their tents; they all stood and watched alertly, even the children, only the dogs still chasing about. Nodding to them I came up to a fire, and felt the warmth and smelled the beans which had been cooking. Only then I realised how tired and hungry and cold I was, as a tall thin man came and steadied me.

"You look done in," he said. "Sit down, take your pack off."

I looked into his face. Lank black hair fell past his eyes almost to his dirty blue-denim shoulders. In one hand he held a greasy rag and spanners with which he'd been working on a black bike. He had a hook nose, and bright glinting eyes. He nodded to me.

"It's okay," he said, "you can relax. My name's Archie."

He saw to it that I got a plate of eggs and a thick hunk of bread to go with a steaming cup of tea. I wolfed it all down, and was not disturbed or asked any questions until I was done. Yet, though as soon as I'd sat most of them had turned back to their work—they were taking down their tipis—I was aware of several of them watching me as I ate, particularly a dark, broad-shouldered girl who didn't drop her intent gaze even when I looked up and met her eyes. As for Archie, he was back at work on the bike, and yes, I think I liked him from the start. He reminded me somewhat of George Gascoigne, who'd pirated the publication of my Discourse, having that same natural generosity and roguish eye. Smacking my lips and looking about as I finished, I saw how efficiently and quickly these people dismantled and bundled up their gear, stowing it away according to its sort in the back of different trucks. Quickly, yes, but without hurry or awkwardness, a raggedly cheerful crew who knew their parts, the old and young as well. So, I found myself suddenly feeling much happier than I had in a long time. "Thank you!" I said, putting down the bowl and going to shake Archie by the hand. "That makes a good deal of difference! My name, sir, is Humf, and I'm much obliged to you!"

He eyed me. "You've been out and about a while, eh?"

"Three months on the moor," I told him.

The dark girl joined us, hunkering down in her boots and jeans and smock and sheepskin jacket, her eyes still intent on me.

"I can't place your accent," she said bluntly.

"Mutatis mutandis," said I, meeting her gaze and somehow having to grin like a monkey, as slowly she did too. "How can you place what no longer has a place? I have been through a lot of changes."

But suddenly I wondered at and doubted this immediate

sense of good communion, and anxiously looked at Archie.

He was grinning too. I heaved a great sigh as the warmth of it rushed through me, a flood of returning faith and memory. It was so strong that I shuddered physically, but could not stop grinning, for it was like rain to a desert, to walk so unexpectedly into family.

So I went with them, the others agreeing, so long as I should pull my weight, finding myself with Lorraine and her two young children perched on the gear in the back of a truck. Yes, that was her name. And again, it happened just like that. And again, consequences unimagined at the time.

"Where are we going?" I was still dazed as we started off.

"Wales." Her gaze was so direct and steady. "Every winter we go to the valley. There's no hurry. We take our time, and give no trouble if we're given none."

Her tight voice told me that recently there *had* been trouble, but she said no more, and it was not until that night at camp in Somerset I learned from Archie that her man, Jake, had lately been killed in a confrontation with police. "They wouldn't let us into a filling-station," he said, "so we blocked the motorway. Worked in the past, right? This time though they brought in an armoured high-speed bulldozer. Fucking thing charged right at us, and Jake got caught." He eyed me sharply. "Take care of her."

"You know, when I saw you coming down off the moor," she went on, suddenly reflective as we bounced and rattled along through the pleasant countryside, "I got this flash, this weird feeling, and I saw your colours . . ."—she took my hand in a sudden urgent grip—"I see peoples' colours, you know, and for a moment when I looked at you I saw this really *old* colour, *really* old, as if you were walking out of the . . ." But there she stopped, letting go my hand and shaking her head in irritation. "Aw, but what am I saying?"

I, embarrassed and marvelling, turned to her children, Colum and Deirdre, two and three respectively, and tried to make small talk.

Colum reminded me of my own eldest son, John. It seemed incredible to remember that I too once had family.

So, on up the road we went, at our ease, but always a tension about the Law, and several confrontations too during the next two weeks as we passed by Taunton, Glastonbury (where we stopped three nights), Bristol, Abergavenny, Brecon, and finally Llandovery. But none of these confrontations came to much, for there was not only dislike between these people and the police, but a good deal of grudging mutual respect. "We can wait," said Archie more than once at our camps after these meetings. "It's coming. They know it, and so do we." And I remembered Masanva, but did not yet speak of that.

Yes, much talk of the New Age, and after Glastonbury, where I was greatly moved in heart and memory by the raising of the Power there, we went through Bristol and over the beautiful Severn Bridge into Wales, stopping many places, meeting other travelers to party and trade, to discuss present purposes and future needs. My fog of disillusion began to lift and I began to remember Tari, finding her spirit in these people, especially in Lorraine. But I could not tell of it, nor of anything much at all. I worked my way, and listened, and tried to get my bearings. Lorraine sensed something deeply frozen in me but said nothing of it. Instead, despite her own sadness, or to forget it, along the way she would talk continually, naming everything we passed, reminiscing, explaining where we were going and how so many folk now lived like this. With tact she seemed to accept my tale of years in exile, but in private she soon began to speak to me as if truly she *did* believe I came from the past and knew little or nothing of the present state of things.

One night in a wood near Brecon (it reminded me of Howell Rees) round a fire with vegetable stew bubbling on it, she and I and some others including Archie sat talking to keep the cold away, and I was prevailed on to say a little about my travels in America. With some heat I described how groups of down-and-outs I'd met had little sense of common cause, it being every man for himself, and how glad I was now to meet folk who had some common sense and unity.

"They all have to Make It in America," said Archie. "We don't."

"Sure we do!" declared Bob, a heavily bearded man. "We're just as individualistic. We just can't afford to make a song and dance about it. We know we're poor. They still think they're rich, or ought to be. They're ashamed if they're not rich!"

So, generalisations flew round the fire, and bottles of cider were opened, then Lorraine was telling me how she'd come to the valley, her folks having left London eighteen years before, when she was six. "... It was part of the hippie thing," she said. "Lots of acid and Love-Thy-Neighbour. Well, that didn't last. I grew up quick, I can tell you, and it was rough as hell, but I wouldn't change it for anything. I'd already started learning about herbs an' that, and seeing peoples' colours. My folks got sick of the road and for a couple of years we had a small-holding up near Llandod. The winters got too much for my mum, so they moved into town, and I ... I took off with ... with Jake and this lot. That was seven years ago. Now ... now there's about two hundred of us in the valley every winter. We've got our own school, some agriculture, and we've built a bit. The bureaucrats leave us pretty much alone now. They spent *years* hitting us with health regulations and building regulations and drug busts—all of it—until finally they realised it's useless, we won't go away, there's more of us all the time. So last year they cut us off the Social, and said, 'Okay, do your own thing and don't ask us for help.' Bastards!"

"The Social?" I asked.

She gave me an amused, secretive look.

"Sure. They've got some new law about the 'Disreputable Unemployed,' so we don't get any money."

"From the State?"

"Right."

"Sounds as well to me," I said forthrightly. "Why remain their slaves? If they don't pay you, they don't own you."

"It wasn't *their* money to start with," said Archie, and then he shrugged. "Sure, money's fucked, but ..."

"How do you think the world goes round?" I demanded. "On moral principle? Money belongs to whoever *uses* it, no matter who or where they got it from!"

"So you don't stand on principle, Humf," said Archie drily.

"I've tried it," I said, "but I always seem to fall through. It's thin ice for making a living."

"Humf, man, you're full of shit!" cried out Sarah from the other side of the fire—and yes, often before we got to the valley I had to put up with this, and learn to take it laughing, feeling I must, and would be better for it, not that I agreed with everything they said and did. But to my mind they are good people, clear and alert, not stupefied, and with a sane understanding of human frailty.

* * *

At length we came to Llandovery amid rainstorms sweeping in, and turned into the wilds past Myddfai towards Black Mountain, then in another direction, and another, until we came to the valley. Down the rough track to a domed building by a river our convoy crawled, some of the trucks by now on their last legs, or wheels, and a crowd of people came out to welcome us in the rain.

We partied all night.

In that poor cold place we partied at any excuse.

The mushroom season was at its height. Someone gave me a handful of little brown growths, pointed like pixie-caps, which I chewed and gamely swallowed. I had a most interesting night during which I discussed the meaning of things with a polite and friendly oak tree.

The valley, sloping gradually up to bare moorland, gives little protection against the weather. Folk live in all sorts of dwellings, from huts and caravans to tipis and benders, which last are but tarpaulins turned tentlike over tied-down branches and staked to the ground. The dome by the river was built by common labour, the lower part being of river-stones cemented, the upper of transparent plastic sheeting stretched over a wooden frame. Here schooling's done, and decision-meetings, and common supper every evening, often sparse, from the stores and riverside gardens. People live with each other or not according to their understandings, and of course on occasion there are disputes, disagreements, what-have-you.

I moved into a well-made tipi with Lorraine, Colum, and Deirdre, and did my best, being agreeable and hard-working, but still saying little of past life, and Lorraine still not asking. There was work to do, it being such a hard, marginal life; and though sometimes I thought it odd that I, once Sir Humfrey Gylberte, should find myself in such a place, I who am Humf put such empty reflections behind me.

Winter came. Cold wet winds turned the poor pastures to mire. There was little food, and often we went hungry for the children. The nights grew long and dark and wild; the outside world seemed scarcely to exist; there was no radio, and few books, and Lorraine grew silent unless she had something practical to say. So, many nights I spent seated on the burlap sacking, staring into the glowing peat fire, watching the smoke waft up through the gap at the ridge, considering the centuries and all I have known. Slowly I came to a perspective on things, about my adventures and all the changes.

In particular I spent many a night considering that weight round the English neck (as I see it now) of the *class system*, whereby each incoming conquering race has thrust down the previous rulers a layer, so that after thousands of years many layers developed, like a cake, which system is now at last strongly challenged and opposed.

Now, once I was a beneficiary of this system, and found no reason to question it, thinking it as fixed and unalterable as the stars in the sky. Yet here at last after all my travels I found myself among folk who admired not the upper classes, nor *any* classes bound into the existing framework of things. No, instead they chose to admire and adopt whatever ways from whatever times most suited them, including the wisdom of those who lived in Britain before the Normans, before the English, before even the Celts and Picts. At first this perplexed me; it seemed unrealistic, another form of retreat, at the same time as they use lorries and such. But gradually I recalled more of what Tari had said, about marriage between Ancient and Modern, and the science of learning what History means. So, while the winds wailed, I began to put a new construction on things.

Only now in Britain, with Empire gone and Order questioned, might the traditional pattern be snapped. But hatreds developed over centuries take a long time to boil out: now the land endures a dull turmoil in which small minds have their way, one thing being over, but the new thing not yet quite born, and a country at the bottom of the turning wheel having much to endure.

Yet when Order's cracked, old dreams spring up anew, demanding marriage with what is lately learned—and it is the heart that beats, not the bones. Clearly the world is caught in great changes; and now with Tari I say that the Phoenix will rise flaming again. Nothing can stop the Hawk taking wing! No number of individual deaths, wars, repressions, or foul bloody massacres can stop the process of History from having its intelligent Light-seeking way. It is written!

I left the valley and Wales in spring of last year. Perhaps I was foolish. Perhaps not. Even if you don't quite see your road, still you will follow it. Lorraine understood what Marianne had not, for she knew I would go before I did. One day she told me so, matter-of-factly. I was puzzled, and asked her what she meant.

"Don't know." Unsmiling, she shrugged. "The way you walk. The faraway look that never leaves your face. You'll have to go. Your feet demand it. They can't stay still much longer."

"What do you think I'm looking for?"

Again, that shrug which accepted everything.

"Don't know. To heal your heart, maybe. To be strong again. But you know what it says in the I Ching. No blame."

She had introduced me to that remarkable Chinese book, and to much else, to healing herbs and serene ways. She never tried to change or restrict me. But on this day a year ago she asked one thing of me:

"Please," she said, "tell me your story before you go."

I knew I must. Her eyes encouraged me. So, with the winds sweeping March rains hard into the valley, I told her all I could or would then remember. I told her of my Newfoundland expedition, of Vulcan and Horsfield, of Tari and Herbie and Masanva. She listened patiently to all of it, and made no comment.

No! I'm wrong!

She *did* make comment! She said something I forgot, or drove out of mind until now. It suddenly flashes back! For when, with difficulty, I spoke of Tari's presumed death, she said the way I talked gave her the odd impression that secretly I *wanted* Tari to be dead.

"What in hell's name do you mean?" I demanded angrily.

"Perhaps she awoke a sleeping part of you," said Lorraine calmly, "but you found it too hard, keeping it awake, so you let it go back to sleep. Whatever it is, your memory of her is a key to it. That's why you don't like remembering. Secretly you're scared it's *you* that's dead. You keep looking for an answer you have already that you ignore, so you can't stop, you can't let yourself find any real peace. Until you do, you won't stay here . . . or anywhere."

Three days later I left. I drove out what she said. God, Gilbert! You persist in aiming at cloudy distant peaks when all the time the truth's like an open barn door ten feet away that a child couldn't miss! Yes, Tari's a ghost now, and no, she is not! She lives in her purpose, and her purpose lives, in myself and others, and it looks now as if I serve it despite my every objection and other intention! Oh, Fool! Why fear and blame others? Look to yourself, to the Light, and step out again!

I wonder if Lorraine is with them at Betws-y-Coed?

⸻❳ 30 ❲⸻

With Red Robbie
on the March to York

Michael just called.

It is late, after midnight, and much still to tell if I'm to be away in the morning, and who would be calling that I might want to hear from? I tried to ignore it, but it went on ringing, until at length I went and snatched it up, cursing the device.

"Thank God!" said a tired voice.

"Michael!" I said. "Michael!"

He told me that he has only just come back from the hospital, has only just learned from his wife that she ordered me out.

"She didn't want me to call you..." God, he sounded so weak! "...I'm sorry, Humfrey, she shouldn't have done..."

"Michael," I said, deciding, "don't speak! Listen! I'm leaving in the morning. The writing's all but done. I'll get it to you, and you can do what you like with it. But that's all. Ursula's right, and I'll bring no more unhappiness on you. The past is the past, so let it be! Sir Humfrey Gylberte is dead and gone—so please forget about him. I'm going, Michael. Thank you for everything."

He spoke a little more, but I stopped him, and said farewell. It is best. Yes. But his voice was so strange.

Well, I marched most of the way up Britain, to Aberdeen, and then I marched halfway down again, to York.

Before I left the valley I took Archie aside and gave him half the money I still had, to go towards whatever was needed. Not much, but I was glad I did it, and it was the only thing I was glad of at all as I walked away with pack on back. I felt an utter fool, thus to obey my legs and abandon such good company, and superstitiously wondered if I had some black spell on me like those put on Flying Dutchman or Wandering Jew. There seemed no good reason to leave at all, but I could not stop myself. I had to go, and did.

Six weeks and five hundred miles later I came through the Highlands of Scotland to the Moray Firth, still jibing at myself for all this senseless, exhausting wandering. Yet during my arduous trek I learned much, and now it's clear that all this walking helped me to what sanity I have. Only by relationship with the natural world, by constant treading of the solid earth, have I been able to come to any sort of terms with the present societies. Yes, so, and on my long walk I met not only trouble and anger, but also that goodheartedness that can spring out of folk when times are most critical. If not for that I'd have lost all will. Luck, or Seven, helped too, for drifters were being checked and jailed, there being threat of riot everywhere in the industrial parts. Yet I had little trouble, and was never stopped. Perhaps I looked too much a shabby ghost to worry about. So many folk were now unemployed that during winter the Social Security system had broken down. Suddenly *everyone* without work found themselves "disreputable." The government said there was no more money, which many refused to believe, so that now in some areas the army was engaged in the time-honoured tradition of protecting rich from poor. But soon, I heard often, there was to be a great march of the unemployed from every part of the land to London.

I felt little connection to any of this and had no thought of joining the march before I came to a fishing-town, Buckie, on the Moray Firth coastline, between Aberdeen and Inverness.

By the time I got there I was in a dream of exhaustion. Even now I cannot recall any of the last hundred or so miles before Buckie. After surmounting the impressive hurdle of the Grampian Mountains I continued north in an automatic daze, and no doubt would have gone further north if not for the sea. One morning after walking on an hour or so, over gentle land with fields of unripened corn, I found the waves before me, and nothing else, but for a line of pale blue mountains seventy or eighty miles away across the water.

Turning east along the road I soon came to a town of neat grey streets, to a large harbour where many fishing-boats were laid up, paint peeling. At a hotel I got a room and slept for thirty hours.

Awakening, I ate, then took my pack and went into the hotel bar for a pint before hitting the road into the night again.

They were hard to understand in there, but cordial. I asked about the laid-up boats. The barman said the industry was ruined because the cod, herring, and mackerel had been hunted virtually into extinction. I could hardly believe this, that now all you could find on the slabs were expensive flat monstrosities from the depths. But apparently it was so. Wondering what Pysgie would have said to all this, I took my pint and sat down, shucking off my pack.

"So ye're a travellin' man too," said a voice.

I looked up and aside and saw along the wall-bench a small thickset man with a shock of red hair and a freckled face. He was dressed much as I, and had a pack beside him too. We got to talking. He said his name was Robbie. He said his last regular job had been as a steelworker, ten years before.

"Could you not find anything else?" I asked him.

He grinned dourly and raised his glass to the light.

"Nivver a chance. The bastards blacked me—Red Robbie they called me—an' whan the steel-mills closed, that was it!"

I asked him what he meant, and got his grin again.

"How lang ye been asleep? Yer name Rip Van Winkle then?"

I spun my yarn about long exile, about my wanderings over America and up the length of Britain.

"An' whit are ye dein' it for?" he demanded. "Hae ye got a purrpose in a' this waakin'? Is it for health, or whit?"

I had no good answer. I could only ask why *he* was on the road.

"No got the bus-fare," he said, nodding vigorously at the barman to set both of us up, "an' need the practiss. Gannin' tae Aiberdeen tae join the Big Marrch tha'll take us doon sooth tae sweep that bloody pairnicious excuse for a government richt oot! Nae a single thing tae lose, an' looks tae me that ye're in the same boat, Jimmy. Ye should come alang an' help thraw the boogars oot!"

Well, he had no bus-fare, but he had drinking-money, and I had a yen to be drunk, and so for unmeasured hours until closing-time I gabbled with Red Robbie, though for the most part he did the talking. He told me much fascinating stuff about

Marxism, interpreting my sufferings as I described them in terms of this philosophy. I was impressed, yet he could not convince me that this Marxian Dialectic of Class Struggle is something new in human affairs. I seem to remember quoting him Ovid and Seneca and Joachite prophecy of the twelfth century, on the Three Ages of History. "Surely," I argued, "this Equality of Man is age-old belief flying in the face of age-old fact: the Corruptibility of Man! These Levelling attempts are nothing new!" And I think I told him the words of John Ball, executed as a leader of the Peasants' Revolt in 1381: *"Good folk, things cannot go well in England nor ever shall until all things are in common and there is neither villein nor noble, but all of us are of one condition."* Robbie wasn't impressed: the last I clearly recall of that night is that he turned my knowledge against me. "Aye," he said thoughtfully, "well, if the notion's been aboot *that* lang, then it's due its day. Man, ye canna haud back an idea wha's time hae come. Those Yanks'll hae to blaw us a' tae smithereens afore they'll stop it. Mind, I'm no sayin' the Russians are ony better, an' there's truth in whit ye say—but ye canna go back, man, ye canna go back."

At closing time we were both turned out, but must have helped each other, for with pounding head I awoke at dawn to find myself in my sleeping bag on the shingle above high tide, and first I saw Robbie's red head sticking out of his bag a few feet away.

Next I saw the policeman who moved us on.

So I went to Aberdeen with Robbie. Why not? I said. Perhaps an old dog can learn new tricks, for I'm no longer the Queen's man, but disreputable, and a low sort. I am Humf. What's to lose?

Aberdeen had lately enjoyed an oil-boom, which now was all but over, and unemployment as bad there as anywhere else. In a few days I heard much bitter talk, and saw much organisation.

Five thousand of us started south on foot a week after Robbie and I got there. We rarely kept company after the march began. To him I was an oddity. I was still in a dream, yet also enthralled by the strange spirit of the movement I'd casually joined. It was defiant, devil-may-care, yet desperation underlay it, though nobody openly admitted it. So, we set off down the road, police patrolling us, and helicopters hovering low and threatening above, which caused much booing and cursing. By night we slept rough in fields along the way. We carried supplies with us and helped each other out; and by day we marched with much singing of songs and chanting of vehement slogans: there was excited talk of what we might gain through the unity of half a million of us from many cities all in London at once. Yet I was confused by the great variety of dissenting organisations on the march, many of whom apparently hated each other, but who had for the time being agreed on common cause. There were Trotskyites, Leninists, Marxists, Maoists, Nationalists, United Fronts against *this* and against *that,* and representatives of many Unions, and many, many more. I was reminded of the great rally in St. Louis where I drank the Pepsi-Cola spiked with LSD—but in fact there was little similarity. The people on this march were mostly socialist, and their material condition much worse than among those at St. Louis; worse even than among those Chicano rioters in San Francisco. Also there were few groups dedicated, as in the States I had found so common, to individualistic causes such as Gay Rights and Jews for Jesus and the rest of it. The loathing of government and cynicism about its intentions were common factors, yes, but where in the States the government was powerful and blatantly corrupt, here in Britain it seemed too weak to be blatantly *anything,* and I could not see what gain the march would bring. Once or twice I tried to argue that perhaps there really *was* no more money in Britain, and that *no* government, left or right, could find a quick solution to such general misery—save perhaps by declaring war on France, which always worked well in the past as a means of diverting popular attention.

But soon I learned I could not say such things if I wished to stay healthy, and I heard many a tirade full of facts and figures proving beyond doubt that Jewish bankers and Tory businessmen had stolen all the money and banked it abroad for their own use. No doubt some of this is true, but what it *did* tell me was that Reason is no more humanity's strong point now than it was four hundred years ago, or four thousand years ago, being still for the most part the whore and slave of Desire, Interest, and Prejudice.

We marched through the depressed grey city of Dundee, where ten thousand joined us, banners flying, and then to Edinburgh, which added another few thousand; three days later we were at Berwick on the English border, and thence to New-castle-on-Tyne, where more than thirty thousand increased us as we went on through Jarrow, South Shields, Darlington, and other towns with a long history of poverty. Thus in time we came near York over sixty thousand strong, and I finding my feet, as it were, yet again forgetting Sir Humfrey, and speaking passionately at our nightly camps on what I'd learned in America, ranting on the struggles of red man, black man, yellow man, and many a white man too, and I did not forget the Woman's Movement. I spoke as if I knew what I was talking about, and indeed came to believe I did, political fever and the desire to be well-regarded both being so seductive. But of Horsfield I said nothing.

Then one night police came and said there would be trouble if we did not disperse. They said the army would stop us if we tried to march through York. They advised us to be sensible, saying we could not succeed in our aims. So in a field we had a great meeting, and nobody knew what to do, until a man named Robert Auld made a fiery speech that roused us. He said we had them running scared, and they could not stop us, more than two hundred thousand marchers from other parts also being on their way to London. "Let them do their worst!" he cried. "What can we lose? How can we turn and creep home now?"

When he had us at fever-pitch we rose and continued at dawn.

The army met us outside a village called Easingwold, attacking us with gas and rubber bullets. Many of us were injured before we were broken up. But a large band of us, over two thousand strong, evaded the troops by striking across country, and we came into York. Many there were eager to help us, and told us that two thousand more were coming from Hull. But the army came after us and caught us near the university grounds where students had joined us. Armoured lorries rumbled among us with blinding gas, and when we were utterly confused and vomiting the soldiers moved in with force.

Now some of us had guns, of which many disapproved, saying use of them would cause tragedy—which is what happened. For temper was utterly lost, guns were fired, several soldiers were shot, at which they exchanged rubber bullets for real bullets, and advanced on us shooting to kill. Over twenty of us were slain, and I was shot in the shoulder. Amid this debacle I crawled into a garden to escape the searching soldiers, and somehow got in through the unlocked back door of a house. I collapsed, bleeding heavily, on the clean linoleum floor of a kitchen. And I remember, as the dizziness rushed over me, hearing the shocked voice of a woman calling out: "Michael! Quick! One of them's in here! He's been shot!"

That is how I met Michael and Ursula Greene.

·──┤ 31 ├──·

Telephones Ringing:
A Circle's Completed

It's after three o'clock and black deep night but the telephone is ringing again! A pox on the pernicious thing! On and on and on! I should have torn the wires of it out of the wall! There's no privacy left at all in this world! Shrilling at me like a shrieking child—no, I will not answer you! God, so nearly done, and I feel watched again, the fear's back on me! Did I claim I'd lost it? Hah! It's still ringing. What if it's Michael again? His voice sounded so strange: what if someone was at his shoulder? Maybe he was trying to warn me, but I didn't listen close enough. No, it feels bad, don't answer it. Perhaps now I should stop and eat and pack my gear in case—no! I'm not tired, and I will finish this, tonight! Complete the circle, cut the knot, or never at all! I cannot flee incomplete! Trust in the Hawk, Humf! Keep on!

The ringing has stopped.

Michael, what will you do with this, *if* you get it? Burn it? Shut it in a drawer? Submit it for publication as a strange romance, with certain names and relevant details removed or changed? Or stick your neck out like a fool still mad for the publication of Truth that is true if you publish or not? I hope you don't do that. Do what you like with this, but don't crucify yourself. You don't have to be a hero, so look after yourself and listen to Ursula.

Michael, you're the only ghost who still haunts me. The others are laid to rest. Your prompting persuaded me to it.

It is so ironic, your ill-luck now. I would never have told you the truth if not for that documentary we saw on TV.

To start with, you knew only that I was a wounded Right-to-Work marcher, bleeding all over your kitchen floor. Neither you nor Ursula had much sympathy with the political spirit or intention of the march, and you had a lot to lose by harbouring me. We were called "common criminals," but you could have been had up for conspiracy. Yes, and I must have looked as "disreputable" as can be imagined. Yet both of you were horrified by what you'd seen of the fighting from your upstairs window, and when I crawled in you realised you had four options. You could throw me out to military mercies; you could call the police; you could take me to a hospital to be treated, then arrested; or you could give me refuge, quietly calling a doctor-friend to come as soon as possible. You chose the fourth. "I don't like seeing that sort of thing in this country," you said later, when I asked you why. Ursula had deep misgivings, but you prevailed on her humanity. "The poor man's bleeding to death," you said. "We should get him patched up at least," and your wife agreed. So you told me. But you realised no mystery about me until, putting me to bed, you saw the scars, and the U.S. passport that slipped out of my pocket. Then again in delirious sleep I started babbling nonsense in strange accent that had you wondering what I was.

Discreetly when the troops were gone you called your friend. The wound was not serious. It was mainly exhaustion and loss of blood. The bullet tore muscle while passing through, but little worse.

Yet the *coincidence* was serious.

Or was it the Hawk again?

Forty-eight hours later, with the nation still in tumult of media-babble about the massacre, I sat with Ursula and yourself in a comfortable living-room. The night was warm, but the curtains were fully closed. My constitution being good, my recovery was swift, though my left shoulder was heavily bandaged and my arm was in a sling. But there was still danger. Twice the soldiers had returned, making door-to-door searches throughout the neighbourhood, and each time you successfully turned them away with your reputable composure. But Ursula was very unhappy about it on grounds of patriotic conscience,

and it was agreed I'd leave as soon as the heat was off and I
could get by without a conspicuous sling.

In fact I planned to leave that very night, secretly, and take
my chances. But it never happened.

Michael, I still didn't know your work. The room held wall-
to-wall bookcases overflowing with volumes on history, and
the only unbooked wall carried gilt-framed reproductions of
miniatures from my time by Hilliard and others. But I was
blank, hardly taking in anything. I had briefly spun my usual
yarn of long exile and recent return, but no more. I felt most
uneasy, wondering only why you were helping me when evidently it caused your wife such distress.

But you were already curious about me. I remember noting
how you started at the way in which, when you turned on the
TV for the News, I promptly reseated myself to one side to
avoid the harmful rays; this precaution by now habitual, though
I no longer felt them so acutely.

So, stiffly, each gripping our little glasses of sherry, we
watched the News with all its riot and fury of battle, Parlia-
mentary uproar, foreign denunciation. The other columns of
marchers had stopped, some had begun to disperse, but the air
in the land was most poisonous, and it was unclear if the
government would survive. Students had been shot amid the
debacle; you groaned to hear again of a victim in your own
department, and Ursula's face was a study in conflicting loy-
alties. I wondered if I should get up and walk out right away.
And when the main story was over you got up to turn the
television off. But even as you did, the telephone rang.

It was a fatal interruption. You went into a neighbouring
room to answer it. Ursula and I spoke not a word. When you
came back, again you went to the TV to turn if off, but even
as you entered the room, the BBC announcer was saying:

*"Our next programme, after a Party Political Broadcast on
behalf of the Social Democrat Party, is a documentary con-
cerning events said by some to have been triggered over five
years ago in the Atlantic by Project Vulcan. The programme
will look at the evidence pro and con the existence of "Distressed Temporal Immigrants," who, some claim, exist and are
secretly held by the . . ."*

"The world's falling apart!" you remarked angrily, hand on
the switch, "and they try to lull us with rubbish like this!"

Ah, the ifs and buts of life. Had the phone not rung, and

had I kept quiet, none of this would have been. Perhaps I should not slander the telephone. It is only a messenger.

"Please!" It burst sharply out of me. It surprised me. I had thought I'd stay quiet. "Forgive me, but... I must see that programme! It is of great personal concern to me!"

That was the first time Ursula met my eyes directly. She is a fine woman, Michael, I imagine her eyes can be very warm, and I do not blame her at all for giving me only ice.

"Why, Mr. Loomiss? Had you something to do with it?"

"Yes." I looked away, regretting my big mouth. "I did."

"You do seem to get involved in the most odd situations," you said, hovering, your tone light, but grey gaze piercing. You appear vague to people, and in some ways you are, but in other ways not. "Are you sure you're not a journalist, you know, the sort who goes into the thick of it for the best story?"

"No... I'm not." I was confused, and wavered, but I'd said it already. I looked up. "Please... I don't wish to impose... but it is important to me to know what they have to say." I hesitated. "It's the first chance I've had to learn... media-opinion about the business. Perhaps you'll know that in America people who tried to speak out on it were killed or intimidated into silence?"

By now you were a most puzzled man. Part of you wanted to laugh it off... but there's a bloodhound in you, and you were on the scent.

"Well!" You turned down the volume but left the set on. "Evidently we'll have to watch it." You met your wife's eye and she sat stiff and upright as you sat and lit your pipe, eyeing me curiously. "Of course we never knew much about it here. I always thought it was something to do with an alternative energy-source, and that all this stuff about time-travellers was on a par with bug-eyed monsters from outer space. Were you on one of the, er, ships involved in the affair?"

"Yes." I was trembling now. "In a sense I was."

"One of the crew, or technicians?" asked Ursula.

"No. No. Nothing like that."

"Do you *believe* in these... Distressed Temporal... whatsits?" she asked, staring now as if I might dissolve at any second.

"There *is* evidence," I said carefully, "that they exist."

She shook her head. You raised your brows and said nothing.

"I have to see to the supper," said Ursula, and left us, and rather than speak you turned up the volume on the political broadcast, and poured me another drink in an almost conspiratorial manner.

But what did you think was coming, Michael?

When the political broadcast was over, Ursula returned willy-nilly and we settled to watch. Rather, *you* settled—I was on the edge of my seat, finding it hard to breathe, and Ursula too was nervous.

And with good cause.

The documentary did not endorse the existence of DTIs. On the contrary. The commentator spoke most skeptically of belief in such unlikely beings, alluding with typical British sense of superiority (even in such times, yes, is it not remarkable?) to the tendency of many Americans to believe naively in escapist nonsense of the most wild-eyed variety. It doubted the authenticity of documents leaked from the State Department and other sources that indicated a coverup, managing at the same time to suggest that U.S. security was not all it could be. It laughed at tales of DTIs held prisoner in a secret institute, and subtly deprecated the testimony of "renegade" U.S. scientists and Navy personnel (at this point you both cast worried looks at me) who'd fled the States in order to speak out. Likewise it scorned claims that U.S. law agencies had arranged the "accidental" deaths of several such "renegades" in the States.

In connection with this came the first of the shocks. Onto the screen flashed the image of a man lying twisted and obviously dead in a city street. When I saw his face I recognised it immediately and could not hold my tongue. "I know that man!" I exclaimed wildly. "I met him in Chaunticleer's last year. In San Francisco. He was a cameraman on the *Slocum* when they . . ."

I stopped. This time you both looked at me as if I were mad. Then came the commentator's explanation. Apparently three months earlier this man had phoned the San Francisco *Chronicle* claiming to have videorecorded DTIs as they were brought on board the USN submarine *Slocum*.

Michael, your eyebrows climbed right up, and Ursula hissed.

The commentary went on. It seemed this man claimed to have deserted the Navy with copies of the tapes he'd made.

He said he was scared that "something" would happen to him. He wanted the *Chronicle* to send a reporter to meet him at a safe rendezvous. He was told this was impossible, that he must bring the tapes to the *Chronicle* offices for assessment. He agreed reluctantly: so said the subeditor said to have taken the call. An hour later, approaching the entrance of the newspaper building, the man was struck and mortally injured by a van that mounted the sidewalk and pinned him to the wall. The driver, later described as "Oriental," jumped out and bent over him as if in horror and to help, but then leaped back into the van, reversed, and drove off through a red light. Before the man died he said enough to confirm him as the voice which had called the *Chronicle*. He was dead by the time police got there. Later the police issued a statement. The dead man was a John Doe, no tapes had been found, the hit-and-run driver had not been caught, and his plates could not be traced.

You stared at me with mounting perplexity.

Worse, or better, came next. The commentator, in the same urbanely sarcastic manner, went on to disparage:

"...chrononuts and their supporters, who claim either that they *are* DTIs, or that they have met DTIs. A person in this latter category—a singer with American rock group KRON-ONUTZ, Sylvia Kasaboulis—recently approached us with videotape she claims to have shot four years ago, in St. Louis, when..."

The shock of it! My shivering was visible and acute. "Are you all right, Mr. Loomiss?" demanded Ursula, half out of her chair, not looking too steady herself as I tried to speak. "You...you had better turn it off," I whispered, "I don't think that what you're going to see will...will help to..."

I couldn't go on. All I'd denied! I thought I would faint.

"Michael, turn it off, please!" said Ursula.

"No!" Your voice had an edge. "Now that it's on we'll watch it, if you don't mind!"

"Michael, I insist!"

"I will watch it!" you stated flatly, setting down your pipe.

I remembered that tape, made in the suburb of St. Louis where we stayed after the rally. Now through a haze of foreboding I saw Sylvia's face. She spoke with a woman interviewer who was offscreen.

Rather, they were arguing.

". . . and so you claim that your band KRONONUTZ—which I assume refers to this cult—met these two 'DTIs' hitchhiking on . . ."

"It's not a cult," insisted Sylvia, "and not *my* band."

"Will you let me ask my question, please?"

"Sure. I just don't like you making it so plain you think I'm a nut. You could at least try to be

Oh God.

The phone's started again.

RING RING RING RING!!! No, I will not speak to you. It's nearly five o'clock, dawn soon, not much more night, and maybe I should go, now, yes, but I must finish this, or I *know* I'll be left undone, I *know* it. Just stop ringing, damn you! If I take fright now and go, I won't finish this—and I must, it must be done, I'll complete the circle, it's nearly there, and all in my mind so strong I can ignore that device, yes, I can!

Stopped. It stopped.

Do it, fool. Get this done.

Yes. "You could at least try to be polite!" said Sylvia. God, I have perfect memory of it, burned in, so now burn it out!

"You say you met these two," the unseen interviewer went on, "in Kentucky, and took them with you to a rally in St. Louis, where one of them got up onstage and took the microphone and claimed to be the Elizabethan sailor-explorer Sir Humphrey Gilbert. Is that correct? You say it's his face and voice on the tape, and that the woman is—or *was*—an Egyptian priestess of Isis, no less? And you believed them and knew them for some six months until the group protecting them in Chicago was infiltrated by the CIA and . . ."

"No, not the CIA. Some branch of the Feds."

". . . and then they went on the run and vanished mysteriously. . . ."

"No. Tari was murdered. Humf was shot in the head, but recovered. People looked after him. Then he went off on his own. We don't know where he is, or if he's alive or dead."

" 'Tari'? 'Humf'? It sounds as if you were on remarkably familiar terms with these . . ."

"Come on! People are people, wherever or whenever!"

"Do you really expect people to believe all this?"

"I don't care. Who believed in space-travel a hundred years ago? I just say what I know. Of course I don't have sure proof. But I'm sure in my heart. Totally."

"Why? What was it about them?"

"A thousand little things. I could go on all night."

"We don't want you doing that. I hear you're playing a big show tonight. Good luck with your band. Thanks for talking to us."

Sylvia shrugged and grimaced at someone off screen. Chris? Vic? Dan? Johan? I sat there in a chill sweat of apprehension, in a sort of spell, my wounded shoulder throbbing. "And now let us see and hear this... *remarkable* tape," continued the commentator. "The donor has taken great care to treat it so that the faces of people in the room you'll see have been blacked out, except for the two alleged DTIs. Ms. Kasaboulis appears to be sincere in fearing danger from her own government, while apparently willing to risk her own safety.

"But the subjects of the tape—said to be Sir Humphrey Gilbert, a half-brother of Sir Walter Raleigh; and Nefertari Mery-Isis, from the Eighteenth Dynasty in Egypt, a century before King Tut—can clearly be seen and heard."

Oh, Michael. You and Ursula both stared at me, sitting there in your living-room; and then you turned and stared *at my face, and at Tari's face,* there on the screen of your television set.

Neither of you said a word. Both of you just looked back and forth and back and forth and back and forth, sang-froid quite gone, and I cannot tell who was more shocked, yourselves or I.

I was clearly recognisable as the same man. On the TV my hair was not so long and shaggy, but my beard and face were the same, and my voice. The two of you stared, and listened, and so did I, and not a word was said while Tari (it hurt, it hurt to see her lovely face and hear the calm of her voice again!) spoke of the cycles of History; of the Marriage of Ancient and Modern...

Then we listened to myself as I spoke of the prophecy the cunning man once made to me at Eton Fair in April of 1550.

"*...He told it all to me when I was but eleven,*" I heard and saw my image say. "*He said from the sea I'd be taken by a power not...*"

Then suddenly, with an oath, Ursula frozen beside you, you jumped up and turned off the TV set with a snap, and your face was contorted with fury and disbelief as you turned on my shivering self.

"HOW...DARE...YOU?" you demanded. "You come bleeding into our house and at great risk we help you and you...DO YOU KNOW WHO I AM? How could you play a trick like this on..."

Then, and I admire you greatly for it, you realised the illogicality of your rage, and controlled yourself with great effort while I stared at the flowered carpet and Ursula breathed in gasps.

At length you grunted in amazement, and shook your head, and went to a bookcase. You pulled out a fat volume and tossed it over the room into my lap, where it arrived with force.

With difficulty I read the title.

Cunning Men and the Occult Tradition in Elizabethan England. It was published by Heinemann, and the author was Michael Greene.

The Hawk, yes, the Hawk. Why not? Either way, it happened. And who knows what will come of all this? With your book in my lap I gazed at you. I was stupefied and unable to move. "I realise," you said slowly, with utmost self-control, "the stupidity of my first suspicion, that you chose deliberately to be shot outside our house just two nights before the broadcast of this programme. But understand—whoever you are—that we are both extremely shocked!"

Ursula muttered assent. I too strove for self-control.

"You may think me mad!" My voice still trembled. "Doubtless I am! Yes, and I understand if you think me but a lunatic playing a low trick on you! But I would never have told you who I am if not for this! I stopped doing that after Tari died, save in two cases."

Clumsily, with difficulty, I stood. "I have no wish to bring harm to you. I will go, now, if you want."

"Michael," said Ursula in a thin voice, "I think...I don't know...that maybe we should...perhaps...?"

"I'll not blame you if you do," I said grimly. "Only give me a few minutes, that's all I ask."

Then I saw you shaking your head, Michael. There was an odd, almost hungry gleam in your eye as you regarded me. "No," you said, and you sounded puzzled at yourself. "No need to rush anything. I think we should at least...sleep on it."

And that's how all this began.

·····❰ 32 ❱❈··

Aquarius:
Vision of the Dancers

And how it ends.

I got away by the skin of my teeth.

Tonight we're camped outside Wrexham, Michael. To-morrow we go on to Liverpool. There are many of us, more than last year, more with each convoy that arrives, and here tonight half-a-dozen convoys stand grouped together for strength. I don't know how many of us there are, but I can see fires twinkling away into the night in all directions. The time has come, the police and soldiers are too busy to pay us the sort of attention they'd like. They're distracted; we should be able to get into Liverpool without too much difficulty. Archie and Lorraine tell me there has been a lot of argument in recent weeks. Some say we should have nothing to do with the fight in the cities, but involve ourselves only where and when it touches us in the country. The majority view (which seems sound to me) is that to sit passively now is to court destruction and waste of much good effort. Most agree we must take what we have into the fight, and breed our spirit into whatever may come of all this. "If we stay out now," Archie said to me just an hour ago, "we'll never find common ground with those folk in the streets. We have to show them we're with them all the way. You've been a soldier, haven't you, Humf?"

"We."

"Our." Yes. I've chosen where and with whom and for what I'll stand, and for more than one good reason! Michael, you know I was once a soldier, and not such a bad soldier at that. The times may change, but not human affairs. Things go

313

in spiraling cycles. Peace and war, peace and war, and Humf knows where he stands now, an it's neither Marx nor Capital, Michael. In my view what's at stake goes far beyond that weary mechanical duality.

Yes, I made it by the skin of my teeth.

It was already after dawn yesterday morning when I wrote those last words (only a page ago, but universes ago, too!) on how you and I met, and how this all began. *"That's it!"* I told myself, *"It's done, let's go!"* Yet very nearly I went on writing for a few more minutes after that, wanting to round the whole thing off with some well-chosen fine-sounding words; such as declamatory description of how Gylberte is now dead so that Humf may live and love and fight again, and making my final judgments on England and America, perhaps with a quotation or two in Latin—all that—but suddenly, with sun near to rising, I had such a strong prickly feeling of imminent inter- ruption, of disaster, that I put down my pen and wrote not another word. In short, I was in a blue funk, with the sense of not a second to be wasted. I bundled up all these pages into the pack with the rest of my necessary gear, pulled on my boots, made sure of the map to Betws-y-Coed, and in ten minutes I was out of that house with dishes unwashed and fire still burning.

Foolish, nervous Humf! Can't answer telephones and flees because of prickles up the spine! So I was scolding myself as I climbed quickly up the pastures, aiming north, up to the standing stone—and was almost up to the top of the hill when from below I heard cars, and quite without thinking threw myself flat behind a bush. When I looked I saw two cars with turret-lights and black-and-white chequer-patterns on their sides come bumping along to the house I'd just quit. Police! Yes, so I scolded myself no more, but got on as quick as I could, stopping just a few seconds at the stone to touch it and give the Hawk my thanks for alerting me. Call it what you like, Michael. And the rest of yesterday I stayed to the land. No roads, and those I crossed I crossed with great care. It's wild land as you know, and I met nobody, but I got caught in a nasty storm. Eventually I knew I wouldn't reach Betws-y-Coed before night. So I stayed in a wood on a lee slope, quite comfortable, really, once I found stuff dry enough to make a fire. I made a shelter and wrapped up tight and was quick asleep.

It's not clear to me why the law came at such a time—early in the day yet late in the month. But I don't have to worry about that.

I slept as sound as a babe, until midway through the night I woke up. You can call it one of these terrifically real dreams I get, if you prefer. For high up the slope above me, through the trees, there was a dancing light.

The rain had stopped. The sky was clear, moon waxing bright, stars like petals, very soft through the wet clean atmosphere; and the land about was layers of dark woody hilly watery presence, all intermingled and vibrant with tremendous sense of lovemaking. The trees rustled soft all about, an owl hooted far away, away a mile or more. And the light—Michael, it was like a will-o'-the-wisp, sometimes two, dancing all over the high pasture, and of course I got up and put on my boots and climbed after it. And so on a high field under the moon I came to them.

Do I have to tell you who they were?

Well, she had her raven hair again, and he as massive as I remembered, magnificent-headed, and I felt those wings that beat above, beating the whole earth, to the beat of which they danced.

They danced the dance of what we do now.

Do you understand me?

When they were gone—or when I awoke—I found myself alone on that slope with dawn. Yes, I had my boots on. I struck camp and made my way the last few miles to Betws-y-Coed.

Once again I found them on the point of departure.

Police were patrolling not-so-casually in the not-so-immediate vicinity of the heath where the convoy was camped. I made my way through them easily enough. I came in, and found a welcome.

Archie took me to Lorraine and when we came to her she turned round unsurprised, as if expecting me, and she was not unhappy about it at all! Neither was I! And she had not one surprise, but two!"

"Oh, hullo," she exclaimed, "your colours look so much better, Humf! Hey, I tried to call you twice, a couple of nights ago, pretty late, but there was no answer. Maybe I got given the wrong number."

Michael, I tell you I was taken aback, and chagrined.

But I can live with it.

It seems that Joe Thomas (Grace mentioned him to me: the local lad who knows these terrible people my friends) told them about the eccentric Englishman staying at Griffith of Gwernacca's old house, so Lorraine knew immediately who it was, and she found the number and rang, late, to be sure I'd be there to answer if there at all. But I wouldn't answer, being so full of bugaboos about the thing.

I told her about it, though not without a cough or two.

She laughed and said she feels the same about telephones.

Colum and Deirdre are well, and were glad to see me. It wasn't until I'd greeted them that she produced her other surprise.

Well! And he has my looks too, the lucky young pup!

She says she knew before I went but decided not to tell me because if she had I wouldn't have gone, which would only have ended up with my blaming her for keeping me. Or something like that.

Michael, this day has been rather remarkable for me. Somehow it completes the whole business. I am no longer a stranger. I have a child in this age. I am a father, and related to others.

I'm still overwhelmed, and perhaps I'm prattling foolishly, but it all seems to me as if . . . how can I put it?—

No. Let's not even try. There are things to do.

As for Liverpool, I had my doubts whether children should go in with us, but discussion has decided that we *all* go in.

Michael, this is a joyous day for me. As soon as I can I'll mail this, to the other address, just in case; also the printed card you gave me to tip you off that it's delivered there.

Be careful, Michael. Godspeed, my friend. Farewell.

Michael Greene
Laughs at Last

After his diet-controlled breakfast, still in his dressing-gown, the pale man slowly climbed the stairs to his study. He looked and moved like one for whom the spirit has gone out of life. At his desk he shuffled papers and scribbled a few notes, but it was only habit, his mind was not on it. Outside birds chattered in newly budded trees; he heard them no more than he noticed or took heart from the sunlight spilling through the windows. Soon, with a sigh, he dropped the papers and took up a dog-eared snapshot of a tall, slim, choleric-looking middle-aged man. No observable expression occupied his face as he studied it.

Some minutes later his wife came in with mail and folded newspaper fresh from the doorstep. "Mail, dear," she said, but frowned to see the photograph on the desk before him. "You're not still worrying about him, are you? He's gone, you know. That man Griffith says he must have left just before the police came to take him in for raping that poor girl. Dreadful business! How you were fooled by him in the first place I'll never know!" She plumped mail and folded paper down over the snapshot. "There's a letter from the Chancellor's office. It must be your formal reinstatement. They've been very understanding, don't you think?"

"Um," he said, not looking up. "Um."

She left, still frowning. After the door shut he picked the bundle of mail up listlessly, and began to slit open the Chancellor's note with a penknife—then tossed it aside.

317

For the first time that day light came to his eyes.

Under the university letter was a postcard, a printed item.

PHILIP OGILVIE, ANTIQUARIAN BOOKS, said the black Gothic script. Address and telephone number followed, then, WE ARE PLEASED TO ANNOUNCE AN AUCTION OF RARE & VALUABLE ITEMS AT OUR . . .

He looked for the mark he'd made. It was there.

His heart began to beat rapidly. *Careful,* he thought, *don't overdo it.* But he felt glad. He felt hope again. His mind, so long sluggish with fear and confusion, began to move. He picked up the local paper automatically. *Have to get to the boathouse somehow,* he was thinking as he opened up the news, *It'll be there now! I'll say I need an afternoon alone at the river to think things out. Tomorrow? Drive me there and pick me up later. I'll get it back here, and . . .*

The headline. The headline caught his eye.

MYSTERY MADMAN CHARGES LIVERPOOL TROOPS!

There was a photograph. Something familiar . . .

"Oh my God!" he uttered, "Humf! No! Surely not!"

His heart. He took a pill. Then he read the story:

LIVERPOOL, *23rd April.* By Our Correspondent.

Soldiers of the Lancashire Fusiliers were driven back from their positions in the Hoxton suburb of Liverpool today following a bizarre assault on their barricades.

At dawn, only hours after the weary troops had driven mobs armed with bricks and Molotov Cocktails out of the disputed area, the men of C Company were awakened by a trumpet fanfare.

"Scared the s . . t out of me!" a private soldier later told our man. "We're used to hearing that coloured reggae stuff, but this sounded straight out of bleedin' John Wayne!"

In the immediate wake of the trumpet call, a rider mounted on a black horse burst out of a side-street fifty yards from the barricades. The rider charged, apparently singlehanded, waving a sword in one hand, and in the other carrying a crude banner with the emblem of what seemed to be a hawk painted on it.

"Our men were confused," our man was told by an officer who requested anonymity, "their training in street-tactics includes no provision for dealing with this sort of thing."

Bellowing a warcry variously described as *"Agelbert," "Agincourt,"* or *"A Gilbert,"* the rider, dressed in pseudo-medieval garb, thundered straight at the army barricade without a shot being fired at him.

"So what would you do?" a disgruntled NCO later demanded of our man. "We know how to deal with blokes throwing rocks and that, but this was like a loony dream! I mean what's things coming to? This f....r just rode right over us. Then the rest of the b......s hit us while we was all watching him doing his Charge of the Light Brigade bit. We didn't have a chance."

Even as the Mystery Rider leaped over the Fusilier emplacement, smoke-bombs were fired into the soldiers from neighbouring rooftops. Next a mob attacked the position, driving the troops back as the Mystery Rider wheeled and charged back into the melee. *"For England and St. George!"* he cried, according to several reports.

Fighting was severe during the following hour. Despite reinforcements the Fusiliers were forced to fall back.

At noon today the Hoxton streets, reclaimed by people who say the troops were an occupying army, are full of rumours about the identity of the Mystery Rider. The strangest tale this reporter has heard is that the man is a 16th-century DTI! Wild times indeed!

So far there is no sign of the Mystery Man himself. In the wake of the fighting he and his black horse are nowhere to be found. Many mouths are tightly shut in Hoxton today.

"These wretched people must learn that they cannot defy authority so easily," stated Col. Blaize-Gore of the Fusiliers this afternoon. He declined to indicate when or whether his troops will be ordered into Hoxton again.

Meanwhile tonight in Hoxton the spirit of
(turn to page 3)

*   *   *

The pale man was no longer pale. He did not turn to page three.

Instead he leaned back. A chuckle escaped him. Then another. He began to laugh heartily.

"Oh my God, Humf!" he exclaimed.

Editor's Note
on Biographical Sources

Much of HG's account is naturally difficult to verify, particularly in regard to his recent experiences, but also where his early years are concerned. He and his brother Adrian *did* have their uncle, Philip Penkewell, for guardian after their father's early death; and he *did* attend Eton and Oxford, but little else about his early life is recorded. However, the events he mentions in connection with his mature years are for the most part verifiable and appear to be accurate, although of course conversational detail cannot be checked.

During initial research with HG, while still highly skeptical of his claims, I gleaned historical information from the following sources: *Sir Humphrey Gilbert, Elizabeth's Racketeer*, Donald Barr Chidsey, Harper, 1932; *The Life of Sir Humphrey Gilbert, England's First Empire Builder*, William Gilbert Gosling, Constable, 1911; *Sir Humfrey Gylberte and His Enterprise of Colonisation in America*, Carlos Slafter (1825), Boston, Prince Society, 1903; *The Voyage and Colonising Enterprises of Sir Humphrey Gilbert*, ed. D. B. Quinn, Hakluyt Society, 1940; and, of course, Hakluyt's *Voyages of the Elizabeth Seamen to America*, De La Rue, 1880; and others—plus a variety of other sources that need not be mentioned here.

Save in minor matters of spelling and punctuation I have not in any way edited or tampered with HG's manuscript. His variable spelling of his name I have left as it is, limiting my functions to those of typist and executor in the publication of this account; except in regard to *Introduction* and *Afterword*, where I have essayed short dramatisations to round the thing out, as it were. I am also responsible for the chapter titles and the Table of Contents, frivolous though some may find these. It is my reluctant understanding that the account cannot be published as *Fact:* the Publisher has requested these items in order to prettify the bald narrative; the responsibility is mine alone.

As he promised, Humf has not contacted me again, and I know nothing directly of his present doings. Yet, if popular rumour is to be believed, he is not inactive!

M. G.
York, October 1990